Secrets & Curses of Crimson

SHAY TAYLOR

WESTWIND PUBLISHING LLC

For those who hate Jesper and Luren.

Enjoy.

Please be advised that this story contains heavy themes that may be triggering for some readers, including but not limited to:

Violence, physical and mental abuse, torture, murder/killing, gore, death, kidnapping, blood, manipulation, betrayal, mental health issues (trauma, anxiety, depression, grief), fighting, and explicit sexual content.

Contents

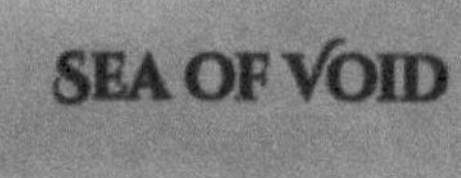

SEA OF VOID
AKECIA
KIZAR
FALGO
CERITHIA
EXILE
CRIMSON
FORBIDDEN WOOD
ELLORYON
SEA OF VOID
ISLANDS OF DEATH

Chapter I

Della- The day Thea died

My chest burned with fury and anguish as I left Thea in Exile again. She was important to me, and I hated to see her suffer. I was angry because my brother, Mikel, was the reason for this. I couldn't believe my own brother was such a cruel, heartless asshole.

Summoning my star mist, its silver glow wrapped around me, taking me to my home high in the stars. Staring at the stunning structure that felt like anything but a home, I felt hatred. The beautiful white stone looked angelic, but it was stained with my betrayal. These walls were once my sanctuary, but now they are my prison.

I barged through the large, glass front door, my footsteps echoing in the silent entryway. My eyes were turning white from grief and sadness. I could not get Cassius' crying and pleading out of my mind. I had once begged

Haden the same way, and I knew how devastating it was when our prayers weren't answered.

"Ardella?" Pia, our housekeeper, pulled me from my rage for only a brief moment. Her big blue eyes widened when she saw me because I never got angry, but fuck, I was sick of this. I stormed past her into the sitting area where Mikel was drowning his sorrows in fae wine. He didn't acknowledge me when I walked into the room, but I was used to it.

He hadn't glanced at me in years.

"How fucking dare you!" I yelled, making the walls shake. One of his favorite tapestries fell off the white wall and onto the black marble flooring. Mikel kept his eyes on the book he was pretending to read and his back toward me. But his shoulders were now tense. I took off my heel and threw it at him, hitting him hard enough in the back that he finally looked at me.

"Have you lost your fucking mind?" he asked.

My brother's eyes, which matched mine, held nothing but hatred. I hope he saw my hatred for him reflected back.

"Why?" I yelled. "What did you do to Thea and Cassius? I know you intervened and made sure she failed." But still, a sliver of me wanted this not to be true. How could my brother be this cruel?

Mikel's face barely changed emotion as he listened to me accuse him.

"Cassius doesn't deserve a fated mate. He killed her. It is his burden to carry. I am the god of judgement, and he hasn't paid his penance."

"Stars above Mikel, he killed her to save her, and you know this. He loves her more than anything; why are you inflicting more pain on him?"

"Why does he get to keep his mate when I don't?" Mikel stood and clenched his fist at his side. "You took her from me. You killed Remiah, and with that, you killed me too."

I wanted to kill him.

"You gave them an opportunity that you never granted Remiah and me. A second chance. You gave it to Cassius, but not to your twin brother!"

This time a portrait fell off the wall from his rage. I deflated at his words for a brief moment.

"Mikel, Remiah's soul left immediately. I did not send her away. She. Left. Thea refused to leave Cassius. She stayed, so I gave them a chance. If Remiah had stayed, then you could have claimed her, and she would have come back. That is not my fault."

"This is all your fault!" His words were full of heartbreak and anger. "You took the only thing I had to look forward to."

I stepped forward in a rage. Pia caught my attention out of the corner of my eye by shaking her head, but I ignored her trying to stop me.

"How many times?" I sneered. "How many times did you make sure Thea didn't break her curse?"

Mikel smiled like a smug prick.

"Every year," he said with a grin that made me recoil in disgust. How could this be my brother, my twin, my only family? "I let Luren know everything that was happening; I made sure Cerithian and Kizar guards snuck into the trials; and I made Thea forget that Crimson had a traitor in their circle. I made her so confused over her feelings for Cassius that she questioned everything about him."

"If I could kill you, I would slit your throat open this second. You will *never* interfere with Thea and Cassius again."

"If we could die, I would have killed myself the day you killed Remiah," he spat back at me. My brother's chest rose and fell in short, choppy breaths. Guilt clawed into my chest because one decision I made had destroyed countless lives. This was all my fault, but this... Mikel was a disgusting excuse of a god.

"Never again; do you hear me? You will not come near Thea and Cassius again. Remiah would not approve of this."

I turned around but stopped when Mikel laughed.

"I'll leave them alone for a trade."

I turned back to him and stared at his menacing face. I would do anything to help them. They were important to Haden, and that made them even more special to me. They had made Haden smile for the first time in years. They gave him a family again.

"I would expect nothing less from you," I snapped.

"I will make a star bargain with you." He stepped forward. Star bonds couldn't be broken, which meant he could not back out and hurt them. "You must give me your star."

Pia gasped behind me.

"My star," I whispered.

"As the god of judgment, it is the only way that I will consider Cassius pardoned for his betrayal," he smiled. "You are the one I want to punish. I agree that I took my anger out on Cassius because of resentment and jealousy, but you are the one I want to suffer. You are the one who should pay for this."

He was right. It was my mistakes that should be punished because Cassius had done nothing wrong. He loved Thea so much that their bond refused to let go even when she died. If my brother had bonded to Remiah, then her soul would have done the same. My eyes glanced over

Mikel's tanned skin which was pale from lack of sleep and eating. His eyes, which once shined brightly, were dull and lifeless. I had practically killed him too.

"I'll be back." I nodded and headed toward my room. Pia was hot on my heels. I could smell her soft lilac scent as she raced in front of me.

"You cannot give him your star. That is meant for Haden." She was more frantic than I was. Her blonde hair swayed as she shook her head. "If you give it to Mikel, you can never solidify a bond with Haden."

I grabbed the star from where I put it eight years ago. The night I killed Remiah was the last time I opened this black velvet box. It sat in my hands for hours that night, and I stared at the beautiful orange and silver glow it emulated. I knew that night that Haden would never accept it from me.

"Haden does not love me. He would never accept being my mate. This stupid rock is useless to me. If it can save Thea and Cassius, then that will be the best use for it."

I tried to convince her and myself that Haden would never love me back. There had always been a shimmer of hope he would, but every time he looked at me, I could see the hurt and devastation I caused him. He didn't love me like I loved him. Pia grabbed my arm as I turned to go back out to meet Mikel.

"Are you sure about this? Maybe Haden will forgive you when he understands you had no choice. Maybe if Mikel knew that Haden is your mate, it would make him understand too."

I loved Pia, but she was naive. I frowned at her.

"If Mikel knew that Haden was my mate, he would use him against me. Haden doesn't need to be pulled into my brother's antics. Haden will never forgive me; he already made that clear."

"You're punishing yourself because *you* can't forgive yourself," Pia snapped at me.

"His judgment against me is valid because I do not regret killing Remiah," I whispered, a thought that had never escaped me. "I would do it all over again, but that does not mean I am in the right just because I love Haden. Mikel loved Remiah too. If I were him, I would have lost any kindness if Haden died. I *am* Mikel's and Haden's villain."

When I glanced at her, I could still see the doubt in her eyes. She needed to understand the depth of Haden's hatred for me.

"Do you know what I wake up to every morning?" I asked. "I hear Haden praying to the stars that he hopes I am unhappy, that I am miserable. He prays that I am unable to find peace. He has not missed one day since Remiah died."

Tears streamed down Pia's face as the reality of Haden hating me settled into her.

"I have prayed to the stars every morning that Haden will find it in his heart to forgive me, but they do not listen to me. The stars have granted Haden his prayer. I am unhappy and miserable. I have not known peace since the last day Haden and I were together. I am unworthy of him. So, I don't think that Haden will forgive me, and I've come to terms with the fact that I deserve it." I let the tears stream down my face as I looked at Pia.

She was sobbing when I turned and left my bedroom.

My star was heavy in my hand as I walked into the room where Mikel was still standing. Surprise took over his face. He didn't think I would do this. Without hesitation, I walked to him and held it out. Mikel was the one to hesitate as he took it from me and opened the box. My star, the one we are given when we come into existence, glowed brightly in his face. So many memories of Haden plagued me at that moment.

We didn't have long enough together before I ruined it. My heart ached as I watched Mikel shut the box. I had dreamt of giving Haden that star since I first saw him and realized he could see me back. He had smiled at me, and I think I fell in love at that very moment, but it was now all tainted by what I did.

"I swear to the stars; you have my word that I will not cause Thea and Cassius any more trouble," he spoke as he held out his hand. I grabbed it, and a small bargain mark burned into our wrists. Its orange glow was in the shape of four stars in a straight line.

"How'd you know I was intervening with them?" he asked.

"Kace told me when I collected his soul. He told me how you threatened his family and gave Cerithia something to use against him."

I still had to tell Cassius that Kace was not a traitor by choice. Kace had waited to leave after he died so that he could warn me, and I was thankful for it. My brother made sure he didn't have a choice because Kace wanted to protect his own family.

Mikel looked at me oddly as I yanked my hand away and glared at him.

"You never being able to form a mating bond will give me great satisfaction. I can't wait to see you suffer alone and watch your mate live a life without you. That is the best torture I can imagine for you."

"Stay the fuck away from Thea and Cassius, or I might find a way to kill a god."

CHAPTER 2

THEA

I sometimes dream of a man I have never met. Sometimes I can feel him watching me in the shadows of Exile as I explore the dead woods. There is nothing in particular that I can recall about his features when I wake up from my dreams. Only the piercing gold of his eyes that watch me like I'm a sight to behold remain clear in my mind during the days. I don't remember his words, face, or anything but those eyes.

I had been in a fog-like haze of confusion for months. I still wasn't sure what was causing it. It was like my mind was trying to claw its way out of a dark cave to tell me something. I was always so confused when I woke up in Exile, which made no sense. I have been here for years.

Even Sybil and the twins were acting strange. When Sybil burst into tears at the sight of me that morning so long ago, it made me feel like I did something wrong.

She never told me why the sight of me coming out of my room that morning had made her sob, and I didn't push it. Because even though I couldn't remember anything, I knew something had happened to me. I was different. I felt different.

I searched the grounds of Exile at night because I felt like I had lost something important. I felt incomplete... lost. Something was missing, and it haunted me with loneliness and heartbreak. It was the reason I was currently sitting in the darkening woods near the shadow border. I was always drawn to this spot of the border, and sometimes I thought of jumping through it, but I knew what would happen if I did. I would die. So, I sat here and waited for something—anything—to happen. It never did.

My eyes looked up at the starless sky, and I sighed heavily. I wished to see the stars and the moon again. The hot, sticky air clung to me, and I wished I could cool off somehow; even the creek was warm. But maybe it would be enough to make me feel clean. I stood and walked farther into the woods. A few yards into the tree line, the wide creek met me. The sound of the rippling water soothed my aching mind.

I stripped off my clothing and laid my bow next to my viper-handled dagger. My eyes lingered on the blade. The vipers coiled their way around the handle, and their eyes bored into me like they knew my secrets. I walked into the creek and sighed at the comfort it brought, even though it was warmer than I would've preferred.

My body was less tense as I lay in the deepest part of it, floating on my back. My eyes closed with exhaustion. My days were not taxing by any means, but I was always exhausted. I felt myself drifting in and out of sleep as I lay there, but I didn't get up and leave. I was too relaxed to get out. My body relaxed for the first time in weeks. I was always so tense, like something bad was going to happen.

★★☽★★

When I finally opened my eyes, I was confused by the landscape around me. I sat up quickly when I realized that I was no longer in the creek of Exile. scanned the shoreline of some sort of hot spring I was in. Something about it seemed familiar. I heard him before I saw him lurking in the shadows. My hand hurried to grab the viper dagger.

"No need for that, my love." His deep voice twisted around my heart and squeezed it.

"Do not call me that," I hissed at the shadowy figure. He laughed softly. I remembered I wasn't wearing clothing. I looked over my skin and paused at the tattoos I had. Pretty crimson-colored flowers and trees surrounded the letter 'C' above my heart. No matter how much I tried, I couldn't remember how I had gotten them. I couldn't remember any-

thing before a few months ago, but I shared that secret with no one.

"Sorry, it's a habit." He paused for a long moment, and I thought he had left. "What a nice hot spring... Why are you dreaming of it?"

I glanced around, and something familiar struck me, but I couldn't exactly say what.

"Come out where I can see you, coward."

"I love it when you call me that," his deep voice sighed.

My heart picked up speed. Was he flirting with me? I guess I was naked and alone, but this was a dream; he couldn't hurt me here. A moment later I could make out his silhouette in the darkness at the edge of the spring. He wore a large, hooded cloak. My muscles relaxed as soon as his golden eyes shone brightly. The darkness that lingered inside of me hummed in approval.

"Is that better?"

"No. I want to see your face."

"Hmm." He paced slowly at the shoreline. "That's probably a bad idea." His voice was almost playful, and I liked it.

"Why? Are you ugly or something?"

He laughed so loudly that I found myself smiling at this stranger in front of me. Something about the noise felt familiar and comforting.

"I think you might like what you see and fall hopelessly in love with me." There was a hint of sadness in his voice.

I scoffed and rolled my eyes.

"Aren't you a cocky son of a bitch."

"Very well, but I did warn you, little viper."

The nickname made my chest heavy with something I couldn't explain. I watched as he slipped the hood from his face, but he didn't stop there. He slipped his clothing off and slipped into the spring with me. I still couldn't see his face as he sat in the water by the dark edge.

"Are you going to stab me with that?"

"Depends," I answered him, even though my grip on my dagger was loose. He nodded slowly. He did not make me feel scared; his presence made me feel safe. Slowly, I sank into the water to cover my naked body from him, but I gripped the viper-handled dagger in my hand just in case he tried any funny business. I stared directly at him as he slowly made his way out of the shadows.

I expected something far more grotesque than what he showed me. Pretty golden eyes stared directly into my green ones. His dark hair was chaotic, and his straight nose led to a kissable mouth pulled into a cocky smirk.

He was devastatingly handsome, and he knew it. My eyes drifted over his muscled shoulders and chest, where all these tattoos decorated him, but my eyes were drawn to one. The letter 'T' with a viper coiled around it sat above his heart. Something in my mind fought and clawed to release, but whatever the tattoo triggered never surfaced.

"Are you hopelessly in love with me now?" He teased me.

I shook my head to stop my gawking. My body begged me to look at him again, but I fought the urge with everything I possessed. I still didn't know who this man was. I should be wary of him always lurking in my dreams, but maybe he was just a figment of my imagination. Maybe my broken and confused mind mustered up his existence, so I wasn't so lonely.

My eyes drifted back to him. Nothing about him made me feel scared. If anything, I felt like I needed to be near him. The darkness inside me urged me forward at the thought of touching him. The man watched me in a way that had my chest tightening. He looked like he missed me.

My darkness urged me forward again, only so much more persistent this time that I had no choice but to listen. Turning, I set down my dagger and looked at him again. I took a small step toward him and saw that it surprised him.

"You aren't real, are you? My lonely mind made you up," I said as I reached forward and felt his warm skin under my fingertips. He felt real. He should feel real, though, if I made him up. When my eyes looked up, he was staring at me. Any sane fae would have stopped my touch if this were real.

My fingers traced the 'T' over his heart, which was beating extremely fast under my touch. I moved my hands to his face and felt the stubble on his chin scrape against my skin. His golden eyes swarmed with flecks of black, making me shiver with anticipation. The man lifted his arm and slowly brushed the hair from my face, but he didn't stop touching me. His hand slid to the back of my neck and pulled me forward hesitantly. He paused an inch from my mouth, so I leaned forward and pressed my lips to his. It was like a tension I didn't know inside of me snapped at the feel of his mouth on mine.

I found what I had been missing.

His big hands yanked me, so I was flush against him. Our wet skin rubbed effortlessly against each other as he deepened the kiss. All thoughts disappeared, and so did the confusion that had plagued me for months. I felt nothing, and it was pure bliss. My arms wrapped around his neck so I could pour everything I could into the kiss. A low hum of appreciation escaped him.

His hands rubbed over my back and thighs like he couldn't help it.

"My love," he spoke with a sadness that had me pulling back and looking over him. "Are you sure you want to do this?"

I nodded because there was no hesitation on my part. It was the only encouragement he needed. His fingers traced down my stomach before reaching where I needed to feel him the most, as his mouth devoured mine. Noises fell from me without permission as the pit in my stomach became heavier and heavier.

"Such pretty noises, little viper," he growled so possessively I locked my stare to his. "Hearing what I do to you may be the closest to the heavens I may ever get."

His mouth skimmed along the skin of my neck and bit me so softly that my orgasm ripped through me so violently that I wondered if the stars above could hear.

"You're so fucking perfect," he sighed as my mouth found his. My body filled with a need I couldn't explain. My lust coiled tightly within me like a venomous viper waiting to strike its prey, and right now this man was my target. A surge of possessiveness cascaded over me in a wave as I took control of our positions. My hands pushed against him, so his back was leaning against the side of the spring. His golden eyes changed to a darkness, which reminded me of the shadows he hid in. I smiled at him as I lifted my hips and sank onto him without warning. My greedy eyes watched him as his eyes clenched tightly and his hands squeezed handfuls of my flesh. His head fell back to rest against the shore of the hot

spring. My movements slowed when he opened his eyes and stared at me.

The look called to something deep within me, something dark. His features were fixed in hard lines as he watched me move faster and faster.

"How's your love doing?" I found myself asking.

A feral growl escaped him as he wrapped his fingers in my hair and pulled me down, so I was face-to-face with him.

"You're doing such a good job, my love. You look so pretty taking what you want from me."

"Fuck," I whispered as his words soaked into me.

"Let me hear you, Thea. Let the realm hear you. Let the gods above know how fucking good we are together. Let them know that they can't keep you from me." His hips thrust up into me at such a delicious pace that my breath caught in my throat.

His mouth possessed mine, his tongue dominating me with the same dominance of his thrusts. It was too much. It felt too good. Whimpering pleas fell from me as I pulled back.

"You're mine," he declared as his hands squeezed my hips tightly. "Only mine. No one ever gets to see you like this. No one else gets to make these pretty noises fall from your perfect mouth. You belong to me, do you understand?"

"Yes," I cried out. "I'm yours."

"Good girl." He clenched his jaw tightly, and the tempo of his hips increased, pounding into me so perfectly that another orgasm tore through me.

"Please..."

"You wanted it, my love, so you'll take it until I'm done with you."

My eyes squeezed so tightly as I called my orgasm into the dark star-painted sky above us just as his release crashed into him. When my breathing slowed, I looked down at him, smiling.

"That was..." I swallowed as emotions bubbled up and tears filled my eyes. "It felt so right." I didn't know how to say what I was thinking or feeling.

He leaned forward and kissed me softly before hugging me.

"I love you," he whispered.

As I leaned back to see his handsome face, my dream shifted to something more sinister. It didn't feel like a dream anymore. I lifted my hands and saw them coated in blood. My heart pounded as I glanced around the hot spring, only to realize the water was red. When I looked at my golden-eyed man, his eyes were black and vacant. Then the large wound on his neck caught my attention.

He was dead.

I fell off him and tried to crawl out of the hot spring, but his hand grabbed my ankle at the last moment, and he dragged me back toward him.

"Are you going to let me die, my love?" he asked with blood seeping down him. I closed my eyes tightly, wanting to wake up from this nightmare.

★★☽★★

When I tried to breathe, water filled my lungs. Panic settled into me as I tried to find the surface of the water. Dark shadows wrapped around me and pulled me up as I gasped for air.

I looked around for the man, but he wasn't there. I was in the creek of Exile again, and it made confusion crash into my mind. I crawled onto the shoreline and tried to catch my breath. My mind flashed to my dream, but the more I tried to remember what the man looked like, the less I could see.

There was nothing about the dream I could remember except the man dying. It was as if I could see his face but not see any of the details. My chest ached painfully as flashes of blood coating my hands hit me.

Are you going to let me die, my love?

My dreams had never done that. I could never remember what he said to me when I woke. So why could I remember this one line? I shook away the overwhelming sense of grief that was taking over my chest. It was just a nightmare.

I frowned at the starless sky above me before rolling over and getting dressed, then heading home. That feeling of missing something overtook me again, but it was worse than before I fell asleep.

I frowned slightly as I stepped into the small house that belonged to Sybil and I. The twins were there, and I greeted them with a small smile.

"We were getting worried about you," Kaz said with a frown.

"I went for a swim, sorry."

They all looked over me oddly, but whatever they were questioning was never spoken out loud. I picked up a piece of bread and ate it slowly to not upset my stomach. We did not have a lot of supplies left in the small town we were trapped in. Soon we would all die from starvation or sickness.

"We should walk the border tomorrow and see if anything has changed," Kai said toward me. His demeanor and tone were odd, but I agreed. My eyes lingered on the blackbird elite magic mark he had.

"Sounds good. We'll meet at nightfall, so others don't see us." I paused for a moment, wondering if I should bother asking questions. "What elite magic do you have?"

"We shift into ravens," Kaz said. Interesting.

He shared a look with his twin and Sybil.

"Were you two the only kids in your family?" I asked.

"No, we had a sister." Kaz frowned like he didn't like this line of questioning. Shouldn't any of this be familiar? I should know these things, but they didn't ask me why I was asking about things that I should already know.

"She didn't have elite magic?"

"No, she did." Kaz stared at me oddly. "She died, though."

"Oh, I'm sorry."

My eyes drifted to each one of them to see their reactions. It was clear by the way they glanced at each other that they thought something was wrong with me. I wanted to ask what it was, but something told me they wouldn't share. Every time I asked why we were trapped here, I was met with an awkward silence. At one point someone said the Crimson kingdom was at fault, but Sybil was quick to shut that theory down. She didn't give an alternative explanation. She said she just knew that it wasn't Crimson, and I believed her.

Although I did not know the names of the kingdoms or who they were, so why would it matter to me? I didn't remember anything, but no one else seemed to remember much either. After I ate, I excused myself to my room. I could hear the harsh whispers coming from the three of them as I left, but I kept going. My room was so small, but something like comfort filled me when I was alone in there.

I stripped off my clothes and lay on the makeshift bed. My eyes glanced up at the crack in the roof. The mud was falling apart, and it would need to be fixed soon. My eyes drifted shut as I tried to recall anything about the man I dreamed of.

CHAPTER 3

THEA

Sybil and I sat in a comfortable silence the next afternoon in our small living space. Her sharp blue eyes glanced at me often, like she was waiting for something. Gods, it felt like she was worried I would combust or something.

"Is there something you want to talk about?" I smiled softly.

"You don't remember very much," she said after hesitating for a long moment.

"No one does." I raised my dark brow at her.

Her frail hands twisted in her lap like she didn't know what to say or how to say it to me. It made my chest tight and breathing difficult because she hadn't looked like this, ever.

"You woke up one morning and you didn't remember anything." She looked back at me. "I know you've hidden it, but I just want you to know that I know you don't remember all the years in Exile."

Her features morphed into sadness. Relief that Sybil knew my secret filled me. But it twisted my heart to think that something was wrong with me or my mind.

"I'm sorry I didn't say anything, but I was just trying to understand for myself." I sighed and leaned closer to the small fire we had made. Watching the flames, something about it called out to me. The colors were so vibrant, and the heat of the fire made me feel calm. "The twins know I don't remember either."

"Yes, we've known that you couldn't remember anything. You seemed more confused than I've ever seen you. Which concerns me."

I frowned at her as she stood and walked toward the kitchen, but she paused with her back to me.

"Has he visited you in your dreams?"

My head snapped up to her.

"Do you know of him? How?" I stood up quickly. He wasn't real.

"You had told me before. I was just curious if he was still around." She looked over at me and frowned again, like she had so much more to say. I wish she would just tell me what was going on. I could help us out of here if I knew what was happening.

"He is a friend. No matter what happens, I want you to know that you can always trust him." A small gasp escaped her as if she was in pain.

"He isn't real." I shook my head and sat back on the small bench. "I can't remember him when I wake up, only his golden eyes."

She smiled slightly at my comment.

"I'm sure he's quite charming and handsome." Her face looked as though she was thinking of a memory or a specific man.

"Why do I get the feeling that you and the twins know more than what you tell me?"

Sybil sighed before working on making bread again.

"I wish I could explain everything to you, Thea, but I cannot. One day you will remember, but until then, just know that the man in your dreams is important. He is *always* the right choice."

Sybil gasped loudly in pain as soon as she said it. Her hands gripped the counter as agony took over her face. I rushed to her, but she insisted she was fine. My eyes drifted over her to see if she had wounded herself.

"Are you alright?" I asked worriedly.

Sybil finally sucked in a deep, shaky breath before looking at me.

"Yes, I said too much." I wanted to ask her what she meant, but she spoke again. "Let's talk about something else."

"No, I want to know what you do," I demanded. I was so tired of not knowing anything.

"Thea, I can't say much. The god, Mikel, forbade it. He tied our tongues with magic. I worry it will only confuse you more." She seemed scared, but I was not letting this go.

"Sybil, you're my family. What are you and the twins so scared to tell me? And what does the god, Mikel, have to do with this?"

"Thea, please."

"No, tell me, Sybil."

"We can't!" She threw her hands into the air. "I've tried to tell you who the man with golden eyes is, and I've tried to tell you what you need to do, but I am silenced each time. If I could tell you, I would."

I wanted to say something to Sybil, but a yell in the distance had both of us glancing at the door. The scream was blood-curdling, making both of us hold our breath for a moment. My body tensed; I had never heard screams like that here.

"What was that?" I whispered.

"Nothing good." Sybil moved to grab a knife. Sybil was not a violent woman, so it surprised me to see her grab a weapon.

We both watched the door as I pulled my dagger out. It was dark outside now, almost as if a storm was approaching, but it did not rain in Exile. Dread filled me as I waited for anything to happen. Another yell somewhere closer to our home startled both of us. I stepped forward so Sybil would be protected. The twins said I was a natural fighter. I could protect Sybil if needed. Our door burst open a few moments later, and before I could lunge forward with my blade, I recognized Kai and Kaz.

"We're under attack," one of them whispered.

"How? We're in a shielded prison." I questioned. They looked to Sybil for guidance or something else. Sybil gave them a nod to their silent question.

"We need to get Thea to the border now. She's who they are after," Kai said. My heart raced quickly.

"Me?" I frowned. "I don't understand what's going on."

Sybil came up to me and grabbed my hands in hers to comfort me, but it only terrified me more. She looked at me with sadness and guilt.

"You don't remember, but you can go through the border without dying."

I shook my head, trying to understand what she was saying. The twins were guarding the door, but the screams were getting closer to us, and I knew we only had minutes before they found us.

"It's been almost a year since you've been back. I'm sure they are here to stop you from the trials."

"Who? What trials?"

Tears streamed down my cheeks as confusion hit me in a new wave.

"We can't say until your curse is broken, and only you can do that. You need to go, and don't worry about us. Once they realize you're gone, we'll be alright."

"They are getting closer. We need to go now," Kai demanded.

"You're scaring me. I don't understand."

Sybil's hand wiped the tears from my cheeks softly.

"I know, sweetheart, but it's all we can say. Break your curse and free us all from Exile. Can you do that, Thea?"

"Yes," I said.

"Yes, you can." She smiled softly. "The twins will take you to the border."

Kaz grabbed my hand and started dragging me to the door, but I pulled back so I could hug Sybil.

"I'll get you out," I promised.

"I know." She hugged me back. "Remember, you just have to make the right choice when the time comes. Red is right, blue is wrong."

I nodded, confused. What did any of this mean? Kaz and Kai rushed me from the house, and we ran towards the shadow border. I could hear houses being ransacked and other fae yelling in fear and pain. I didn't look back. I couldn't because it would make me want to stay and protect Sybil.

The twins led me through the field of dying grass to the spot by the border I always sat by. Once we were there, they stopped and turned towards me. Both of them bowed at me like I was superior to them.

"We can't go with you, Captain, but you'll figure it out this time."

This time? Captain?

Kaz grabbed me and hugged me tightly, and then Kai did the same, but as Kai released me, he shoved me hard, so I stumbled through the border. I tried to grab the dead branches of trees to stop my falling, but it was no use. A searing pain shot through me as I hit the ground on the other side of the shadow border.

I called out into the night sky and to the stars twinkling above me. My body couldn't move as the pain coursed deep within my bones. No doubt trying to kill me for crossing. After a long minute, though, the pain started slowing down. My lungs pulled the cold night air into them, and it was such a pleasant feeling after breathing in the hot air of Exile.

I stared at the stars for a moment, admiring them before rolling onto my stomach and standing. I leaned my body against a large tree that looked like no others around it. My hand traced the large 'X' carved into the side. Someone had marked the shadow border. My eyes drifted into the distance. A tall, intimidating black castle sat high on a hill with red light illuminating it.

It was so stunning that I took a step towards it so I could admire it more. The city below was lit up in the night sky, and I tried to remember if I had ever seen anything so breathtaking before.

My instincts were to go toward it, but I stopped myself. I didn't know where I was or who that kingdom belonged to.

Panic shot through me. I didn't know where to go or how to stop whatever curse I had. How had Sybil known about my curse, and why couldn't she tell me more?

Suddenly, I heard a stick break somewhere in the distance, and I held my dagger in my hand tightly. Instead of heading toward the black castle that called to me, I went in the opposite direction and away from the sticks breaking.

I needed a plan. I needed a way to find out information. Where was I from? I knew my name was Thea, but I knew nothing else. I dreamt of nothing but a man whose face I couldn't even remember. My feet seemed to have a mind of their own as I wandered farther into the woods. I walked for miles in the dark with nothing guiding my way.

Something in front of me caught my eye before I heard the soft voices in the dark. I stood behind one of the trees and held my breath. The voices seemed to be getting closer, but then suddenly they were gone.

I peeked around the tree to see if they were still coming. As my eyes adjusted to the moonlight, I could see a tall man ahead of me. Then a silhouette of a smaller man appeared too. My eyes widened when I saw black shadows swarming around the tall man. I stared, mesmerized by the way they tangled around him angrily. There was a dead body at his feet. I held my breath. It was a woman.

"We can't cross Cerithia's boundary until war is officially declared," one of them said. "We're running out of time. We need to find her before they do."

"Did we kill all the witches responsible for the attack?" the man with shadows spoke.

"Yes, there were only six."

The man with the shadows held his hand up to silence the man next to him. My breath caught when the man turned his head in the direction I was hiding. If he could see me, he didn't let it be known. After a long moment, they both walked in the opposite direction of me.

Suddenly there was a soft green flame floating above the ground. It mesmerized me as it flickered towards me like it was happy to see me. A moment later, my senses kicked in, and I ran from whatever the creature was.

I didn't stop until the cool air turned hotter and the trees were different species. Then I kept going until a cave caught my attention. My eyes drifted around me. Someone or something was watching me; I could feel it. I climbed into the cave entrance and found a hidden crevice to squeeze into. Once I was sure that I was completely out of sight, I wrapped my dark green cloak around myself as I curled into the ground and prayed for sleep.

★★☽★★

I scanned the darkness surrounding the field of flowers that I found myself standing in. I could feel the waterfall in front of me before I could see or hear it. The power of its roar made the ground vibrate under my feet. It was breathtaking in the moonlight. The field held every shade of red and orange flower I had ever seen. Something moving in the shadows caught my eye.

"Come out, coward." I smiled.

"Are you flirting with me, little viper?"

I shrugged. His golden eyes glowed in the darkness. He watched me like prey as he stalked toward me. He only stopped watching me to look at our view. Something tender crossed his features as he gave me a big smile.

"Pretty view."

"Yes, it is." I smiled. "You didn't visit me last night."

"You wouldn't let me." He frowned. "You put up some sort of wall that wouldn't let me see you. I thought maybe you were upset with me."

"How can I be upset with an imaginary man I made up?" I laughed, but he didn't. His eyes flashed something like hurt in them.

He took a hesitant step towards me and wrapped me in a hug. This is what I had been looking for. I wrapped my arms around his strong body. He smelled like forest and rain.

"Did you miss me, my love?" he whispered next to my ear. "Because I missed you terribly."

I smiled as I pulled back to see his handsome face.

"Yes. I did miss you, my coward." His eyes flashed with amusement. "Why can't I remember what you look like when I'm done dreaming?"

His eyebrows knitted together.

"What do you mean?"

"I can only remember your golden eyes, but nothing else."

"I'm not sure," he sighed as his gaze looked over the water-fall. His hand held tightly onto mine as we stood in silence.

He turned his head, so his pointed ear was toward the woods, like he had heard something. I glanced behind us, but I couldn't see or hear anything.

"Where are you right now?"

I opened my mouth to answer him, but a weird noise behind me had me turning to see what it was.

"Fuck," he whispered as he looked over where I was watching. "Something is wrong; I need to wake up."

"Wh-what? I want to stay with you."

His eyes filled with a deep emotion before he leaned down and kissed me possessively. I felt the shift again. No. Not this.

When I pulled away from his kiss, his eyes were vacant. The man fell to his knees in front of me. Blood poured from a neck wound.

"No." I kneeled and caught him as he fell. But it was too late; he was dead again. I leaned my head against his chest, sobbing loudly. I was begging him to come back. That's when I felt it. His cold hand circled my wrist, making me look at him.

"Are you going to let me die, my love?" he asked.

"No."

"Then save me."

★★☽★★

I gasped for air as I sat up in the cave, trying to stop the tears from flowing down my face. Why was my mind torturing me? My breathing was too quick. I couldn't steady my breathing. I tried lying down as the dizziness enveloped me.

That is when I noticed the floating green orb as she moved toward me. I prayed to the stars that she was friendly and wouldn't kill me after I passed out. My eyes fluttered shut, and I fell into darkness.

★★☽★★

When I opened my eyes, I was rocking gently in a chair, the cave still nowhere to be seen. I was surrounded by blackness, but then a small flicker of flames ignited. The roar of the fire in front of me was so comforting. After a moment, the black walls around me shifted into a small, inviting space with trinkets and art on every inch of it.

The rug under my chair was soft against my bare feet. I sensed him before I saw him. But I could not stop rocking back and forth. I did not feel any danger. The chair next to me began rocking in tandem with mine.

I smiled when my eyes met the frail older man smiling at me. His wild white hair seemed to fit him, even if I didn't know who he was.

"*Thea, my dear,*" *he said with a smile. I watched him.* "*My name is Brim, and we are friends.*"

Brim. His name was so familiar.

"*I don't remember dreaming of you before.*" *I frowned.*

"*You aren't dreaming.*" *He glanced away from me and to the fire.* "*You have been having visions like your mother used to, and you are about to have another one. I am here to guide you. You called to me for help.*"

I did?

"*My mother...*" *An image of a woman who looked similar to me popped into my mind but was gone before I could appreciate her beauty.* "*A vision of what?*"

Brim looked at me curiously.

"*I am unsure. But your mother had them to show her events that would alter her life forever.*"

"*You look scared.*" *I frowned. Why was I getting worried all of a sudden?*

"*It's going to feel like a dream. You need to try and remember every detail possible, but it will be hard. Visions do not like to give us a straight answer to anything.*"

When I turned to ask him a question, he was gone, and I was standing in a field. There was an arena in front of me filled with loud cheering that pulled my attention toward it. They were chanting my name. Hundreds of fae shouted.

Thea! Thea! Thea! But for some reason, I was angry about it. I sucked in a lungful of dust and hot air.

The sun was too hot. I glanced down and saw I was wearing a dark blue dress. There was blood on my hands. The veins in my arms were black. I felt fucking furious. There were so many fae standing by me in the arena, but they were a haze. I couldn't make out anyone's face.

I felt nauseous as time faded and blurred my vision. As it came back into focus, I was staring down at my leg as a dagger stuck out from it. My eyes pulsed red.

"Thea!" His voice boomed through all the chaos—deep, peaceful, perfect. It distracted me from the man coming up behind me. "No!" His voice echoed in the space around me. My eyes snapped up to where I heard the deep voice coming from. The man with golden eyes was trying to get to me. His magic was ripping and tearing against a barrier I couldn't see. Suddenly, his shadows burst from him as someone hit him with something that I could not quite make out through the haze. He fell to his knees, wounded.

Another blade sliced across my back, but I turned and killed the man who was hurting me. Then time faded away again, and when I looked forward, the man with golden eyes was kneeling in the dirt, bleeding still.

A sense of urgency filled me. I needed to get to him. I needed to save him. Nothing else mattered but him living.

But as I took one step closer, he glanced up at me. What I saw in his eyes would haunt me for a lifetime. They were filled with regret, sadness, and longing.

"No!" I released my darkness to shield him.

"I love you," he called out to me before a man, whose face was blurry, swung a sword and beheaded him. My whole body burst into flames.

I was too late. I was too late.

I ran toward him, desperate. A sharp pain on my wrist caught my attention. I gasped as my crown tattoo broke and shattered on my arm.

"No!" I was frantic. I was devastated. Time faded again before I was standing right where the man died. I couldn't look at his dead body. I wanted to burn the realm down in my grief. I turned and let all my magic tear through me as a vicious scream tore from my throat—destroying everything in its path.

I gasped for air as my vision pulled away from me, and I was rocking with Brim again. Tears were streaming down my face as I tried desperately to catch my breath.

"What did you see, Thea?"

"He died," I cried. "The man from my dreams. The one with golden eyes was killed."

Brim didn't say anything, and I couldn't hear the rocking of his chair anymore. When I glanced up at him, he was in shock.

"Are you sure that is what you saw?"

I nodded. I couldn't breathe.

I glanced at the crown tattoo on my wrist to see it still intact, and the sight brought me comfort. Tears burned and fell from my eyes unrelenting. My chest squeezed so painfully at the man's haunting golden eyes that I started hyperventilating. I was going to pass out or die.

"That can't be right." He stood up and began pacing. "What else do you remember?"

I closed my eyes tightly, trying to remember what I had been doing, but my mind and chest ached with grief.

"I was fighting in an arena. There were lots of fae. I was hurt, and he tried to help me." I began crying again.

"Why would the stars do this to you?"

I looked up at him as he became furious. He was muttering something about the gods and how I had given enough to the realm that I didn't deserve to lose him.

"Who is he? Is he real? I thought he was just in my imagination."

Brim stopped and gave me a look of pity.

"He's real, and he is going to die."

CHAPTER 4

THEA

I was crying when I woke up. My vision of the man with gold eyes dying in front of me plagued me. Even if I couldn't remember his face, his eyes haunted me. The way they were filled with sadness when he looked at me right before he died. I felt an overwhelming sense of devastation. My chest ached so much that I rubbed it with my hand to make sure I wasn't dying. I could remember everything about Brim, but why couldn't I remember the man with golden eyes? He was going to die, and it would shatter me.

My body raced with adrenaline. Suddenly, dark tendrils of magic swarmed from me in a frenzy. I was mesmerized by the beauty of it, but also the power that pulsed from it. It acted like it was... angry. Before I could react, they had merged into a semi-solid form and lifted me off the ground, giving me a push as if to tell me to get my ass moving. So, I listened and started walking the same way as yesterday.

My stomach growled and my feet ached. Maybe I would starve to death out here instead of in Exile. My stomach growled again as I wandered through the hot, sticky air of whatever kingdom I had wandered to. I focused on the hunger pain—anything to distract me from him dying.

This was fucking torture. All I could think of was that man being killed. The way his eyes were watching me before the sword came down. I closed my eyes tightly and tried to think of anything else. I tried humming and thinking of Sybil and the twins, but it wasn't working. That darkness inside of me was seething.

It was determined to kill someone for stealing that man from me.

My mind felt as if it were aching from trying to remember him and my past. The last year in Exile was hazy at best. Sybil said I laid in bed and hardly left. Why was I so sad when I woke up that day? Then my mind switched to trying to find something. I was missing something important, and I never could find it. Sybil had told me I had all of my possessions, but I didn't. I couldn't. Something in my chest didn't feel right.

It kept telling me to find it, over and over in my mind. But maybe I was losing my mind because even now I could feel that same sense of loss.

"Thea, look up." A deep voice said from somewhere next to me.

I froze when a figure appeared in front of me without warning. My darkness hummed with anticipation. It had to be eight feet tall with a slender frame and a large, white oversized cloak. Their beady red eyes stared at me, tilting their head as if to study me. I hadn't heard them approach me, but someone had and tried to warn me. Glancing around the woods, I did not see who that deep voice belonged to.

"What do you want?" I spoke firmly.

"You are in our forest, yet you question us?" It did not speak harshly, but the tone was unfriendly. My eyes scanned around us to see where the others were, but I couldn't find them. My gaze landed on a man who stood on the edge of the treeline. He was extremely tall with kind brown eyes. There was a woman next to him, but I couldn't make out her features before she was gone. I focused on the creature in front of me as it slipped its hood off, revealing female features. The tall woman had hair so blonde it looked white, and she was beautiful in a melancholy way. She was far too thin to be a fae, but I didn't know what she was.

"I didn't know this forest belonged to you; I was under the impression that it belonged to the king." Which king? I had no idea.

The woman's head nodded slightly before smiling, but her smile did not comfort me. Her mouth opened far wider than mine would, and her teeth were sharp and pointed. There were so many that went all the way back to her throat. Something stirred deep inside of me.

"Well, the king does own the land, but we have free rein if we stay on this side of the wall."

The word 'wall' triggered a memory of me sneaking around one and running into the forest. A forest that looked similar to the one we were in now. I shook the thought away.

"What do you want with me?"

"We're hungry." The woman smiled again. "You look very satisfying."

My heart rate picked up, but I did not show any signs of the fear I felt. I could feel something like an itch under my skin as the woman got closer. She smiled when I didn't try to run.

"Don't run. You can overpower her," the man said, drawing my attention toward him. He was still a good distance away. He wore simple clothing, but he seemed to glow slightly around his body.

"If you let me by, I'll let you live," I bluffed.

The woman's laugh floated through the air like a melody that did not match the disgusting beast she was.

She lunged at me before I could react, but her blow never hit me. A bright light burst in front of me, making me close my eyes instinctively. As I opened them, they had to adjust to the fiery mist that was now surrounding me. My eyes followed it to see it was coming from me. I have magic. Fire magic. Mixed with the fire were dark shadows, flitting about the fire and twisting in on themselves in a fluid motion.

I could hear the woman screeching on the other side of the fire mist, but I wasn't sure if it was in pain or frustration. With a simple flick of my wrist, my fire magic exploded around me. Then in an instant, it stopped swarming and came back to me. I glanced at the woman who lay burned on the ground. Her red eyes shifted to my face.

"Princess," she muttered to me.

"What did you call me?" I looked down at her, but she had already died. Something about the term 'princess' pissed my darkness off, making it swarm around me with fury.

The trees around me crackled and popped as they slowly burned. How could I have caused so much damage with such little effort? I summoned my fire magic, and it came forward again, but this time it sat in the palm of my hand. It was beautiful to witness the immense power it held, even in its small form. But then the black shadows tangled with the small ball of fire, causing the flames to burn black. Something about the two things entangled together had me smiling at them.

It wasn't long before the sounds of horses running at a fast pace caught my attention. I wouldn't be able to outrun them, but I could get away from them with my magic if I needed to, so I stayed where I was. When I looked for the brown-eyed man, he was gone.

Within a few minutes, dozens of men on horseback burst through the forest and through the smoke. Their light blue uniforms reminded me of the sky, and the crests on them were gold like the sun. The leader halted his horse immediately at the sight of me. The rest of the men followed suit, and for an intense minute, they all just stared at me. Then the leader rode closer and dismounted a few feet away. All of the men followed his lead.

Nothing had prepared me for what they did next.

They all bowed to me like I was important, just like Kai and Kaz did. My brows creased at the gesture.

"Captain," they all echoed into the small clearing. "Your family will be so happy to see you back home."

"My family?" I questioned.

"We will take you home immediately." The man stuck out his hand for me. He was tall, with untrusting eyes and no hair on his head. His tanned skin glistened with sweat as his dark eyes watched me closely.

"Thea," I whispered.

He chuckled softly.

"Yes, I know."

Right. He knew exactly who I was, and I didn't know anything apart from my name. I took his hand, and he helped me mount his horse before taking another man's horse for himself. Then we were sprinting in the direction they had all appeared from. In the short distance on top of a large hill sat a castle made of grey stone with blue flags waving in the breeze.

It filled me with a sense of unease when I looked at it. There wasn't a familiarity about it like I thought there would be. No excitement or happiness. I felt indifferent at the sight of it. Even as we rode closer, it still didn't feel right. Perhaps it was my lack of food or sleep in the past few days that made me feel like this.

"Home sweet home," the man sighed.

"The castle is my home?" I looked at it again, but nothing surfaced. No memory or comfort.

"Yes, I'm sure your family will be waiting at the doors."

Princess. That is what the woman had called me. The word didn't sound right to describe me; 'captain' sounded more proper for whatever reason.

"How did you know I was in the woods?" I asked.

"The fire exploding."

As we rode through town, I saw the way the fae in the streets stared at me. They did not seem happy to see me. Their whispers were undoubtedly at my expense. It did not feel very welcoming. I felt more like a spectacle than a fae.

When the gates to the castle came into view, I noticed the long stone wall that ran around the perimeter of the castle grounds. It was the same one that flashed in my mind earlier. I could see them standing through the gates at the door of the castle. A king, queen, and two women who were dressed in light blue, gold, and white attire.

When we dismounted the horse, no one said anything to me. They all stared at me in a way that I didn't know how to decipher. They almost looked scared of me. Something inside of me hummed at the sight of their fear. I liked to see them scared of me.

"You don't recognize us," the king said. "We're your... family."

I looked like the king in some ways, but I shared no resemblance to the queen or the women next to her.

"So, I'm a princess?" I crinkle my nose at the term without thought.

The queen's eyes nearly popped out of her pretty face when I spoke. The two women next to her scoffed softly.

"Y-yes, you're my eldest daughter," he stuttered over himself, which I found odd. He did not look confident in himself. "You were never fond of the term princess. You were—are the captain of my army."

That seemed right. Something about the sentence rang truer than any of this. I noticed they did not hug me; they did not say they missed me, but I kept that concern to myself.

"Aren't you wondering where I've been?" I questioned them.

"Of course, but we did not want to overwhelm you. Let's get you settled, and you can tell us over dinner."

I nodded and followed them inside, keeping my unease to myself. I kept my face indifferent as they walked in front of me. Their bodies were stiff and tense. The castle was pretty with the expensive decor and tapestries that cluttered the walls. The king turned and smiled at me over his shoulder, but it looked forced. We took a left to a grand staircase.

"My room is this way?" I glanced to the right and saw a door with stairs leading to a floor below us. That seemed familiar.

"Yes, we left your room just as you left it," he said, almost irritated. I nodded and followed without questioning it again. He stopped at the first door on the left and opened it. When I stepped into the room, it was mostly white with pops of blue and gold.

My mind flashed to a dark forest green bed and decor. I shook my head to clear it away. This room looked... dull.

"Did my room used to be green?"

"No."

"Hmm. It's not what I pictured for myself." I shrugged and looked in the drawers to see the blue uniform the guards wore. The color seemed wrong. My mind raced with thoughts of confusion. This didn't feel right, but why would they lie to me?

"Should I wear a dress to dinner?" I asked just to break the awkward silence.

"That would be good." The king smiled softly. "We will give you an hour to bathe and get ready."

I nodded and watched them leave. As soon as they left the room, I locked the door. When I turned back to the room, I saw a flash of dark green decor again. This was not my room. I would not like something so sterile and ugly. I slipped off the dark green cloak I wore and tossed it on the white bed.

I pulled out the darkest dress I could find in the closet. A dark blue that looked like sapphires. The bath was a welcome relief, and I didn't want to leave it, but I settled on getting out and getting dressed. I was eager to talk with my family and figure out some answers. When I went back to my room, I walked to the one window. I had pictured a vast garden with black fountains when I looked out, but I was greeted with a view of men training in a large field below me. I shook off the feeling of uneasiness as I finished getting ready.

I didn't bother getting too fancy before heading out of my room. A guard waited for me at the bottom of the stairs to lead me to the dining room. I paused at the doorway when I heard them whispering. I couldn't hear what was being said, so I walked in, and the whispering stopped. My eyes immediately went to the good-looking guy with dark blonde hair and pretty blue eyes. He wore gray instead of this kingdom's colors.

"You look wonderful, Thea," my father said. The younger man stared at me, specifically the tattoos that covered my arms. I ignored the stares and sat down away from them all, so my back was protected by the wall, and I could see the doorway and them. My darkness hissed at the younger man who watched me, then seemed to chuckle when I saw the large scar gashed into his cheek.

"What is everyone's name, and who am I related to?" I looked around when they continued to stare at me.

"Of course." The king stood up. "I'm King Luren of the Cerithian Kingdom; I'm your father. This is the queen, Gwyn, your stepmother, and our younger daughters, Tally and Mae. The man next to Tally is King Jesper of Kizar. He and Tally are to wed soon."

Brim had mentioned my mother.

"My real mother is where?"

The look of disgust on Gwyn's face couldn't be covered quickly enough. This was obviously a touchy subject. My eyes narrowed on her, and she swallowed hard when she noticed I was watching her. The darkness inside of me hummed at the fear I could feel from all of them. They were scared of me.

"Dead, for many years," my father snipped as if the topic was done being discussed. I nodded slightly as the first course was placed before us: a large steak and vegetables. My eyes drifted around the room, and I almost gasped when I saw the green flame floating behind my father. It wisped around the room and flashed between black and red. It was the same floating orb that had been by the man with shadows. Was this his pet or something? At my thought, it flashed gray, making it seem like it knew I called it a pet.

"What are you staring at?" One of my half-sisters spoke, but I didn't know which one it was.

"Nothing." I don't know why I didn't mention the floating orb, but it was clear that no one else saw it. Gods, it was a persistent thing, flashing like crazy as if it wanted my attention. Shit, I might have lost my mind. All of a sudden it rammed me, making me and my chair slide back slightly. The noise of the chair on the floor was awful. I wanted to glare at it and strangle the thing, but it moved far enough away that I couldn't reach it. Everyone stared at me oddly as I glared at an invisible being that seemed pissed off at me.

"So, what do you remember exactly?" Jesper was the one to ask.

"Nothing really. I remember being in Exile with others, but nothing before that. Even Exile is fuzzy. I knew my name, and that was it."

"And you escaped Exile, how?" the queen questioned.

"I jumped through the border." I shrugged. "It hurt, but didn't kill me. Then I just walked in a direction that felt right." That was a small lie because the black castle still haunted my mind.

It was silent for a long moment. Everyone stared at me like they were trying to see if I was lying. The tension in the room was awkward, but I did my best to ignore it.

"No one from the Crimson Kingdom saw you?"

"No one saw me." Crimson Kingdom. The black castle must have been Crimson. A castle that was far prettier than this gray one. "How did I end up in Exile?"

Everyone turned their eyes to the king.

They didn't even ask me what or where Exile was. My senses were on high alert. I didn't need memories to know that this was not my home. My eyes focused on the floating orb. She moved closer to me, and I could see the silhouette of a woman within the colorful flames. I glanced around the room when I felt that feeling of being watched again.

"We don't know. You were leading the army against Crimson, and we assumed you and the other elite magic holders had been killed. We didn't know you were being held prisoner by Crimson all this time."

Sybil's words rang in my head. The Crimson Kingdom was not responsible for our entrapment. She had been so adamant that it wasn't Crimson, and I trusted her far more than anyone in this room. Besides the fact that their reaction to seeing me did not look like a family who was devastated that I had died and miraculously survived.

"Was I cursed?"

The queen dropped her silverware on her plate, causing us to jump at the loud noise. They all glanced around at each other as they spoke without a word. The orb was flashing purple and green. What the hell was its problem?

"Yes, by Crimson. That is why you were fighting the war against them. You needed to break the curse, and to do that, you needed to win the war. You needed to kill their bloodline off."

Sybil still defended Crimson, and she knew of my curse. My eyes drifted around each fae as they stared at me oddly. I really didn't seem to like anyone here. The orb flashed red and black, and for some unknown reason, I knew it was angry at my father's words. But that wasn't what had me freezing to my spot. The man from the woods was standing next to the angry ball of light. He stared at me before glancing at the orb.

"Don't ask too many questions," he warned. "You're in danger here."

Before I could react, he disappeared. It was clear that my family didn't see or hear the man. I waited for him to reappear, but he didn't.

"Jesper," my father spoke in a tone that seemed strange. "Did you speak with Cassius?"

It wasn't lost on me that they all stared at me as they spoke. They were testing what I knew. Who was Cassius, and why would I care? My chest ached at the mention of the name, but I ignored it and focused on my food. The floating orb turned dark green, and the darkness inside of me started swarming at the name. It was...happy?

"No."

I continued eating. I had been so hungry, but I couldn't enjoy the food. I was not asked anything else at dinner until the end. Still, no one told me that I had been missed. No one hugged me. No one touched me. But I also found it odd that I didn't care. I didn't seem to miss anyone here either.

"Did I have a boyfriend or husband before I disappeared?"

The man with golden eyes was going to die. Tally made a noise of irritation towards me, and her eyes narrowed on me before grabbing Jesper's arm tightly.

"We were engaged." Jesper looked over my face slowly to gauge my reaction, but all I could focus on was his eyes. They weren't gold. And nothing about him appealed to me. I made a look of disgust before I could hide it.

"Oh," I sighed.

"This is probably awkward for you." Jesper started like he might apologize.

"It's not in the slightest. I have no idea who any of you are," I said honestly as I downed my drink. Jesper glared towards me but didn't say anything else. I excused myself to go to bed, but I paused outside of the dining room to see what they would say when I wasn't there.

"She really doesn't remember anything," Jesper sighed.

"No, it seems like she doesn't remember anything at all this time. She should get back to her old role of captain before the war starts; she is our only hope at winning against Crimson."

"I'll walk you to your room." I turned to see a guard staring at me. I nodded and pretended to not be eaves-dropping.

CHAPTER 5

THEA

"*I love you,*" *he called out to me again right before the sword descended on his neck.*

"No!" My voice shook the ground below me as I stared into the man's golden eyes as he kneeled, wounded. I had released some sort of barrier magic, but it did not reach him in time.

That sharp pain on my wrist let me know that I had not been able to save him again.

When I looked up, he was dead.

Dead.

Dead.

Dead.

Never coming back.

Gone.

He didn't exist anymore.

Dead.

A scream tore from me as I fell to my knees and self-destructed.

★★☾★★

A sob tore through me as I sat up in bed. I was sweating from my dream...vision. My face was wet with tears as an aching consumed my chest. He's going to die, and I won't save him in time.

Harsh whispers came from the hallway outside of my room, so I slipped out of bed and crept to the door. I opened the door and was greeted by two guards, but nothing else.

"Captain." They bowed.

"Why are you lingering at my door?"

"The king requested that you have protection." One of them stuttered out.

"Is everything alright? I thought I heard a noise." I lied.

"Fine." They both assured me. Their eyes stared at me, probably because of the tears soaking my face still.

"Protection from whom?" I asked. Did the guards stand outside everyone's bedroom?

"Cassius and Crimson." One of them spoke. The other guard gave him a look like he had said too much.

I nodded before shutting the door and going back to my bed. Cassius. I lay in bed and tried to remember the dream man's face, but I couldn't. I could still feel the pressure in my chest at his death. It felt all-consuming, and I couldn't sit there. It would kill me to think about him dying, even if I couldn't remember anything about his face.

His gold eyes flashed in my mind, and I groaned loudly as pain coursed through me. When I opened my eyes, I glanced around the room before getting up and dressing in my captain's uniform. The floating orb was in my room again, her color a melancholy gray. I stared at her and swore I saw a reflection of myself in it.

"Are you friendly?" I asked.

Her color turned vibrant green as she twirled around me. It made me feel comforted to see the color.

"Is there a reason only I can see you?"

She flashed orange, but I didn't know what that meant.

"You don't speak," I sighed. She flashed brighter orange, but then she disappeared when a knock on my door startled me.

Quickly, I walked to answer it, thinking it was one of the guards. The door swung open to Jesper standing too close to me. Fuck, why was he so close to my door?

"Your father would like you to meet him in the throne room. I will show you where it's at."

"Alright," I agreed and glanced over my shoulder once more for the floating friend I had seemed to make. She was gone.

"This must be overwhelming for you," Jesper said as we made our way downstairs.

"Honestly, not really. I thought I would be overwhelmed or maybe even upset, but I don't feel anything." I didn't like it here. I glanced at Jesper and saw his jaw clenched tightly. He looked angry, and I wondered what he was thinking. As soon as the thought crossed my mind, voices penetrated my mind, making me flinch.

"Are you alright?" Jesper asked. I nodded even though voices practically screamed into my mind. Jesper stopped me and stared into my eyes like he was concerned.

She is already acting weird. Something is wrong, and she's already lying to us.

"I'm fine. It's just a headache." I lied. I stared at him and waited to hear his voice again.

What has she remembered that she is already lying about?

My eyes dropped to his mouth to see if he was talking, but he wasn't.

She wants me to kiss her.

My face contorted with disgust because I did not want such a thing.

"You have food on your face." I lied. Jesper seemed to snap out of it, and his cheeks heated as he wiped off the nonexistent food and kept walking. My chest was tight with worry and confusion. I did not hear his thoughts—did I? I tried to keep my composure. He was suspicious of me, and that put me on high alert. My body was rigid and tight as I scanned around me for danger. As we approached the large wooden door at the end of the hallway, something about it filled me with dread.

When we entered the room, my father stood in the center of it, staring at me. His throne room fit him somehow. It was flashy and had an ungodly number of jewels in it. Not to my taste at all.

"Thea, thanks for coming in." My father's booming voice startled me. "I know you've been gone for quite some time, so if you would like a few days to rest, I understand. However, Crimson is planning on declaring war in the coming days, and I would like you to lead the army so that you can break your curse."

Seriously? I've been back for less than a day. I stared at my father, who looked like he was trying to keep his composure. Something dark lurked deep in me. I could feel it coiling tightly inside of me at the sight of him. It was angry and disgusted. I tried to shake the feeling, but I couldn't.

"You need to go." That deep voice said from somewhere to my left. "I know it's odd that they are sending you away already, but you have to go. You can feel it, can't you? That you do not belong here."

The man stepped forward enough that I could see him in my periphery. I nodded slightly as I watched my father closely.

The more I looked at my father and the throne room, the more I wanted to run away. *Leave. Leave. Leave.* A feminine voice purred into my mind. It was not my own voice or anyone I had heard before. I glanced around the room to see if someone else was there, but I couldn't see anyone. The man had disappeared again. Why the hell was my father thinking of sending me away after a few days? With the thought, his voice seeped into my mind as I stared at him.

Just take this mission and leave. She better not make this difficult this time. I need her gone before she starts asking questions.

"Actually, I would prefer to do something with my time. Should I head to the training field?" I agreed because something told me I shouldn't be here.

Thank the fucking stars.

"No, I have a task for you. You were always the greatest warrior I had—smart, tactical, and clever. We need to know how armed Crimson's territory is. You and a handful of guards will go to Crimson and see how far you can penetrate. I want to know anything about their army you can gather. This mission is to stay under the radar, no killing unless necessary. Do not get seen by anyone."

And stay the fuck away from Cassius.

"Alright." I nodded. Cassius, that name made my chest tight with longing again. "Are you sure I'm ready? Shouldn't I train first?"

"I think your skills will come to you effortlessly. If you're not up to it, I can appoint Palo as captain of my guard until you feel prepared."

Just agree to this and go.

"No. I'll do it." I was desperate to leave and try to figure things out on my own. They hadn't even sat and had a conversation with me about everything that happened. It was almost as if they didn't care. The darkness lingering inside of me hissed at the thought. Did they not miss me in the slightest? They had no questions or curiosities about where I had been or who I was with. It was almost like they knew it already. Sybil had said I would break my curse this time. Did that mean I had tried before? Now I'm pretty sure I wasn't losing my damn mind when I heard their thoughts.

"Good, now go."

Alright, prick. I turned on my heel and headed for the doors, where I was greeted by four guards. They bowed, but I ignored them and headed for the stables outside. My father had yet to mention my fire magic, and I wondered if he even knew I possessed it. Was the ability to hear thoughts another form of elite magic? What was this darkness that lived inside of me?

My mind was constantly filled with questions about my family's odd and unwelcoming behaviors as we rode toward Crimson. None of the guards spoke to me, but I noticed how each of them watched me too closely. What were they looking to see?

★★☽★★

We made it to Crimson by nightfall the next day. We waited on the territory line that night to see what patrols would show up, but none did. My men sat away from me and did not engage me in conversation, but I didn't mind. I stayed up all night because I was restless, and I didn't trust these men with me.

At first light, I woke the men and led them into Crimson territory. We were met with no resistance. Either this was a trap, or Crimson did not think Cerithia would be stupid enough to cross their borders. We watched for guards all day, but none made an appearance. It wasn't until we got closer to the city below the black castle that we saw our first soldier.

His crimson-red uniform left no mistake as to who he was. We watched as he seemed to be watching the city border, but not intently. He did not expect anything to lurk in the shadows. He was big and burly; he looked like he would be mean, but something about his face made me... happy.

"Zade!" someone yelled. I watched the man who had been patrolling. Something about his name stuck with me. His face broke out into a comforting smile when he saw the other guard coming toward him.

"Haden, I thought you were off patrol for a few days," Zade said. Haden's dark blonde hair was chaotic, and his eyes looked directly to where I was hiding. I held my breath, but he looked away without noticing me in the shadows. I watched them both as they laughed with each other. Something about the two of them mesmerized me. Their faces seemed familiar, and that only made me more concerned because they were our enemies. Why did they seem more familiar than my family?

"Cassius is going to be a real dick at training tomorrow." Haden frowned.

Cassius, my darkness hummed.

"This has never happened. Hopefully, we don't have to cancel the trials." Zade looked worried. Trials. Sybil had mentioned them, but what had she said about them?

There had been too much going on to remember exactly. My men were standing with me, listening intently.

"Why do you think Cassius is losing his shit every day that passes?" Haden looked directly at where I was again and looked confused. "I think there's someone over there." He cocked his head to the side like it would help him see me. "I can sense something."

Shit.

I didn't actually feel in danger, but my men were insistent that we leave immediately. I headed toward them but stopped when the man appeared in front of me.

"Wait, you need to see him," he said softly. "He is almost here."

"Who?"

I took a few more steps forward until I heard a third man speak behind me, and something about his voice made me look back. My mind practically ached as if something was trying to break free, but it couldn't. The man's black uniform stretched across his broad shoulders. Gods, he was taller than any fae I had seen. Even though I could not see his face, something about him drew me in. I could not stop watching him.

"Cassius," the men spoke as they bowed.

This was Cassius. My eyes widened as I watched him closely. I took a hesitant step toward him. This was the man the guards insisted might come for me, so they kept guard outside my bedroom. The fae my father wanted me to stay away from, but he didn't actually warn me against him. That darkness inside of me swarmed feverishly inside of me at the sight of him. It was happy to see him.

"Don't fucking bow at me," he huffed. His voice soothed me like a warm hug. I could listen to him speak all day. I couldn't see anything about him but his dark hair. His shadows swarmed around him like an angry cloud. "Training is two hours earlier tomorrow."

"For fuck's sake," they both groaned.

He laughed softly. I swallowed hard as I stared at Cassius' back. My eyes locked in on him, hoping he would turn so I could see his face. Show me your face.

"I can't sleep, so no one will. Not until we find..."

One of my men yanked my arm, so I couldn't hear what he said. I glared at him. The darkness inside of me wanted me to slit his throat for interrupting what Cassius was going to say.

"There are more guards coming; we should retreat."

I nodded and glanced over my shoulder, but the three of them were gone. My chest squeezed with emotion, but I didn't understand why. Haden and Zade had seemed familiar, but they were Crimson soldiers. How could I possibly know them? Perhaps I met them in battle before. The whole way back to Cerithia, I just thought of their faces and the man with shadows. Cassius. My father had talked about him briefly at dinner, like he and Jesper would talk, but that made no sense if he was an enemy. The man who followed me made sure I saw him. Cassius was important, but I didn't know why.

"Did anything look odd to you?" one of the men had asked me. I found his question strange as we dismounted our horses when we were back in Cerithia the following night.

"Just that they didn't have guards at the border. They aren't expecting an attack. We got extremely close to their city. I suppose that is odd."

The guard nodded. I watched him carefully as we were ushered to see my father almost immediately. The king stood in the throne room as we went in, but his eyes drifted to the soldier who had asked me the question. The soldier gave him a subtle nod as if to say no.

"So how was it?"

I want to hear my father's thoughts.

Please don't make this difficult.

"Fine, their forces are not waiting around for an attack. It's like they don't realize war is coming," I said. "Are they? Or are *you* declaring war?"

"It depends on if Cassius decides to attack before we plan to in a week's time," my father answered without looking at me. "You must be exhausted. You are dismissed."

It depends on what you do.

I didn't know what he meant by that. I nodded and started to leave but paused when the guards didn't follow.

"Are you guys coming?" I asked.

"I have to get them their wages for going with you. We'll see you tomorrow." My father stared at me intently.

Get the fuck out.

"Alright."

The four guards that accompanied me stayed behind. Once I was out the door, I waited to hear them talking.

"She didn't seem to know anything," one of them spoke. "We even saw Cassius."

"Interesting," he said. "She didn't remember him?"

Remember Cassius? I knew Cassius, and my father seemed worried about it. I slipped that nugget of information away for later.

"No."

"Perfect, we will plan on leaving for war in a few days. She needs to kill Cassius."

My darkness swarmed at the thought of Cassius dying, and I thought it was odd.

"What are you doing?" I turned to see Jesper.

"Snooping." I shrugged. I figured acting nonchalantly would throw him off my trail, and when he smiled, I figured it had worked.

"Sounds like you," he chuckled. "You were always a bit of a troublemaker."

I nodded but took that as my cue to leave. I hurried past him and pretended to go to my room, but instead, I waited around the corner until I heard my father's throne room door open. Peeking around the corner, I watched the guards shuffle out of the room and disappear down the hallway before Jesper walked into the room with my father. I hurried forward and stood at the cracked door.

"Well, she saw Cassius and didn't remember him." My father said happily. "Maybe all of our plans will come together this time."

"Don't get too hopeful; she still has to kill Cassius."

My father sighed heavily before he spoke. "You can have a little optimism."

"Every time we have optimism, our plan goes to shit," Jesper snapped. "We have sacrificed enough. We can't afford to keep doing this, so it better work this year. My mother won't help another year."

"You sound like your bitter mother," Luren said angrily. "No one has sacrificed more than I have through this damn curse. Do you need to remind your mother that she owes me her cooperation for what she did to *my* sons?"

Jesper scoffed.

"Your bastard sons. Sons that you didn't care about until you could use them to hold over my mother's head."

Shock coursed through me. I had brothers.

"You little shit." My father began, but Jesper cut him off.

"I would tread very carefully, Luren. You need me and my mother to make sure this all goes in your favor. My mother has sacrificed too, or did you forget *who* you had those sons with? They were *her* children too."

What in the actual fuck was happening? My father didn't say anything in return, but I could feel their tension from in the hallway. Did Gwyn know that my father had sons?

"Get out of my sight," Luren demanded. I hurried away when I heard Jesper coming toward the door. It wasn't until I was safe in my room that I let out a deep breath. When I turned toward my bed, a woman stood near the window watching me with her red eyes. But it was the fact that she looked just like me that made me let out a startled scream.

"Shit," she muttered before disappearing. My bedroom door burst open as two guards stormed in.

"Captain?" they asked while looking around.

I opened my mouth, but I couldn't get the words out. My friendly dark green orb appeared in the room and flashed between black and red. I don't know how I knew she was warning me to not say anything, but I did.

"I saw... a spider."

They looked at each other before looking at me suspiciously but didn't question me any further before leaving my room. What the hell is happening?

CHAPTER 6

CASSIUS

Forty-nine. There were still only forty-nine partici-pants standing there. My heart pounded violently as I glanced around at each one, hoping that I had missed her somehow. But as I stared into the group of men, I knew she hadn't come. Her green eyes were not hidden behind her green cloak. I didn't feel her close by.

She had missed the trials.

This was the first time she had never made it. Panic was taking over because I felt helpless. I didn't know what to do. I didn't know where Thea was. My father stood to my left and Haden to my right. But my eyes stared at the gate, waiting for her to walk through it. She still might show up.

"Cassius." My father had turned to face me. "Maybe…"

"We can wait a little longer." I cut him off. "Maybe she ran into some trouble."

I didn't need to look at my father or Haden to know they were staring at me with pity. The trials were supposed to start yesterday, but I postponed it until today to give her more time. Haden's hand gripped my shoulder.

"She isn't coming."

I broke my trance on the gate and looked at Haden. He frowned when he saw how distraught I was becoming. Thea was missing. She never broke out of Exile to steal from the villages. Not once in the past year had she left Exile. My chest squeezed tightly. I was losing it.

"The trials are canceled this year; we apologize for the inconvenience. If you need a place to stay and food, we will open the commons area in the castle for the night," my father said.

It was like a knife in the heart.

No one complained too much as they shuffled past us and took advantage of the free meal and bed. Once they were gone, I finally looked at my father.

"Son." He frowned.

"She's never missed the trials." I started pacing because I was losing my fucking mind. "What if Luren killed her before she ever left Exile?"

Flashes of watching Thea die hit me, each one making me feel sick. I couldn't lose her again, but I especially couldn't lose her before we had a chance to fight for our lives back.

"Cassius, let's not think the worst," Haden said. I turned my body toward him.

"Why not? It's a very real possibility, Haden. Thea never came out of Exile this time. She never stole from the homes. She never killed any guards we had stationed in the Forbidden Woods. She *never* came out. Sybil would have talked her into leaving by now." I froze. "Unless Luren has her."

"Are those the only two options?" Haden sighed. "Maybe she is still sitting safely in Exile."

"She hasn't let me in her dreams for days. I don't feel her through the bond. I'm losing my fucking mind here." I ran my hands through my hair. "What if she didn't even get a chance this year because those fucking witches that attacked Exile got her?"

They didn't say anything because they knew too. They knew something was wrong. My chest was heavy with longing and desperation. I missed Thea, and it felt like it was going to kill me. Where the fuck was she?

I was suffocating. If I didn't even get to see her this year, I was killing Luren. I didn't give a shit about the fucking prophecy. I would cut his fucking head off and stake it up for everyone in the realm to see. Della told me that it was not in the cards for me to kill him, that it would be Thea, but I was hardly containing this rage inside of me.

My shadows seeped from me as I walked into the castle and straight to my father's throne room. I gripped the wooden table as I glanced over the map of Elloryon. Where are you, my love? My eyes were pulsing black as I looked over the map, like it would mark her location magically. I paused on Cerithia before closing my eyes and trying to calm myself down. I was spiraling.

My father, Haden, Leer, and Zade shuffled in and shut the door.

"Maybe we should declare war so that you can see if Luren has her?" My father looked at me. "We can declare, and you can cross into Cerithia to search for her."

I contemplated it for a moment but honestly didn't give it much thought at all.

"Then let's declare." I glanced up at them staring at me as I lost my fucking composure. I was hardly keeping it together before, but now I was feeling a sense of urgency.

"Is that crazy?" I sighed and pinched my nose, closing my eyes tightly to control myself. "Tell me if I'm being irrational."

No one said anything, so I opened my eyes and glared. I knew I was being irrational. Haden stepped forward.

"No one here is stupid enough to tell you that you're being irrational when it comes to Thea." He gave me a small smile. "We will do whatever it takes to find her. If war is what needs to happen to find her, then let's do that."

"We are going to assume that Luren has kidnapped her at this point." I nodded and took a calming breath. Suddenly, Wisp, as I had taken to calling her, appeared in front of me. She had been gone for days, and that also worried me. She was twirling around, her color purple. I wasn't sure I had ever seen her this color before. But as soon as she made herself known, she disappeared again.

Damn it.

"What happens if we find her? Since the trials are canceled, how do we convince her to get the bloodstone?" Leer asked.

I had no fucking idea.

"Let's worry about finding her first," my father sighed. "If Luren has her, then we don't know in what capacity. Maybe she escaped and went to Cerithia on her own."

I froze and narrowed my eyes on my father. He gave me a look that let me know he was ready to fight if I really wanted to. "Don't look at me like that, Cassius. She doesn't know any better. If she went willingly, that would be the best-case scenario. Luren would think he could use her, so she'd be safe."

He had a point, but I still didn't like it.

"We will take a few days to train and get ready, then head out." I nodded, feeling good about the plan.

This year would be different. Mikel was no longer interfering with us, thanks to Della. I would not let this happen another year. Thea was mine, and I wasn't letting anyone keep her from me. Not the stars, not the gods, not her father.

A strong sense of hatred filled my blood bond, making my thoughts scatter.

"Fuck," I breathed.

"What's wrong?" Zade asked.

"I just felt Thea through the bond, and she really fucking hates something."

Haden let out a sigh of relief.

"So, she's alive somewhere. That's a step in the right direction. Are you sure it was hatred you felt?" Haden asked.

"Yes. She is really fucking angry too." The feelings were overwhelming to the point I had to grip the table and bow my head at the onslaught of rage she was pumping down the bond. "Fuck, what would make her feel like this?"

Flashes of what Jesper did to her last time plagued me. No. She would feel scared or anxious if that were happening. This was white-hot rage and hatred.

"Probably not something in Exile, so she's probably out," Leer said, hopeful. I agree with that. My first thought was Jesper or a member of her family.

The emotions down the bond cut off abruptly. I would rather feel her rage than nothing. I glanced up at all of them staring at me.

"Let's get ready to find my wife."

We thought we had been sneaky for the past few weeks. We destroyed an enemy scouting camp, but we had managed to stay out of sight of the Cerithian army. Palo, their new captain since Thea killed Jeb, was not known for being strategic. It was odd for him to play this game of cat and mouse. But when I found my empty scouting camp burned to the ground, I realized that Palo was on to us.

Then I found another one burned down a few days later. Palo had grown a pair recently because he usually wasn't so aggressive with his tactics. I had gone to the Cerithian castle last night to try and find Thea, but I couldn't. Her room hadn't been slept in; dust coated the bedding, so I didn't think she was there. My mind had been distracted since I didn't find her. Maybe she was in Exile.

But now I had declared war, so I had to fight until I pushed Cerithia back to their lands. This should be easy because Palo was a spineless captain, but for some reason, he decided to be a pain in my ass these past two weeks.

I glanced around the burned scout camp we came upon. This was the third one he destroyed, and it just irritated the fuck out of me. How did he know where our camps were, and how did he do it without being caught?

"What do you want to do?" Haden glanced at me.

"We need to make this a face-to-face battle. Let's find the Cerithian bastards and end them. I will handle their coward of a captain, Palo, by myself."

We headed back toward the base camp we had set up. The temperature was dropping with the setting sun. All I could think of was going back to Cerithia tonight to spy on Luren and figure out where Thea was. Suddenly, something in the air shifted, making me glance around us. But I heard them before I ever saw them. I stopped and held up my hand so that all the men halted too. We were on the edge of a large clearing, and across it I saw Cerithian guards on horseback.

I slipped on my helmet to get ready for our attack. It was clear that Cerithia didn't expect to see us either because they were loud as they talked and rode through the woods. A moment later their captain halted. Gods, Palo was much shorter for a male than I remembered from our one brief meeting. I was instantly pissed off that he was on Kaida. That was Thea's horse, not his.

Onyx seemed to recognize Kaida as he became frantic to get over to her. He wouldn't move, though, until my command. I decided I was stealing her fucking horse after I killed Palo.

Palo wore a helmet that covered his whole face, but I could feel his eyes on me. He was waiting to see what I would do.

"Their captain is mine," I called out.

Palo's horse took a step towards us, and I took that as my signal to meet him in the center of the field and end him so I could go find my wife. Palo hesitated for a moment before charging straight for me, his men following. Onyx was much faster than Kaida, so I met him a little past halfway through the field. I unsheathed my sword. Palo copied me, and we collided.

The force of our swords knocked us both from our horses and to the ground. I recovered quickly with my sword in my hand. I charged at him, not giving him one second to spare. He tripped over his feet but then regained his fighting stance as we swung at each other. Palo met me blow for blow, which surprised me because men didn't last long in a sword fight with me. The clanking of swords around us let me know that our men had followed us and were now in full battle.

Palo ducked low and pulled a dagger out, almost spearing me in the stomach. For fuck's sake, when did Palo become a worthy opponent? I barely dodged it, but I managed. Palo and I stared at one another for a long moment before we both charged again, but this time we did the same moves. I narrowed my eyes on him. Did he learn my technique to fuck with me? If I was being honest, it was working. Palo stumbled back, getting caught up in his own feet because his stance wasn't wide enough.

We fought, just the two of us, amongst the chaos of all the soldiers. It was clear our men knew that we would fight each other, and no one bothered us.

I could hear the screams of dying men behind me. Magic blazed through the fields, but I could not tell who had the upper hand—us or Cerithia. A strong scent of burning overtook the space around us, and it was so foul that my eyes burned with disgust. Their captain stumbled backward as I swung my sword toward him.

He was getting sloppy and fell over the body of a dead fae. I smiled triumphantly as I sent my shadows for him. They wrapped him up, ready to crush his body into dust at my command. My eyes shifted to Wisp, who was suddenly in front of me. Her flames flashed from dark green to purple.

I don't know what that means, little viper. I watched her for a moment before turning my attention back to Palo. I stepped forward and sneered at him. I raised my dagger toward him, but Wisp got in between us again, this time flashing red.

"Any last words, Captain?" I hissed.

Wisp expanded at my tone. What was she so damn worried about? I glanced around, hoping that Thea was here for some reason. Why else would she be freaking the fuck out? I didn't see Thea. I took another step toward Palo, but Wisp refused to let me get close.

Then Wisp expanded and exploded between us, ripping my shadows from Palo and shooting me back. Fuck, I landed on my back and tried to catch my breath as I stared at the stars. The wind blew across my face, letting me know I lost my helmet. I stood, fucking furious that Wisp was being a psycho over Palo. Jealousy that Thea's soul was protecting another man made me enraged.

I stood up, ready to go kill Palo solely on the fact that Wisp was attached. She was mine. I wasn't sharing her affections with anyone. My eyes landed on Palo as he stood. He was fucking dead, and I would make it painful. He hadn't lost his helmet in the explosion, but it was clear he was watching me. I took a step toward him, but I stopped when I felt a rush of lust and desire through the bond. Gods, it was crippling as I tried to walk to Palo. I physically couldn't move because of Thea's emotions; she pumped down the bond.

What the fuck was Thea doing that made her feel like this? A new layer of jealous rage coated me as I stood frozen on the battlefield, staring down Palo.

Chapter 7

Thea

Fucking Cassius. His damn shadow magic had me in a death grip. They tangled around me so tightly that I dropped my weapon. He stood, towering over me. I didn't need to see his face to know he was smiling, but not in a kind way. My darkness inside that had protected me all week did not stir with concern. It seemed content to be this close to their captain. My eyes shifted to the floating orb of light behind his shoulder. She was burning bright green, which I had come to learn was her being happy.

Why was she happy? Did she want me to die?

"Any last words, Captain?" He muttered softly. Fuck, his voice was perfect. Strong, cold, and indifferent—powerful. The floating orb was between us in a flash. Her color turning from green to purple. I knew I was mistaken, but I swear Cassius was watching her. He glanced around before turning his attention back to me.

"Fuck you," I answered, but the floating orb expanded so large around us that she exploded, and he didn't hear what I said. His shadows ripped from me as all the fae went flying from the explosion. My head pounded as I lifted myself off the ground. Sitting up, I looked around the field of dead guardsmen. Red and blue uniforms littered the field and the forest surrounding it. Shit. How many men did I just lose?

My eyes caught a movement from my left. Cassius stood in his black armor. His helmet had been lost in the explosion. Fire blazed behind him, only adding to the pure rage on his face. His black eyes flickered around him. When he faced me, I could have sworn my soul left my body.

Of course, he was a handsome bastard. His tanned skin glistened with sweat. Blood ran down the side of his face. But it was his shadows that swarmed around him that made him look like the most beautiful monster I had ever seen. Stars above, I couldn't look away from how beautifully menacing he looked. Cassius looked like a god standing in hell.

His jaw tensed and his hands fisted so tightly that I knew I would not be able to overpower the wrath that was currently consuming him. He started to take a step toward me, then stopped for no particular reason. Something dark stirred deep inside me. It practically purred at the sight of

Cassius. Fuck, I was practically drooling over my enemy. My darkness wanted him to come over here and touch us.

He took a small step toward me before stopping like he couldn't move.

"Crimson!" His deep, terrifying voice boomed into the dead silence. "Fall back!"

I was too busy gawking at Cassius to realize some of my men had also stood, and they rushed to me. At least this damn helmet kept my face hidden from them as I admired our enemy.

"Captain, let's get the fuck out of here." They helped me stand. But Cassius just stared at us without attacking. Why didn't he keep attacking us? I headed for Kaida, but the bastard grabbed her reins with his shadows and stole her. He took my damn horse, and something about it just felt like a slap in the face. Probably because she went willingly, looking happy as she nudged his black horse, he climbed on. He gave me a sneer as he turned and left.

We retreated quickly to our base camp.

I sent a few men to let my father know what happened and hoped he would send more guards before Cassius decided to attack us in our weakened state. That was days ago. Most of the men who survived were wounded, and I was surprisingly unharmed. My eyes darted around the woods to see if anything was lurking, but so far nothing. My mind kept replaying Cassius standing so terrifyingly in the field. Lust was consuming my thoughts, and I needed to realize Cassius was not someone to swoon over.

"Thea."

I turned with my viper-handled dagger in my hand and nearly stabbed it through Jesper's eyeball. The thought made me happy.

"What the fuck are you doing here?" I looked around and realized I had been so distracted by that Crimson prick that I hadn't even heard Jesper. The sun had come up, and I hadn't noticed. I was exhausted. I was distracted by Cassius. Over Jesper's shoulder, I saw the man with brown eyes watching us concerned.

"Your men came back and said it was bad. I brought Kizar men and wanted to check on you." His eyes looked friendly, and everything about Jesper appeared friendly, but an overwhelming sense of hatred consumed me at the sight of him. My darkness did not like him, and that made my guards go up.

The floating orb appeared behind him, her color a wisp of black. She was pissed.

"Isn't being in a war below a king?" I raised my brow at him.

"Yes," he agreed. "I was just worried you were hurt and needed to see for myself how bad the damage was."

My neck prickled with uneasiness. He was here to spy on me. What was he and my father so damn worried I would do? Or find out? I glanced around at his men before turning back to him. I was in a war; what kind of trouble could I get myself into?

"I'm fine. You can go back to the safety of your castle."

I turned from him, but he gripped my wrist and yanked me back. A memory flashed so quickly that I didn't register it at first. *Jesper beating me. His handsome face twisted like a sadistic monster as I begged him to stop.*

"Thea?" Jesper's concern pulled me out of the memory. I yanked my arm from him instantly and backed away. His eyes narrowed on the movement as his jaw clenched tightly. "What's wrong?"

"I don't like to be touched. Now leave; I have a job to do."

He stared at me so angrily that I gripped my dagger tighter in my hand to the point of pain. I would slice him open if he thought of hurting me. His eyes fell to where my dagger was before the anger disappeared in the blink of an eye.

"I'm going." He smiled, but it did little to comfort me. "Just remember that we're watching everything you do. So, tread carefully."

Before I could respond, he turned and left our camp. He was threatening me. My eyes flickered at all the men in gray uniforms staring at me now. I swallowed hard. I had hardly slept and wanted to rest, but that would be impossible with them watching me. I was so uncomfortable that I went to my tent and slept with my dagger in my hand.

★★☽★★

Crimson had never come to attack us, and I was thankful because I hadn't slept well in the week that Kizar guards came here. They watched me closely—too closely. I was sick of waiting for the war to find us, so today we were looking for Crimson. The sooner I could end this war, the sooner I could get away from these lurking spies my father and Jesper had.

We had packed camp this morning and slowly made our way through the thick forest between Crimson and Falgon. I was so lost in my thoughts that I almost missed how silent the woods became. My horse stopped, and I immediately glanced around us. The stupid helmet my father gave me severely limited my sight. My eyes caught movement in the trees ahead of us. I narrowed my eyes on the men hiding.

"Fall back!" I yelled, but it was too late. A cloud of arrows cascaded down on us. I flinched, waiting for the arrows to kill me, but they never hit. When I looked up, there was some sort of barrier magic above us. Thank the gods someone here had used their magic. Crimson guards had started advancing and were already almost to us. I urged my horse to run forward as soon as Cassius came into my view.

He didn't wear a helmet today, which sucked for me because he was still distractingly handsome. Lust instantly coiled in my stomach. His dark hair blew back in the wind, and his black eyes narrowed on me. He was fixated on me, not bothering to try and fight anyone else near him. It would be a shame to kill him. I ignored every other guard around me too, and Cassius' focus never wavered. He gave me a smile full of hatred as he closed in on me.

He repositioned himself on his horse, but before I could understand what he was doing, he leaped from his horse and tackled me off of mine. His arms had me in a death grip as we soared through the air. Fuck, this was going to hurt. My body cushioned his fall, and his muscled body nearly crushed me to death. Wheezing, I stood as he did. He pulled out a dagger and swung it at me, not giving me a second to try and catch my breath.

Dodging it, I pulled mine from my boot and swiped at him. He almost didn't dodge my strike. His surprised face looked at me before he made his next move. Cassius was fast for how tall and built he was. He missed me narrowly but struck again quickly with a second dagger. I groaned when the blade sliced my thigh.

Fuck.

I was panicking as blood seeped down my leg. I tossed my dagger at him, and it missed when he turned his shoulder slightly. Well, that was a stupid move. Cassius smiled at me before charging forward. I reached down and grabbed a sword from a dead fae. For fuck's sake, this thing weighed as much as I did. I swung it as best as I could to deflect his daggers. The man was going to kill me. He was charging at me without relenting. I was too exhausted to keep up with him.

My sword tangled with his daggers, pulling me close to him. His eyes were black as night as he stared at my armored face.

A vision of Cassius and me in this same position hit me like an arrow. Only that time he smiled at me in a way that had lust pumping through me. The memory was enough to distract me from his violent shove backward. I stumbled, trying desperately to keep my balance. He moved forward and kicked me so forcefully in the chest that my feet lifted off the ground as I flew back.

My lungs lost all their air when I landed on my back. I stared up at the dark sky, feeling dazed. I could hear swords clanging, and the smell of smoke assaulted me. Cassius was moving for me quickly. He would overpower me, especially since I hadn't been training for long. I wouldn't go out without giving him hell. Taking a deep breath, I waited for him to get close enough to me, and when he was, I swiped my foot out, taking his legs out from under him.

He landed with a grunt, and I was crawling on top of him. I punched that handsome face twice before he shoved me off. We both stood, our breathing labored. His brow was bleeding slightly down his face.

"Why don't you take off that helmet and face me like a man, Captain?" He sneered at me. Stars above, at least his face would give me a pretty view as I died. Neither of us had daggers. Where did his go? I glanced around, but I didn't see them.

"You're a gifted fighter," he breathed heavily as he stayed in his fighting stance. "Most men don't last ten seconds. Who trained you?"

I didn't know who trained me. Maybe I taught myself. That damned memory of Cassius and me sword fighting hit me again.

"Fuck," I muttered as my head became dizzy at the onslaught of the memory playing repeatedly. My broken mind was going to get me fucking killed. As I steadied myself, Cassius just watched me curiously. A moment later, the floating, colorful orb appeared between us. She was flashing bright purple. Cassius could see her too. Maybe she was his pet. His brows furrowed as he glanced at her and then at me. Something like confusion filled his features.

"I don't feel like beating you to death. Let's use daggers," he sighed as he looked around the field at his men. Cassius seemed bored fighting me, and it hurt my feelings for some unknown reason. That damn purple orb was twirling in front of Cassius, and he was watching her again. Confusion filled his eyes before he glanced around like he might see someone.

"How fucking gracious of you," I snapped. This had him twisting his body toward me quickly. His black eyes cascaded over me as if he could see through my stupid armor. Cassius tilted his head slightly to the side as if trying to decide if he heard me right.

"Where is Palo?" he questioned. "The captain of the Certhian armies?"

"I'm the captain," I answered.

This time I could see his body tense when he realized his worthy opponent was a woman. Through the slit of my armored helmet, I could see his chest rise and fall quickly. The purple orb calmed down now and just floated calmly between us.

"Give me my dagger and let's get this over with," I demanded.

"Find your own," he muttered, but it was more confused than angry. My eyes drifted to the viper-handled dagger he was holding.

"You find your own and give me my damn dagger." I pointed to the viper-handled blade and held out my hand for it. Cassius glanced at the dagger before turning around and looking over the ground. A moment later he leaned over and plucked my dagger, which I missed him with, out of the ground. He lifted it and inspected it.

They were the same daggers. He glanced at me, and I swore I saw a smirk grace his face. What the fuck was he so happy about? An overwhelming feeling of relief and happiness flooded me, but it wasn't my own. Cassius tossed my dagger between my feet, and I picked it up. Cassius smiled brightly at me. Something in the air shifted as he watched me. His eyes flickered to the floating orb, and I swore his smile widened at it.

He focused on me again before he charged me. I twisted away from him, but he knew what I was doing and moved from my swipe. Cassius rushed me, and we both made the same moves. Everything I did, Cassius mirrored me. What the fuck was this—some sort of weird magic?

"What's wrong, Captain?" He smiled without hatred this time. I charged at him, and my body seemed to remember how to fight because I did things without thought. My blade stopped an inch from his ribs as his hand wrapped around my wrist, and he yanked me so I was against him. Fuck, I could feel his muscled body perfectly.

"This helmet is doing you no favors, Thea." He had wrapped me in his shadows and ripped my helmet from me. Shit. My father said they would know me. Cassius' handsome face looked over me like he was assessing something sacred. His eyes dropped to my mouth briefly before meeting my eyes. His hand brushed my braid over my shoulder. My heart hammered in my chest at his odd gesture. He released me, and I stumbled back.

"That's much better." His eyes glided across my face. "I've been looking everywhere for you."

A moment later, I heard someone else coming up behind me.

"Stop!" Cassius ordered. "She belongs to me. Go get Haden, Zade, and Leer. Tell them to come here immediately."

The guard scurried away. While he was distracted, I stepped forward and stabbed his leg.

"Fuck!" he groaned. His wild, black eyes pinned me to my spot, but gods, he looked proud of me.

"That's for cutting me earlier," I breathed out with a vicious smile.

We both took our stance, and Cassius smiled as I rushed him first. Again, we did the same moves. It was like a never-ending sparring match. We both breathed heavily, but neither of us was stopping. Sweat ran down my back as I tried desperately to keep up with him. I'm sure he had worked and trained much harder than I did for this. There was no way I could win. He looked like he was hardly sweating.

"Fucking hell." I heard from my side, and I made the mistake of turning toward the familiar voice. Haden from the scouting mission stood staring at me, but then two overly large fae appeared too.

"Shit." One of them muttered as he looked at me.

Cassius leveled me onto my back and pinned me down. He pointed his dagger at my throat.

"Dead." He gleamed at me.

"That's not fair. They distracted me," I spoke like this wasn't a war. Cassius shifted, and I groaned under his weight. Gods, his weight felt good on top of me.

"You should know better than to get distracted, little viper."

My heart pounded, but I wasn't sure if it were because of how completely inappropriately attractive I found this man or because I knew he would kill me in a moment. *Gods, please let Exile be free if I die.* I squeezed my eyes shut tightly, giving in to my fate.

"What are you doing?" Cassius asked. His warm breath fanned over my face. Stars, he smelled good, like rain and forest.

"Just kill me quickly," I spoke.

It was so silent, besides the men still fighting around us. So, I cracked my eyes open, and Cassius was smiling at Haden. They were talking without saying a damn word. He was happy. Cassius glanced down at me. Then he leaned close to my face and gave me a chaste kiss. My heart hammered quickly as I tried not to kiss him back.

"What the fuck?" I thrashed under him so he wouldn't know how much I liked that.

"My prize for winning this match." His smile was so bright that I stopped moving so I could admire him. "If you win the next one, I'll let you choose your prize."

"How about killing you? I won't stop; I'll plunge that dagger into your heart."

His face fell for a moment.

"We'll see about that, Thea."

He glanced over my face slowly once more before standing up. I stood up quickly and got in my fighting stance. Cassius kept his back to me as he walked to Haden. There was not a fuck given that I could stab him right now. My eyes shifted to Haden as he gave me a small wave and a friendly smile. What the fuck was this?

"Widen your stance." Cassius looked over his shoulder at me. "That's why you lose your footing so often. Widen it. I taught you better than that."

He was giving me fighting advice. What the hell was happening here? I glanced around and saw our men were pretty evenly matched as they still fought.

"I look forward to sparring with you again soon, Captain." Cassius smiled at me before his shadows burst out into the field, covering everything in sight. They caressed my face softly before they disappeared, taking all of the Crimson guards with them.

I stared at where he had been and felt confused about why I felt... sad.

Chapter 8

Thea

"Again," I demanded.

"Cap—"

"Now! That's an order." I breathed heavily. The Kizar guard looked at me like I had lost my mind. I had. It had been a week since Cassius let me go, and I trained every day in the base camp. I had to keep my mind busy because Cassius haunted my every thought, whether I was awake or asleep. At least I wasn't dreaming of haunting golden eyes watching me as they lost their light. Now, Cassius consumed everything.

He was in every thought. He was in every breath I took. He was in every damn thing I did. I'm sure he was having fun teasing me until he could catch me off guard and sink his dagger into me. But gods, I couldn't stop thinking about him kissing me. A heavy ache had settled over me, and I desperately needed a release, but I would not give my enemy the satisfaction of getting off to his handsome face.

The guard swung for me, but I dodged him quickly. I was getting quicker and not tripping over myself. I widened my stance.

"Such a good girl." Cassius' voice took over my thoughts. A flash of him smiling at me took over my vision.

His face disappeared as soon as the guard punched me in the face.

"Oh shit." The guard came over to me to help me off my back. "I'm sorry."

What was wrong with me? Was I daydreaming about my enemy, or were these memories? It had to be daydreaming. It didn't make sense to have memories with that man.

"I'm alright," I grunted and wiped the blood from my face. "I was distracted. Rest up. We're hunting down Crimson in the morning." I smiled because I couldn't wait to see Cassius. When I walked into my tent, the man with brown eyes who had been stalking me was waiting. He was wearing the same simple clothing as he had been the first time I saw him. He ran his hand through his hair as I glared him down.

"Why the hell are you following me around?" I glared. He gave me a big, friendly smile.

"I'm making sure that you are staying on track." He cocked his head to the side as he watched me. "Since Mikel isn't interfering this time, we can help you. But Della will not be pleased if she finds us."

"Who the fuck are Della and Mikel?" I asked. "What do you mean, keep me on track?"

"They are the gods. Don't worry, you are on track. You can hardly keep your emotions for Cassius in check. A blind man could see how much you like him. Don't let your father know of your affection for Cassius."

I gaped at him. Excuse me. He laughed softly as I stared at him.

"He is my enemy. I don't even know him."

"My mate was once my enemy too." His eyes twinkled mischievously. "Don't worry; you are doing exactly what you need to do to break your curse."

I watched him disappear before I could ask what was going on.

★★☽★★

Cassius apparently had the same thought to hunt us down because I woke up to my men screaming that we were being attacked. I slipped on my trousers and boots, tucking in my black camisole as a shirt before leaving my tent. Cassius and his men were headed straight for me. My dagger was already in my hand when Cassius jumped off his horse and immediately started fighting me with a giant smile on his face.

I dodged his first swipe, then his second, then his third. My training had been paying off. He smirked at me when I readjusted my stance wider. His eyes drifted over my outfit before he clenched his jaw.

"Did you want to put on a shirt or armor?"

"No," I said. My cheeks heated under his intense gaze. His eyes glanced around at our men fighting before coming back to land on me. I rushed forward, thinking he was distracted enough, but he knew and pinned me to the ground with little effort. Fuck. Cassius' weight pressed into me as he straddled my hips.

My cheeks heated more when a small moan left me.

"Dead," he breathed as his dagger sat at my throat. My chest throbbed with anticipation. My eyes drifted down to his mouth as he smiled. "That was too easy, little viper. Did you let me win so I'd kiss you again?"

My eyes narrowed on him out of fear that he could see exactly how much I thought about him kissing me, among other things. Fuck, my mind was a traitor. My darkness was swirling quickly inside of me at the thought of his lips on mine.

Mine. It purred into my mind. I closed my eyes tightly as I tried to control myself.

"You just got lucky." I lied.

"What happened to your face?" He raised an eyebrow at me. Cassius shifted slightly, and I nearly closed my eyes to focus on the feeling of him moving against me. I was too attracted to him. My face heated as I realized how much I had been looking forward to this.

"Training," I breathed.

He stood and helped me up. He was so odd. Cassius stepped forward and planted a kiss on my lips, but it was fleeting. It made my skin hot. Bright swirls of red and orange appeared as my vision pulsed black. Gods, I was losing control of myself, and Cassius seemed to know exactly what was happening as he gave me a knowing smile. He tried to stifle his smile, but it was impossible when my swirls glowed brighter at the sight of him. He barely fucking touched me, and I was spiraling.

"You've been practicing." He watched me as he got into a fighting stance again. "Again, little viper."

I widened my stance as I glanced at the three guards watching us in the distance. Haden and two large fae males. Leer and Zade, I think. When they saw me looking, they turned like they had been caught spying. Cassius used my distraction to make a move on me, but I knew he would. I crouched down and swiped his legs out before crawling on top of him. Cassius rolled us, so I was on my back.

Both of us lost our daggers.

Cassius' black eyes moved over my face. When he leaned down like he might kiss me, I head-butted him.

"Fuck!" He groaned as he fell off of me. I rolled, grabbed my dagger, and moved behind where he kneeled. My fingers slipped through his dark hair and yanked it back forcefully, making a moan escape him. Fuck, is that what he sounded like when he was turned on? Swallowing hard, I tried to mask my lust and desire. My vision was pulsing with black as I admired the muscles in his neck flexing.

His eyes were watching me, but he didn't look scared of me. His tongue darted out to wet his lips, and I swallowed hard as images of him using that perfect mouth to make me cum plagued me. Fuck, I was breathing heavily as I stared at him. He made no move to get away from me. His hands fisted tightly at his sides.

I put the blade against his throat as I leaned down.

"Dead," I whispered, and I felt him shiver at the contact of my lips on the shell of his ear. The three guards were moving closer to us, but Cassius waved them off.

"Are you going to plunge that dagger into my heart, Thea?"

I should. I should have sliced his throat open, but an uneasy feeling filled me at the thought. My darkness swarmed in a frenzy inside of me. It was worried for Cassius. So, I moved in front of him. Cassius' eyes darkened as he kneeled before me, bleeding from his cut brow.

"I want to know what kind of sick war game this is."

Cassius lifted his hands like he might grab me, but then lowered them and smirked.

"This has nothing to do with the war."

"Then what—"

"I thought it was foreplay." His deep voice confessed in a whisper. Lust immediately coiled deep in my belly. My breathing was uneven, even to my own ears. Something about Cassius on his knees in front of me was making me feel crazy with need. "You like me kneeling in front of you, don't you?"

Yes.

"Again," I muttered because I didn't know what else to say. "Fight me again."

Cassius stood, and I turned around so I could start in my spot. When I turned back, Cassius was watching me like there was nowhere else he'd rather be. Neither of us moved at first, then we were both charging each other.

Like our first fight, Cassius and I mirrored each other's fighting moves. The sounds of war around us had faded, and all I could focus on was him. The way he moved, the way he smelled like rain and forest, the way he made me question my own loyalties to Cerithia. Because I wanted to pull him into my tent and have my way with him.

"Distracted?" He smiled like he knew exactly what I was thinking.

Fuck. His black eyes drifted down to my crown tattoo before meeting my eyes again. Something zapped through my arm where the crown tattoo sat. Lust and longing. For the love of stars, I could not stop thinking about Cassius doing a lot more than kissing me. Part of me wanted to lose so he would kiss me, and that concerned me. We kept fighting. We were equal in nearly every stance and move. My eyes watched as Cassius breathed heavily. Sweat ran down his neck as he watched me like prey.

This was dangerous, so I put all I could into winning this round because I couldn't kiss him again. I kicked Cassius' chest when he spun away from my blade, and he fell back into a tree, but he just used it to bounce off and come at me. His jaw was tense as he swiped and swiped until he finally got my camisole strap, making it fall dangerously close to showing him my chest.

His eyes traced the deep dip near my breast. When I tried to adjust it, he struck. His move forced me to move back into a tree.

My camisole slipped again, but his dagger was pointed under my chin.

"Dead," he whispered.

My body hummed as he pressed into me harder. Cassius stopped a few inches from my mouth. I felt myself leaning slightly into him instead of away.

"Did you think of me this week when we were apart?" he whispered.

My eyes found his.

"No."

A sexy smile tugged at his lips. "Such a liar." His focus moved to my mouth again. "Did you think of me kissing you? Or maybe you thought of me touching you?"

My chest moved quickly with wild breaths. Gods, he was a confident bastard.

"You know, if you want to make your thoughts a reality, all you have to do is tell me," he whispered. "It can be our little secret."

My mouth opened like it was going to tell him to take me to the tent, but I shut it quickly and stared at him. When I didn't say anything, he pulled away from me and turned away, gathering his daggers. He headed toward the three gawking guards.

"That's it?" I called out, making him turn toward me. "You aren't going to take a prize?"

His eyes filled with sadness when he looked at me this time, and it made my stomach drop. Why was I playing this game with him? I would lose.

"Until next time, little viper."

I stood there wondering what the hell was wrong with me as he walked away. My darkness urged me forward, and I listened because I wasn't ready for him to leave yet. Cassius must have sensed my attack coming because he turned and blocked my daggers with his own. His eyes dragged over me slowly before I shoved him away from me. Cassius stalked around me like he was about to fucking devour me. My stomach filled with lust as I watched him. Images of him and I touching and kissing each other filled my mind.

I shook my head to get rid of the intrusive thoughts. When I focused again, Cassius was smiling at me like he could see every dirty thought I had about him.

"You wanted me, Thea, so come get me."

I charged at him, and he stepped forward to meet my attack, but this time I wasn't losing. At the last moment, I released my fire mist and used it to swipe his feet out from under him.

"Oh, fuck," he grunted as he fell to his back on the ground. I hurried on top of him and smiled as I pressed my blade to his throat. A flash of Cassius in the same position plagued me. *I will wait for you in the next life.*

My thighs squeezed tighter around him. My hand wrapped around his throat as my other hand held the blade under his chin, barely. I found I didn't want to hurt him. I just wanted to feel him against me. He hummed when my hand squeezed his throat. Fuck, he was beautiful. Cassius watched me, waiting to see what I would do.

A sharp, angry pain in my thigh pulled me from the thoughts. I groaned when I saw a small throwing knife buried in the side of my thigh. My gaze met the Crimson guard who had thrown it at me. Fuck, it hurt. Cassius looked at the wound on my leg before his eyes locked onto his guard.

His body stiffened as his shadows swarmed from him. He looked terrifying with his solid black eyes and jaw clenched tightly. He was pissed.

Cassius used his shadow magic to wrap around me and lift me gently off of him. I pulled the small knife from my leg and tossed it to the ground without looking away from Cassius.

"One second, my love," he mumbled to me as he set me on my feet. Surprisingly, he released me from his shadows, but I didn't move. I was too mesmerized watching Cassius stalk toward his guard.

He grabbed the man by the back of his neck and dragged him over to me. Cassius kicked the back of the man's knees, making him kneel in front of me.

"Apologize to Thea for wounding her, now!" he bellowed.

The guard's eyes widened when he looked at me.

"I am sorry, princess," the man trembled.

Cassius grabbed his dagger and plunged it into the guard's back, killing him. When he looked at me, his chest was heaving with shallow breaths. Gods, he was fucking unhinged as he smiled at me.

Cassius used my moment of shock to wrap me in his shadows again. He moved us over to the side, away from the dead body, where he proceeded to lay back down on his back and dragged me over him, so I was straddling his hips again.

"Where were we, little viper?" He watched me as I stared down at him. "Oh, that's right." He grabbed my wrist and yanked my blade up to his throat, smiling. "You were flirting with me."

I stared down at him with no thoughts running through my mind.

"You killed your own guard," I whispered.

"He hurt you."

"Isn't that his job? That's *your* guard."

"Exactly; he should know better than to hurt you. He's lucky I made it quick." Cassius stared at me with a longing in his eyes as his hands gripped my hips tightly. His fingers dug into my flesh, and a small sigh escaped me, making Cassius squeeze me tighter.

"So, you killed him because he did his job?"

"I killed him because no one hurts you and lives." Cassius reached up and brushed my hair over my shoulder. "Are you going to kiss me now? Since we both know you want to."

A wicked smile spread over his lips when I sat up quickly, moving away from him. I thought he was going to force me back to him with his shadows, but he chuckled softly as we both stood up.

"Don't miss me too much, my love," he proclaimed as I watched him use his shadows to wrap around himself and his guards before meeting my eyes and disappearing.

I could have killed him. I should have, but the thought made me feel sick to my stomach. I focused on where he had been standing with his men, but he didn't appear again. Disappointment filled me, but I put on a mask of indifference as I slipped on a shirt and assessed how many men died this time.

Chapter 9

Thea

It had only been two days since Cassius attacked my camp. Only two days, I told myself, so why did it feel like I missed a man that I didn't know? I longed for him to come attack our camp, and that was such a stupid thing to think of. I couldn't help it. Even my darkness seemed to be encouraging it. I was a fucking traitor to Cerithia, and it didn't bother me in the slightest. If my prize was Cassius, I would hand over my own kingdom. I would give him my family.

Did that make me psychotic?

Probably, but again, I didn't fucking care. I was losing my mind the longer he hid from me.

I dreamt of him. I dreamt that he didn't just give me a fleeting kiss. I dreamt of an all-consuming kiss. When I woke up, it was as if I knew exactly how his mouth would dominate mine, how his hands would touch and grip me, how he would whisper dirty words into my ear as he filled me.

"Captain?"

I shook my head and stared at the men in front of me. My cheeks were flushed, and my breathing was at the rate of a hussy. Fuck, I was losing it.

"We did not see any Crimson armies close." They reported. Damn, I had hoped he was planning another attack. Stars above, I was a sick and twisted fuck. I was hoping for a battle so I could see Cassius. No wonder my father wanted me to stay away from him. Maybe my father knew I would not be able to resist him.

"Alright." I nodded. "Let's rest up today, and we'll move on to them tomorrow." Because I was going crazy sitting here thinking of him. They bowed to me, and I went to my tent to stew in my lust away from peering eyes.

My eyes dropped to a dark green envelope sitting on my bed. I lifted the small envelope and glanced around. It was forbidden to be in my tent, so I wasn't sure what soldier thought they were clever in leaving a note in my personal space. The envelope was soft. The paper was high-end, and the color was stunning. I opened it slowly, like it might explode. A small white card fell into my hands. The writing on it was definitely a man's.

Captain,

I'm disappointed at how easy it was to infiltrate your camp, let alone your tent. With how well you fought, I expected you to be impenetrable. You've made this war more interesting... more fun. If you want to forfeit, let me know. Or you may always choose to fight with me. I promise to treat you so well, Thea.

Captain of Crimson Armies,

Cassius, aka coward

That smug prick. How did he have time to get here and put this in my tent without being caught? I have been here all day. Did he walk right past me as I daydreamed of fucking him? I glanced around to make sure he wasn't lurking in my tent, but nothing was amiss. I should feel threatened that he had been here. But this somehow felt like a game of cat and mouse. It made me excited. I sat at my desk fiddling with the envelope and card before grabbing a piece of paper. My heart pounded in my chest as I quickly wrote my response. Two could play this game, Cassius.

Coward,

Do you think entering my tent while there are no guards is impressive? How pathetic. I want you to know that unlike you, I can put this letter in your tent while your men guard it. You and I are not on

the same level. I will always be a step ahead of you. If you would like to submit to me, you are more than welcome to beg on your knees, but I will still slaughter you.

Captain of Cerithian Armies,

Thea

I smiled to myself as I folded the paper into an envelope and scribbled 'smug prick' onto the front of it. When darkness fell, I slipped my green cloak on and trekked through the woods in the direction of Crimson. My darkness had crept from me for the first time since the cave. It did so without permission, and I was dazed by it looking for something. Suddenly it exploded and expanded through the forest as it became frantic.

Then I realized it was searching for Cassius. I could tell the moment my darkness detected his magic because it practically dragged me along with it. It was excited to see him, maybe more than I was.

The only signs of the Crimson armies were smoke from fires. Once I saw the camp, I bided my time. A large black tent stood at the center of camp, and I knew that was where Cassius was. So, when his men switched guard detail, I hurried to the camp, undetected by anyone, and slipped inside.

I paused when I saw him sleeping in his big bed. His space smelled like rain and forest, like him. His smooth, tanned skin lifted slowly with each breath he took. My eyes cascaded over all the black tattoos covering his chest. His face was hidden by his arm draped over it. My body hummed at the sight of him. An overwhelming sense of need pulsed from me. It felt like torture to see him and not touch him.

I pulled the envelope from my pocket and set it on his black uniform, which he tossed onto the chair. I wanted to see his reaction so badly. My eyes scanned his body once more before turning to leave.

"Leaving so soon, Captain?"

His smooth voice stopped me. I smiled brightly as my back was turned. I lowered the green hood of my cloak as I turned to face him.

"Just dropping off a gift." My voice faded as his handsome face came into view. His eyes were black as night, which seemed wrong. But gods above, his face was made to be admired. He gave me a small, lopsided smile when he saw the envelope on his uniform.

"You are quite impressive," he said. "Did you come to catch a peek of me?" He moved the blanket off of him, showing off a body made of muscles and tattoos. Gods. My eyes drifted over all of him without giving a shit if he saw. Even his legs had black tattoos covering them. After a moment, I collected myself.

I rolled my eyes and scoffed.

"You're as smug as I imagined."

"So, you've been thinking of me?" he smirked. I turned around to leave but paused for no reason in particular. When I turned back, his smugness was gone. His head tilted as he examined me slowly.

"You could have killed me on the battlefield; why didn't you?"

"You didn't kill me either, Thea."

I nodded because he was right. My eyes traced over his face. Something ignited in me at the sight of him. Something primal and feral clawed at me when I saw the red crown tattooed on his arm. An urge to go to him overwhelmed me, but I didn't move. He was my enemy. He was an obstacle that kept me from my task, killing the Crimson bloodline.

"Nice tattoo," I muttered before I stopped myself. My words were breathless, and I knew he noticed it too.

A slow smile spread across his face as he lifted it up as if he were inspecting it. Something about it called to me. I took a step forward, then another, before stopping.

"It's my favorite tattoo I have." Tenderness crossed his face as he watched me. My heart was racing, and I didn't understand why this man was making me feel crazy with lust.

"If you find yourself getting lonely, you can come back anytime you want." He smiled brightly.

"Don't mistake this for anything but psychological warfare." I lied. Cassius stood up so quickly, but I didn't move. I stood my ground as he stood close enough that his chest pressed into mine. Then he grabbed me and tossed me onto the bed. My heart pounded as he stalked at me.

"You have never been a good liar," he breathed. "Tell me how much you've thought about me these past few days."

I rested on my elbows as he stepped between my legs.

"Every day," I confessed on accident. His eyes seemed to become more black. "I thought of all the ways I would kill you." I tried to backtrack.

Cassius laughed softly as he leaned down to crawl over me.

"Oh, my little liar, you don't have to hide from me. I can see how much you want me in those pretty green eyes of yours. All you have to do is ask, and I will gladly give you anything you demand of me."

Gods, this felt too intimate for this to be the first time being close to him. I didn't stop him as he pinned me to the bed. I swallowed hard as my eyes bounced back and forth between his.

"Lust is hardly a feeling." I tried to sound bitter, but I failed miserably.

Cassius' eyes darkened. Gods, he was impossible. I could call him the worst thing I could think of, and he would probably still look at me like I hung the moon.

"Lust is better than indifference." He smiled. "I'd say we're making progress, little viper."

I rolled my eyes and scoffed.

"Are you so desperate that you are willing to accept my meager feelings?"

Cassius' eyes dragged over me slowly.

"I'll take every scrap you throw my way, Thea. I can wait."

I waited a moment before deciding what to say. I should leave, but that wasn't what came out of my mouth.

"You still have a prize for winning our fight," I whispered.

He nodded before he leaned down.

"So do you," he breathed.

Cassius stopped an inch from my mouth, and it was the worst torture he could inflict on me.

"We are enemies; this means nothing," I said with as much conviction as I could. "Don't let it get to your head."

"If you feel the need to call me your enemy, then so be it. As long as I am *something* to you."

My heart went crazy in my chest. Cassius didn't make any movement. My mind was spinning with all the things I wanted him to do to me.

"Tell me what you want."

"Kiss me," I demanded. Cassius let out a noise of approval as his lips descended on mine. But he gave me just another fleeting kiss, like he was purposely teasing me. I growled, frustrated.

"I want a real kiss," I breathed, not caring that I was weak.

"Then kiss me," he demanded.

I lifted my mouth to take his. This kiss was all-consuming. He released my wrists so that he could grip my jaw tightly. Cassius' tongue dominated my own. This kiss was more than want and need; it was full of longing and passion. I gripped him to me and rolled my hips up to feel him hard against me.

Cassius pulled away and stared down at me. Something intense took over the look he gave me, and it scared me, so I shoved him off me and stood. This was too much connection and emotion for a man I shouldn't know. But I knew deep in my heart that I did know him. He felt familiar. He felt safe. He made the feeling of missing something go away.

"I'll see you on the battlefield, coward."

I turned and left as he called out to me. My heart pumped rapidly as I made my way back to my own camp, to my tent, where I tossed and turned for hours. Cassius' black eyes haunted my mind whenever I closed my eyes. Lust cascaded through my veins whenever I saw his face behind my eyes. This was so forbidden—to feel anything towards this man, but it only made my body want more.

"Fuck it," I sighed as my hands skimmed my skin. My fire magic glowed as I touched myself where I pictured Cassius' hands. My eyes squeezed tightly as I pictured a different scene than the one in his tent.

No, this time I didn't leave. His big hands skimmed my naked skin. His eyes turned completely black as he pushed me onto the bed. His mouth claimed me, devouring me. It was as if he couldn't hold back from what he wanted to do to me. He felt the same thing I did—an unbridled need to just feel him.

"Do you feel that, Captain? Do you see what you do to me?"

I nodded as my eyes clenched tighter. The image of Cassius leaning over me. Thrusting his hips into me so perfectly.

"Please."

"Beg me, Thea. I want to hear how undone I make you."

I couldn't keep it together any longer as my orgasm crashed through me like a violent storm. My face buried deep into my pillow to stop the noises from being heard. Sweat coated my skin as I stared at the roof of my tent. Fuck, I was screwed.

Chapter 10

Thea

It had been a week since Cassius and I kissed in his tent. Each day that passed only made me feel like a traitor because I couldn't stop thinking about him and touching myself every night. It was sick. I had a real problem.

An overwhelming sense of longing filled me. This had been happening a lot. Random feelings that did not feel like my own constantly plagued me. My eyes glanced around the dark forest we had stopped in tonight. We were still on Crimson lands; I could tell by the tall pine trees and the air that seemed to be the perfect temperature. My lungs sucked in the air that smelled like rain and forest.

I liked Crimson's lands. Not that I would ever say that out loud. My men had gone to sleep a long time ago, besides the dozen who kept guard. I had been sitting by the fire when a sudden urge to look around the woods overtook me.

"I'm going to look around," I told the guard closest to me.

"Do you want me to follow?"

"No. I won't be long."

I made sure my viper-handled dagger was in my boot before heading to the woods. My eyes darted around when I felt as if I was being watched. Maybe monsters lurked out here. Adrenaline pumped through me, and I liked the feeling of this unknown danger. I glanced over my shoulder at the camp, disappearing into the darkness as I walked farther into the forest. When I turned forward, I ran into Cassius' hard chest.

I grabbed my dagger and pointed it at him, but he was one step ahead of me. He grabbed my wrists and slammed them above my head into the tree behind me.

"Miss me, little viper?" His handsome face instantly sent lust through me. Damn him. He plucked the dagger from my hand. "You don't need this right now." He tossed it to the forest floor.

"What are you doing?" I breathed as he held me in place with his own body.

"Watching you." His black eyes stared at me like he could see every dirty thing I had ever thought about him in the last week. This position we were in was going to haunt my fucking fantasies.

"You disappeared."

My eyes flickered down to his mouth when he smirked.

"So, you did miss me."

"No," I scoffed. "It's just a very cowardly way to fight a war." I lied.

His smile grew. Gods be damned, I was not doing myself any favors by being out here with this handsome monster.

"Have you thought of me, Thea?"

"I've thought of stabbing you." I smiled wickedly at him. His smile reflected mine, and it made lust shoot through me again. Cassius shifted as something made his body soften against me.

"You came into the woods; why?"

"I felt like I should. I didn't know you were lurking like a creep."

He laughed at my insult. My eyes took in the sight of his happiness, and it made me feel good to see it. Confusion flooded me.

"What's the matter?" His brows knitted together.

"Why are you flirting with me? We're in a war, and you seem to not give a damn."

His black eyes traced over me slowly. The grip on my wrist lessened, and his hand grabbed my jaw gently.

"Why do you like me flirting with you, is the real question?"

My traitorous body leaned closer to him. Cassius' jaw tensed as he watched me. He was struggling with something.

"I don't like you flirting." I tried to sound confident, but it came out breathless and exactly the opposite of what I tried to convince him of.

"I think we both know how much you're lying, my little liar. If I reached my hand into your trousers, I know you would be fucking dripping wet for me."

Oh shit.

I lost all ability to function. A war raged inside of me. I wanted to tell him to reach into my trousers and find out for himself, but then I also wanted to shove him away from me. I was lying to myself; there was no way I would shove him away from me. I was a mess the past few days when he hid away from me.

"You are a cocky prick, aren't you?" I smirked.

"And you're a very bad liar." He leaned forward so his mouth was an inch from mine and stopped. His eyes bounced between mine. Cassius smelled like Crimson, rain, and forest. Fuck. I wanted him to kiss me.

"Kiss me, Thea. We can add it to our list of secrets."

"I'm supposed to trust you," I whispered. Cassius' hand holding my jaw pulled me closer to him, and he kissed me.

Immediately I pulled him to me and kissed him back, but then he was pulling away.

"I missed you too, little viper."

My eyes glided over his face as he watched me in a way that made me feel safe. He had moved a few feet away from me. The sleeves of his black tunic were rolled up, exposing that damn red crown again. My vision pulsed red as I looked over him.

"Thea," he breathed.

"Cassius." I stepped forward. His shadows burst out from him as I lunged at him. My mouth crushed his as he yanked me against him. Cassius lifted me and pushed me up against the tree. His hips rolled forward, and I moaned at the feeling of him. Fuck, this was better than anything I could think of.

"What are you doing?"

Cassius dropped me to my feet as soon as the man appeared next to us. My eyes moved from Cassius to the Kizar guard who had stumbled upon us. "Shit," he hissed when he realized the man I was kissing was Cassius.

My darkness lashed out of me without permission and grabbed the man, squeezing until his body exploded. Chunks of his body fell to the forest floor, and I stared at him before looking at Cassius. What would he think of my magic? I was too worried, so I grabbed my dagger and slipped it back into my boot, readying to leave.

When I glanced at Cassius, his shadows swarmed around him in a frenzy. His eyes focused on me. For the love of gods, he was fucking beautiful and terrifying.

"Where are you going?"

"Running away so I don't have to see you look disgusted at my magic."

His eyes glided over me so slowly. Fuck.

"Run, my love." He smiled. "I'll give you a head start, but just know if I catch you, no one will interrupt us until after I've made you cum."

"Fuck," I whispered and took off into the dark woods. My lungs burned as I looked behind me to see Cassius watching but not moving from his spot. I smiled as I disappeared down a small embankment and out of his sight. Shit, maybe I should just stand here so he catches me. His heavy footsteps made me hurry into a thicket of willow trees and kneel. My heart pounded as I waited for him.

My breath caught as I watched him walk around the woods. I saw a smile tug at his lips.

"I thought maybe you would be waiting for me out in the open. Gods know how much you've thought about me making you cum in the past few weeks. Tell me, Thea, did you start touching yourself after that first kiss, or did you torture yourself and pretend like you didn't feel something for me? How long did you hold out for?"

Shit, I almost walked out of my hiding spot, but the anticipation of him stalking me and hunting me down like prey was making me stay put. He kept walking past me.

Cassius disappeared behind trees a good distance away. Smiling smugly to myself, I turned to move spots, but instead, I walked into his chest. He smiled down at me.

"Found you, love," he whispered as he hauled me over his shoulder and carried me out of the trees to the small clearing by the creek. I thrashed around, not trying very hard to get away. Cassius set me on my feet, and I backed away from him. His eyes dragged over me slowly, teasingly.

"Fuck," he breathed as he came at me, forcing me against a tree by my throat. His mouth dominated mine as his hand slipped into my trousers, and he moaned when he found me wet. He pulled his lips from mine and looked at me as I breathed heavily. "You are perfect, Thea." He admired me as my hips rolled against his fingers.

"Cassius," I breathed.

"Tell me how much you've thought about me making you cum." His voice was demanding that I answer.

"Every fucking time I close my eyes," I confessed.

His mouth crushed mine, and his tongue dominated mine. He consumed me and turned me inside out with that kiss. His fingers gripped my throat as he pulled back to stare me in the eyes. His eyes drifted down to where his fingers were sinking into me. His thumb circled my clit with a pressure that was making me see stars.

"Cassius," I moaned loudly.

"That's right, my love, let me hear how good I make you feel."

I closed my eyes tightly, and his movements stopped.

"Keep those pretty eyes on me. I want you to remember this moment and touch yourself later, picturing how perfect we are right now."

"For fuck's sake, Cassius. I like it when you say shit like that," I moaned.

"I know you do." He smiled like he had a secret.

My hips rolled into his fingers as he leaned forward and gave me a hard kiss.

"You need to cum before more guards come to find you."

I didn't want this to end.

"Please, I want more," I begged.

"Cum for me, Thea. I want to see you come apart on my fingers. Next time, I promise I'll give you whatever you want."

"Fuck." I squeezed my eyes shut as his hand gripped my throat tightly. I focused on anything but how good this felt because I wanted to live in this moment forever.

"I know what you're doing," he groaned. "Be a good girl and finish. Quit holding back."

"Cass—" his lips crushed into mine to silence my orgasm. I was a whimpering, pleading mess as I tried to prolong this moment. Cassius hummed his approval against my mouth, swallowing down every moan that escaped me. His chest rose and fell quickly as he moved away from me.

Before I could demand that he come over and kiss me again, his shadows swarmed around us. When they pulled away, we were in my tent. Cassius looked at me once more before leaving without a word. Before I could ask him to stay.

CHAPTER II

CASSIUS

A movement in front of me in the woods had me tensing. Someone was already spying on Thea's camp. Silently, I moved through my shadows, so I was directly behind them. I stared at the back of Palo's head until he felt my presence. He turned quickly toward me. His eyes filled with terror when his mind registered who I was. I had come alone tonight, not expecting to see anything—except Thea.

"What the fuck are you doing here, Cassius?" Palo stood up and stared me down.

"Spying." My eyes narrowed on him. "Why are you in the woods?"

His body tensed slightly.

"Scouting."

I gave him a vicious smile.

"You're scouting your own men?"

Palo clenched his jaw tightly as if to say he wouldn't tell me anything. Fine by me. I punched him in the face as my shadows wrapped around him.

"You're coming with me, Palo." I grabbed him by the collar of his uniform as my shadows took me home. Palo was yelling and thrashing around once he realized I had taken him to Crimson. My father and Haden came running to see the commotion.

"Cassius?" Haden questioned.

"I found Palo here spying on Thea, and he will be telling me why he is watching her instead of trying to protect her."

"Fuck you."

My chest rose and fell quickly as I thought of all the reasons he would be watching her. Had he seen her and I talking? Did he tell Luren? I would get my answers one way or another.

"I'm going to the dungeon with Palo. Haden, would you like to help me beat the shit out of him?"

"Fuck yes, I would."

My father let out a long sigh before giving me a look that let me know I was becoming unhinged, but he wouldn't stop me. My shadows forced Palo to lie down on his back. I didn't say anything to my father as I dragged my prisoner behind me. Haden followed eagerly. I didn't give Palo the decency of lifting him down the stairs that led to the bottom floor of the castle.

I made sure his head hit every fucking stair on the way down. He was already whimpering by the time we got to the room I would torture him in. I set him in the chair that was bolted to the stone floor. I used the leather straps on the armrest and tightened them painfully to him, then did the same with his ankles.

Haden was smiling as I grabbed my shirt collar and slipped it off so Palo's blood wouldn't ruin it. Thea loved this tunic, which is why I wore it tonight, hoping to see her. Palo's scared eyes watched me as I circled around him like prey.

"You're going to tell me everything that you know. You will answer every question I ask; do you understand?"

Palo clenched his jaw but didn't answer me. I smiled as I stepped forward and punched him in the face; his blood poured from his nose, spewing across the room and onto me.

"I suggest you answer me, Palo, or the next hit will be with my blade."

"Yes, I understand." He glared.

"Now," I sighed, irritated. "Why were you spying on Thea?"

Palo hesitated, and this time Haden stepped forward. His knife rested in his palm as he stared at Palo. Whatever Palo saw on Haden's face scared the fuck out of him.

"King Luren has me follow her."

"If you continue with these short, stupid answers, I will just start cutting your fingers off now. Details, Palo." I stepped forward so I was at eye level with him.

"He wants to make sure she isn't being strange." He stopped, and Haden stepped forward, slapping Palo across the face. "She was acting odd as soon as she got to Cerithia. Luren doesn't trust her, so he made me follow her around."

"How long was she in Cerithia?" She didn't come to the trials, and that had never happened. Was she there for months, and I had no idea? What did her father fill her head with this time?

"We found her in the woods by accident when she lit it on fire. She was at the castle for only one day. Luren was worried she would notice things weren't right, especially after she made the comment about her bedroom."

I gave him a look that let him know he better keep talking.

"She recognized that her bedroom wasn't hers because it wasn't dark green. We're assuming she was picturing *your* room."

Damn straight, she was picturing our bedroom. I gave him a knowing smile, so he knew that was exactly what she pictured.

"That, and she sneers at Jesper every time he speaks."

I laughed softly. That's my girl.

"What exactly are you hoping to find on this little spy mission of yours?" I asked.

"Luren wants to know if you two speak at all."

"What have you reported to him so far?" I stepped forward with my dagger. Palo didn't speak. I was done giving him warnings, so I plunged the dagger into his forearm and pushed it all the way through so that it stuck into the chair.

"Fuck!" Palo screamed into the dungeon. His screams made my shadows burst out in a frenzy. Scream for me, Palo; it only makes me want to hurt you more.

"Answer," I demanded.

"Nothing. I just started tonight."

I tilted my head as I watched the blood pour from him onto the floor. He didn't continue to speak; he just sobbed like a baby.

"Was someone else spying before you?"

Palo's eyes widened. This little motherfucker thought I would be so stupid to not ask that. I grabbed him by the throat and squeezed it until his face started turning purple.

"Who the fuck is it, and where are they?"

He was desperately trying to breathe.

"I don't think he can answer you." Haden interrupted my rage. My black eyes flickered at him before shifting back to Palo. I released him.

"A Kizar guard. I relieved him tonight, and he is headed to Cerithia on horseback. He left Thea's camp two hours ago."

I looked at Haden.

"Watch him; I'll be back shortly."

My shadows wrapped around me, and within a moment I was standing in the forest of Crimson, listening for the rider. I didn't hear him, so I moved through my shadows several times until I finally came upon him. The Kizar guard had made it a lot farther than I thought he would in a short time, meaning Palo was a fucking liar. This man had probably left Thea's camp a half day ago. I knew the moment he saw me standing in the darkening woods, blood dripping down my hands and chest from Palo.

The guard widened his path around me like that would protect him from me. I shot my shadow magic out and clotheslined him. His horse kept running as he scrambled to his feet, trying to grab a weapon.

"I've been looking for you." I smiled.

He tried to run, but I used my shadows to move in front of him quickly. He ran into my chest and fell to the ground.

"We need to talk."

My voice was laced with venom as I reached down and grabbed the man, moving both of us with my shadows to the dungeon. I tossed him to the ground by Palo's feet.

"That was fast," Haden chuckled.

The guard tried to scoot away, but he wouldn't escape me, especially knowing that he was going to report Thea, and that would have cost her life. But before I started questioning him, I walked to Palo, yanking my dagger out of his arm so I could cut off three fingers. When I inspected my work, I slammed my dagger into his other forearm.

"That is for lying about when you traded places with him. He was almost to Cerithia when I found him."

Palo was crying hysterically. I glanced up at Haden, who was leaning against the wall, flipping his dagger in his hand, watching. Something vacant filled his features before he looked at me and stepped forward, coming to my left.

"You're going to tell me what you planned to relay to King Luren."

The guard's dark eyes widened as he looked to Palo for guidance. Palo nodded for him to tell me.

"That I saw you two having a conversation and you kissed her," he muttered, terrified of me. He should be. He almost cost me my wife.

"You've already kissed her?" Palo sneered.

I smiled at him. My fists clenched tightly at my sides. Gods, the rage that was coursing through me was enough to make me spiral and go on a killing spree. I could hunt down everyone who kept Thea from me and slaughter them. To hell with the prophecy.

"We've done more than kiss."

Palo's face reddened with his anger.

"What's wrong, Palo?" I teased.

"Didn't take long for the Crimson whore to spread her legs for you, did it?"

"That was very fucking stupid to say to him," Haden muttered.

My shadows crept toward Palo, grabbing his hands and twisting them until they snapped at the wrists, but that wasn't good enough. I kept twisting and twisting until his hands pulled from his body. My chest was tight with rage as he screamed to the gods to save him.

"The gods won't save you, Palo." Haden smiled. "She is on our side."

The Kizar guard had run to the corner farthest from me, cowering in the corner.

"I will skin you alive if you disrespect my wife like that again." I moved toward him as his sobs filled the space. I knew the moment my words sank into him. His eyes were wide with confusion.

"Wife?"

"That's right, Palo. Thea Valeska. My wife."

Palo started praying to the gods again, and it made me laugh. I turned my attention to the Kizar guard.

"Who else saw or knows that I kissed Thea?"

"No one." He was a mess, crying with snot running down his round face.

"Good." I released my shadows toward him and snapped his neck before turning my attention to Palo as his dead body hit the stone floor. Palo's eyes were losing focus as his blood poured from where his hands used to be attached to his body. I slapped him to wake his ass up.

"What is Luren planning with Thea this time?"

"I'm not telling you," he groaned. "I'll be dead soon anyway; do your worst."

Hmm. He had a point. Maybe I should have left his hands attached to him. A moment later I saw his eyes widen as a glow filled the space. When I turned, Della stood next to me. Her eyes were staring at Palo.

"You will tell Cassius what Luren's plan is now." Her voice was darker than I had ever heard before.

Palo shook his head no. Della pushed me aside and grabbed the man by the uniform, getting in his face.

"I will force your soul to stay in your body until you tell him. Do you understand me? I will refuse to let you die. As the Goddess of Life, I will stand here and hold your soul inside of you until Cassius has you begging for death. I will keep you alive until you give him everything he is asking for. I will not let you die."

Fuck.

I looked at Haden, who was staring at Della in awe. She was fucking terrifying when she was pissed. Palo didn't answer her, so she grabbed the dagger I speared through his arm and ripped it out. He cried out, but she stabbed it right back into the same wound.

It shot blood out and onto her fancy dress, but she didn't move.

"I suggest you start using your words, Palo, or I will break every bone in your body one at a time."

I crossed my arms over my chest as I stared at Palo. Haden stepped toward Della as if he couldn't help it. Della glanced at him, and he just stared into her pure white eyes. But Della hardly gave Haden the time of day as she focused on Palo.

"He..." Palo gasped for breath, and his eyes began rolling back.

"I don't fucking think so." Della raised her hand before shoving it into his chest, breaking through his skin and bones. The sound made me flinch. "You see that, Palo? You were supposed to die just now, and I'm not letting you," she whispered.

Remind me not to get on Della's bad side. For fuck's sake, she and Thea could probably kill everyone in the realm with their power.

"Luren told Thea that she has to kill the Crimson bloodline to break her curse," he wheezed out barely. "Then he will kill her. She will be useless to him, and he will make a spectacle of her death to instill fear in the fae so he will control all of Elloryon."

My eyes narrowed on Palo.

"He thinks he can control the prophecy and force her to kill Crimson, Falgon, and Akecia."

"Well, Luren's a fucking moron," Della sneered. Stars I don't think I had ever seen her so fucking pissed. Haden was still watching her closely as I glanced at him, taking a small step closer to her.

"Jesper is trying to convince him to just hunt her down each year and kill her so she will never break her curse."

That little fucking bastard.

"That's it?" Della asked. "Why is he so confident that she will kill all the royal bloodlines and not him?"

Palo's nostrils flared.

"The witches are helping him."

My shoulders tensed. We had already killed the witches that tried to kill Thea in Exile, but we could not figure out where the others were hiding or what coven it was.

"Yerma from the Ravenstone Coven, now let me die," he begged Della.

She looked at me for permission. I nodded, and she yanked his soul from his body violently. She was breathing heavily and angrily. Della was losing control.

"Ardella." Haden's voice made her shoulders tense, but she still refused to look at us. Her breathing was uneven. Haden looked at her back worriedly.

"Little viper," I called out. Thea's soul appeared in front of me in the form of Wisp, her face smiling within her dark green flames. "I need you to make sure Thea finds out about the Ravenstone Coven. Can you do that for me?"

She flashed purple and disappeared.

When I looked back at Della, she was staring at me oddly.

"Sorry, I took over your torture session." She frowned.

"It's alright. How did you know what we were doing?"

She tensed again; her eyes flickered at Haden briefly before looking back at me.

"I just sensed that you needed help."

Haden was still watching her, but Della refused to look back at him.

"Do you know anything about Ravenstone Coven?" Haden asked her.

She shook her head. Her eyes were still solid white. She was struggling with something, but I figured it had something to do with Haden.

"I'm going to go introduce myself to Thea." Then she left.

Haden stared at where Della had been for a long moment before looking at me. I was tense and fucking irritable. This time was different, and I wouldn't let anyone stand in the way of getting Thea back.

Chapter 12

Thea

The Crimson army had disappeared. It had been weeks since Cassius got me off in the woods, and we could find no trace of them anywhere. An insistence to search for him took over me the first few weeks, but then I stopped. Cassius was good at hiding, and I would not search like a dog. So, my army waited for him to come out of hiding.

But he never came back. Crimson had vanished into thin air, and their border had doubled its protection. Disappointment filled me. I missed a man who was supposed to be my enemy. For all I knew, this was a sick and twisted game of manipulation on his part, but if it was, I was sick and twisted because he could use me however he saw fit.

Did he think of me too, or was this all a game for him? Fuck, I felt like this was some sort of test he was doing. If I had a way to get to him, I would let him know that he didn't need to play this game. I lost any semblance of restraint the first moment I saw him on the battlefield without his helmet on.

My father's annoyed breath reminded me that I was being scolded and should not be thinking of Cassius. My skin heated as I shook away his memory.

I shouldn't have been so surprised when my father called us back to Cerithia, but it wasn't my fault. A waste. That's what my father called me when I returned this morning. A waste of resources. A waste of his time. A waste of potential. I should have killed Crimson's bloodline by now.

I stood there and took it because I didn't care what he thought of me. His words rang through my mind. They bounced around in there, but somehow, I wasn't surprised by them. It was like my mind could remember the harsh words he had spoken to me before and didn't let them hurt me. Even now, as he blabbered on, I ignored him.

Images of Cassius and I shot through my mind, but it was as if they weren't my own thoughts. Gods, longing and lust zapped down my arm. My darkness hummed in approval as the onslaught of Cassius kissing, touching, and saying dirty things to us played through my mind. My cheeks were heating.

"Are you listening?" My father glared.

"Honestly, no." I stared at him. Oops, didn't mean to say that out loud. "It's just that you act as if Crimson's disappearance is my fault. It isn't my fault that they ran like cowards." Unless Cassius was running because we were traitors to lust after each other. Then yes, it was a hundred percent my fault. Gods, was he this consumed by thoughts of me too?

My father's eyes frosted over before Gwyn stepped forward with her hand clenched, as if she would strike me. I wish she would because I would lay her flat on her back with one punch. Fuck, I was more irritable than normal, and I knew Cassius was to blame. I didn't understand why he disappeared. Was it easy for him to resist whatever connection we had?

"You disrespectful little shit," Gwyn hissed.

"Oh, shut up," I scoffed. "If you two think you can do it better, then get your prissy asses out of your castle and go fight this war yourself," I snapped. My darkness practically chuckled at my reaction. Hatred filled their eyes, but it made me so fucking happy to see.

"Thea!" my father yelled. "Show us respect."

"I'll show you respect when you give me the same courtesy."

"What is your problem?" Jesper asked. This prick was lingering around too damn much.

"You are all ungrateful. That is my problem." I clenched my fists tightly. "You sent me to war after being home for a day and get pissed off because I haven't broken a curse? Get off your high horse and fuck off unless you'll be joining me on the battlefield."

They all gaped at me as my eyes pulsed red. I could feel the swirls on my skin heating below my uniform.

"I will not take criticism from three fae who have never done a day of hard work in their life, especially about war. This conversation is over, unless you want me to really lose my shit at all of you. I am ready to fight, and I guarantee that you will fucking lose."

No one said anything as I turned and left the throne room, slamming the wooden door so violently that I swore I heard it crack.

★★☽★★

Things at Cerithia were different after my outburst. No one even tried to be friendly or talk to me about being family. Was this what life had been like before Exile? A sense of not fitting in or belonging? The queen and my half-sisters hated me, and I hated them too. Something in my bones ached with hatred when I saw them. I hated my father and Jesper as well.

"Thea?"

I shook my head from my racing thoughts. Jesper stared at me from the other side of the counter. I had snuck down here after everyone was sleeping to eat, so I didn't have to talk to any of them.

"Jesper."

"How have things been since you've been back?" He smiled at me, but it made me step away from him. The feeling of leaving the same room as him consumed me.

"Fine." I lied. I had been trying to find a way to go see Cassius in Crimson for the past two days. But none of my excuses for showing up in Crimson made sense. I was sure the Crimson royal family would have me killed on sight.

"Do you ever remember flashes of your life?" He tilted his head to study me.

"Lie to him." The man with kind brown eyes said from somewhere close to me.

Jesper was bad news. When I didn't answer, he reached out and grabbed my wrist. When I tried to pull it free, he gripped it tighter and examined the black trees tattooed on my arm. His finger traced something under my tattoo.

"What did you do to Palo?"

Palo? Why the fuck would I know where he went?

"Let go of me."

"Why do you look scared of me?"

"I'm not, but I don't want anyone touching me." His fingers gripped my arm slightly tighter. "I will burn your fucking hand off if you don't let me go in two seconds."

He gave me a look of irritation but dropped my arm. But I decided that it wasn't soon enough and sent my fist into his smug face. Jesper fell into the wall behind him before falling to his knees as blood gushed from his nose. My darkness and I watched as he cried like a fucking baby.

"You will not touch me again, or I will slit your fucking throat."

"You fucking bitch!" he yelled. "You remember something, admit it!"

I crouched down and stared him in the eyes.

"I don't like you very much. In fact, I kind of want to slit your throat open right now." I grabbed my dagger, and he sobbed loudly. I laughed as I stood up. "This is actually really embarrassing for you; get up and quit being such a baby."

"Fuck you, you cunt."

"Stay the fuck away from me," I warned as I glared at him and slowly made my way past him and to my room. Once the door shut, I locked it and listened to see if he followed me, but nothing made a noise in the hallway. I lifted my arm to inspect my tattoo. Why was Jesper always asking about and looking at these tattoos? My finger skimmed it, and I could feel the lifted skin under it.

Letters. I could feel letters covered by the dark ink. I traced them once, then twice. My stomach churned with disgust. Jesper's name was on my arm. So many things swarmed in my mind, but none of them were good. Pain shot through my mind as images of Jesper cutting my flesh with a knife hit me. I stumbled into the wall and caught myself as my head pounded.

What was happening to me?

Through my panic, I saw a flash of movement in the dark corner of my room. I froze where I was because I thought perhaps I had imagined it. A moment later, though, a woman as pretty as the heavens stepped out. She held up her hands.

"I'm not here to hurt you," she whispered. I grabbed a candlestick and held it back, ready to swing and hit this intruder. How had she gotten in here?

"I'm a friend; you just don't remember," she said quickly. My darkness didn't stir inside of me at this warning. A flash of dark green let me know the friendly orb was back. She was floating calmly next to the woman.

My eyes shifted back to the woman with golden skin and eyes the color of twinkling stars. She smiled when she glanced at the floating green orb.

"You can see the light?" I asked.

"Yes," she smiled. "You named her Wisp; she is a friend too."

"Wisp," I spoke softly. It did sound familiar. Slowly, I lowered the candlestick and stared at the woman. Something about her was peaceful—familiar.

"My name is Della, the Goddess of Life."

A laugh escaped me at her words. Her face fell into an unamused expression as I struggled to control myself. Her hands rested on her hips as she narrowed her eyes at me.

"I'm friends with a goddess?" I chuckled.

"Why is that so hard to believe? We're friends."

"Okay, why are you friends with a mortal fae?" Gods, I really shouldn't provoke this woman; she was clearly not right in the head.

"Because I helped my brother, Mikel, curse you to have no memories." She frowned. "I did it unintentionally, of course."

Her confession was like a slap in the face.

"What?" I remembered the man who stalked me saying their names. "Wait... the man mentioned you."

"What man?" she asked with concern.

"I don't know who he is. He has been watching out for me. He said you wouldn't be pleased to see him."

Her eyes flickered pure white briefly before she glanced around like she might see him here. He wasn't, but I could see she knew exactly who the man was. Della stared at me for a long moment as if she were contemplating telling me something or not.

"Who is he?" I asked.

"I don't have time to explain the details, but I needed to check on you after Cassius said he found you...fighting for your *father*."

By her tone and expression, I could tell her words had a different meaning to them, but what? I nodded my head at her.

"Cassius, my... arch nemesis?" I deflected the feelings of longing so she couldn't see them on my face.

Della gave me a big smile.

"I'm pretty sure enemies don't kiss and flirt like you two do. Or touch each other." Her eyes narrowed on me as my cheeks heated like I was being scolded by a parent. Stars above: how did she know about that? "How are you feeling?"

"Fine..." I spoke cautiously. "Why is Cassius talking to you about me?"

"I can't tell you outright." She frowned. "But you're smart; you'll read between the lines."

"So, you are trying to tell me something about Cassius?"

She shrugged her shoulders. What a pain in the ass woman.

"Is he *not* my enemy?" My heart pounded. I hadn't realized how much I wanted that to be true, but that was impossible. Stars above knew that I would march to Crimson right now and demand he keep me, but I don't think the Crimson royal family would allow it.

"He's something." She smiled.

"I'm sorry, why can't you just tell me what the hell you're hinting at?" I rested my hands on my hips and watched her.

"My tongue is tied with magic."

I was tired of this. I rolled my eyes and turned to leave.

"Where are you going?" she asked.

"Leaving because you have not said anything I believe."

As my hand touched the handle of the door, she shoved me away. I stumbled into the wall before turning and glaring at her. Della looked around frantically as I readied myself for a fight.

"Please," she begged. "I'm on your side."

"I don't know how I can believe a strange woman who snuck into my room. Especially one who says she's a goddess."

"Ask Haden," she spoke quickly, her eyes flashing with pain as she spoke of him. "He knows who I am. He can confirm I'm not lying to you."

"Haden, as in, Cassius' guard?"

"Yes, he's a very good friend of yours." She winced a little as if she were in pain. I took a step to help her, but she backed away from me. Tell me what she is thinking, I demanded from my magic. Nothing came to mind. Odd.

"That magic doesn't work on gods." She wheezed in pain toward me. How had she known I tried?

"Is this some sick joke that Cassius put you up to? Why would I believe Haden? He's probably in on this weird act you have going too."

"He hates me!" she yelled. Tears filled her eyes, and I gasped as they fell down her cheeks. They were illuminated like the stars in the sky and glowed brightly. Well, that is not normal. "He hates me; he will not lie for me."

"Why does he hate you?"

"Because I killed his sister to save him," she whispered. "I'm in love with a man who wishes he had never met me. He curses my very existence every day of his life."

I opened my mouth to say something, but she sobbed into her hands.

"I still don't know how this will make me believe you." I frowned.

"You will be able to tell by the devastation on his face that it is not an act." She looked away from me, ashamed. "He will tell you how much he hates me, and you'll know he is telling the truth. You can ask Cassius too."

Shit, I believed her, and I wasn't sure if I was desperate to have any indication that Cassius was important to me or if I was gullible.

"Why did you have to kill his sister to save him?"

Della's shoulders stilled at my question before turning to me. Glowing tears still falling from her eyes.

"Because he was the one who was supposed to die, and I couldn't lose him, but I needed to collect a soul to keep the balance. So, I took hers instead, even though he begged me to save her. It's the reason my brother Mikel cursed you, but I cannot tell you the details. Cassius is the only one who can."

My mind reeled with everything she was saying. I believed her.

"Why wouldn't you just take his soul like he asked?" I didn't blame him for being so angry.

Della stared me right in the eyes as she took a shaky breath.

"Because he is my fated mate, and I couldn't lose him, but in the end, I lost him anyway."

I gaped at her.

"He doesn't know he's my fated mate, so don't tell him, please. He will have a new reason to hate me."

"I won't," I promised.

"I've never told anyone about Haden being my mate," she confessed. "Besides my housekeeper, Pia. It feels good that someone else knows."

She stared at me with devastation on her face. Something about the look made me think of Cassius. Like I had seen a similar look on his face before.

"Can I ask you a question about Cassius?"

This seemed to jar her from her thoughts, and she perked up.

"Yes."

"Cassius is important to me, isn't he? My mind can't remember him, but my heart does. When I was in Exile, I always felt as if something was missing, but that feeling went away when I saw Cassius and only returned when he was gone."

Della smiled.

"Yes..."

A knock at my door startled me. Della glanced at me before disappearing from sight. Damn it, there were more questions I had. I ripped open the door to a guard staring at me.

"What?" I snapped with my dagger in my hand, angry enough to kill him.

"Who are you talking to?" His dark eyes moved past me and into the room to see if I had a visitor.

"Myself. Sorry, I'll keep it down." He looked at me as if I were crazy. I glared and slammed the door in his face before locking it. I went and drew myself a bath and soaked in the water, replaying Della's words in my head. There was something about Cassius I was supposed to figure out. I closed my eyes as images of Cassius pinning me to the ground and kissing me plagued me. Suddenly, the crown tattoo on my wrist zapped, making me feel wild with lust, but it felt as if it weren't my own.

"I need to fucking find Cassius before I lose my shit."

Chapter 13

Cassius

Why did I do this to myself? I paced my father's throne room as my parents, Haden, Leer, and Zade, stared at me. I was antsy, and I could not fucking relax.

"For fuck's sake, man. You need to chill; I'm starting to doubt this theory of yours." Haden broke my racing thoughts. When I looked up, he bit into an apple and shrugged at me.

"Son." My mother walked to me and put her hands on my shoulders, staring me in the eyes. "Haden's right; you need to calm the fuck down. She will come."

"It's been almost a month," I sighed. "Don't we think she would come to find me by now?"

"She tried to find you for weeks before she went back to Cerithia." My mother reminded me. "She will come; she probably just needs a little push in the right direction."

"Ardella is keeping an eye on her," Haden said. He always refused to call her anything but her full name.

I knew this was my idea. I would pull Thea in by hopelessly flirting with her, then disappear. It was fucking torture, and each day that passed, and she didn't come to find me, the more I doubted her feelings for me. This could all be lust to her. I thought by me disappearing she would face the reality of her feelings for me. But she didn't come.

I started pacing again, and Haden groaned as he threw a chunk of his apple at me. Glaring at him, I kept moving around. I needed to be busy, or I was going to go mad. If she didn't come find me in the next few days, then I would have to go find her because I couldn't fucking stand this distance. My marriage bond burned because it knew that I could see her, and it wanted me to get my ass out there and force her to come home.

But this time was different. Not only the way she watched me but also because Della had told me what her brother did—sabotaged us every year. My shadows swarmed out of me without permission as my anger took over. I would fucking kill him if I could.

"Cassius," my father's voice pulled me from my dangerous thoughts. He pointed behind me, and I saw Della. Her eyes found Haden immediately, and she looked away when he refused to acknowledge her existence.

"Della." I stepped toward her. "Please tell me something; I'm losing my fucking mind," I begged.

Della smiled.

"She's on her way to Crimson, alone." Della hesitated as if she were contemplating telling me something. "She is distraught. Her father hit her."

My shadows exploded from me and filled the room again. That motherfucker. My eyes pulsed black as rage filled every shallow breath I took.

"Why did he hit her?" Leer asked. "Isn't he trying to get her on his side?"

Luren had never been good at convincing Thea. Thea always came back to me. Della's eyes flickered to mine before she smirked slightly.

"She broke Jesper's nose for grabbing her, and when her father demanded an explanation, she told him that her reason was that she found Jesper's existence unpleasant. But then she was asking about her life before Exile. She wants to know why she feels like something is missing, and her father refused to answer. When she kept asking, he blew up at her and told her she had nothing before, that he owned her entire life. She told him that she did not belong to him, and he hit her. She did tell him to fuck off and spit blood at him. Then she started running, and

Wisp is making sure she is headed to the border, but she was already headed this way."

Are you what I've been looking for?

Her words haunted me. She felt I was missing.

"I'll go watch for her and call for you when she gets here." Haden stood and walked out of the room. Della's sad eyes followed him until he was out of sight.

"When are you going to tell her that you cursed her? You will have to at some point so she can break the curse and fulfill the prophecy," Della said.

"I know." It was the one thing I didn't know how to do. I had to make sure she loved me and would listen. "I think a few more visits, and I'll tell her. I have to know where her feelings are before I risk saying that to her. I am not losing her again."

"I'll let you get ready for her to come. She should be here any minute. I'll keep checking on her and let you know of any new developments."

"You can stay," I told her.

Della frowned at me.

"He would prefer to not see me," she whispered. Haden didn't want to be near her, but he would put his anger aside so she could help Thea. But I knew that Della didn't want to stay and keep getting looks full of hatred from Haden.

"Thank you for helping her." I smiled, and she nodded before disappearing.

I started pacing back and forth with a new worry. How the fuck was I going to tell her I killed her and have her listen to me? Gods, I felt like I did when I used to follow her around during our previous war and flirt with her. Anticipation filled me. I couldn't wait to see her. No matter how brief it was, I was happy.

"Cassius!" I heard Haden's voice boom in the distance. Immediately I left in my swarm of shadows. When I stepped out of them, my heart beat wildly at the sight of her. She was very distraught, her green eyes red and puffy from crying. Her blue uniform made me sick. Blue didn't suit her. But it was the trail of dark red blood down the front of it that made my vision pulse black. My hands fisted tightly as I tried to control myself. Her pouty lip was cut, and so was her cheek.

"Don't move." One of the guards demanded of her. I watched as she lifted her hand, trying to evaporate him with her fire, but nothing came out. I immediately looked at her wrists to see if her magic was bound, but it wasn't. She was just tired. She had to run for over a day to get here.

"It's alright, Thea." Haden stepped forward. She quickly unsheathed her viper-handled dagger and held it toward him. She didn't realize she had come to Crimson. Disappointment filled me. I shook it away and focused on her. She was sending all sorts of emotions and thoughts down our bond, so many that I couldn't understand what she was feeling.

"Everyone but Haden, leave," I demanded without looking away from my wife. Thea's chest rose and fell quickly, but it was slowing down as she watched me.

"Did you run all the way here to stab me?" Her eyes never left mine. "I admit this is a surprising war strategy, but again, you always had a way of keeping me guessing."

I smiled at her when she blinked slowly at me. Her pretty green eyes widened, letting me know she liked me flirting with her. Gods, all of the worry I had earlier disappeared when she looked at me like this.

"It was a mistake. I did not mean to cross into your territory. I was just running." Disappointment filled me again. I took a hesitant step toward her, and she moved her dagger toward me instead of Haden. I lifted my hands to show her I wasn't going to hurt her.

"Running from someone? Or running to someone?" She didn't answer. Interesting.

"Or perhaps you are taking me up on my offer? Are you lonely?"

She opened her mouth to speak but shut it after a moment of not finding something to say back, but she didn't need to. I could feel her desire through our bond. She lowered her blade. Good, we were making progress.

"We're friends, aren't we?" she asked Haden.

"Yes." Haden smiled smugly at me. Why was she asking that? Was she having flashes of memories?

"Haden," she whispered his name as if she were remembering it. Then she turned her attention back to me. "We're more than friends."

"Something like that." I nodded and smiled at her.

Her green eyes traced over me slowly, and I couldn't help the longing that flooded me. I missed her so fucking much. She was trying to figure something out in her mind. Talk to me, my love. Ask me more questions so I can understand what you're thinking. Haden stared at me before looking at Thea. He could tell she was struggling with something too.

She sighed heavily and rubbed her forehead with a soft groan. I tilted my head and tried to see what she was feeling through the bond, but it was as if she blocked me completely. I hated when she did that, even though she didn't do it intentionally.

"I will leave Crimson. I did not mean to intrude into your territory. This is not a strategic war move. It was simply a mistake," she finally spoke.

I nodded slowly as I stepped closer to her. Haden moved toward her other side. I needed her to stay a little longer; this was not enough time. Thea's eyes watched us as we moved toward her.

"Thea," I whispered as I went to grab her.

She stabbed her dagger into my thigh.

"Fuck!" I groaned and let go of her. "You fucking stabbed me." I accused.

"I'm so sorry," she muttered immediately. Guilt filled her eyes as she looked at me bleeding. Haden stood off to the side, dying of laughter at the scene unfolding in front of him.

"You're apologizing?" I ran my hands down my face, both in pain and confusion. "Why?" Her face turned to something tortured at the sight of me. She didn't answer me. My eyes stared at the viper-handled dagger sticking out from my thigh. Thea stepped forward and ripped it from my leg. Fuck, that did not feel very fucking good. Blood rushed from the wound. I went to hold my hand to it but stopped when she kneeled and pushed her hands against the wound. She stared up at me, and my jaw clenched at the sight of her on her knees.

Then I saw the glow from her hands and watched it seep into my leg. The blood stopped pushing through her fingers, and the pain disappeared immediately. Fear filled her eyes as she backed up.

"What the fuck was that?"

She didn't know she could heal.

"You used healing magic." I squatted down to her level. "You have a lot of magic inside of you, my love. You don't need to be scared."

Her breathing was rapid, and I cursed myself for calling her that. It was hard to control the habit. Her lust pushed through the bond, and I closed my eyes tightly to keep myself in check. She was going to fucking be the death of me if she kept looking at me with those eyes and her desire pumping through the bond.

"I should go." She stood and started walking toward Cerithia. I was hot on her heels, desperate to just be near her for a little longer. She walked silently beside me at a painfully slow pace. She was exhausted, and I just wanted to take care of her.

"You know, Cerithia is quite a walk from here. You can stay the night if you'd like."

"Did you hit your head recently? We are at war. We are... enemies?"

Her answer was exactly what I expected as I smiled at her. She watched me, though, as if the word enemies did not feel right.

"We can take a break from pretending to hate each other," I said the words that I did to her all those years ago.

"We do not hate each other. We can't even pretend." Her body stiffened like she hadn't meant to say that out loud. My heart pounded faster.

"You're right. We can't even pretend to dislike each other. I mean, what kind of enemy would make you cum on his fingers?"

Thea's face burned bright red as her mouth fell open. She had stopped walking so she could gape at me. I just gave her a big smile. She told me once that my smile was one of her favorite things.

"You can't go around and say things like that," she muttered and started walking again.

"But you love it when I say things like that to you."

She refused to acknowledge me, but her cheeks were tinged pink from her desire.

"I'll make you a deal, Thea. I'll get you back to Cerithia in less than a minute with my shadow magic if you tell me why you're blushing so much right now."

"I'd rather walk." She lied. Okay, she was playing hard to get.

"Let me guess it then." I scratched my chin as if I didn't already know. "You think I'm handsome. No, that wouldn't make you blush. You want me to kiss you. No, that wouldn't make you blush either. I know…" I stopped walking, and so did she. "You pictured me naked."

"No," she said too quickly. "I wasn't blushing for anything like that. I'm just…flushed from exhaustion."

My little liar.

I grabbed her arm to stop her from walking and turned her, so she was watching me.

"Is it me you picture when you touch yourself at night?"

Shock filled her features. But fuck, her eyes were turning black as she stared at me. I knew she pictured me because she sent images down the bond accidentally. And she thought about it a lot.

"You've lost your mind," she scoffed.

"You didn't deny it, my love." Shit, I didn't mean to call her that again. Her eyes fell to my mouth when the name registered.

"Do you flirt with everyone?" she asked.

"Would that make you jealous?" I asked as I watched her closely for any reaction.

"Why would I care what my enemy does?" She lied quickly, but not before her eyes flashed red without her permission, showing me exactly how she felt about that. I lifted her into my arms because somehow she was getting slower.

"You need to work on your lying, my love. If it makes you feel better, I picture you when I touch myself."

Lust shot through me from the bond. Gods above, I was drowning in desire. I watched her face as my shadows swarmed around us and took us to Cerithia. Being this close to her instantly settled my racing thoughts. She had always been my safe place, my anchor. She smelled like these little purple flowers that grew in Crimson—sweet and intoxicating.

Her fingers fiddled with the dark hair on my neck out of habit. A moment later my shadows moved, showing her that we were in the forest of Cerithia, but she didn't let me go, and I made no move to put her down.

"Are your eyes normally black?" she asked.

I didn't answer. Brim said to keep my golden eyes from her until I needed to show her. He had been frantic that day he came to see me but refused to say why. I knew she didn't remember anything about me but my golden eyes from her dreams. I felt like it would confuse her to know it was me. So, I kept my eyes black as I leaned forward and pressed my lips against hers.

My gentle kiss only lasted a moment before she pulled me closer to her and turned it hard and needy. I moaned as she twisted in my arms and wrapped her legs around my hips. Her hands snaked through my hair, tugging it.

I fucking loved when she did that. It was like her body remembered exactly what I liked because she did small things like this all the time.

I kissed her once more before setting her down on her feet. Disappointment filled her eyes, but I needed to understand where her mind was.

"Why do you think you ran to Crimson?"

"I don't know. I just felt like I was suffocating here." She paused before frowning. "Do you ever feel like you've lost something or misplaced it? I feel like that all the time, and no one in my family has been helpful. I've asked my father. I've asked my half-sisters. I even asked my sister's fiancé, Jesper."

"Stay away from that monster. Do you hear me?" I warned, but silently told myself to get a grip.

"Thank you for bringing me back. I guess we can go back to being enemies on the battlefield. Unless you will continue hiding?"

I smirked. She wanted to know if she'd see me again.

"I'm not hiding, Thea. I was testing out a theory. Maybe if you wanted to sneak into Crimson again, I would let you."

"Be careful, Cassius; I might use that invitation to stab you again." She glanced over at me, and that feeling of wanting to be close to her consumed me. I didn't want her to leave yet. "Did your theory work?"

I smiled softly at her, and I wondered if she felt this tension between us.

"In fact, it did tonight."

Her full lips tilted into a curious frown as she watched me. Her eyes looked over me as if she were trying to figure out what I meant. She took a step forward but stopped herself and turned towards the castle of Cerithia.

"I need you to promise me something," I said.

"Depends on what it is."

"When you get back to Cerithia, do not tell them you made it to Crimson lands."

She looked confused at me.

"It was an honest mistake. They would understand."

I was suddenly in front of her, holding her chin up, so I was staring at her pretty face.

"Believe me when I tell you they would not understand. They will know you found me, and you will not be around anymore. They will punish you, Thea." My eyes closed tightly as images of what Jesper did to her last time plagued me. "If you promise me anything, let it be this, Thea. You will lie to them."

"Okay." She agreed. "I'll tell them I ran into the woods after my father struck me and got disoriented from it. I was lost in the Cerithian forest."

I sighed relieved as I let go of her.

"I want you to do another thing." I was silent for a moment because I was wary of saying too much and not enough. "I'm about to tell you something that no one but Crimson knows, so if you speak of it, they will know you've come to see me." I turned with my shadows swarming around me. "Crimson will be asking for a meeting of the kingdoms in two weeks to discuss a negotiation for peace. All of the kingdoms will meet in Cerithia. You should be in attendance as the captain of the guard, but I do not doubt that your father and Jesper will try to keep you busy, so you aren't in attendance. You will do everything in your power to make sure you are there, but more importantly, you will see that the king will not tell you about the meeting at all.

"And in these two weeks as you're in Cerithia, I want you to notice how no one tells you anything. How you are kept in the dark about everything. They will whisper about you when you're present and speak of you when your back is turned."

She stared at me like she was seeing me for the first time. Something about the look disarmed me. What did she see when she looked at me?

"We knew each other before I disappeared." She frowned. "That is why you seem so familiar."

Devastation filled me at how sad she sounded.

"Yes, and your father did not like it. You'll start having memories soon. It always happens when you leave Exile for too long."

"I've left Exile before. Sybil had said the same thing."

"Yes, this is your eighth time trying to break your curse, and I hope you do this time, Thea."

I watched her closely.

"They won't tell you anything about your life, and if you ask too many questions, they will start thinking you remember." I stepped toward her and grabbed her hands. "I would keep your memories to yourself. They will not be happy to know that you remember."

"What am I going to remember?"

My face softened as I looked at her. Us. Me.

"The real reason why you fled to Crimson tonight. It was no accident, Thea; it was destined."

My answer caught her off guard. A tortured expression overtook her face, and I pulled her to me and kissed her deeply. She pulled back and stared at me intently.

"Tell me why I miss you when you're gone," she whispered. "You are all I think about, Cassius, and I should feel bad because your king is my father's biggest enemy. But if I'm being honest, I really don't like my father."

A laugh escaped me at her words. I loved this fucking woman with every fiber of my soul.

"Because you love me, even if you don't remember." I decided to give her a sliver of the truth to see how she took it. Her face didn't change. "You don't look surprised."

"We love each other," she answered back. "Della said I needed to read between the lines when it came to you. But I can see it when you are near me that you miss me, but you have been missing me for a long time."

My chest rose and fell as she talked.

"Gods, what am I babbling on about?" Her voice panicked as her cheeks heated instantly as she looked anywhere but at me. I grabbed her jaw and forced her gaze to meet mine. Maybe I should tell her about how I cursed her. She didn't deny loving me.

"Thea!" someone called out close by.

Fuck.

"Shit, they're looking for me."

"I'll see you soon." I smiled but frowned when she looked at me with tears in her eyes. "What's wrong, my love?"

"I... I don't know; I just feel overwhelmed by you leaving me."

"I think I see her!" Someone interrupted us. I took a step back, but Thea glanced to my left, making me look too. I saw nothing, but she nodded her head as if she were answering a question. When I looked back at her, she was looking at me again.

"Do you see him like you see Wisp?" she asked.

I glanced to where she had been looking and saw no one. Worry filled my chest. Why was she seeing things?

"Who is it?" I asked. She frowned at my question.

"I don't know; he won't tell me. He has been following me for a while." Her eyes drifted to him again, and she smiled. "He said to tell you that..." Her brows furrowed. My heart sank when Thea looked at me. "Bayla? Does that name mean something to you?"

I opened my mouth to speak, but a guard coming through the trees stopped me. I stepped back and left in my shadows, but I didn't go to Crimson. I went to Cerithia. My shadows disappeared, and I was hidden behind the blue velvet drapes in Luren's throne room. I had to make sure she was alright. I had to make sure she lied to them. Adrenaline pumped through me at Thea's words. How had Bayla sent a man to help her?

Her words raced through my mind. This was the year. She was coming back to me, and the excitement I felt was overwhelming. I stilled when I heard Luren clomp into the room. A moment later, a commotion followed. I could feel her hatred through the bond. I peeked through the small gap in the drapes and saw her glaring at her father.

"Where the fuck have you been for three days?" His voice was soft, but in a cruel way.

"In the forest." She lied immediately. Good girl. "I was upset after you hit me, so I ran into the woods to get away from you, and I became disoriented and lost."

Jesper's beady blue eyes stared at her in a way that made me want to cut them from his fucking sockets. He had always looked at her like she was a piece of meat, and it enraged me more than anything. He glanced at Luren, and they exchanged a look I didn't like.

"Did you go to Crimson?" Jesper was the one to ask. My heart raced; my shadows were ready to attack them if they tried anything. Thea stilled, but her eyes flickered to where I was, but she didn't see me. Shit, her darkness could probably sense my magic.

"Why would I go to Crimson?" She scoffed like it was the most stupid thing he could have suggested. "Besides, if I went to Crimson, I would not be back by now. That would take me longer than three days to get there and back."

The guards watched her closely, like she might explode, their hands gripping their weapons. Suddenly the bond filled me with rage and anger.

"So, you didn't go to Crimson." Jesper glared. "Did you talk to anyone?"

"Like who? The monsters in the woods? What is with these questions? Who do you think I'm meeting in the woods?"

"No one." Luren glared at Jesper like he had said too much. He had. Thea wasn't stupid; she would have known this conversation was odd even if we never talked. Her anger doubled.

"Well, I'm tired, hungry, and cold, so is this interrogation over?" She snapped. Her father waved his hand to dismiss her like she was unimportant.

She was the most important fae in this realm, and he treated her like trash. Thea left immediately, and I instantly missed her.

"She's right; she wouldn't have made it all the way to Crimson and back this quickly," Luren sighed.

"I still think she's being strange." Jesper winced when he scratched his black and blue nose. I smiled at the damage Thea had done to him.

"You always think that." Luren rolled his eyes. "We will keep an eye on her. We'll need her gone for the meeting; she cannot be close to Cassius."

Too late for that. I waited for them to say more, but they didn't, so I went home. My father and Haden were waiting for me.

"How was that?" Haden asked.

"I need to talk to Della," I said.

"What, why?" Haden asked worriedly.

"Thea just told me a man is following her, and he told her that Bayla sent him." I glanced at my father.

"Thea's dead mother?" Haden looked at me. All I could do was nod. Something was happening to Thea, and I hoped Della knew what it was.

CHAPTER 14

THEA

The castle had no secrets or clues hiding anywhere I had found in the days following my return. Searching had proven difficult with the guards my father had watching me. He thought I didn't see them lurking in the shadows or following me when I left my room. It was easy to lose them—they were idiots.

That was how I had found my way into the bottom floors of the castle. It had simply started with me hiding from the guards, but now that I was down here, something felt right. So, I wandered until I came across a small wooden door. There was nothing in particular about it. In fact, there were dozens of doors that matched it, but this one called to me.

When I opened it, I was met with a very small room. A bedroom by the looks of it. The bed was small and unslept in by the dust that had settled everywhere. I sat on the bed and closed my eyes as an image plagued my mind. An image of me crying silently in this bed played on repeat, or maybe it was different memories rolled into one. Then I could hear myself counting, but somehow, I knew what I was counting as I opened my eyes and looked around the room. There were sixty-seven nails. I was so sad.

I looked around the room, but nothing else happened. Standing, I headed for the door but stopped when I saw her. I turned when I spotted Wisp floating by the bed. She was her usual color of dark green, but then she shrank in size. She was so tiny that she swarmed the side of my bed and disappeared into it before reappearing again. I walked to her and watched her disappear into a slit in the mattress.

She was showing me something. I reached my hand into the bed and pulled out a letter. Something felt familiar about seeing it. Wisp disappeared into the mattress again, so I shoved my hands into it and found another sheet of paper.

The blood-red envelope sat heavy in my hand as I stared at my name on the front of it. I glanced around to see if anyone had followed cure down here. I hurried and shut the door, using my fire magic to make sure that no one could enter. I ripped open the envelope, and my heart plummeted as I read the words.

I read the letter three times. I stared at the last part of it the most. A man with golden eyes watches me. The man from my dreams. The one who had seemed to disappear altogether. *Blood witch. Never trust my father. A deal with the gods. Cursed to die young.*

My hands shook as I unfolded the other sheet of paper. My eyes glided over the words of a contract. My blood boiled when I realized it was a contract to attack Exile. I stared at my father's and Gwyn's names scribbled on the bottom. Then I focused on the other name. Yerma from the Ravenstone Coven was scribbled on the bottom too.

Sweat beaded off my forehead as I paced in the room. Who left that in the mattress? Was it me? I begged the gods for a moment of clarity, but nothing happened. Sucking in a deep breath, I pulled my shit together because I knew that my father had secrets, but I had my own, and he couldn't know that I was suspicious.

Those words swarmed my mind as I shoved all of it back into the mattress. I was a fucking witch. Who was the man with golden eyes, and where did he go? *Never trust my father.* Somehow, I felt like that was the most important thing I read. I would find Yerma and figure out what the contract was.

Wisp appeared in front of me. She hadn't been around for a few days, and I thought maybe she had disappeared. She flickered red and moved down the hallway before pausing.

"Do you want me to follow?"

She burned bright orange and twirled happily. My darkness hummed as I followed Wisp toward my father's throne room. The door was open and the room empty, which I thought was odd. Wisp moved back behind my father's throne, where velvet drapes hung. Was something behind there? An urgency filled me as I darted behind them only to be met with... nothing.

I looked at Wisp, who burned bright purple.

"I don't know what that color means," I whispered harshly.

"We don't have much time." My father's voice had me holding my breath. Wisp burned bright purple still as I slowly peeked around the drapes.

A woman with hair as bright as my fire magic stood in the room with him. Her eyes were an odd shade of purple as she looked around. Her ears were not pointed like a fae, but I could feel her power pulsing from her. Her cloak was purely a style choice, as it was made of black lace and thin. I could see her soft yellow dress through it.

"Where is Thea?" The woman hissed my name with hatred. Bitch.

"Who fucking knows?" My father sighed. "But guards are watching her; don't worry, she won't recognize you even if she sees you."

"What do you want me to do this time?"

"I need you to trap Cassius and his family in their castle so that they cannot escape."

My heart pumped anger through me. What was my father doing? My darkness seeped from me in black tendrils, ready to kill anyone who meant harm to Cassius.

"When?" she asked, bored.

"Around the wedding. I will give you specifics when I get them. I just wanted to make sure you will be available."

"Fine, but this is the last time I want to do this. You will take care of Thea too because I will not lose my coven to that bitch."

"Calm down, Yerma. Thea doesn't even know that she is part blood witch, let alone who you are." My father rolled his eyes.

Yerma, the name from the contracts I found to hurt Exile.

"If she breaks her curse, she will kill me too. So, make sure she can't," Yerma snapped viciously at my father. "Did you hide her bloodstone like I told you to?"

"Well, if you do what I ask, then she will never break her curse. Take this and get the fuck out of my castle." He shoved a small velvet sack toward her. I could hear the coins clanking. Payment. Yerma sneered at my father before snapping her fingers and turning into a raven, flying off.

My father left, slamming the door on his way out.

Stepping forward I glanced at the map that Wisp was twirling around. The map had nothing marked on it, but Wisp shrunk herself down and illuminated a small section of the woods in Cerithia. I didn't know what she wanted.

My darkness hadn't given me a chance to think about this. It had twisted around me, and suddenly I was standing deep in the woods. Wisp was not with me. The night was falling, so it made it difficult to see anything until the soft glow of light appeared through the trees. I walked quietly toward the fire but stopped when I realized it was a small village. Cottages lined a cobblestone path.

The small homes were charming. The moss and flowers growing over them made them blend into the nature around them. A moment later I saw a raven appear, swooping close to the ground. Then suddenly it transformed into Yerma. This was her coven. She began walking away, and the witches on the path moved quickly from her.

Shit.

When she disappeared, I continued to hide in the woods. I didn't know how many witches were there, but my plan was to break into a cottage and get answers from one of the members.

I watched as an older witch moved into her cottage. I waited patiently to make a move. It wasn't until I saw smoke barreling out of her chimney that I crept to her door. I slipped in, ready to pounce, only to turn and see her watching me as if she had been expecting me.

"Thea." She greets me.

My brows furrowed as my darkness didn't reach forward and wrap this woman up. "Lock the door, will ya?"

I did as she asked before watching her cover the window blinds.

"You knew I was watching you." I accused.

She chuckled. Her purple eyes took in the sight of me. Her dark blonde hair was starting to fall out of place as she sat down.

"I knew you'd come someday."

"Do we know each other?"

"Yes." She frowned at me. "I assume you're here to claim your right as the queen of the blood witches."

Confusion plagued me. This wasn't the blood coven.

The woman frowned at me when she saw how confused I was.

"If that isn't why you're here, then why are you?"

"I'm looking for Yerma."

"The queen of the Ravenstone coven." Her voice was soft. "What for?"

"Why would I tell you?"

My darkness wasn't warning me that this woman was a danger. She smiled at me when I tried to read her mind.

"That won't work on me, my queen. But do not fear; you can simply control any of us with a command. We cannot defy you."

My darkness swarmed around me, but with a happiness I had never felt before. When I glanced at the woman, she smiled brightly at me.

"You are a sight to behold."

"What is your name?"

"Genia."

I took a steady breath before telling her what I found in the mattress. I wanted to collect vengeance for what she had done to Exile. Genia was very silent as she stared at me. My eyes had turned red during my story. I was pissed and could hardly control myself.

"You don't believe me," I sighed.

"No, I do, and I know why she helped your father."

I sat up straighter as she admitted that. Her eyes faded from purple to red like mine. She lifted the sleeve of her dress up to reveal swirls like mine, but hers were smaller, and she didn't have as many.

"You're a blood witch." I shook my head. "I thought everyone died."

"Your mother gathered the coven one night. She was frantic and scared. I had never seen her like that before. She demanded that we all pack our things and come here to the Ravenstone coven because your father was on his way to kill all of us. We told her to come with us, but she kept talking about how your father had you and was keeping you from her. When she commanded that we leave without her, we had no choice but to listen. She said that she needed to free your magic and get you away from your father; then she would join us. Apparently, she had made a deal with Yerma that she would watch over you until you were old enough if she didn't make it back to us."

Genia frowned at me.

"We waited for her, but she never came for us. Eventually, we went back to the blood coven and found her dead. We loved your mother. She was such a wonderful woman, Thea, and she loved you."

"So, my father killed her." Sadness filled me before anger and rage took over.

"Yes. He didn't want her to let your magic out. We told her we would stay and fight. We all love you too, but she said she couldn't risk us, but she was also terrified that your father would kill you."

"How many blood witches are here?"

"All of us, around a hundred. We would have more, but Yerma doesn't let us leave Ravenstone. She is cruel, and I believe she's helping your father because she doesn't want you to claim your right to become the queen of blood witches. If you do that, then she loses power, and all of us, and Yerma loves power. She is nothing like your mother was. She has refused to let us go out to find mates. It's like she knows if there are too many of us, she won't be able to control us. She is cruel even to her own witches."

"So, you're a prisoner here."

Just like Exile.

"Yes, but I knew you'd come for us. Gods, you look just like your mother." Her friendly eyes looked me over.

"I came to kill her," I confessed. "That was my plan before I heard all of this because of what she had done to Exile, but now I want to because she has kept all of you prisoners."

Genia smiled brightly at me.

"Then let's kill the bitch."

We stood, and Genia grabbed some daggers from a small drawer before walking over to me.

"You don't have to do this," I told her. "I can manage her on my own; I don't want you to get hurt."

"Oh, I know you can handle her. I'm just going as back-up, and honestly, I just want to see her take her last breath."

I smiled at the woman before we snuck out of the cottage. It was darker now; the last fading beams of sunlight had completely faded behind the trees, leaving moonlight to guide our way on the pathway. We didn't need to walk for long before Yerma's home came into view. I knew it was hers simply because it was huge.

The large home was white with a large green yard surrounded by a black fence. It was far nicer than the small cottages everyone else was living in. She didn't have any guards outside, so I assumed it would be fairly easy to break in. When I turned to Genia, though, there were dozens of witches coming out of their cottages. I stood up straight as I looked at all of their red eyes watching me before they all bowed to me.

I smiled at them as I forced my eyes to shift to red. They gasped. Faint whispers of how I looked like my mother spread through them.

"I'll be right back," I whispered to Genia.

Then I hurried to the house and peered into the window, only to see the bottom floor empty of any guards. I slipped through the front door. The house smelled like these small blue flowers that grew by my father's castle. It instantly put me on edge. I should have asked Genia what kind of magic I was up against, but she didn't seem too worried for me. A soft moan from upstairs caught my attention.

I crept up the stairs, careful not to make noise. The sounds were clearly those of pleasure, so I followed them. The bedroom door was wide open, and I paused when I saw her. Yerma was beautiful, her hair a fiery red, and her skin pale. But that wasn't what made my eyes go wide. It was the three men she had in bed with her. Gods, they were really going at it. I tried not to look at them, but a small red wound on Yerma's shoulder grabbed my attention. It looked infected and...

I let my darkness out to see what magic it pulled, but I was met with nothing. Interesting.

"Sorry to interrupt," I called out, making all of them freeze. Yerma's purple eyes looked at me with so much hatred in them.

"Thea," she snipped. "For a second I thought you were your mother, but then I remembered that she's where she should be... dead." Her full lips pulled into a wicked smile.

"Now see, why did you need to go and say that?" I huffed. "I was just going to kill you quickly, but now I think I'll draw it out."

Yerma was still straddling one of the men, just staring at me oddly.

"You can't kill me." Her eyes flickered over to something, but I didn't take my eyes from her. "You think I'm stupid? I knew you'd come someday, and I'm prepared."

"Let's hope so, because if not, I'm going to drag your naked ass outside and gut you in front of all the coven, and then I'm claiming all your witches too."

This pissed her off, her jaw tensing, but she just glared.

"Good luck getting past my ward. If you step foot inside my room, you'll die."

I smiled as I sent Cassius' shadows from me and grabbed her with them. Her pretty eyes widened as I wrapped her up and dragged her toward me. The men just stared at the scene unfolding without moving. At least they knew better than to get in my way.

"You really think a ward would protect you?" I laughed as she dangled a few feet in the air as I headed down the stairs. She was trying to talk, but my darkness wrapped around her mouth so she couldn't.

As soon as I walked outside, it was clear every witch that lived here was waiting, watching. My fire mist exploded from me, twirling around all of us so that I could see everyone. Slowly, my eyes looked over the witches to see if anyone was going to attack me. No one moved. I was hoping that Yerma had been such a bitch that no one wanted to defend her.

"If you don't want to witness me killing Yerma, then you should probably leave now," I warned. My darkness was swarming around me in a frenzy, excited to get revenge for Exile and my mother. Not a single witch left.

I released my darkness from around her mouth.

"Anything you'd like to say?"

Yerma glanced around at all the peering eyes.

"What are you all doing? I am your queen; kill her!"

Looking over my shoulder, I smirked when no one moved toward me. I glanced back at her and glared. Shouldn't her witches move forward to protect her if she commanded it? My eyes glanced around the witches, but still no one moved. Maybe that was just a blood witch thing.

"Looks like they don't like you very much."

"Fuck you!" she screeched. "Go ahead and kill me, but just know that you will fail to break your curse. Your father will win, and I hope he guts Cassius in front of you!"

There was a gasp from behind me, but I didn't look. My darkness froze at her words. It was pissed.

"You say a lot of stupid shit," I muttered before my darkness created a wall between me and Yerma. It slowly moved toward her, and as soon as it touched her, she began screaming. I couldn't tell what it was doing until she started emerging through the darkness with her skin missing. Fuck, it skinned her ass alive.

Her screams were deafening. Cassius' shadows released her, and she fell to the grass. I knew I should feel disgusted, but I was fucking proud of my darkness. I turned toward the crowd.

"This is for Exile and for my mother the former queen of the blood witches!"

I flicked my hand open, causing fire to create a ball in my palm. Then I turned and lit Yerma on fire, not giving her the mercy of killing her quickly. I stared her in the eyes as she burned alive at my feet. Once she was dead, I turned.

"I have come to claim my coven, and now Ravenstone will be a part of it."

They all bowed to me without protest. Genia moved toward me quickly, smiling.

"That was quite the show. Where would you like us to set up our coven?"

I opened my mouth before shutting it. I didn't know what to tell her.

"Crimson?" she asked as the others moved closer.

"Why would you think Crimson would be a good choice?"

Dozens of the blood witches smiled at me like they all knew a secret that I didn't. What did they know?

"It's just that your mother mentioned you fancied the prince, Cassius."

"My mother is dead," I scoffed.

"Yes, but she told us one night that she finally pieced together who the man with golden eyes was." Confusion filled me. "We do not keep secrets in the coven. We share knowledge so that we may all be prepared for what comes at us."

"My mother thought I liked Cassius?"

Wait, what did Cassius have to do with my golden-eyed man?

"She saw it in one of her visions. Your mother thought the stars made the best selection for you."

My eyes glanced at everyone without understanding. They were all staring at me oddly.

"Selection for what, exactly?"

Genia's eyes widened at me before she looked around at the other witches.

"For your fated mate."

My what?

"Cassius is my fated mate..."

"Shit, sorry, I thought you were here because you broke the curse," she muttered. "I don't think I should have been the one to tell you."

"Way to go, Genia," someone grumbled.

"How was I supposed to know!" Genia argued back. I could hear them bickering back and forth, but their words jumbled together.

My breathing was coming out in choppy breaths. Gods, I was going to pass out. I stumbled forward, and several of the women caught me before blackness overtook me.

CHAPTER 15

THEA

My head was pounding when I opened my eyes. Fuck, what happened? I groaned as I sat up and was startled by a dozen women staring at me. I was in bed, my boots and cloak gone.

"For the love of the gods, Thea, we thought we killed you," Genia scoffed.

Her words came back to me quickly.

"Oh gods, Cassius..." I was hyperventilating again. "Cassius is my... my mate."

"Breathe." A witch who looked like Genia, only much younger, held my hand and fanned me with her free hand to help my sweaty forehead. I was going to be sick.

"Maybe you should lay back down," someone else said.

I shook my head, trying to understand what this meant.

"Does my father know that Cassius is my mate?" I asked.

All of the women physically tensed at my question. Their eyes seemed to glow a violent red. Okay; they clearly hated my father.

"No, and if you tell him, he will kill Cassius."

"Does Cassius know?"

The women smiled brightly.

"Yes, he knows." Genia smiled. "Your mother said he would love you so strongly that the gods wouldn't be able to keep him from you. A love so grand that it would break a curse, save a realm, and outlast time itself."

My mind flashed with all my encounters with Cassius since I left Exile. Stars above, he seemed so happy to see me. He had never hurt me. My eyes drifted to Wisp, who was floating in front of me, her color a dark green.

My darkness swarmed inside of me as I thought of Cassius. It was happy at the thought of him, instead of being angry or disgusted like I was with my father. At this thought, Wisp burned dark purple.

"Fuck," I whispered. "What am I supposed to do?"

I glanced at them expectantly.

A woman stepped forward from behind the others. Her blonde hair was in a tight updo, her figure was filled out, and her face was pretty.

"You break your curse and get your man." She smiled. "We will help you any way we can."

"Do I tell him that I know?"

"We can't answer that for you." She frowned.

Something inside of me told me I shouldn't tell him. If I belonged with Cassius and Crimson, then he would try to protect me. Wait… I was supposed to kill the Crimson bloodline.

"You called him Prince Cassius." I glanced at them.

"He is the Prince of Crimson." Genia looked over me oddly.

No, no, no. I refused to kill him. I would give up all my memories if that was the only way I could get them back. Wisp burned a bright purple at me like she agreed with my thoughts. My father would demand I kill him. What the fuck was I supposed to do?

"Why can you guys tell me things and everyone else has magic tying their tongues?" I asked.

They all glanced at each other.

"Technically, Mikel bound the fae from talking, not witches. That, and we were in a ward because of Yerma, so I'm sure that stopped it too," Genia said.

"So, you can tell me everything?"

Genia hesitated before glancing around at the women. Her eyes met mine, and she nodded. Genia sat down on the bed and held my hand tightly as she told me everything she knew. I listened carefully. But it wasn't until she re-vealed that Cassius had killed me that her words sank in.

"What do you mean he killed me?" I stood up and began pacing around. I waited for the betrayal or anger to course through me, but I felt nothing. Why the hell wasn't I upset about this?

"He did it to save you." A pretty woman spoke. "He is not a bad guy."

Genia narrowed her eyes at the woman, like she said too much. I froze and stared at all of them as they watched me like I would explode.

"Are you alright?" Genia frowned. "You aren't freaking out."

"I don't think it's sunk in yet." I lied because the words definitely sank in, but I didn't care that he killed me. I was relieved that Cassius was mine. Fuck, how long had I been gone for?

"I need to go before my father knows that I am missing," I said, panicking.

I stood quickly but paused after getting my boots on. Turning to the woman who looked at me like I was some-thing fascinating.

"I will come check on you guys soon. I have some things to figure out."

They smiled and bowed to me. Something about the gesture made me sad.

"Use the bloodstone to call us if you need us. We will be there immediately." Genia smiled. I don't know where my bloodstone is. "We will stay here until you have broken your curse and called us."

"If something happens to me..." I paused and swallowed hard. "Genia will take over as queen."

Genia's eyes filled with tears as the women behind her gasped.

"You will do great. Your mother would be so damn proud of you." She gave me a tight hug before releasing me. A moment later, Cassius' shadows swarmed around me, and when they moved from my vision, I realized they hadn't taken me to my room. I was in Cassius' room; my eyes flickered around the room, and I sighed relieved when he wasn't there. I glanced over the portrait he had on his nightstand and picked it up. Gods, I looked fucking happy in it. I set it down and closed my eyes. My darkness crept out of me as I told it to find Cassius. It moved silently throughout the castle, searching for him.

I smiled when it located him on the floor below me. Slowly, I walked out of the room and into his living space. Pausing, I looked over the space and had an overwhelming sense of comfort. Smiling to myself, I headed out of his room and downstairs. When I reached the bottom of the stairs, I glanced around the corner to see no guards. My heart pounded with anxiety about getting caught, but I was also excited to see Cassius.

His deep voice floated through the hallway, and I followed the sound. I came to a door that was open and heard him speaking. I glanced in cautiously. Cassius stood with Haden, Leer, and Zade. The king sat quietly on his throne.

"Maybe we should attack the castle while they sleep," Haden said.

"Or we could take Thea as a prisoner. She obviously feels something for you." Leer smiled. Gods, that was the understatement of the century.

"No, we don't want to complicate this. Thea loves me; she just doesn't understand. She has blocked me from visiting her dreams, and she does not communicate through our bonds."

Bonds. Dreams.

He rubbed the crown tattoo, and I glanced down to mine. They were nearly identical. What kind of bonds were these? Fuck, Cassius looked good. The sleeves of his black uniform were rolled up, showing all of his tattoos, and his dark hair was messy and chaotic. I couldn't help myself, as I admired everything about him. Was this because he was my mate? All these feelings felt overwhelming, and I wanted to march into the room and demand that he take me to bed. Cassius ran his tattooed hands down his face. Fuck, seeing him now after the witches told me he was my mate made me instantly long for him. I watched everything about him. The way his dark hair was messy, or the way his hand rubbed his stubbled chin. My eyes widened as if they needed to be bigger to watch him lick his lips as he concentrated on the map in front of him. Gods, why was I so feral with lust?

A moment later, Cassius froze before rubbing his crown bond that matched mine. His eyes were solid black as he smiled softly to himself.

"What? Is she communicating through the bond?" Haden asked.

"Yes." Cassius closed his eyes as he gripped the table tightly in front of him. His fingers turned white at the strength he was using. Gods, the muscles of his arms flexed, and his jaw clenched. He was fucking perfect.

"Oh..." Haden chuckled softly. Oh shit, he could feel how turned on I was. Closing my eyes, I tried to focus on anything that wasn't him, but all that flooded my mind were images of Cassius kissing me, smiling at me, and fucking me. Stars above, I was making it worse.

When I opened my eyes, Cassius' eyes seemed more black, and his shadows swarmed him as if he had no control over himself or his magic. His chest rose and fell in short breaths. I smiled to myself at his reaction.

"So, take her prisoner and tell her the truth," Leer spoke again as if he had no idea what was happening. "Thea loves you, and she will understand, but we can't draw this out much longer."

"I know she loves me, but she still hasn't brought up the bloodstone or breaking her curse. I don't know how much she knows. I don't know how I'm supposed to tell her I killed and cursed her. I was thinking that waiting until she hands me the bloodstone, that way she doesn't have time to lose her shit. She'll remember I did it to save her."

Is that what I felt when he was near me? Love. Cassius was the only one who made me happy. He was my fated mate. Something about that made me feel untouchable. It made me feel like I could take on the whole realm.

"I just don't want to lose her again," Cassius admitted to all of them. "This time has been so different. Besides, Bayla has sent extra help. Thea will break her curse and fulfill the prophecy."

Bayla. The man with brown eyes said she had sent him to help me. I had seen how hearing that name affected Cassius. He looked as if he had seen a ghost. He didn't seem worried about it, though.

"Does the curse allow you to take the bloodstone too? That way we can take her and the stone and make her give it to you so the curse can be broken." Haden asked.

"No," Cassius sighed. "She has to bring it to me herself. It has to be her choice."

Bloodstone.

My mother's bloodstone. My bloodstone. I didn't know where the fuck it was.

"Well, you should tell her how to break her curse. Maybe she will come to the decision on her own," Leer said hopefully.

"My concern is that her father or Jesper will kill her before she decides that she is willing to try. Thea is smart; she will see how that kingdom treats her, and she will start to ask questions. I just worry that it will raise their suspicions, and I will lose her again."

Gods, he knew me well, but he didn't know that I had already reached that conclusion myself. Deep down, I knew that something wasn't right. The moment I saw Cassius, I had lost that feeling of something missing. He was what I was searching for. He was why I felt so lost in Exile and why I felt it whenever I was away from him.

"Thea will find her way home," the king said. "She always finds her way back to us, son, even if it is short-lived." He stood and walked to Cassius, grabbing his shoulder.

"Her heart knows that you are her home. The gods could not take away the fate of you."

Cassius nodded.

"I just want my wife back."

Wife.

My darkness vortexed inside of me. I gasped when he spoke the word. Feral need wrapped around me as the word wife pierced right into my heart.

"Someone is in the hallway," Zade muttered.

Fuck.

I immediately used the shadows and disappeared as their loud footsteps came towards me. I collapsed on the floor in my room. My head just repeated the term wife over and over in my mind. Wife. I was Cassius' wife. I should be freaking out, but I just sat on my floor smiling to myself because he was mine.

The handle to my room jiggled, and I hurried out of my cloak and boots before diving into bed. I pretended to be sleeping. A moment later, I sensed someone in my room.

"I told you she was here," one of the guards said. "We make sure she doesn't leave."

"Well, she's sneaky, and I wanted to double-check. Double the guards outside of her room from now on."

Jesper.

Asshole. They left a moment later, and I sighed heavily into the room. My body was on fire with lust and need. I closed my eyes as I pictured Cassius. All mine.

I couldn't even think about everything that happened with the witches tonight. All my mind kept thinking about was Cassius being my husband, my mate.

CHAPTER 16

THEA

The next day, Jesper appeared at my bedroom door as soon as I left it to go to training. His blue eyes stared at me in a way I didn't like.

"What?" I didn't hide my dislike for him.

He cocked his head to the side as if he were trying to see something. The sun shone brightly from the window behind me, making Jesper's eyes appear purple as he flinched away from the light. He smelled like liquor.

"You remember something." He accused me. I didn't even flinch at his accusation because he was drunk and a moron. I stepped around him, but he grabbed me and smiled at me.

"Tell me your secrets, and I'll tell you mine. We would be so good together, Thea."

Gross.

"You're drunk."

Tell me what he's thinking.

I may be drunk, but I'm not stupid. I can see how much you hate it here. My mother warned me that you were going to be a problem. I just didn't think you'd be this big of a pain in the ass.

"What secrets do you have that I could possibly care about?" I asked, hoping he would think about them and reveal them.

We want the same thing: your father dead.

"I'll share when you start being honest with me."

Mother said that you know about Cassius, but I can't confront you without blowing my own plans and secrets.

I stilled at his thought. Jesper's parents were dead. So, was he referring to something from a long time ago?

"I have nothing to tell you."

"You should have chosen me over Cassius. We are more alike than you know."

"My father needs me, so piss off."

"You could've learned to love me," he whispered. When my eyes met his, I could see that he truly thought that. His eyes filled with something close to guilt or regret, but I didn't feel bad for him. I opened my mouth to respond but shut it when I felt him. Cassius was spying somewhere close to us. I could feel his possessiveness, and I could only imagine it was because of what Jesper had said. A moment later, I couldn't feel Cassius anymore. I shook Jesper's grip from me and left.

My father had wanted me so that he could send me away for the meeting of the kingdoms. I accepted eagerly. A few days into our mission, we were closer to the castle of Crimson than we had ever been before. We hadn't run into a soul. We hadn't even seen an animal. That should have been my first clue that something was wrong, but we kept pushing through Crimson lands like no one knew.

Guards were stationed outside the castle as we sat in the shadows and watched. We did that for the first night, but something just seemed weird. The guards never switched duty, and they kept glancing into the trees like they were expecting someone. Us, maybe.

Even with my instincts telling me that they knew we were here, I didn't warn my men. Gods, I wanted to be fucking caught so I could see Cassius.

"Hello." I turned to see Haden looking at us. The two large fae were with him. "Don't reach for any weapons, or we will kill you."

He spoke directly to the guards but didn't seem to be talking toward me. The other fae smiled at me the same friendly way Haden had. The same way they did in my memory. They held their weapons to our backs as they led us to the castle. It was far prettier up close. The black stone that it was made from was stunning with the stained-glass windows.

It was like a portrait, and the gardens were vast, with hundreds of flowers of all shades of red. We stopped when the doors to the castle opened. The king greeted us with his tall crown and pretty red and black robes. He was tall and handsome for an older fae, and he was staring daggers into me.

"Captain Thea of the Cerithian Armies, what a surprise."

He didn't sound very surprised. I glared at him, and it only seemed to make him smile.

"Take them to the dungeon and make sure they are comfortable." The king demanded of Haden and the others. "Thea will be placed in the jail room."

"Yes, sir." Haden bowed.

Once inside, my men were taken to the right, and I was taken in the opposite direction. My eyes took in the castle and how different it looked from what I pictured.

"Where's Cassius?" I demanded.

Haden gave me a smug smile before stopping at a wooden door and ushering me in it. I tried to leave, but they locked me in. When I turned, there was a small bed with dark green bedding and a large window. I went to the window to see a beautiful view of the gardens and fountains. The drop wasn't far down. I could leave if I wanted to, so why didn't I?

The door opened a moment later, and Haden stood inside.

"I could burn you to a crisp," I threatened.

"Easy." He held up his hands. "You won't do that." Haden was so sure of himself. I held up my hands and formed a ball of fire, but Haden just flicked his wrist, shooting frost out. It froze my ball of fire and made it fall to the floor, shattering. I opened my mouth to say something, but I didn't know what to say. I was impressed.

"No need for magic right now. You should rest."

"You think I'm going to sleep while you watch me creep?" His smile widened at my insult. "Or in Crimson?"

"It wouldn't be your first time staying the night." He winked at me. "Cassius isn't available, and he trusts me to look out for you, not that anyone here wants to hurt you."

"Well, I don't trust you."

He frowned slightly at me but shrugged and pretended to do something. I rolled my eyes as I looked around the room. My legs were tired, so I sat on the bed. My eyes wandered around the room before I remembered my men.

"Are my men still alive?"

"Of course, and well fed."

I narrowed my eyes at him, but it didn't seem to bother him.

"Where is Cassius? Can't the shadow boy just appear in places?"

Haden started laughing so loudly that I smiled at the comforting sound. Haden's big smile got bigger when he saw I was smiling too.

"He's going to love the nickname."

I knew without a doubt that Cassius would not like that nickname. After hours went by, I started snooping through the drawers of the desk. I paused on the book of family crests. Something about it made me set it on the bed. At least it would help me pass the time. My eyes were growing heavy, but I fought with everything I had not to fall asleep, but then I heard Haden snoring. He had sat on the floor with his back leaned against the door.

Seriously? He didn't think I would hurt him. Oddly enough, I didn't have any desire to. I nibbled my lip as I ripped a page out of the book and crumpled it. I tossed it at Haden, and it hit him in the face, startling him awake.

He glared at me.

"Why'd you do that? Cassius has been running us ragged; I'm exhausted."

My heart pounded.

"I want to ask you about Della."

Haden stood up quickly, his eyes wide with uncertainty. His hand rubbed the back of his neck before looking at me.

"What about her?" he frowned.

"She came to visit me, and I didn't believe that she was a goddess or my friend. She said you would tell me that she was real."

Haden had stopped moving and stared at me with a look of longing in his eyes that made me sad to see.

"She's telling the truth." He nodded. "Did..." he stopped for a moment. A war seemed to be going on in his mind. "Did she say anything else?"

"She said you hate her. She told me how you wake up each day and curse her existence. You hope that she is unhappy and miserable." I frowned. "She said you haven't missed a day since your sister died."

Haden's eyes filled with tears, but he turned away from me quickly.

"I didn't realize she heard my curse." His voice was cold, but it seemed forced. "Now that I know that, I'll make sure to remind her how much I wish I never met her."

He turned to me, his eyes filled with hatred, but lurking under that was a deep sadness.

"Did you love her?"

The question made Haden's anger dissipate instantly.

"Yes." He nodded. Gods, why didn't she just tell him they were mates? "I didn't think I could feel more passionate about anything as I did when I loved her, but I was wrong. It turns out my hatred for her far surpasses any love I ever had for her."

"Gods, that seems harsh." I frowned.

"What is harsh is watching the woman I love rip my sister's soul from her body, killing her, even after I begged her to save her. The day she killed Remiah is the day she killed me too."

His hands balled into fists as he looked at me.

"I'm sorry," I said, regretting bringing this up. Especially seeing how much Della still loved him and how much he hated her. I couldn't imagine hating Cassius for any reason. He could have killed my father, and I would probably thank him. Fuck, he killed me, and I'd still get on my knees and crawl to him if he asked me to.

"I need to go for a walk," he said angrily. "Leer and Zade are standing guard outside the door if you need anything." He stormed out of the room. I stared at the wall, feeling like an asshole for bringing it up.

CHAPTER 17

THEA

I could hear harsh whispers somewhere in the room. My mind was confused when I opened my eyes and saw I wasn't in Cerithia.

When I turned around, Haden was talking with one of the other fae, Zade; I think they had called him that before. They both stopped and looked at me for a long moment.

"Good morning, Thea." Zade smiled.

"Good morning, Zade."

I laughed when both of their faces fell in horror. I was not supposed to know his name, but this was well worth learning it on my scouting trip.

"You remember me," he stuttered.

"No." I looked up at the ceiling of the room. "We did a scouting mission a few months back, and I overheard it."

When I looked back, he frowned at my confession. Haden chuckled and patted his friend on the shoulder. A moment later, the big fae, whose name I couldn't remember, walked in with breakfast.

"Thank you." I smiled. "What's your name? I can't remember."

"Leer." He raised his bushy eyebrow at me. "You recognize me?"

"Yes. I recognize all three of you."

Their faces lit up like this was the best news they had ever heard. All three of them stayed in my room and talked amongst themselves. It was a nice distraction from the fact that I was a prisoner and that I had upset Haden last night. Better here than Cerithia, I supposed. At least they like me here. My eyes watched the storm moving in over the castle. I loved the rain and the dark gloominess it brought.

The guys stopped talking suddenly, and I looked over to see what was wrong.

Cassius was glaring at me from the doorway, dripping wet from the rain outside. I stood up and looked at the guys. They all just stared at me and then at him with big smiles on their stupid faces. Cassius leveled a glare at them too. He was mad, but fuck, I could hardly keep myself in check knowing he was my mate.

Husband.

"Leave," he ordered, and they took off without a word. Cassius looked back at me with black eyes. His fists were clenched tightly.

"If you're going to kill me, then get on with it."

This seemed to snap him out of his angry glare. He blinked slowly at me and then took a step toward me. Gods, it was difficult to be near him without touching.

"Did you believe Jesper when he said you could have learned to love him?"

He was jealous.

"No."

Something murderous flashed in his eyes as he moved toward me. His hand grabbed the back of my neck so he could pull me an inch from his face. "You know I would never let you belong to anyone else, don't you?"

"Yes," I whispered as I swallowed hard. He searched my eyes like he was seeing if I was lying.

"You stayed the night?" He raised his dark brow at me.

"I didn't have a choice. Besides, Haden said it wasn't the first time for me." I narrowed my eyes on him. This made him chuckle to himself. "I suppose that doesn't surprise me."

"Haden said you were hardly hiding with your men. Practically stomped your way to the castle. Were you trying to get caught?"

My cheeks heated, and his smile widened.

"You did want me to catch you." He flinched as if he were in pain. I pulled back; my eyes shifted to his stomach when the drops of blood hit the floor. My eyes snapped up at him, but he looked unfazed.

"For the love of stars, Cassius, why are you flirting with me when you're wounded?"

Grabbing his hand, I pushed him onto the bed. He looked up at me from his back. A seductive smile tugged at his lips as I lifted his shirt.

"What happened?" I traced the large gash in his side, and he winced in pain.

"I was ambushed. A soldier got a good swing with his sword," he groaned. His head fell back, and his eyes squeezed shut.

"Shh. It's okay; I'll fix it."

I put my hands on his wound and concentrated until the glow of red and orange transferred from me to him. Cassius watched me in awe. I glanced up at him as my fingers brushed against his warm skin. There was no reason to be touching him still, so why was I not removing my hands? Cassius watched me closely as I moved my hands over his warm skin. I couldn't stop myself, and he didn't seem to mind either.

"Do you feel better?" I whispered.

"Much better," he whispered back. He swallowed hard as I shifted on my knees so I could see his face better. "I think I have another wound right here." He pointed to his upper chest, and I smirked to myself as I lifted his shirt. Cassius sat up and lifted his arms so I could pull his shirt off. His face was just a few inches from mine as he smiled.

He lay back down and watched me as I inspected him for wounds we both knew he didn't have. But I used this excuse to run my hands over his smooth skin. He hummed in appreciation as I explored.

"It's kind of hard to see from where I'm at." I lied as I straddled his hips. Cassius' shadows burst from him and around us in a flash. They caressed me like they had missed me. His hands ran up my thighs and rested on my hips. I glanced at the tattoos covering him. There was a 'T' above his heart with a viper coiled around it. I traced the letter before moving down to the red viper coiled around his arm.

Cassius' breathing was shallow as he watched me move toward the crown tattoo on his forearm. It looked like mine. Something about this mark on his skin made desire course through me. Fuck, what was wrong with me? It was just a crown tattoo. He called it our bond, but what kind of bond?

"Are you hurt?" he asked. "Maybe I should take a look."

I smiled as he tugged my Cerithia uniform off of me and tossed it to the floor. His hands rubbed against my skin slowly. Cassius sat up so our faces were close again, but this time his mouth claimed mine. Our tongues tangled as our hips rubbed against each other at an unbearable pace.

"Tell me you missed me," he begged.

"I missed you," I confessed.

Cassius turned us so I was pinned beneath him. His black eyes traced over me slowly, and that feeling of longing zapped up my arm again.

"I missed you too." He smiled as he pulled my pants from me. I should feel self-conscious as I lay naked in front of a man that I couldn't remember, but he looked at me like I was better than anything he had ever seen.

His rough hands ran over my thighs as he knelt on the floor. Cassius spread my legs and kissed the inside of my thighs. I couldn't look away as he softly bit my flesh, making my fire magic burst from me.

Cassius smiled at me as his hot mouth clamped around me. I moaned loudly into the quiet air. Cassius hummed as noises fell from me. He wrapped his arms around my thighs and pulled me up to his face so he could devour me. His tongue licked slowly before flicking across my clit. Then he sucked me into his mouth. I watched every move he made propped up on my elbows.

Cassius acted like a starved man who just found the best meal of his life. I moaned loudly as I grabbed his hair in my hands.

"Fuck, Cassius."

He pulled his mouth away and slipped two fingers inside of me. His thumb rubbing me perfectly.

"Gods, I've missed the way you sound, Thea," he whispered. "I've missed watching you come apart in front of me."

Gods, I knew we had done this before, but my mind was too filled with pleasure to think about it.

"More, my love, I want to hear more of what I do to you."

His fingers pushed deeper into me as his mouth found me again.

"Fuck," I moaned. I tried to close my legs because this felt too good.

"No hiding from me. You're going to take everything I'm giving you like the good girl I know that you are." His teeth grazed my sensitive nerves, and I bucked my hips up so that they rolled into his face. A low growl escaped his throat. He licked lazily before pulling his mouth away.

"That's my girl. Take what you want, Thea. Use me. Fuck my mouth with that pretty pussy that belongs to me," he said in a way that I nearly came from his words alone. I stared at him before I shoved his face back down and did exactly what he told me to. Gods, I was close. Cassius pulled away from me before lying on his back on the bed. I went to protest, but he yanked me over his face and wrapped his arms around my thighs, pulling me down to his tongue.

"Sit," he demanded.

"Fuck Cassius." I rode his mouth with quick movements. Cassius gripped my thighs tighter and slowed down my movements, so his tongue moved across me slowly. He pulled back slightly.

"My needy girl," he growled when I gripped his hair and circled my hips. "I want you looking at me when you cum, Thea. I want you to remember this moment and never forget it."

Then he was devouring me again. This time he pulled me roughly against his mouth, and I could hardly breathe.

"Cassius, please," I begged. "I'm going to cum," I breathed heavily.

His movements became faster. My stomach coiled tightly before it finally exploded, and waves of pleasure rippled through me. My moans filled the space as my hazy eyes stared down at Cassius.

"Gods, you're fucking beautiful," Cassius muttered. I shuffled down his body and ripped the trousers off of him

just enough to free his erection. Cassius watched me closely as I crawled back over him, sinking onto him without
warning. We both moaned into the silent room.

Cassius' hands gripped my hips tightly as I moved in
steady movements.

His eyes watched where he slid into me, and he cursed
softly at the sight. His eyes met mine.

"You take me so fucking good," he whispered.

Fuck. Lust shot through me.

"I like when you say things to me," I whispered.

Cassius smiled as he flipped me onto my back and thrust
into me deeply.

"I know you do, my love. You like knowing that I can't
get enough of you, and I love hearing what I do to you.
You whisper my name like a prayer. You look at me like I
am your heaven and stars. I love the way your pussy takes
all of me, and yet still you beg me for more. You were made
for me."

I groaned as his hips pounded into me.

"Cassius..." I pleaded. Small moans tore from my throat
as I stared at him.

"Let me hear you," he begged. "Every noise belongs to
me, Thea. You are mine; you just don't remember." His
jaw clenched tightly as I stared at him. His confession had

my eyes filling with tears. "You are mine," he whispered again. "I have missed you so much."

I was his.

"Cassius..." I searched his eyes for understanding. Husband. Mate.

"It's alright. You'll remember when you break the curse this time. But you know it's true, don't you? You know that you are mine, and I am eternally yours."

"Yes," I whispered as tears spilled from my eyes.

His hips were relentless as he watched me. I felt the release building inside of me quickly, but I didn't want this to end. The orgasm washed over me without warning. I gripped Cassius to me as he buried his face into my neck and came with a possessive groan.

We didn't move.

We didn't speak.

We stayed connected as tears spilled from my eyes.

After a long moment, Cassius pulled back so he could look at me. He wiped the tears from my face.

"I hate it when you cry," he whispered.

"You know about my curse." I wanted to have this conversation with him. Something somber crossed his features before he nodded.

"Yes."

"My father said I have to kill the Crimson royal bloodline to free myself from it."

This had him pulling back in shock. Something angry passed through him. I wanted to see his reaction. I would never hurt him.

"Your father is such a bastard," he scoffed as he stood up. "That is not how you break the curse."

My brows furrowed as Cassius stared at me.

"Then what do I need to do?"

My heart pounded as I waited for him to tell me. Cassius glanced away from me before running his hand through his hair. He let out a long breath before meeting my eyes.

"You must get your mother's bloodstone from your father and give it to me."

"You know my mother is a blood witch?"

He nodded.

"I know everything about you." He frowned at me like it broke his heart that I didn't know anything about him. "I meant what I said. You don't remember, but you are mine, and I will always be yours."

"You could be lying to me." The words slipped from my mouth, but I didn't actually think he was. I was panicking. Tell me what he's thinking, I demanded from my magic.

Please don't look at me like that. I should tell her I cursed her. That she can't remember us because I killed her. I should tell her it's me she dreams of.

I stilled at his thoughts and backed up slowly. His eyes watched me confused.

"Thea?" He frowned.

No, please don't run. I'm trying to get you to break your curse. I miss you so much. This is the year that we break it, and you can come home.

His eyes being black always bugged me. It was wrong, and I knew it.

"Show me your real eyes," I demanded. He swallowed hard, but the black faded into the prettiest shade of gold. No. No. Images of him dying plagued me. Tears fell from my eyes as I tried to control myself. Cassius was going to die. I felt nauseous.

"I need to go." I needed to figure out where the blood-stone was, but now I had a bigger fucking problem. *Are you going to let me die, my love?* I groaned as I stumbled against the wall. There was an urgency inside of me to leave and go find the stone right this second. I couldn't stay here even if I wanted to. The need to find the bloodstone was too much to resist.

"Please," he whispered, and it tore at my heart.

When I looked back at him, he looked gutted.

"You're scared." He seemed to be convincing himself and not me.

I froze and stared at him. His chest full of tattoos rose and fell in steady breaths. I did trust him, and that is why I needed to leave. *Find the stone and break this curse. We will save him at any cost.* My darkness was frantic inside of me.

"I'm not scared." I slipped on my boots.

"Are you worried that you're a traitor because you love me?"

"No." *You are my husband, my mate.*

"You look at me like you're terrified." He frowned.

Don't leave me again.

This was too much. I walked around him and hurried from the castle, not giving a shit about my men. Cassius followed me, but I ignored him as I headed into the woods towards Cerithia. It took little effort for him to catch me, and when he did, I saw the tears in his eyes.

"Please, my love, don't be scared of me."

I couldn't think of anything to say back to him. I was overwhelmed.

"Let me go. I'm not scared of you," I demanded, and he immediately dropped my arm. "I'll see you at the meeting."

His shoulders slumped, but he nodded and watched me walk away. I was terrified when I looked at him, but it was because I couldn't lose him. I was leaving so I could figure out where my bloodstone was, and I needed him to be at a distance because if my father suspected anything, he would kill us. Cassius was destined to die, and I had to figure out how to stop my vision.

CHAPTER 18

THEA

Della stared at me, her mouth hanging open, at a loss for words. My heart raced as I watched her reaction. Was this good or bad? My breath caught as she shut her mouth and lightly cleared her throat. I was on my way back to Cerithia when I begged Della to find me.

"My apologies. I lost my composure," she whispered. Her star-like eyes seemed to glow more brightly. "And how did you come to this conclusion so quickly?"

Her eyes were giving away her excitement.

"I know I am Cassius' wife."

She opened her mouth before shutting it again, at a loss for words.

"And his fated mate. I know he killed me, but he did it to save me. I know I am a blood witch. I found the blood witch coven."

"For fuck's sake, Thea, when the hell did you learn all of this?" Della looked around like someone else would pop out and fill in the gaps. I chuckled softly.

"The witches told me that he was Prince Cassius, and they said he was my mate. They told me a lot, and everything kind of just fell into place."

"How did the witches tell you? There is magic that forbids it." Her eyes narrowed on me skeptically.

"They've been kept behind a ward."

Her mouth opened, then shut, then opened again. Della began pacing back and forth in front of me, her pretty black dress trailing behind her. Why was she always so fancy?

"This is great news, Thea." Her words instantly calmed my nerves. Cassius was the right choice.

"I just need my bloodstone, and I will break the curse and fulfill the prophecy. But I searched for it before and couldn't find it anywhere."

"Well, part of the curse is that your father must have in his possession in the castle. So, it's somewhere in the castle. Have you tried using your darkness to feel its power?"

"Yes, every day since I found out about the stone, but it doesn't feel it anywhere. I've looked so much that I do not know where else it could be."

Della frowned.

"That's odd."

"I thought so too. Is it possible that he got rid of it?"

This was so frustrating. For the first time in a while, I felt like I had clarity about what I wanted and needed to do. I wanted Cassius, and nothing was going to stop me... well, except this damn bloodstone missing.

"No. He physically cannot get rid of it. The only one who can take it from the castle is you; that is part of the curse."

Mentally, I began thinking of all the places I might have missed, but I knew I checked every room in the damn place.

Della was silent, making me turn my attention to her. Her hands were clenched tightly by her sides, and her eyes were bright white as she looked up at the sky, and her whole body trembled.

"Della?" I hurried over to her, but there was some type of shield around her, so I couldn't touch her. "Della!" I called out to her, worried she was dying or something, but then suddenly she blinked, and her normal eyes were in place.

"Fuck," she muttered like she hadn't just been possessed.

"What the hell is happening?" I demanded.

"Brim needs to see us." She looked at me frantically. Brim? Della didn't give me a chance to ask any questions. Her starlight mist shot around us, and I felt like I was going to throw up. I fell to the forest floor on my hands and knees when her mist left.

"Sorry," she grunted as she tried to help me up. I threw up, and she let go of me.

"For fuck's sake," I moaned in agony.

"I forget that moving at the speed of light makes others nauseous, but we don't have time to waste. Get your ass up."

My eyes snapped up to her with a glare. She was being bossy as fuck. But my glare disappeared when she looked terrified.

"Brim wouldn't call upon us unless it was bad news."

I stood on shaky legs and glanced around. We were still in Cerithia. The castle was behind me a short distance. When I looked ahead, a shambled shack that was rotting away was in front of us. Della immediately walked into the shed, and I followed without questioning anything because her face terrified me.

As soon as we were both over the threshold, the rotting wood faded into pretty walls covered in art and shelves of trinkets. Something about the space was familiar and calming. The stone fireplace was oversized for the space, but the fire burning in it caught my attention. I turned to Della but looked back to the fireplace when I heard a male voice.

"Thea, you look far better than the last time I saw you." His eyes were friendly as he stared at me from a rocking chair that had been empty a moment ago. "Sit," he gestured to the other chairs across from him. Della and I sat down quickly.

"You came quickly." He looked at Della.

"You said it wasn't good," her voice trembled. Her eyes met mine, and she must have seen how confused I was. "This is Brim; he's a seer. He was a friend of your mother, and he was the one who told your prophecy."

I nodded and glanced back at him. His unkempt hair was long and crazy-looking, but he seemed just as friendly as he did the first time.

"I remember you from my vision." I nodded.

"Vision?" Della looked from me to Brim. "You had a vision."

"Yes."

Brim gave me a sad look before looking away. Della was looking confused and pissed off.

"You've made a decision about your curse," he said confidently. How did he know? "I had the vision this time.

You've learned who the man with golden eyes was, and it set into motion our visions."

His eyes darted away from me, and it made my insides burn with anxiety. Brim seemed to be trying to find the words he needed to tell me.

"For fuck's sake, just spit it out," I snapped. "Sorry," I sighed when it came out harsher than I meant it to. Did he have the same vision I did?

"Cassius is still going to die because he knows you are breaking your curse." He looked me in the eyes as he said the words. Della and I didn't move as his words soaked into us. Cassius was still going to die. *Die. Die. Die.*

I had tried to not think about this fucking image of him kneeling in the dirt before dying. If I thought about it, I couldn't function. *Die. Die. Die.*

The word wouldn't stop ricocheting around my mind. Flashes of Cassius hurting and lying dead in front of me played in my mind, but I couldn't move. If I did, I might explode.

Della stood up quickly. "No, I will not allow it." Della's power pulsed around us as my mind froze. As Brim's words sank into me, my chest felt like it was going to cave in. My magic swarmed from me in a colorful storm. Darkness, shadows, light, fire, and other magic I didn't recognize swarmed around us in a frenzy as my eyes turned red.

Della and Brim didn't move as they watched my magic create an angry cloud above us on the ceiling, cracking and popping with power. It was fucking furious, which was odd because I felt like I might be dying. My breathing was shallow, and my heart physically ached to the point of pain. My limbs were numb, and my throat closed in on itself. But this anguish in my chest seized my lungs as tears fell from my eyes silently.

"Thea?" Brim called to me, but it felt like he was much farther away than he actually was. My vision tunneled as I watched the flames moving in slow motion in the fireplace. There was a hole in my chest, and the more I thought of Cassius dying, the bigger the hole was getting, threatening to swallow me entirely.

I would never allow that to happen. He would not die.

"No," I finally spoke after what felt like an hour but was less than a minute. My voice sounded foreign—nothing like me at all. I still couldn't physically move. "I can stop it."

"Yes, so far the vision has not changed. He still dies." He frowned. "The vision came to me as soon as you decided to break your curse and give him the stone." Brim looked truly sorry. I wondered how much he knew Cassius and I to hold such pity in his eyes. "I summoned you to see if your vision matched mine. Every decision you make could change his fate for the better. But if I'm being honest, I am seeing the vision multiple times a day, which is not a good sign."

My eyes moved to Della as she frowned. Her power zipped around her too, but my power was overpowering and suffocating in the small cabin. Della's eyes were solid white, and I could feel her anger.

"If breaking my curse kills Cassius, then I will gladly not do it."

"You must," Della frowned at me. "If you don't, then Exile is stuck, and the prophecy will not be fulfilled. Do you know what your father does if he isn't stopped?" She stepped forward. "He slaughters every fae that isn't from Kizar or Cerithia. Children. Women. Innocent. Crimson. Cassius. They will all die. You have to break your curse so that the prophecy happens. Cassius will die that way too."

My mind was too filled with my darkness talking quickly about saving Cassius. I couldn't fucking think. Thank the stars that Della came with me because she took control of the conversation.

"So, he will die if she breaks the curse? How the fuck is that happening?" Her eyes narrowed on Brim. "I want the details of your vision. How does he die? Why?"

Della was fucking furious.

"Ardella…"

"No, tell me. You said it's a vision, not a prophecy, so it can be changed."

"You know I'm not supposed to say too much." Brim glanced at her.

"I am your god, and I am demanding that you tell me every detail you know!" Her power expanded around us, and I knew that Brim would not deny her again.

Brim nodded.

"Give me a moment," he said. "Visions are not always clear. Prophecies give clear details, and visions are like small snippets of information that make up just a sliver of what you need."

My heart was racing. I didn't want to hear how he would die, but I had seen it play out in my mind hundreds of times. Part of the reason I wanted Cassius to stay away was because I saw an image of him dead each time he stood in front of me. All I could think of was never seeing his smile again, never feeling him, never hearing his voice, never having a life together.

"He dies trying to save Thea. He goes into the next life, or rather waits for Thea so they can go together." Brim stood and paced in front of us. "Thea breaks her curse and goes to fulfill her prophecy, but there is some trouble;

that part of the vision is unclear. Something about him breaking free of restraints. It was almost as if he had been taken by Luren and Jesper, but Thea was already fulfilling her prophecy. Perhaps him being taken is what triggered her to see the prophecy out. Because he is in danger.

"But he tries to help Thea when she is injured and..." Brim swallowed hard. "Luren has a fae with magic that captures him so he can't move, and Luren beheads him."

Hearing my father's name was the final straw. I stood quickly and furiously, my fists clenched tightly.

"I'll go slice my father's head off right now if that will stop this from happening."

"You must break your curse before you go and kill the kings. You need your bloodstone to fuel your powers. Without it, you will not be able to fulfill the prophecy. You will be overpowered and will die." Della frowned. "How can we stop this, Brim?"

I would die with him. I would not exist without him. But I would burn this whole fucking realm down with me when I went. No one would escape my wrath. I wouldn't be able to hold my darkness in or control it.

"Cassius feels like he must save her because he knows she broke her curse and worries that she will die, and he will lose her forever. She gets wounded, and it triggers his mate bond to act, and he can't stop it because he knows she will not go to Exile this time."

"Okay, so I won't tell him." I looked at both of them. "I won't tell him, so he doesn't try to help."

"He's still going to try and help." Della looked at me, and I knew she was right.

"No, actually Thea's right. If she doesn't tell him, he might not intervene. He intervenes because he *knows* she will die for good, and that is the thought that makes him react. But maybe if that thought never goes through his mind, then he won't."

"I won't tell him." How the fuck was I going to break this fucking curse without him knowing? "When did this happen? If I know, then I can use my magic to make sure he can't interfere with me and the prophecy. I couldn't tell when it happened in my vision."

Della looked at Brim expectantly.

"I don't know," he sighed, defeated. "It gave me no indication of anything particular happening, so I can't pinpoint the day."

Fucking wonderful. I gripped my forehead tightly. My crown tattoo on my arm burned so much that I couldn't help the painful sob that escaped me.

"If Cassius dies, the whole realm dies," I promised, my eyes pulsing violently between red and black. I was losing control of myself.

"You have enough details that we can make sure it doesn't happen." Della nodded, trying to sound hopeful, but we both knew that there was a chance. A chance that Cassius dies.

Brim frowned at me, and I could feel his sadness for me. This tiny man cared for me even though I didn't know him. He stepped forward and gripped my hand in his.

"I believe in you, Thea, my dear. But you need to make sure you don't tell Cassius, no matter how much you want to. Because this will be far more difficult than you can imagine. Your bond will demand that you tell him."

I squeezed his hand back.

"Losing Cassius is not an option," I said truthfully. I felt sick to my stomach as I thought about it.

Della was still next to me.

"They are getting ready for the meeting of the kingdoms. Thank you, Brim; if you learn anything more, summon me."

Her starlight took us back to the forest outside of the castle so quickly that I felt dizzy. The sun was up now.

"Thea?" she asked, concerned.

"I can't lose him."

"Why didn't you tell me you had a vision of him dying?" She was angry.

"Because I didn't know it was him until he showed me his golden eyes. He just told me a day ago, and I immediately ran from him so I could figure out how to save him."

Della frowned.

"It's fine. We have enough details that we can protect him."

Tears rolled down my face.

"Della, what if I can't save him? You will have to kill me because I will destroy the realm." I stood up and stared at her. "Promise me, if he dies, you take me too."

"Thea…"

"Promise me! My vision shows me destroying everything around me when my bond breaks."

"I promise." Her eyes filled with tears.

I nodded as I headed to the meeting.

CHAPTER 19

CASSIUS

My body hummed with anticipation as I looked around the room. Thea wasn't at the meeting. Where the fuck was she? The meeting had been going on for twenty damn minutes, getting nowhere. Jesper smiled at me like he knew I was looking for her.

"If you're looking for Thea, just know that she will not be attending. We made sure of that." Jesper sneered and interrupted whoever was talking. Everyone fell silent as I stepped toward him.

"If she gives us any indication that she remembers you, I will cut her fucking head off in front of you." He smiled when my shadows burst out of me.

"Let me be very fucking clear to you and Luren. If you harm Thea in any way, you better pray to the stars, the heavens, and the gods to save yourself from my wrath. I will storm your kingdoms and gut anyone who is important to you. If Thea dies, no one else deserves to breathe. I will eradicate your bloodlines from our realm, and I'll make both of you watch me do it. Then I will bargain with the gods to bring your souls back so I can fucking kill you over and over again."

Jesper stepped forward and glared. But I could see him thinking of whatever he could to piss me off. After my last encounter with Thea, he would be smart to shut the fuck up, but Jesper had always been stupid. He was being brave today as he stopped only a few feet in front of me before whispering.

"I think I'll fuck her before I kill her."

I lost it.

Jesper's eyes widened when I reared my fist back and punched him square in the face. I didn't stop. I grabbed his hand and snapped his fingers, one at a time, making him yell. He punched me, cutting my eyebrow.

"How can you touch her if you don't have any fucking hands?" I called out as I grabbed my daggers. Jesper's eyes widened because he knew I wasn't bluffing. "Say goodbye to your hands, and then I think I'll cut out your tongue so I do not have to hear you say stupid shit ever again."

I moved for him as the door slammed open, and Thea walked in looking disheveled and exhausted. Gods, did she not use magic to come back? She walked all the way home.

She stopped when she saw Jesper and I in the middle of the room, clearly having just fought. I punched Jesper and grabbed him by the collar, so he was looking at me.

"You're lucky she showed up because I would have made good on my word. Maybe I still will when you least expect it. Touch her, and I will fucking end you." I shoved him, and he stumbled away like a coward.

"Thea, you're back?" Her father snapped. "I thought you were going to be gone a few more days."

"We realized Crimson was gone." She lied as she came and stood next to him. Her eyes drifted around the room and paused on King Sybrien, and I wondered if he seemed familiar to her. My breath caught when she looked at me. I could feel her heartbreak from here. She hated that I was the man that visited her dreams and that destroyed me. Her grief was consuming our bond.

Jesper stepped up to her and whispered something that made her eyes flash red in anger. She whispered back, and his whole body tensed. He glared at me and didn't try to hide it, but I couldn't glare back at him. I was too busy wishing my wife would look at me and I wouldn't see fear in her eyes.

"We are here to talk about a peace treaty so that our realm can finally have some damn peace." The king of Akecia spoke. "Crimson is willing to negotiate with Cerithia and Kizar for peace."

"Why would we ever agree to a treaty when we can't lose?" Luren's voice echoed in the space.

Uh...to stop losing men and resources. I could feel Thea's darkness around us in the room before she frowned, and it disappeared. What was she doing?

"Kizar and Cerithia stand together in this." Jesper backed Luren. I stepped forward, desperate to have Thea.

"How about a proposal for an allegiance?" I spoke to Luren. "A marriage alliance. I want to wed Thea, and we can call peace."

"Have you lost your fucking mind!" he yelled.

Thea's cheeks heated at my proposal, not knowing we were already married. That we were bound in this life and each one that followed. Jesper sneered at me. His blue eyes looked almost purple from this angle. He always wanted Thea for himself, but he would never have her.

"Aren't you tired of fighting and losing our men over this?" I asked. "Our kingdom does not want to keep killing our men for this war." *But I will if you don't give her to me.*

Thea's face softened toward me when I looked at her. Then she flinched when our eyes met, as if she was seeing something she didn't want to see.

"Absolutely not," her father snapped. "What have you remembered that you didn't tell us?" His eyes narrowed on her.

"Nothing." She frowned.

"You can have Thea the day my body rots into the ground," Luren growled.

"That can be arranged." My black eyes shifted to him. My hands fisted at my sides as my chest rose and fell quickly. Fuck, I might actually kill her father right now.

"Father—" Her sentence was interrupted by his backhand.

"Stop arguing," he hissed. My shadows swarmed around him with anger.

"You better watch yourself, Luren," I warned as my shadows begged to snap his fucking neck, but I knew Thea deserved to kill him after everything he had done to her. So I settled with punching him using my shadows. Luren stumbled backward into his guards. Thea's lips twitched slightly as she tried to not smile.

"I should kill you for laying hands on me!" Luren yelled as blood poured from his nose.

"Then come down here and try," I taunted. Thea let out a painful noise and gripped her head as she reached out blindly to steady herself. Unfortunately, that meant she grabbed onto Jesper.

"Thea?" I asked.

She realized Jesper was what she had grabbed and yanked away from him with disgust.

"I don't feel well," she whispered.

"This discussion is over," Luren declared. "My daughter will never belong to Crimson. She is a weapon of Cerithia. The prophecy still stands, and until it comes true, I will not let her out of my sight."

Her confusion came through the bond. She didn't know about the prophecy. I took a step toward her when she glanced at me, but Cerithia and Kizar guards stopped me. My guards stepped forward and tried to shove them away.

"King Luren, this has been going on for eight years. Don't you think it is time to give up on her ever choosing you?" I didn't know who said it, but it was a king.

"She always chooses me. Then she is tricked into going to Crimson by that delusional Prince Cassius!"

Fuck. Her eyes glanced at me as her father revealed I was the prince. I waited for the anger and betrayal to flood those pretty eyes, but it didn't come. Did she already figure that out about me? Thea blinked slowly before looking at her father and forcing herself to be confused.

"I'm sure the marriage proposal is just some twisted way to use me against you," she spoke so coldly. "I will gladly fight this war for you and Kizar if that is what you wish." Fuck, those words made my stomach roll with disgust and betrayal. My crown tattoo burned with such violence that I had to bite my lip to keep the painful sob in.

Her skin burned with bright swirls of orange and red, making her father step back away from her. Everyone visibly took a step away from her but me. Jesper stepped forward and made her look him in the face.

"You will kill the Crimson bloodline to break your curse?" he asked.

"Yes," she said. "Crimson is my enemy. I am a princess of Cerithia, a soldier of my kingdom, and my loyalties lie with Cerithia and my father."

"Thea..." I began to beg. "This is no trick. I just want peace, and I want you."

Her red eyes found mine.

"You probably want her so you can kill her again," Luren announced. "You are the whole reason she is cursed in the first place."

No. Time slowed as I watched her reaction. I should have fucking told her myself. It should never have come from Luren.

"What is he talking about?" She glanced around, refusing to look at me.

I turned around to look at my father and the guards in attendance. I turned back to her and took a shaky breath.

"You are cursed because I killed you eight years ago," I said so calmly. "I cursed your soul, and you've been trying to break the curse ever since. I plunged that viper dagger into your heart, and the gods cursed us for it. But I did it to save you."

Thea didn't give any sort of reaction to this either. Shit, she was in shock. I didn't dare to look away from her. Her darkness burst from her and swarmed around her in a frenzy. I was losing her. My jaw clenched tightly to keep my emotions in check.

"Then I guess I will return the favor and plunge the dagger into your heart next." Her father smiled at me, knowing that he had the upper hand.

My body deflated at her words.

"Thea, don't do this," I pleaded. "Choose Crimson, and I will explain everything to you. There is more to the story than this."

"Choose Crimson? I don't know you or Crimson. Why would you ever be that stupid to think I would fall for this weird act you have going on?"

Tears blurred my vision. She fucking hates me.

"My love," I whispered in anguish. The term of endearment made her face fall for a brief moment.

"Don't ever call me that disgusting name again. You are the last male I would ever be with."

It was like a punch to the stomach to hear those words from her. My marriage bond burned with heartbreak, but I blocked it from her. I was trying not to confuse her more. So, I took her venomous words and watched her walk away.

"Cassius," she spoke loudly to me, making my heart jump like she would take back her words. "I'll see you on the battlefield."

My shoulders slumped when she turned and walked away without a glance back. My body wanted to follow her. My heart didn't understand why I wasn't running for her. *She belongs to me, with me.*

"Cassius..." my father spoke softly.

"Let's go," I demanded without saying goodbye to the other kingdoms. They would understand. My shadows swarmed around us, and we were all standing back in Crimson a moment later. I knew I should have just walked away, but I looked at my father, then Haden, Leer, and Zade. Pity was evident, but I didn't want their pity.

"Son."

"Please, just don't," I muttered as I clenched my fists tightly. "It was different this time. She looked at me differently when we sparred. She loves me." I didn't know who

I was trying to convince—me or them. We fucking slept together; she couldn't stay away from me for long. It was different this time.

"She will come around. Give her time to process that you killed her," my father pleaded. But my mind was a dangerous thing. It had already conjured up losing her again. Images of Thea dying plagued me immediately. I would lose her again. I wouldn't survive it this time. It would swallow me whole.

"She hates me." She left me when she found out that I was the man from her dreams. Thea walked away.

"No, she doesn't." Haden stepped forward so I could focus on him. "She loves you. Don't trick yourself into thinking that she doesn't. Even today she didn't look like she hated you, and she found out you killed her. Maybe she is up to something."

"She's slipping through my fingers," I snapped back. "It's turning into all the times before."

"Cassius, she hasn't looked at you like she hates you once. For fuck's sake, she kissed you more than once." Haden lowered his voice. "She slept with you. She practically gave herself to you on a silver platter when she came for her scouting trip. You can see it in her eyes that she misses you even if she doesn't understand why. She loves you."

But I showed her my golden eyes, and she didn't change her hurt expression. Did she notice it was me in her dreams? She had to, and I saw the disappointment in her eyes when she realized it was me.

"Lust and love are two different things. Now she knows who I am and what I did. She might choose to have nothing to do with me ever again."

"We don't know that. You are going to drive yourself crazy by thinking the worst." Haden frowned.

I knew she loved me, deep inside her soul, but she couldn't remember.

Just then, Thea's soul appeared in front of me. I could see the silhouette of her in the soft green glow. Her eyes were staring at me like she wished she could hug me, but she couldn't. She flashed a series of colors, and I wasn't sure if she had done that besides when Thea had been in trouble. Wisp was warning me about Thea.

Immediately my shadows swarmed around me, and when they lifted, I realized that I was hiding in the corner of her father's throne room behind the drapes. There were perks to being at war with Cerithia. I could now cross freely into their lands.

I froze when I saw Thea walk into the room. She looked irritated, but she was trying to look as if she wasn't bothered.

"I'm going to town today," she declared to her father.

"What for?" He raised an eyebrow.

"I haven't been since I returned. I want to explore our kingdom, and I'm bored. You won't let me go fight."

I smiled softly at her eagerness to come fight me in a battle. He nodded like it made sense. Her hands fisted tightly at her sides when her father turned away from her. What was she up to?

"That's fine. Do not leave the city and be back before dark. We will meet in the next few days to talk about a strategy for war."

"Alright. I'll see you at dinner."

She turned and immediately headed out of the castle. I used my shadow magic to go into the forest that surrounded Cerithia. I watched her walk cautiously through the streets. The city was bustling with fae, and some of them avoided Thea as soon as they saw her, choosing to cross the street or duck into the shops. I'd fucking kill every fae who treated her like she was a monster.

Her pretty green eyes glanced around before she frowned and looked down. The fae whispered and pointed at her, but Thea seemed to be trying to ignore them.

"What are you doing, my love?" I whispered to myself as I followed silently in the woods. Thea stopped and glanced around as if she could sense me close by. Gods, she looked so lost and confused. I just wanted to go tell her that I love her, but I didn't know how she would react to seeing me. So, I continued to watch her as she lingered in the streets of Cerithia, seemingly trying to find something.

Thea's soul appeared in front of me, flashing between green and orange. I didn't know what that meant. She didn't usually use those color combinations. She flew from me and drew my attention to a small cleft in between two trees. Small flashes of light seemed to be coming from within the space. I cautiously walked over and peered inside, only to find a small child who was using elite magic. He was a brave boy to use elite magic in this kingdom. It was obvious he was hiding from the prying eyes of the other fae by practicing in the woods.

I paused for a moment and watched him turn from a small child into a grown man. Illusion magic. A moment later, he turned into a boy again. Thea's soul was still flashing colors at me, and I took a step forward. She burned a dark green, which I knew meant I was doing what she wanted from me.

The boy froze when he saw me approaching. I doubted he knew who I was, but I approached cautiously.

"I'm sorry I was using magic; please don't tell the king." His soft voice trembled.

I kneeled so I could talk to him quietly. It made me sick that a boy this young was scared of his king.

"That was very impressive." I smiled. His dark eyes moved over my face as if he were trying to sense any danger that lurked. I would never hurt a child, but I did want his help.

"Mother said I shouldn't use it because the king will be very angry with me," he whispered. His clothing was ripped and torn. His golden skin was covered in dirt. What kind of king lets his fae live in squalor like this? Especially children.

"I'll make you a deal. If you help me by using your magic, then I won't tell anyone that you used it."

He hesitated, and his stomach growled. I frowned.

"And I'll pay you so that you can get some food." I smiled.

"What do I have to do?"

"Can you make me look like a different male? Maybe an older one with dark eyes and white hair?"

"Why ya want to be different?" He raised an eyebrow toward me.

I glanced over my shoulder at Thea walking toward the edge of the woods. Shit. She could sense me close by.

"Because I want to talk to a girl and see if she likes me, but I don't want her to know it's me."

The boy studied my face for a long moment before smiling at me and looking over my shoulder toward Thea. She was getting closer.

"That girl?" he giggled.

"Yes. Will you help?"

He glanced over my face and smiled softly.

"I already changed you, but I have to be close, or it stops working."

"That's fi–."

"What are you doing?" Thea's voice was like a warm hug. I turned toward her, and her eyes glanced over my face. Fuck, I hope this kid really did what he said he would.

"My... grandson and I were looking for wildflowers." The lie came off my tongue without thought.

She glanced at the boy as if he would protest before she relaxed, putting her dagger away.

"I'm sorry. I'll let you be." She turned, and I panicked.

"Thea, wait."

Her shoulders tensed as she slowly turned toward me. She rested her hand on her dagger as if I would attack her. My heart broke at the thought of her thinking she was in constant danger. Her eyes glanced from me to my left, where I knew her soul floated. I couldn't help the smirk on my face as she asked Wisp if I was a threat.

Whatever she picked up from Wisp made her relax. My body tensed as her eyes glanced over me slowly, as if she thought she might recognize me.

"What do you want?" she asked.

"I'm Atticus," I whispered. I looked around us to make sure no one else followed her. My marriage bond burned with the lie. "Sybil's husband."

"You're Sybil's husband? I'm sorry, I don't remember." She took an eager step toward me.

"It's alright, I know. I had hoped you would wander into town so I could try and speak with you. You and I are not allowed to talk, so if we are caught, I will be killed."

"Why would—wait, you know information about me?" My chest squeezed at how hopeful her eyes were. She just wanted answers.

"Yes." I nodded. The boy shuffled away from me a little bit so that he could look at a bug crawling up the oak tree.

"Should we go somewhere else to talk?" She looked around, her eyes trying to see if there was any danger. I felt exposed out here, like they would find us, but we had no choice.

"We need to stay here. I'll tell you what I know, and then we'll go our separate ways like we never talked." I kneeled to the ground behind a tree and smiled when Thea immediately came over to me and kneeled next to me. "You know of your curse?"

"Yes, Cassius killed me and cursed me, but nothing more." My need to tell her that I did it to save her almost slipped out. I bit my cheek to collect myself. I needed to remember that I wasn't Cassius right now.

"The prophet?" I asked, and she shook her head.

"My father mentioned a prophecy in passing, but I know nothing about it."

"A prophet came forward about eight years ago and told of a woman with great power, magic beyond anything the realm had ever seen. They spoke of how she would kill kings and crumble kingdoms. It was you he spoke of, and ever since, your father and that little shit from Kizar have been trying to keep you here to use for war. They want everything, Thea. They want control of the realm and will try to use you to kill the rest of the kings."

"That's what this war is about?"

I nodded.

"Well, that is why Cerithia and Kizar are at war. Cassius is just trying to bring you home to Crimson."

Her eyes widened at my comment. Fuck, she was beautiful. My eyes traced over her slowly before looking away. Stars above, I can't check her out when I am Atticus.

"I know Cassius wants me home," she sighed.

My brows furrowed.

"Then why are you here?"

Her big green eyes stared at me.

"I have a few things I need to do before I can leave."

She *is* up to something. What could she be doing that she needed to be here for it?

"Do you need help? I'm sure Cassius would come to help you. You don't remember, but you two love each other very much."

The look she gave me made my stomach churn. Luren was such a fucking dick. How could he look at her anguish and not care about her happiness? Finding her happiness was my biggest goal in life.

"I can't risk Cassius. He needs to stay away from me."

"But..." I was at a loss for words. "If you're in danger, he can help you." Why didn't she want me to help her? Sadness pumped into me. Did she not trust me?

"You don't trust Cassius."

"What? No, I trust Cassius. If I could go to Crimson now, I would." She paused and took a long breath before looking at me. "I knew my father was a fucking liar the moment I was in his presence for longer than a minute." Her eyes widened as she looked over my shoulder. "I'm sorry, I forgot your grandson was here. The moment I saw Cassius on the battlefield, everything felt... right."

I wanted to ask her why she ran from me. Why did she look so devastated when she saw my golden eyes? But there was something in her eyes that made me feel panicked. She looked devastated and heartbroken.

"What's wrong?"

She looked away from me and shook her head like she was trying to get rid of an unwanted thought. When her pretty green eyes looked at me, I lost my ability to breathe. She was crying.

"I'm scared of Cassius dying."

The tone of her voice made my heart squeeze. Why would she say that? I had no response to her words. Maybe her father had a plan to kill me or something.

"I will break the curse and bring Sybil home to you. I promise." She gave a fake smile, and it made me feel like shit because I didn't know where Atticus even was these days. After Sybil got trapped in Exile, he lost his mind in grief. I didn't blame him.

I reached forward and squeezed her hand in mine out of habit, but she just gave me a small smile in return.

"You need to stay safe and trust no one in Cerithia. Your father will tell you anything to make you choose him, but he is the wrong choice."

Her brows furrowed at my words.

"Sybil said I needed to choose right this time." She frowned. "I didn't know what she meant, but then she said blue is bad and red is good. Do you think she meant that as the kingdom colors?"

Fucking Sybil, what a magnificent woman. She couldn't tell Thea outright who to pick, but she still told her something that would be a hint.

"Yes, I believe that is exactly what she meant." I smiled.

"Thank you, Atticus." She hesitated. "Do you know Jesper?"

Jealousy instantly made my face redden.

"Yes..."

"Is his mother dead?"

What an odd fucking question.

"Umm, yes. She died when he was a baby."

Her brows crinkled in confusion, letting me know that my answer was not what she expected.

I didn't want to leave her yet, but I knew I needed to. Before I could stop myself, I asked, "Do you still hate Cassius for killing you?"

Her green eyes widened with a look of longing.

"I've never hated Cassius." Thea's lips pulled into a frown. "I have to save him."

Before I could ask her what that meant, she looked panicked.

"Guards are coming." She stood up, making me drop her hand, and I headed into the woods. I spotted the Cerithian guards making their way toward her. Shit. Quickly, I ducked behind a tree as the little boy followed. I glanced around and saw Thea pulling flowers up, pretending like she hadn't even noticed the guards; she jumped as if she were surprised.

"Fuck!" She yelled, overly dramatic.

"Sorry, Captain." They bowed. "We were trying to see where you went."

They eyed the bouquet of flowers in her hand. My magic simmered. If they tried to hurt her, I would gladly skin them alive.

"What? Is picking flowers forbidden or something? I thought they'd look nice in my sterile room."

They said nothing to her. "Nice to know my father sent you to spy on me," she muttered, and I laughed silently at her bad attitude. A moment later she disappeared with them, glancing back to see if they were gone.

When they were out of sight, I breathed heavily.

"Did you tell her you love her or what?" The boy pursed his lips at me.

"No, but I think that worked."

He held his hand out and gave me a sassy look.

"Pay up."

"Strictly business, got it." Laughing, I put his payment into his hand and watched his eyes widen at how much I gave him. "You should go home, and don't use your magic where others can see it again."

He nodded and took off like I would take his money right back. Thea's soul floated close by, and I smiled at her.

"Good idea, little viper." She twirled around me as if she wanted to hug me but couldn't. "Let's hope you listen to Atticus."

"I have to say, you always were a clever one, Cassius. Truly, I am impressed."

I turned quickly with my dagger drawn before rolling my eyes when Della stood close by. I hated it when she snuck up on me like that.

"I want this shit to be over."

"Me too." She frowned.

I used my shadows to move back to Crimson. When they disappeared, I was standing in the hallway where I was earlier. My eyes narrowed on Della when I realized she was following me.

"What do you want?" I asked suspiciously.

She wrung her hands nervously in front of her. The gesture was not something I had seen from her before.

"Can I ask you something about Haden?" she whispered. I should tell her no. Haden had shared what she did to him, and he was devastated about it. I couldn't blame him. She killed his sister. But when her star-colored eyes met mine, I saw my own devastation and the longing I had for Thea reflected in hers for Haden.

"I can't promise you I'll have an answer."

She hesitated before glancing down to the floor.

"Do you think he's happy?"

She glanced up at me, and I froze at her question because I had expected something else.

"I think so," I answered. She nodded and frowned. "Sometimes I think he pretends to be."

Tears filled her eyes as she swallowed hard.

"Thank you for giving him purpose and friendship. He was so sad before, and now I see him smiling, and that's because of you. I just wanted to thank you for making him smile again." Della tried to hold her tears in, but they fell silently down her cheeks.

"Della…"

"He hates me, doesn't he?"

Her eyes looked at me, pleading with me to tell her that he didn't. There was a small sliver of hope in them, and it gutted me for her.

"Yes," I said with a frown. "Can you blame him?"

She shook her head and cried out loud, and for some reason, I felt bad for her because she clearly cared for him.

"What would you do to save Thea?" She asked as she met my eyes.

"Anything," I answered without a thought. "You know that."

"Including killing someone she cherished? Even if she begged you to save them instead of her, would you have done it?"

"I would never choose anyone over Thea."

"And I would never choose anyone over Haden. I do not regret taking his sister's soul instead of his, but I do regret hurting him so deeply."

I still didn't understand how Della and Haden came to be acquainted with one another. But it was clear that she loved him, and he didn't want to love her. Something about her statement made me wonder if she meant they were mates. Haden didn't say that—unless she kept it a secret.

"When you came and told me about Kace, you told me you made a bargain with your brother for him to leave Thea and I alone. What was the bargain?"

Della's sad eyes looked at me for a long moment.

"I had to give him something in exchange for him to leave you be."

I could see on her face that whatever she had given devastated her. I hadn't realized she had given something for us. But what could have been important enough that Mikel thought it was worthy of leaving me the fuck alone?

"Della, what did you give him?"

She shook her head and frowned. The tears were streaming down her face in a constant stream.

"My star," she whispered. When I stared at her confused, she continued. "When a god or goddess is brought into existence, we are gifted a piece of the star we come from. It is sacred, and we only get one. We hold onto it until we find..." She trailed off and stared at me with a tortured expression. "Until we find who it belongs to."

"Your mate."

She nodded as she swallowed hard.

"He's your mate."

She nodded again.

"You didn't tell him."

"How could I? I killed his sister because he was meant to die, and I would never choose anyone over him. I would've killed my own brother to save Haden, but he wouldn't listen to me. Telling him that he is my fated mate would make him hate me more. He does not want to love me."

I agreed with her. He would be pissed to know he was tied to the woman he hated and loved at the same time.

"So, if you don't have your star..."

"I can't solidify the mating bond with Haden. It's a perfect punishment because Haden's sister, Remiah, was Mikel's soulmate."

This bit of information made me understand Mikel's asshole behavior toward me, but it still was unforgivable.

"Do you think he could ever forgive me? Maybe with time…"

Stars above, I wanted to lie to her to make her feel better, but I couldn't.

"No."

My one word made her stop talking and sob loudly into her hands.

"I used to pray for Haden's forgiveness every morning I woke up, but now I pray that the stars will break our mating bond so that he can be happy. I just want him to be happy, and I know that I won't ever be the one to do that for him. But it's so hard to let go."

Her shoulders shook with every shaky breath, and her body trembled in her grief. A noise coming down the hall had me panicking. Haden was walking toward us, but he wasn't alone. Some woman with blonde hair and dark eyes was clinging to him. Fuck. He had never shown an interest in anyone. Now it made sense; he had a mate, so he wouldn't want anyone besides them. Haden slowed down when he saw I was talking to Della. Then he frowned when he realized she was sobbing.

Della heard his heavy steps coming toward us and looked up. Gods, I felt like shit when her eyes drifted from Haden to the woman hanging off him. I thought I saw true devastation in her eyes earlier, but now I could feel her heartbreak surrounding us. I didn't think she took a breath as her eyes took in the sight of Haden standing close by with the woman.

I knew what that felt like. When Thea kissed Jesper last time, I was fucked up for days over it.

Haden glanced at her but masked his concern with hatred. Della stared at the woman, but the woman hardly glanced at her. She was too focused on touching Haden's arm and hugging him to her. Della just stared at the woman without saying anything. Sadness and jealousy were clear on her face.

"What's going on?" Haden asked me, completely ignoring Della.

"Nothing." I shook my head.

"Is Thea alright?" He frowned with genuine worry.

"Yes, she's alright."

Haden's jaw clenched tightly as he turned his focus to Della.

"Why are you here? No one wants to see you; you've done enough damage to last four lifetimes," he hissed. Shit, I don't know if I had ever seen Haden so angry.

"Haden..." she whispered so softly. She took a step forward like she couldn't help herself. Haden took a step away from her, and she flinched as if the movement burned her. Thea had done that to me before, and it broke me. "If you let me explain, then maybe—"

"Maybe what? I would forgive you?" This made him step toward her furious. "That will never happen. I can't wait for Thea to break her curse so that you no longer have a reason to annoy us with your existence. I meant what I said that day; I never wanted to see you again."

The woman that came with Haden glanced from him to her, then to me, like I knew what the fuck was going on. She took his anger, but fuck, I wanted to protect her. Della's tears glowed like starlight down her cheeks as she watched Haden reach back and grab the woman's hand while staring her in the eyes. Gods, he wanted to hurt her, and he was succeeding. Della was the one to look away from him. She turned her back to us as she tried to hold her sobs in.

"I'll stay away," she whispered as she turned once more, her eyes focusing on their hands clenched together. She didn't look up at him.

"Thank you, Cassius." She frowned at me. "I guess you were right."

Then she was gone. I glanced at Haden, whose chest rose and fell in short breaths as he stared at where she was.

"Haden?" the woman spoke.

"Leave," he demanded as he let go of her hand. She went to protest, but he turned to her. "Now, this was never going anywhere anyway."

"Asshole," she hissed but left.

Haden's frosty eyes met mine, and I glared right back at him.

"What did she want?" His voice gave away the sadness he was hiding.

"She wanted to know if you were happy." Haden's anger melted away instantly. "And she asked if you hated her."

"I can't forgive her." He sounded like he was convincing himself.

"Della asked if I were in her place if I would have saved Thea, even if she begged me to save someone else."

Haden frowned at me.

"I would never choose anyone over Thea, and she said she would never choose anyone over you," I sighed heavily as Haden seemed to stop breathing at my words.

"It's different." He clenched his jaw before turning away from me and leaving toward his room. He stopped when I called out to him.

"If you and Della switched roles, would you have let her die or saved her brother if she asked?"

I don't know why I was involving myself. Part of me felt indebted to Della because she gave Thea and I a chance at happiness. The other part wanted Haden to stop lying to himself. He still loved her, and it was as if he couldn't help it. They were mates, and Della had a bravery that I could never possess. She was willing to give him up and spend her eternity alone if it would make him happy. Haden opened his mouth before closing it.

I was the one to turn and walk away from him.

Chapter 20

Thea

I was confused when my father demanded my presence this morning. He and Jesper waited for me in the throne room. I glanced over the matching scars across their cheeks, and my darkness seemed to chuckle inside me. My eyes wandered around the room, looking for any sign of my bloodstone. I had been scouring this damn castle every day for it, and I couldn't find it. I couldn't ask about it because I was not supposed to know anything. It was making things difficult for me.

I needed it so I could go home to Cassius.

"Thea, we are starting our war against the other kingdoms." My father waved me over nonchalantly, as if these weren't living beings we were talking about. Hesitantly, I stepped forward to the map. My gaze drifted over Elloryon and all the places marked on the map.

"We are starting a war with everyone." I glanced up. Why?

"Yes, but it's more like we will be assassinating the royal bloodlines." Jesper smiled.

My darkness swarmed inside of me at this news. Why would we do that?

"Tonight, we will be sending someone to Akecia to kill King Sybrien and his wife."

"What for?" I asked. "I didn't realize we were not friendly with any kingdoms."

"Power," my father said. "I will be the king of all the lands, but that can't happen unless the royal bloodlines are gone."

Instinctively, my eyes flickered to Jesper. I would gladly kill his bloodline right now.

"Jesper is not on the list. He will not qualm to my place as king. After all, he will inherit it all when I step down and he and Tally are married."

That's what you think, asshole. I will rule the realm, and my mother will help me.

Jesper took a hesitant step away from me.

"Who is going to kill them and when?"

"They're already on their way." My father looked at me as if he were expecting some sort of reaction to this news. I didn't show him how disgusting I found his plan. My face remained neutral. "We will let you know when it is done."

"Sounds good." I nodded. "When will you attack Falgon and Crimson? If they hear about the attack on Akecia, they may go on the defense and attack us before you can kill them."

My father's eyes filled with pride, but I was just trying to throw him off my scent.

"Likely, tomorrow night." Jesper smiled at my father, speaking without saying a word.

"Let me know when it's done." I smiled. "Should I prepare the men for war just in case?"

"Yes," they spoke together.

"Very well." I gave them a curt nod and headed for my room. My darkness was not relenting inside of me. She was pissed. When my bedroom door clicked, I fell to my knees at the pain my darkness was causing. I let it out, and she swarmed around me, angry as fuck.

"What should I do?" I muttered.

My darkness stilled and seemed to be watching me. Its dark tendrils of magic darkened until shadows swarmed around me. I closed my eyes. My own magic was going to fucking kill me. I didn't understand what I did to piss her off.

The temperature change had my eyes flickering open cautiously. I was kneeling in the snow. What the fuck? I whipped my head around. My mouth fell open at the beautiful white castle behind me. My darkness urged me to get up. Where were we?

My foot crunched into the snow as I started for the castle. A sound of pain stopped me in my tracks. Glancing around, I saw a guard lying in red snow. He was bleeding. Hurrying over to him, I kneeled.

"How many of them are there?" I asked frantically.

"Two," he muttered.

"Is this Akecia?"

He looked at me like I had lost my fucking mind but nodded. Shit. Magic swarmed from me and toward the man who was dying in my arms, but it stopped. He had already died. I laid him down gently before heading inside. Two more guards were lying dead. My stomach churned. Gods, I hoped I wasn't too late.

A moment later I heard the unmistakable noise of a dagger cutting through flesh. As quietly as I could, I headed up the grand staircase. When I got to the top, I glanced down the hallways on both sides of me. To the left, I could see two figures opening doors quietly. To the right, I saw nothing but darkness.

I turned to go after the two figures, but my darkness circled around me and forced me towards the right.

"They are this way." The man with brown eyes appeared in front of me. He had disappeared, and I thought I wouldn't ever see him again. His soft golden glow illuminated the darkness in the hallway. I nodded and kept silent as I crept through the dark hallway until I saw a room with two doors decorated in gold and jewels. Shoving the heavy door open, I slipped inside. When I turned, someone punched me in the face.

"Fuck," I groaned as I stumbled into the door.

"Oh shit." My stalker muttered.

A light flickered on, and standing in front of me was a large male fae. Very large, with white hair and beard. His dark eyes widened when he saw me. A movement in the bed drew my attention to a petite woman with red hair and large brown eyes.

"Thea?" The man whispered harshly.

"I'm assuming you're the king." I wiped the blood from my nose. He nodded. I sized him up. He was fit, and I wasn't sure if he even needed my help.

"Whatever your father told you isn't true. You don't need to harm me or Petra." He was practically begging.

It dawned on me then; he thought I was here to kill him.

"I'm here to help. Someone is here to kill you and your wife."

There was an uncomfortable pause of silence.

"Did you break your curse?" The king looked oddly at me.

"No," I sighed. "Your guards are already dead. The men will be here any moment."

The king looked at me without moving.

"What?" I asked self-consciously.

"I just thought maybe you remembered us." He frowned. I knew them. My gaze flickered to his wife, and she smiled and gave me a small wave. They seemed familiar, but I didn't know why.

"Were we friends?"

He smiled brightly.

"Yes. Great friends."

Before I could respond, I heard the soft creak of someone sneaking up to the door. He heard it too.

"Go to your wife and pretend to be sleeping. I will kill them when they both come in," I whispered.

He opened his mouth like he would argue.

"Cassius will kill me if something happens to you," he whispered back.

I flashed my eyes red at him, and he didn't look scared. The king gave me a sassy look, like he couldn't believe I would try that on him. After a short stare-down, he sighed in defeat before turning to the bed and crawling in, holding his wife closely. Something about his wife glowed. It was odd, but I forced myself to focus. I grabbed my daggers and hid behind the door.

It only took a few seconds for the doors to slam open.

These are the worst assassins. The king and his wife sat up and stared at the men.

"King Sybrien. Queen Petra."

One of the men chuckled and did a half-bow.

"What the fuck are you doing?" Sybrien barked at them.

"I think you know what we are doing," the other man said. I couldn't see anything about them with their backs to me. They were dressed in all black with hoods on.

"You won't get away with this," Petra snapped.

"We will. By the time Crimson or Falgon realizes what happened, our men will be sneaking into their homes and killing them too."

My darkness was fuming inside of me.

"Hello, fellas," I said as they approached the bed. They stilled and twisted to me immediately.

"Thea," one of them muttered.

They slipped off their hoods and stared at me. Their faces were familiar.

"Did your father send you to do the honors?" The one with black hair asked, confused. But the one with blonde hair glared at me.

"You came to protect them?" he questioned.

I smiled.

"Fucking Crimson whore." He charged at me. The insult made my darkness explode from me with anger. I humored him by using my daggers against his. He swung and swung, too angry to fight well. Shoving him off of me, I readied my dagger for the killing blow, but before I could, my darkness seeped from me. It shot through the man like an arrow, leaving a gaping hole in his chest as he fell over dead.

The next man stared at me, terrified. Taking a small step backward, he tried to show that he was no longer a threat, but I could never let him go willingly.

"I'll leave," he begged.

"Too late for that," I answered. "You'll tell my father what I did."

"I won't," he cried out. "Show me mercy."

This made me angry.

"Show you mercy," I snarled. "Like you were going to show them? You came here to kill an innocent couple because of greed. I will show no one mercy."

I wrapped him up in my darkness, squeezing him until he cried out. Then I summoned my fire magic, focusing on the man's heart. His cries stopped instantly, and it made me smile as he burned from the inside out. His charred body fell to the floor. My skin felt hot, my eyes blurring with rage.

"Thea." I heard Sybrien speak, but it was as if he was far away, not right next to me. "Thea." He tried again.

It wasn't until Petra stood in my line of vision that I blinked out of the rage that was taking over me. Her red hair fell in pretty curls over her nightgown. She was glowing, and for some reason, it concerned me.

"Are you ill?" I finally asked her. Her big brown eyes widened when she realized I was asking her. My magic didn't hum like she needed healing, but something was odd with her.

"No." She hesitated. "Do you see illness in me like you did with Sy?"

I glanced at him but didn't see anything coursing through him. It was her that I was drawn to.

"You're...glowing." I looked at her and didn't understand what was happening. Petra's eyes looked over herself oddly. She didn't know either. A moment later, I saw Della appear behind them. She was smiling, but Sy and Petra didn't seem to see her.

"She's with a child," Della answered. "You can see a new soul forming; that is what the glow is."

"What do you mean?" I asked and realized that Sy and Petra were going to think I lost my mind because they couldn't see her.

"After Cassius killed you, you needed part of my soul to make sure you could come back each time you died, so you can see souls—life. Just like I can."

I just stared at her. There was a lot to unpack about that, but now was not the time.

"You need to get back to Cerithia; they are going to be checking on you to make sure you aren't interfering."

I nodded and turned my attention to Sy and Petra again. I smiled softly when I saw the faint golden glow around her. My smile dropped when I realized the man who followed me also glowed.

"I need to go." I panicked.

"Wait!" Petra stopped me. "Who were you talking to?"

I swallowed hard as I turned back around.

"Ardella, the Goddess of Life. She's a friend of mine." Gods, I sounded like I had gone mad.

"What did she say?" Petra frowned. I realized that she was worried about the glowing.

"She was telling me why I see you glowing," I answered.

"Is it bad?" Sy panicked.

"No."

"Tell us," Petra begged. "I will go crazy thinking I am dying, and you aren't telling me for some reason."

I nibbled my lip nervously. I didn't want to ruin this moment for them.

"I don't know if I should. It might ruin the surprise," I said honestly.

"You won't," Sy promised.

"You're pregnant," I confessed. "I can see the glow of your child's soul."

They both gaped at me. Obviously, this was a surprise to both of them. A second later, Petra reached forward and squeezed me tightly in a hug.

"It's so special that you told us," she cried softly. "We miss you."

I pulled back and looked over both of them as they held each other tightly. They were familiar, but no memories surfaced. I turned to leave the room, but Sybrien pulled me back so he could stare me in the eyes. His dark eyes glanced into mine like he was looking for something.

"You don't remember?"

I shook my head.

"Then why did you do it? Why would you care if we died?"

"I don't have an answer for you. It just felt wrong. I have to go before anyone knows I'm missing. Please tell Falgon and Crimson that my father and Jesper plan to send assassins to kill the royal bloodlines in the next few days."

"I'll tell them." He frowned as he let me go.

I headed for the door again but paused for a brief moment.

"I hope I can remember being friends with you both someday and meet your child." I glanced at them as they held onto one another. "Triple your security." But paused. "Is Jesper's mother alive?"

"No, the Queen of Kizar died soon after he was born." Sybrien looked at me oddly. I nodded, then turned without a word and walked around the corner, willing my magic to take me back home.

Chapter 21

Thea

It had been three days since I saved Petra and Sybrien. My father had not said anything to me, so I didn't think he would suspect that I killed his men. But every day that passed, the more paranoid I became. Did they know that my magic let me travel in mere seconds? They would've killed me by now if they did.

I focused on the men fighting but could not stop thinking about my father and how atrocious I found him to be.

"Thea." I froze when Jesper spoke from behind me. My face remained blank as I turned to look at him. "Your father needs you."

"Alright." I nodded before turning back to the men. "You're excused for the day!"

They stopped combat immediately to salute me. I followed Jesper as we silently moved toward the castle.

"You've been training the men extra in the last few days." He looked at me oddly.

"We're expecting war. Isn't that what you do when you need your soldiers to be the best—train them?"

Jesper didn't say anything as we stepped into the throne room. My father dominated the space with his height and fancy robes. He was glaring at me as he stood at the map of Elloryon. Fuck. What did he know?

"Thanks for coming," he sighed and looked away from me. I relaxed as soon as he looked concerned.

"What's wrong?"

"King Sybrien and his wife are still alive." He watched me closely, like he expected some sort of reaction. I gave away nothing. "Our men never got to them and didn't come back like they should have yesterday."

"Well, maybe something happened, and they had to put it off for a few days." I offered, knowing I had murdered both of them. Flashes of my darkness punching a hole through the man made me smile to myself.

"No, these were some of our best men. They would have been in and out. Something happened when they got there."

Jesper's eyes were staring intently at the side of my face, but I refused to look at him. I pretended to be thinking about something, but all I could picture was the guard I burnt to a crisp.

"Alright, then attack Falgon or Crimson before word gets out. If our men were killed by Akecia guards, then he will likely warn the other kingdoms, right? Move in before he gets the chance."

Jesper's gaze finally turned to my father, and I saw him give him a surprised look. They hadn't expected me to plan another attack, which was good for me.

My eyes glanced around his throne room. I had ripped it apart the other day searching for my bloodstone so I could break my curse, but I didn't find it. It had to be in this room. My father was always here, and it was always guarded. My darkness crept from me undetected and searched the area for its power again, but I frowned when it felt nothing.

"We have men scouting the borders of Falgon and Crimson now. We should know by the morning which kingdom is our next move. Akecia locked down their border, so they are not an option."

"Alright, well, let me know what you need from me when the scouts return."

"We will." My father smiled at me like he was proud.

Prick.

Turning, I headed for the door but stopped when my father spoke again.

"I'm so glad to have you back home, Thea."

I wanted to vomit, but I turned back and smiled.

"Me too."

Swallowing back the bitterness I felt saying it, I headed for my room.

★★☽★★

I kept my eyes shut, but I heard something moving around in my room. I had laid in bed for hours after my talk with Jesper and Luren and had only just relaxed when the noise caught my attention. Where had I left my dagger; was it on my nightstand or in my boot by the bed? Whoever moved around was almost completely silent. I thought maybe it was Della, but she would have made herself known.

My eyes flashed open when I felt something touch my face. I sat up quickly. The only thing that I was met with was complete darkness. I could feel someone watching me, even if I couldn't see them. Standing, I grabbed my dagger and headed for the door to see if the guards were there. I opened the door to both of them.

"Is something wrong, Captain?"

I shook my head.

"Sorry, I think I was having a weird dream." I lied and shut the door, locking it. When I turned around to scout the room, I was ambushed. The man's hand clamped around my mouth as he ripped the dagger from me and set it down quietly. I was about to scream, but the scent of rain and forest surrounded me.

Cassius.

He pressed me against the wall with his body before I saw his glowing golden eyes.

"It's just me, my love."

He slowly removed his hand from my mouth before dragging me toward the window, where the moonlight shone brightly enough to see his face.

"What are you doing here?" I snapped. I hadn't seen him since my father told me that he killed me. Honestly, it was probably for the best because I was trying to plan my prophecy. But I also needed to break my curse and couldn't find the damn bloodstone.

"I wanted to see you, but more importantly..." He stepped forward, trapping me between him and the wall once again. His eyes stared into mine intently. "I want to know why you saved Sy and Petra."

Gods, I couldn't concentrate when he was touching me this much. His hands caged me to the wall, but that didn't stop him from leaning his body flush against mine.

"I don't know why I did it."

He leaned down so he could look into my eyes. What was he looking for?

"Did you break your curse?" He whispered like he was scared I'd say no.

"Of course not." I breathed. "Why would you think that?"

"Because you saved our friends. Because you told him to warn me and Falgon about the assassins. You're betraying your father and Jesper."

"I don't want to be a monster." I glared. "I will not let my family take all of Elloryon for greed."

Something in his eyes changed as he listened to me.

"You have never been a monster." He leaned close to me. "I had hoped you somehow broke your curse and remembered me, us. I was hoping to take you home with me tonight."

His lips pressed into my neck softly. I sighed as his stubble rubbed my skin as he kissed down my neck.

"I think you deserve a reward for being a good girl," he whispered as he leaned forward to press his lips into mine.

No thoughts came to me. Cassius smiled against my lips before pulling away from me.

"You won't be needing all of this." He waved his hands over my clothing. I immediately discarded my camisole, making him chuckle softly. I should probably resist him a little bit, but I couldn't. There was something about this man that made me lose my fucking mind. Cassius hooked his thumbs into my underwear and slowly sank to his knees as he dragged them down my legs. His mouth leaving a trail of soft bites and licks down my stomach.

He tossed them to the side before lifting my leg and devouring me. Fuck. His tongue swirled around me as he plunged two fingers into me at the same time. My fingers dug into his hair as I tried everything in my power to not make any noise. He was fucking relentless. I did my best to hold out, but it was useless. The man knew how to use his mouth for more than flirting. It didn't take long for me to cum. Cassius smiled as he sat back.

"Fuck, Thea. I barely touched you."

"Get up," I demanded.

"Yes, ma'am." He smiled and stood in front of me.

"Take it off." I waved to his clothes. Cassius smiled at me as he slipped from his boots. Slowly, he unbuttoned his shirt and slid it off his muscled body. My eyes immediately dropped to the crown tattoo before looking over the red viper going up his arm. I could feel him looking at me as I watched him undress.

"We've fucked in a lot of places, Thea, but we've never done it in *our* enemy's home."

My eyes glanced up at him. Gods, he looked like I was his prey.

"What would they do if they walked in here and saw you bent over the bed moaning my name?"

"Kill me," I answered his rhetorical question. His lips twitched slightly.

"Are you really worried about anyone catching us?"

He stepped forward and traced the 'C' tattooed over my heart. I shook my head no as my eyes found the 'T' above his heart. Cassius and Thea. It had a viper coiled tightly around it. Little viper. His finger lowered, circling my breasts. Goosebumps gave away what his light touch did to me. Cassius stepped forward, his hand tangling in my hair so he could drag my mouth up to his.

Cassius was not gentle. His mouth dominated mine, his tongue dancing with mine as his other hand slid down to find me wet.

"You always were ready for me, Thea," he sighed. I leaned forward and kissed his neck. My mind was flashing with an image of him dying. I flinched, but he let out a soft moan and leaned back so I had better access, making the image disappear. My hand wrapped around his hard length, and I smiled when he flexed his hips.

"Seems you are always ready for me too." I smiled before kissing over where I could feel his heart beating. Cassius stilled at the touch before yanking me back up to his mouth. Cassius pulled away from me, spinning me so I was facing the bed, and pushed me down, so I was on all fours. His hands rubbed over my naked back before grabbing handfuls of my ass.

I could hear my heavy breathing in the room, but nothing else as Cassius slid into me quickly.

I moaned before he yanked me up, so my back was flesh with his chest. His hand wrapped around my jaw as his mouth brushed my ear.

"Be quiet," he demanded.

"That is going to be impossible," I sighed as he thrust up into me again. Cassius sighed heavily into my ear as he picked up his pace. My eyes squeezed shut, trying my hardest to be quiet. My head shook back and forth as his hips pounded into me. There was no way I was going to cum quietly. His tattooed hand covered my mouth.

"Fuck, I need to hear you," he groaned as his shadows swarmed around us. My skin prickled when the cool air hit me. I opened my eyes to see we were in a meadow, the bed gone.

"Cassius," I moaned. "Don't stop."

"That's it, Thea. Tell me what you want." He shoved me back down on all fours, his hands grabbing my hips tightly and slamming me back against him. His fingers flexed so tightly into my flesh that I knew it would bruise.

"Oh fuck."

"You're about to cum, aren't you?" he ground out. I moved my hips back to meet his thrusts. "Such a greedy fucking girl. Always wanting more."

I moaned into the dark night.

"Cassius, please," I begged.

Cassius' thrusts became more erratic behind me, his breathing heavy and uncontrolled. Without warning, he flipped me, so I was on my back under him.

"I want to see you," he muttered. His eyes, black as night, stared at me hauntingly. His shadows swarmed around him. He looked like he did the first time I fought him on the battlefield. My mouth opened, but nothing came out as my orgasm teetered on the edge of release.

"I love seeing you like this. You look at me like I am all you need." He slammed into me.

"You are all I need," I moaned.

Cassius lost it. He slammed into me as his orgasm overtook him. He thrust into me deeply, making my own orgasm follow. I held him to me as he softly groaned into my neck. He kissed me as his shadows swarmed around us. A moment later, we were lying in my bed in Cerithia. Cassius frowned slightly as he stood up.

"What are you doing?" I asked.

"I should go," he whispered as he looked for his clothing.

"You could stay."

He stilled and stared at me. I asked my magic to tell me what he was thinking. Cassius' voice flittered into my mind instantly.

She wants me to stay. How could I say no to her, but why does she want me around?

"Do you want me to?" His eyes searched mine for something. *Gods, she's looking at me like she did before her curse. I've missed sleeping with her next to me.*

"Yes."

He let his clothes fall from his hands instantly as he crawled into bed and pulled me next to him. I could feel his heart racing under my hand and glanced up at him. He was nervous.

"I killed you," he whispered. *Why did I remind her?*

"I know."

But gods, I really didn't fucking care.

"You should be upset with me." *Please don't hate me.*

"I know." I frowned as I traced my finger down his chest and over his tattoos. Cassius turned so he was facing me. My breath caught when his eyes met mine. He looked pained and tortured as he watched me.

"I don't want to lose you again," he confessed. "I don't want to wake up tomorrow and have you hate me again because of what I did." *I did it to save you. I love you and would do anything to bring you back home.*

My hand ran over his face.

"Let's have tonight. I don't want to think of anything but the way it feels when you are close to me."

Cassius leaned forward and kissed me.

"Cassius..." I looked deep into his eyes. "I could never hate you."

Thank the fucking stars. I just want you back home.

Chapter 22

Cassius

"This is a stupid idea." My father gave me a pointed look. "He might just kill you."

I shrugged.

"Jesper would be dead before he could get his hands on me. Thea has been avoiding me for a week, and when I go to check on her, it's like someone tells her I'm coming so she can leave. I need to know what is going on."

"Why would Thea actively avoid you to that extent?" Haden asked.

"I don't know, but I think there is something she isn't telling me. Every time she looks at me, I can feel her sadness. I feel grief from her, and I don't understand why."

The room fell silent. My mother stared at me like she understood why I wanted to do this. Everyone else clearly thought I lost my mind.

"Why Jesper?" she asked.

"Because I overheard him talking to Thea, and I think he is hiding things from Luren. Maybe he and I can agree to get Luren out of our way."

Haden whipped his head toward me.

"You want to team up with Jesper?"

"No, not really, but if I can convince him that I want to, maybe he will open up and tell me what the hell is happening with Thea. She doesn't want to tell me something is wrong with her."

Haden glanced around the room as if he were looking for something.

"I know you're here, Ardella," he sighed.

Della appeared in front of me.

"Leave Thea alone," she warned. "Nothing is wrong with her, but she is getting closer to the prophecy."

I stared at Della and frowned.

"Why are you lying to me too?" I whispered. "Please just tell me."

Della's eyes filled with uneasiness. She had become my friend over the years, and I knew when she was lying.

"Cassius, she is busy. Please just let her be. This is the year she comes home to you." Della stepped forward and hugged me so she could whisper, "Sometimes we have to keep things from those we love in order to protect them."

Haden glared daggers at me when our eyes met over Della's shoulder. It made me wonder how he didn't realize they were mates. With Thea, I can't stand any other male touching her even if they are a friend. Did he feel the tugging in his chest that I felt with Thea? What did he think that was?

"She's avoiding me." I glanced over at Della's face so I could see if she knew this.

"Yes."

"Is it something I did?" My chest tightened.

"No." Della frowned and almost turned toward Haden but stopped herself. "She's doing it because she loves you."

I sighed defeatedly and closed my eyes tightly as my bond told me to go find my wife and my logical side told me to give her space.

"She misses you too, but give her more time to do this."

Della left before I could respond again. Fuck.

"I still want to talk to Jesper and see if he lets anything slip." I knew Thea was on to something, especially since she asked me about Jesper's mother, who died a long time ago. Then she asked me again when I was Atticus, and Sy said she asked the same question to him. What was the fascination with this dead woman? I would stay away from Thea for as long as I could, but at some point, my mating bond would demand I find her, and I would not be able to stop myself.

"Alright, what do we need to do?" My father asked.

My gaze flickered to each fae standing in the room with us. They were all willing to support me and Thea even if my ideas were crazy.

"I'm going to find Jesper and take him to Kizar, but I will need to scout Cerithia to take him when he's alone." I looked at Haden. "I'm going to go alone."

"That's not a good idea," Haden protested.

"Della will let you know if something happens to me. I'll go tomorrow."

Haden wanted to argue, but he knew I would not be persuaded with reason. I was barely gripping onto reality right now. No one but maybe my wife would talk me out of it, and she was actively avoiding me.

"Fine, but I don't like it."

"If it helps me understand what's going on with Thea, then it will be worth it."

My gaze followed Thea as she walked into the throne room where Luren and Jesper were waiting. My chest ached at how pretty she was. She was in a black uniform with her green cloak on. Her hair was in a neatly done braid. I didn't dare look away from her because I knew she would be gone in a minute and I would miss her even more.

Thea glanced around as if she sensed me, but her eyes didn't linger where I hid in the shadows. Then I felt the power of her darkness humming through the room as if it were searching for something. At first, I thought it was me it was looking for, but when her darkness caressed me softly before continuing to look around, I knew she was trying to find something else. Whatever it was, she didn't seem to find it when her lips tilted into a small frown.

Wisp appeared in front of me, flashing red and black in warning. Great, even her soul was warning me away. I frowned at her, and Wisp turned dark green and twirled happily in front of me before disappearing.

Luren was warning Thea about some plan he had pretended to hear about me taking her. So he ordered her to stay in the castle under close supervision. Thea's face gave away nothing, but I felt her hatred through the bond.

"Fine. Is that all you needed?" She was impatient. What was she in such a hurry to do?

"Yes." Luren clipped.

Thea glanced at where I was hiding, and her eyes flashed red like she was telling me she knew I was spying. When she was gone, Luren sighed and stood up. He straightened the ugly crown on top of his head.

"Have you talked to your mother recently?" Luren glanced at Jesper.

His dead mother?

"No, I haven't had time to go see her." Jesper's face gave away his lie, but Luren wasn't looking at him. He was too busy looking at a map of Elloryon.

"This is the only warning I am giving you, Jesper." Luren stared up at him. "If you and your mother try anything to get me out of your way, I will kill her in front of you, and then I will lock you in the cells to rot away."

"Why would we do that? We are getting everything we wanted from this arrangement. Well, except Thea." Jesper glared. "I told you I wanted to marry her, not Tally."

"Thea would gut you the moment you let your guard down," Luren said matter-of-factly, but I barely heard over the possessiveness pounding in my ears. Why was Jesper so damn persistent on taking my mate? Did he care for her, or did he want to use her for something? It didn't matter; she was mine, and no one would ever take her from me.

"She could have learned to love me." Jesper barked back. Luren laughed loudly.

"You?" He chuckled. "It is clear that Thea loves Cassius. It doesn't matter how many times her memory is wiped; she always finds her way back to him. She will *never* choose you. You are lucky I am letting you marry Tally. She will be a good wife to you."

"She isn't Thea." Jesper frowned. Damn straight she wasn't. Jesper and I could agree that Thea was exactly what we both wanted—smart, funny, kind, loyal, and pretty. Jesper knew no one else could even come close to her. Too bad for him, the stars made her for me.

"You will get over this infatuation with Thea. She does not want you. Besides, she is a bastard child. Why would you taint your bloodline with a bastard? A witch bastard, no less."

Jesper became enraged at this. His face turned red as he walked toward Luren. I don't think I had ever seen him this angry, especially toward Luren.

"I am a witch bastard too, or did that escape your memory?"

I froze at his declaration.

Jesper was a bastard child? And part witch? What the fuck was happening? I glanced around like someone would explain what was happening.

"Your father is royal, and your mother was a witch. You still have a good bloodline."

So Jesper's mother wasn't the Queen of Kizar. Thea must know this, but why was it important to her? Jesper smiled smugly at Luren.

"By that logic, you are saying Thea has a good bloodline too. Her father is royal, and her mother was the fucking queen of blood witches. By your logic, Luren, Thea has a better bloodline than you."

I smiled to myself because Jesper was defending my wife, and I knew that would piss off Luren more than anything. Luren's face turned bright red in his fury. His hands fisted by his sides, like he might punch Jesper. I would love to see it.

"That's why you don't want me to be with her. It would make me more powerful than you. That's why it kills you that she loves Cassius. He is already powerful without her, but with her... they are unstoppable."

This had never been about power for me. I knew Thea was powerful the very first time she used her fire magic in front of me. This attraction to her has always been about Thea and the type of woman she was. Even if she was magicless, I would not have been able to stop my need for her. She is all I have ever wanted since I first saw her in my dreams as a child.

Thea destroyed any other woman's chance at catching my attention before we ever met. And it wasn't her power and magic that did that. It was everything else about her. It was why I never dated, never touched another woman. I knew Thea was mine before I knew she was real. I saved everything for her: first kiss, first date, first hug, my gods-damn virginity. I belonged to her the moment my heart first beat.

Mate bond or not, I would have never been able to resist her. And if she had been fated to someone else, I would have wiped their existence from the realm before she knew about them. Because I was not selfless like Della was with Haden. I was selfish. I wanted Thea happy, but I wanted her happy with me.

Every day, I will question why the stars thought I was the one who was worthy of her. But maybe it wasn't about being worthy. Maybe the stars knew I would be nothing without her. I would be lost. Thea loving me made me the man I was. Without her, I would not have a purpose. The realm is a better place because Thea found me worthy of loving back. There was no doubt in my mind that Thea saved me. She was the reason I was a semi-decent man.

"Which is why we need her to kill him before she realizes she loves him. No one will be more powerful than me."

Jesper looked pissed.

"I have to take Gwyn to a stupid play she has been bugging me about." Luren left, and Jesper stood fuming in the throne room. Perfect.

I stepped out from the shadows, and before he could register what was happening, I had him in a death grip in my shadows and was moving to Kizar.

"Let me go!" He thrashed around. I released him and took a step back so he could recognize we were in his home.

"What the fuck are you doing, Cassius?"

I wanted to demand who his mother was, but I also knew I couldn't give away too much. So I stuck to my original plan.

"I want to give you a chance to switch sides before Luren gets you killed." I lied. Jesper was a dead man walking even if he decided to help me now. What he had done to Thea would never be forgiven or forgotten.

Jesper laughed.

"Team up with you and your whore wife?"

Wife.

He fucking said 'wife.' My shadows formed a fist and punched him in the face.

"Don't ever disrespect my wife like that again."

Jesper spit blood from his mouth and onto the floor. His eyes were crazy as he stared at me. My heart pounded because Jesper knew way more than he should.

"How did you find out?" I asked.

"My mother."

"Your mother is dead." I reminded him.

He didn't say anything but gave me a smirk that had me more on edge.

"Why haven't you told Luren?"

Jesper smiled, and I thought he wouldn't answer me.

"Because as much as Luren thinks he's the big player in all of this, he isn't. I don't answer to him."

"I don't understand why you involved yourself in all of this. You could have stayed in your own kingdom and minded your business. But now you will die as a consequence of being a follower of Luren."

Jesper glared at me, his blue eyes void of any emotion.

"Thea was always meant to be mine," he said like he truly meant it. "You stole her from me on the blood moon all those years ago. She was mine first. If you had just stayed away, then all of this would have been avoided. All I ever wanted was Thea."

I glared.

"No, all *you* ever wanted was her power. All *I* have ever wanted was her." I took a small angry step toward him.

"Despite what you think, I do care for her, but she is too damn stubborn to do what she should. She needs to be tamed. She is dangerous otherwise."

I stepped toward him again, and he backed away.

"She is perfect the way she is. Thea is not some animal to be tamed."

Jesper rolled his eyes.

"This conversation is done. I am not teaming up with Crimson. I won't lose. Luren is just a means to get what I want, and he is playing the puppet so well that he doesn't even know what is happening. He won't make it out of this alive, but believe me when I say I will. And I'll convince Thea to be by my side."

Jesper was not smart enough to pull this off, which means his mother was the mastermind behind all of this. Who the fuck was she, and why did it make Jesper so confident that he couldn't lose? It was someone who knew way more than they should about Thea and me.

"I look forward to the day I watch my wife murder you as you beg for forgiveness."

Jesper's jaw clenched before I used my shadows to move him back to Cerithia without me. My chest was tight with worry and longing for Thea. I glanced around the room I was in before taking a deep breath, knowing what I was about to do was the act of a desperate man.

I walked out of the wooden door and was immediately met by three guards who drew their weapons on me, and I let them.

"Don't move, Cassius!" One of them yelled loud enough that more guards came. I lifted my hands and let them cuff me.

"Get word to King Jesper that we caught Cassius in the castle." A guard demanded. That would take days, and by then Thea would have come to save me. They dragged me into a large room where the floor and walls were made of stone. They kicked my legs so that I sunk down in the middle of the room before tying both my wrists outstretched to my sides.

"Why are you here?" one of the men asked.

I ignored him and sent an image of what was happening to Thea. The guard smiled as he moved behind me, and I heard the whip unravel before I felt it slice through my tunic. I groaned in agony as the hits kept coming. Still, I said nothing to them. Della appeared in the room, and I could barely see her through the threat of unconsciousness.

"Damn it, Cassius," she sighed before disappearing.

I smiled because I knew Thea would come for me. Then I couldn't fight anymore, and everything went black.

Chapter 23

Cassius

I groaned when I opened my swollen eyes. Kneeling on a hard floor overnight was starting to hurt. I tugged on the chains that had my arms stretched out to the sides. I could escape this easily. Della appeared in front of me again.

"I'm starting to think your plan isn't working." She glared at me. "I told you that Thea is busy."

She gave me a pointed look and huffed.

"It'll work. I passed out, so she didn't sense I was in danger through the bond."

Della began pacing back and forth like she was worried too. I laughed quietly, making Della stop and stare at me.

"What?" I asked.

"I can't believe this is your plan. Who in their right mind would willingly be taken as a prisoner, and to Kizar no less? Jesper's guards are a bunch of morons." Della was not impressed.

"A man who is desperate for Thea to recognize the depths of her feelings for him," I said smugly. I hadn't seen her in too long, and Della said she was too busy to come see me. Della hadn't filled me in on how Thea was doing, so I knew they were up to something. But why would Della keep things from me now? She wanted Thea to break her curse, but why couldn't I be involved?

"Thea needs to focus on what she is doing. I told you to give her time." Della gave me a disapproving look.

"I did." I watched her closely. "It's been well over a week. She hasn't come for me; she hasn't let me in her dreams; she hardly communicates through the bond. I'm going fucking crazy."

"So, this is your plan? She'll feel you through the bond and come rescue you, making her realize that you are more important than anyone else."

"Yes." Della looked off to me. Why wouldn't she look me in the eyes? "Do you know something?"

"Of course not," she spoke quickly. "Thea knows her depth of feelings for you, which is why she is staying away."

Before I could ask her about why she was lying, the wooden door opened and a dozen Kizar guards walked in. I watched them circle around me, weapons drawn. They had whipped me last night until I passed out. My back was sore and uncomfortable, but Thea would fix me when she came.

"Who are you talking to in here?" Their captain narrowed his eyes on me.

I glanced at Della, who stood next to him unbeknownst. "Myself."

The captain stepped forward and kneeled in front of my face, his dark eyes piercing into my own. I had sent an image of being beaten to Thea, but she still hadn't shown up. It hadn't been that long, but I would prefer not to get my ass kicked again.

"You are mad, aren't you?" The guard spoke. "Our king always said you weren't right in the head. A madman he called you."

I leaned forward and headbutted him, his nose breaking. They had no idea how fucking crazy I could get. The captain stood and punched me as hard as he could. Fuck. Instead of showing him the agony I was feeling, I laughed.

"You'll pay for that," he hissed. "Give me the whip," he barked at the guards without looking away from me. Della suddenly stood straight up and smiled at me. All the guards froze when the lights flickered violently. Thea.

The guards in the room didn't feel the shift in the air. They didn't realize that Thea's power commanded all the energy around her. That she made the realm bend and mold to her for her use. Her power demanded attention so everyone would see how fucking perfect she was. The guard in front of me unraveled the whip and drew his arm back as if he would whip my chest. But he paused.

Screaming was coming from outside the door now, and the guards quickly turned their attention to it with their weapons drawn. It sounded like a fucking massacre out there. I could hear bones breaking and men begging for their lives.

"What the fuck is that?" One of the guards cried out into the room.

I chuckled, making them look at me.

"That would be my wife." I smiled. "And she sounds very angry."

"Wife?" One of the guards looked around as if the other guards knew who I was talking about. His curiosity ended when the wooden door splintered and exploded. Thea, in all her glory, stepped into the room. Fuck, she was beautiful, but something about seeing her like this, completely lost in her darkness, seized any ability to breathe. My eyes dragged over her. Her eyes were dark red, and the swirls on her arms glowed so brightly. She wasn't just pissed; she was enraged. Her darkness swirled around her like my shadows did but seemed darker and more intimidating than mine ever could be.

Her eyes flickered around until she saw me, and I swear the ground shook in her fury. My wife was about to lose her shit.

"Thea?" The captain said with a tremble in his voice.

"What are you doing to Cassius?" Her voice was laced with anger, which only made her more menacing. Gods, I fucking loved this woman.

"He's a prisoner."

She nodded before glancing away from me for the first time. She glanced around the room, assessing how many guards there were. Her eyes lingered on the whip in the captain's hands. With a flick of her wrist, she evaporated every guard in the room with her fire magic, except him. Fuck, I was mad, because this was not the time to be turned on.

She took a step toward him, and he cowered down. When she glanced at me, I smiled at her. I felt it in our bond—her longing to help me. It stole my breath.

"You whipped him?" she tisked. Before he could blink, she moved behind him and kicked his legs out from under him. He cried out in pain when he hit the ground. Thea wasted no time pinning him to the floor with her darkness before dragging him directly in front of me.

He was pleading with her, but she was too lost in vengeance to hear him. Her eyes locked onto mine, and she gave me a wicked smile as she pulled out her viper-handled dagger, cutting the man's hands from him.

"You fucking traitor!" he yelled at her.

She stood up and glared down at him, and I worried that it would make her second-guess what she was doing. But she kicked him in the face.

"If I had more time, I would skin you alive," she snapped. "But I want some time with Cassius before I leave. I've missed him." My stomach clenched tightly with anticipation. Her fire magic glowed as she lifted her hands and focused on the man before his body went up in flames. Thea stood and watched him until he took his last breath.

"My love," I spoke to help her pull out of her darkness.

Thea shook her head and stared at me for a moment before hurrying over. She unchained me and instantly helped me out of the room. There was chaos happening everywhere. Thea pulled me into a random dark room. She gently pushed me down to sit. What the fuck kind of chair was I sitting on? I turned to see I was in fact seated on Jesper's throne. It was hideous, silver with ugly gray stones. Her darkness was circling all around us, so no one could enter the room.

"Cassius." Her voice was frantic. "Fuck, what did they do to you?"

Her hands were running over the wounds on my bare chest.

"I should have drawn out their deaths." Her eyes flashed black again, and I was mesmerized by her. Worry and anger zapped through the bond. She was becoming erratic.

"It's alright." I grabbed her hands and slowed down her movements. "You disappeared. I've missed you."

She was kneeling between my legs where I sat. Her eyes faded back to dark green as she looked at me. A moment later, her healing magic seeped from her and closed all my wounds, but we didn't break eye contact.

Thea's lips parted as she let out a shaky breath. Desire pumped into our bond, and it was crippling.

"You had me in our enemy's castle; now I think I should have you on our other enemy's throne," she whispered.

Fuck.

Her eyes swirled with black as she pulled her hands from mine and ran them over my thighs and up to the waistband of my trousers. She smiled at me when I leaned back and lifted my hips so she could yank them down. Her eyes never left mine as she gripped my hard cock, moving her hand down its length. I moaned at the sight of her.

"My love," I sighed when she leaned forward and ran her tongue up the length of me. My hands gripped the arms of Jesper's throne as she pulled me into her mouth. I didn't dare close my eyes. The sight of my wife on her knees while I sat on a throne that didn't belong to me was enough to make me cum. My hips surged forward, making her take me deeper. Her plump lips wrapped around my cock were a sight to behold. Thea opened her eyes and glanced at me through her dark lashes.

"Fuck, your lips were made to be around me."

Thea moaned at my words, and she used her hand to move down my length in tandem with her mouth extremely slowly. She was teasing me. I tried to lift my hips to get more friction, but she pulled away slightly. I gripped her hair in my hands and pulled her off me, so she was staring me in the eyes.

"You don't want to play this game, my love. I will have you begging for release in less than a minute."

"That sounds like heaven," she breathed.

Gods, this woman was perfect.

She smiled at me as I leaned forward and took her mouth with mine, my tongue dominating hers. Thea was a whimpering mess when I pulled away. Then I shoved her mouth back down to my cock.

"Open," I demanded. She listened, and I filled her mouth, but I was losing control of myself. I pulled out quickly, then slowly glided back into her throat, making her gag. Thea moaned around me, making my sanity snap. My hips surged forward at their own pace. She took it eagerly.

"Look at you, so eager to please me," I ground out. My words only fueled her enthusiasm as she whimpered around me. Her hands reached forward and scratched my bare skin on my stomach. "Fuck, you're such a good girl," I praised her. Her fingers dug into my flesh, and I knew it would bruise. "Do you want me to cum in your mouth or inside of you?"

I yanked her back so she could answer.

"In me," she begged.

I forced her to stand so I could reach forward and yank her trousers down. Thea took control as soon as she was naked from the waist down. She straddled my hips as she grabbed the back of the throne and sank onto me quickly. I had to hold her hips so she couldn't move. Fuck. Fuck. Fuck. I was not going to last long.

Thea gripped my hair and pulled my face back so she could kiss me. When she pulled back, her hands yanked her tunic up and over her head, so she was naked.

"I need your mouth on my skin," she demanded, and she yanked me against her breasts. She slowly slid up my length as my hands grabbed her breasts, sucking and teasing her.

"Oh fuck," she moaned into the silent room.

My arm wrapped around her back and pulled her closer to me. Her fingers ran through my hair and pulled on it as she rolled her hips into me.

"Fuck," I muttered when I stared into her black eyes. Her soft pleas were echoing in the space. "If I could only hear one noise for the rest of my life, it would be this."

"Cassius…" She was close. "You feel so good."

I leaned my head back against the throne and watched her face as she fought her orgasm. She never wanted this to end. She never got enough of us. Her mouth parted as she stared down at me, her hips moving at an unbearable pace.

"Cum for me, Thea," I begged. "I need you to cum."

She leaned down and took my mouth with hers as she clenched around me. Thank the stars. I moaned into her mouth as I buried myself deep inside of her and came. Neither of us moved. Our labored breathing filled the silence around us. Thea pulled back, and I always worried she would regret this, but she gave me a heart-stopping smile.

"Every time I see Jesper, I'll picture fucking you on his throne. Fuck, we should have done this in Cerithia too."

I smiled at her. I loved her so fucking much. Thea's eyes cascaded over my face before she hesitated.

"I love you too," she whispered.

I froze. Not because of her words, but because I know I didn't say that out loud. Thea watched the confusion mask my expression. Then she smirked at me.

"I didn't say that out loud."

She stood and started getting dressed so nonchalantly. She smiled at me when I pulled up my trousers and stared at her.

"No, you didn't say it out loud, but I still heard it."

"What do you mean?"

"I can read minds." She shrugged like she was talking about the fucking weather.

"Since when?"

"I don't know. It happened when I first escaped Exile. I heard Jesper's thoughts. At first, I thought I was losing my mind, but then I realized I could turn it off and on."

I was at a loss for words. Thea smiled at me innocently.

"I need to get back before my father knows I'm missing. I'm sorry it took so long to get to you; I was in a meeting."

She stepped forward hesitantly before hugging me. Her lips pressed into the skin above my heart. When she pulled away, I grabbed her wrist.

"Come home with me."

She smiled brightly at me. Gods, did she break her curse? She looked at me like she used to before she forgot. There was no way she broke it; she didn't give me the stone.

"I didn't break the curse," she answered my thoughts. "I'm working on it."

Emotions clogged my throat.

"You're really going to do it this time, aren't you?"

"I hope so, but I have to figure out where my bloodstone is first." She frowned at me. "My father hid it, so I'm trying to find it."

"I can help find it." I offered, but she frowned at me.

"I need you to stay away, Cassius." Tears filled her pretty eyes. Why would she say that? "Once the curse is broken, I have to fulfill the prophecy. You will be in the way if you try to help."

"But I want to make sure you succeed."

"I know, but promise me you won't interfere." She was serious as she stared at me. Something was bothering her. "Promise me, Cassius. What is the point of all of this if I lose you at the end anyway?"

I didn't want to promise her.

Her face softened as she stepped forward again. Thea's fingers traced my face softly.

"You need to trust me."

Her words made me flinch.

"I trust you more than anyone." I frowned. "But what if you die again and I could have prevented it? I will die with you."

"You can't always protect me, Cassius. This is one of those times that I'm asking you to let me do this on my own. I'm telling you I need to do this without worrying about you."

"I just love you so much," I whisper. "My biggest fear is seeing you die again."

"And my biggest fear is forgetting you again or losing you because you want to save me. You have saved me countless times before, my love. Let me save us this time."

I didn't know if I could promise that I could stay out of it. She was everything to me.

"Then at least try," she answered me.

"I don't know how much I like this mind-reading," I confessed, which made her chuckle softly.

"I like it quite a lot."

"I will do my best to stay out of your way," I said. But I knew that I would have a very hard time not helping her. Especially if she broke her curse. If she died, then that would be it, and I would follow her into the next life because I refused to live in a realm where she did not exist with me.

Thea's eyes softened, letting me know she was reading my mind.

"Cassius…"

"I mean it. You own me, mind, body, and soul. In this life and in every life that follows. I cannot exist where you do not. You are my entire existence."

Thea leaned forward and kissed me possessively.

"I love you," she whispered. "I will remember you soon."

She disappeared before I could respond.

Chapter 24

Thea

"**Y**ou want me to pretend to like Cassius and then stab him?" I glanced around at my father and the guards. This was the most stupid plan I had ever heard. "He won't ever fall for that. We're enemies." *Tell me what he is thinking,* I told my magic.

"Cassius is fond of you. He will fall for it." My father waved his hand as if to dismiss me. *Don't be fucking difficult, or I'll start this curse over again.* "Once you've gotten into the castle, you will use your magic and destroy it—with the royal family inside." *And finally, get rid of Cassius forever.*

"How am I supposed to convince him not to kill me and that I like him?" I acted appalled, but my stomach was clenched with anticipation. As soon as I glanced at Jesper, images of Cassius fucking me on Jesper's throne made me feel dizzy with longing. I knew he was pushing those images into my mind through the bond.

"You're clever; you'll figure it out." My father pinched the bridge of his nose in irritation. *Because he fucking loves you, and I will use that weakness against him.*

"This is a terrible idea." Jesper stood. "Cassius could fill her head with lies!" I glanced at Jesper and focused on his thoughts.

"For once, I agree with Jesper," I said.

Luren has lost his fucking mind if he thinks that Cassius won't convince Thea to be with him. She fucking can't stay away from him. Thea will never choose us; we should just kill her each year and stop trying to convince her to be on our side.

"She knows that he killed her, and she won't fall for his manipulation. Right, Thea?" I glanced at my father and focused on his thoughts. *If you do, we will just kill you again.*

"Of course, but I'm more worried that this is an obvious plan, and he'll slit my throat open or something."

My father and Jesper seemed to contemplate this plan again. It was sick to sit here and think that they were manipulating me. They knew Cassius was important to me, yet they used it as a weapon. Did my family and kingdom hate me that much?

"Let Jesper and I discuss. I'll come find you when we know a better plan." My father dismissed me. Quickly I left the room, but I did not leave without hearing what they had to say. I waited at the door.

"What do you think?" My father asked Jesper.

It was silent for a long moment before I heard someone walking around.

"Well, she thought it was a bad idea, so she must not remember him," Jesper sighed. "But Thea is also clever; she could be putting on a whole show. Someone killed all the guards in my castle."

Shit.

My mind raced with what I would do if they knew I was protecting Cassius.

"It was probably Cassius. Thea can't get to Kizar, kill all of your men stationed there, and be back in a short time. The guards said she didn't leave her room. Besides, you saw Cassius at the meeting. She devastated him; that was no act." My father laughed. I just smiled to myself because my father had no idea how much I had seen Cassius since that meeting. I needed to find the bloodstone. "We've never been in a position where she does not choose Cassius. It seems the gods are in favor of us."

Rage simmered under my skin. They think this is funny. My life is just a joke that they can use as they see fit. It was sick.

"What happens when she kills the family and realizes we lied?" Jesper questioned the king.

"We will worry about that when the time comes. Besides, it will be easy to blame it on Cassius or his family. Maybe a different curse that cannot ever be broken."

"Alright." Jesper breathed heavily. "But she can't pretend to like Cassius. If she spends any time with him, then she's going to start remembering him. Maybe we should lock her up until we can get the Crimson family prisoner. Then she can kill them."

"If we lock her up, then she will know what is going on. Besides, we don't know all the magic she has inside of her or what she's collected. She could escape. We need to just keep pushing the war off."

I didn't even know what kind of magic I had. I was severely at a disadvantage here. Half the stuff they talked about went right over my head. One thing for certain was that I did not belong here. My heart pounded as I turned and left. I went to my room even though all I wanted to do was run far away from here.

Cassius was not going to stay out of my way. He would try, but I knew he wouldn't be able to help himself. So,

I needed to break the curse without him knowing. By the time he realized I remembered it, it would be after I fulfilled the prophecy.

Cassius was much safer without me telling him anything. I lay in bed and stared at the ceiling of my ugly, white, sterile room. The weight of everything settled on my chest, making it difficult to breathe or concentrate. My father was going to keep me prisoner here by any means necessary. All the lies and deceit were enough to make my darkness swarm around me.

I would need to use my magic to trick my father into telling me where my bloodstone was. I had no idea what magic I had, and I had no idea how I could figure it out. Maybe tomorrow I will try to use some. My darkness would help. At the thought, my darkness hummed in approval. This was ending very soon; I missed my husband.

★★☽★★

It had been two days since my meeting with my father, and I hadn't seen him once. In fact, he was purposely avoiding me. So today I snuck out of the castle in the night and deep into the dark woods. My magic stirred frantically in my chest as if it knew I would be using it today. My body hummed in wild anticipation.

When I was far enough away, I glanced around the small clearing. I'm sure there were monsters out there that wanted to eat me alive. I flicked my wrist, and fire illuminated the space. Alright, now what did I do? Shit, my fire magic had exploded out of me without warning before. Maybe my other magic would too? I stood in the middle of the clearing, waiting for something to happen. "Gods, I feel stupid," I muttered to myself.

Breaking sticks alerted me that I wasn't alone. My gaze darted around the dark woods. At first, I couldn't see anything, but then dozens of creatures burst through the tree line.

"Fuck."

Their ear-piercing screeches let me know that they were not friendly. Their small bodies were camouflaged into the tall brown weeds of the field, making it impossible to see them. A painful scream tore through me as one jumped on my arm and tore it open. Power like nothing I felt before rippled from me as I fell onto the ground.

Blood gushed from my wound, and I held my hand to it tightly to heal it like I did with Cassius. When I glanced up, I realized the creatures had not attacked me again. Then I realized why. There was some sort of invisible boundary around me that they couldn't get through.

Had I done that? Wisp's green flame caught my attention as she floated outside of the boundary. The small creatures seemed to see her as she flickered away from me, taking them with her. When she reappeared a minute later, she was alone and twirling around me. I released my boundary magic and glanced around.

"I'm not sure how to summon magic when I don't know what kinds I have," I sighed. Wisp continued to float around, but her color switched to purple. What did that mean? My darkness was urging me to be released. At first, I refused to let it out because I wanted to focus on my magic, but she was persistent.

After struggling with my darkness for a few minutes, she refused to be locked up and burst from me. Her inky tendrils swirled around me until she gripped me tightly, seeping into my bones and clawing her way through my body. I was frozen, helpless, as my darkness took over me. Trees swayed at the force of her. She forced my mouth open and made me swallow every drop of her. When she was done, I fell to the forest floor.

My breathing was labored as I looked around, slightly confused. All of a sudden my darkness burst from me again, but this time she forced my magic out of me too. I was not in control of my body as it summoned my fire, making it swarm around me. Cassius' shadows entwined with it, making the flames burn black. Then a ball of light formed in my hand. My darkness forced me to grab it and stretch it before forcing me through it. When I stepped out, I felt dizzy, but I had moved across the small clearing in a matter of seconds.

My hands raised without my permission, and I felt them pulsing. Suddenly my dagger and other metal objects rose into the air before dropping. My body whipped around and shot frost out, freezing a little creature that was sneaking back toward me. Like Haden's magic.

My body pulsed violently as my darkness drained all of my energy into showing me the next magic.

I watched as the forest turned into a lake. I glanced around as my magic slowly seeped over every surface, changing it right before my eyes. Illusion magic. Fuck. My darkness tried to show me something else, but I collapsed on the forest floor, drained of energy. Wisp was flashing between dark and light purple.

"Wisp, I don't know what purple means."

"It means you're taking a step in the right direction." Della appeared next to me. "You're trying your magic."

"Well, my darkness didn't give me much of an option." I groaned as I stood on weak legs. "I haven't seen you in a while."

Della smiled.

"I was helping Cassius." Her eyes traced over me. "He said you told him you loved him."

"I do love him," I sighed.

"I know you do." She frowned. It made me feel bad because somehow I knew she was thinking of Haden. I got the sense she wanted to talk about him.

"Not that it matters now, but Haden said you were real." I glanced at her. She nodded sadly. "He was really angry."

Della glanced into the stars and sighed heavily. Her mind seemed to be remembering something that was painful for her. Her eyes squeezed tightly before she zoned out on the ground.

"As gods, we wait an eternity to meet our mates. We never know when it will happen, just that it will. I dreamed of my mate for as long as I could remember. I had this idea in my mind about the kind of life we would have. Those thoughts only tripled when I met Haden. He was so much better than I could have dreamed up for myself. Strong, funny, handsome, selfless, and kind. But I managed to ruin it in months. All my dreams went out the window the night Haden told me he hated me, that he wished he never met me." She swallowed hard. "I have nothing to look forward to anymore. Our existence as gods means nothing until we meet our other half. They give us a new purpose, a reason to want to wake up in the mornings, but now I have absolutely nothing."

"Della..."

"This is going to sound terrible." She paused as she turned to meet my face. "A part of me hates you and Cassius."

Her words should anger me, but I knew what she meant.

"How much you two love each other makes jealousy bloom deep in my chest. He killed you, and you have forgiven him. There have been so many mistakes made between the two of you, but your love has never wavered. Haden did not think I was worthy of forgiveness. He did not love me like I loved him."

"But maybe he can forgive you in time." I wanted that to be true. The thought of Della alone for the rest of her existence hurt my soul to think about.

She laughed humorlessly.

"Do you know what he said the last time he saw me?" Her jaw tensed. "He cannot wait until you break your curse so that I do not have to be around anymore. And it made me realize that part of me dreads you breaking your curse because he is right. I will no longer have a reason to be around, let alone near him. You must think I'm awful for thinking like this."

"No, I don't." I stepped toward her and turned her, so she was looking at me. I grabbed her and hugged her. "You will have a reason to be around. You are my friend, and that will not end because my curse does."

Della was crying silently as she held onto me. Her heart was beating rapidly as she pulled back.

"I came to tell you that your bloodstone cannot leave your father's castle unless you take it. So, wherever it is, it is here. Let's find it. I want to help. I'm surprised that your darkness can't feel its power." Della seemed to be thinking of something when her face broke into a smile. "Use your illusion magic. Turn into Gwyn or someone and ask your father about it; even if he refuses to tell you, he will likely think about it, and you can hear it with your mind reading."

"Can I make myself someone else?"

"Yes," she chewed on her bottom lip. "I've seen someone do it recently. Try it." My eyes narrowed on her because she seemed suspicious.

"I thought your tongue was tied with magic."

"It is, but I haven't actually told you anything that you didn't already know. Besides, I'm looking forward to watching you fulfill your prophecy." A wicked smile took over her face.

A noise in the woods had both of us freezing in our spots. A moment later, Cerithian guards emerged from the tree line. They drew their weapons at me; Della was standing next to me, but I knew they couldn't see her.

"Don't move."

"What are you guys doing?" I demanded an answer.

"You need to come back to the castle."

I glanced at Della; something was wrong. She followed me as the guards refused to lower their weapons. I didn't bother demanding any more answers. Something felt... off with them. Della followed me silently through the woods. If something happened to me, she would tell Cassius. I was confident in that.

When we entered the castle, I expected to go into the throne room, but instead, the small group of guards led me upstairs to my room. They shoved me inside and closed the door.

"What the fuck!" I yelled when I jiggled the doorknob to find I was locked in there. A noise behind me had me quieting down. Della was next to me, not saying anything, so I wasn't sure what to expect.

"What the fuck?" Della finally muttered. "Bayla?"

I turned toward the noise and froze. She was smiling at me with her red eyes and hair that matched mine; in fact, everything about her matched me. This was the woman I saw in my room before. Della referred to her as Bayla... the woman who sent the brown-eyed man to protect me. She was standing by my bedroom window. Bayla's arms opened as if she expected me to go and hug her.

"Thea, darling, come hug me." She smiled. My back hit the door behind me as I tried to get away from her. Why did she look like me? And why did I not feel safe with her? "Thea, come hug your mother," she said, irritated.

"My mother is dead." I glanced around to find understanding but saw nothing out of the ordinary. Well, besides my dead mother trying to hug me.

Her face fell, but she stepped toward me. I grabbed my dagger and held it toward her. Something in her eyes shifted.

"I've come back to help you break your curse. I had not moved on to the next life yet; I didn't want to until you regained your memories."

Della hadn't moved at all. I wasn't sure if she was even breathing at this point.

"Why did my father's guards bring me here to see you?"

My heart was pounding in my ears. This wasn't my mother. It couldn't be her. As much as I wanted it to be, it was impossible. My father had her killed.

"He wants you to break your curse, so he called upon my spirit to help guide you."

Okay, lying sack of shit.

"I need to kill the Crimson bloodline. I don't know how you can help with that."

She took a small step forward as if it would be undetected.

"Please give me a hug." She frowned.

"No thanks." I stepped backward, and the image of my mother was clearly irritated. "This is not possible. My mother moved on years ago."

Della looked at me with a look I didn't like.

"It's not impossible," Della whispered. "Killian waited for your mother when she died, but when their souls met, they... disappeared."

"What do you mean, disappeared?" I hissed, not caring if this woman heard me.

Della began fidgeting, which she did when she was nervous.

"Your mother is a stubborn woman, and so is Killian. They refused to go on to the next life, and their souls vanished. I could never track her or him down. I'm assuming your mother wouldn't move on until she knew you broke your curse."

I looked at the woman who was claiming to be my mother.

"Della's right, I didn't move on." The woman smiled. "I'm worried that Cassius is tricking you again. Have you spoken to him?"

"No, of course not."

She took another step toward me. Why did she want to be closer to me? Fuck, I realized my magic was not stirring in my chest. My darkness was not there either. Something about this thing was keeping me from using my magic, or maybe I used all my damn energy trying to see what magic I had.

"I'm pretty disappointed you won't hug your mother." She pouted. "Let me at least see how beautiful you grew up to be."

She moved toward me quickly. I darted from her touch and held out my dagger.

"Who the fuck are you, and how did you block my magic?"

"I'm your mother."

"No, you aren't. My mother would never help my father. He murdered her. So, I'll ask you again, bitch, who are you?"

Her face contorted into a wicked smile as she advanced on me again.

"She's a vatori!" Della yelled at me. "She can see your memories and thoughts by touching you. One small touch and she can see everything stored in your mind."

Fucking wonderful.

"So, who hired you? Gwyn, Jesper, or my father?" I glared.

"None of them." She smiled. I glanced at Della, confused. "Are you looking at your little friend, Ardella, over there? I can see you, goddess."

"Who the fuck are you?" Della snarled.

"Well, that's not very ladylike for a goddess." The woman smiled.

"Answer me now!" Della spoke with so much authority that I felt myself shrink down from her wrath. The woman just stared blankly at her.

"You can call me Val." Her focus returned to me. "I just want a peek inside that memory of yours, Thea. If you do that, then I will let you go."

"Fuck you."

"Well, that's also not very ladylike for a goddess either." Goddess.

I looked at Della, who stared at me.

"You're a goddess, but you chose to stay in Elloryon and be with Cassius. You'll remember when you break the curse."

I nodded like I hadn't been told I was a goddess.

"Who hired you?" I asked Val.

She ran at me, but I couldn't even fight her without her getting what she wanted from me. I stumbled into the wall, smacking my face into my side table. Val smiled at me as she stalked toward me; just as she was about to touch me, Della tackled her ass to the ground.

I looked behind her when I saw movement by the door. Cassius and Haden stood in the corner of the room. He must have felt something through the bond. Della's pained sob filled the air. Haden's face contorted into fury when he saw Val had Della by the throat. Val smiled as she focused on Della as she lifted her off the ground and slammed her into the floor. She dropped her and stood over her.

"My, my, Ardella, what a sad and pathetic life you lead."

Val's eyes flickered to Haden and Cassius. Cassius looked at me for answers.

"She's a vatori; she can see every thought and memory by touching you." I groaned as pain radiated down my face.

Val smiled when her eyes landed on Haden.

"Look, Ardella, it's the man who takes up most of your thoughts," Val sneered. "The one you broke. The man who curses your very existence each morning he wakes up. The one you wish to the stars would love you back."

Haden glanced at Della, who was in pain on the floor.

"Ardella!" Haden called out. "Are you alright?"

She didn't say anything as a painful sob tore from her. Haden glanced at Val when she circled back for Della. He ran at her.

"Haden, don't!" I called out. Val immediately turned and let Haden's fist connect with her face, but he immediately withered in pain as she latched onto him. He fell to his knees as pain took over his face. Val's smile widened as she let go of Haden and shoved him on the floor next to Della.

"Man, you two are quite the couple. A woman who loves a man more than the realm itself, and the man hates her just as much. A woman who wants forgiveness and a man who can't stand the sight of her. The mere thought of her makes him disgusted."

Della cried out loud, but it was no longer because of pain. It was knowing Haden's thoughts of her. Val looked at Della and smiled.

"Should I tell him your biggest secret?"

Oh fuck. I couldn't let her do that. Haden couldn't find out that he was Della's mate like this. Before I could offer myself up on a platter, Cassius stepped forward and glared at the woman.

Val's attention immediately turned to Cassius, and she whistled as she admired him. My jealousy didn't like her looking at what was mine.

"You're as handsome as she said you'd be."

She?

Cassius glanced at me before his eyes darted to our friends lying on the ground. Did he know that Della and Haden were mates? Why would he offer himself? Val didn't grab him, though; her focus turned to me.

"I'll keep her secret for your thoughts and memories."

"Deal." I stood and let Val walk toward me. She reached out and touched me; I could feel the burning sensation coursing through me. It felt like the shadow boundary had. It was quick and intense, making me fall to my knees. Val released me, and her eyes glowed with excitement.

"You've been a very busy girl, Thea." She smiled and turned to Cassius. "It seems your little friend here is also keeping secrets from you."

Cassius' face fell when he looked at me. This bitch.

"Are you keeping secrets from her too?"

Yes, he was, but I already knew of them. Val circled Cassius without touching him. Her eyes flickered at me, and she smiled when she saw me ready to fight.

"She told me to leave you alone; don't hurt Cassius," Val mocked the woman's voice. "She just wants Thea out of the way."

Cassius' body went rigid. His eyes refused to look at me as he stared at the floor. Val smiled even bigger.

"Thea dies, and you get so lonely during those times. She wants you to know that she can warm your bed. She is willing to marry you, bear children, and not *forget* you. She can offer you a full life." Val purred to Cassius. He didn't ask her who she was talking about. He knew. Cassius knew who hired Val.

"Cassius?" I asked.

His golden eyes found mine, but they didn't reveal anything to me.

"You can tell her I'm not interested, just like I wasn't interested the dozens of other times she approached me." His voice was even, but his eyes were burning with rage.

"You were promised to her, and you backed out."

"Promised for what?" I snapped, my jealousy knowing exactly what he had promised to her for.

"Cassius was supposed to marry another woman before you came along. He even agreed to it."

I felt it, my darkness stirring in my chest angrily. Jealousy and hatred toward a woman I didn't even know made me sick.

"My parents agreed, and I didn't even know you yet." Cassius frowned at whatever he saw on my face. "Making Thea jealous is only going to work against you," he snapped at Val.

Val's smile vanished when she looked at me. My darkness had seeped from me.

"Your magic isn't supposed to work in the room."

My red eyes flickered at my husband as he smiled.

Val started to speak, but I walked forward and grabbed her by the hair, yanking her along with me. Her magic no longer crippled me because she had seen my thoughts and memories.

"Who sent you here and why?"

"Flora," Cassius answered for her. "Falgon Princess."

The name sounded familiar in the sense that I hated it.

Haden stood and tried to help Della, but she refused his hand and went as far away from him as possible. He frowned at her back.

"Perfect," I snarled, and my darkness wrapped around me and Val. When it moved away, we were standing in Falgon's castle. The guards all raised their weapons at me as the royal family sat down for dinner. Cassius appeared next to me a moment later.

"Cassius?" Valor asked, confused. I used my metal magic to rip all the swords from the guard's hands, and when I squeezed my fist tightly, all of the weapons twisted and mangled on the floor.

"Tell your father what you did, you stupid bitch," I demanded of who I assumed was Flora.

Flora looked at Val and paled.

"Flora?" Her father glared daggers at her. "What did you do?"

"She's lying."

Cassius stepped forward, and I saw the way she fawned over him. Her eyes shone like he was about to confess that he loved her. Stars, she was fucking psychotic. My dagger slammed into Val's chest, making her yell in pain as she bled out at my feet, but my eyes never left Flora.

"Flora, tell your father now, or I will let Thea kill you," he demanded.

Valor glanced at me, and I could feel his fear pumping through him. He didn't look surprised that Flora had done something.

"He was promised to me, and I thought if Thea was out of the way, then he could see we were meant to be together!" Flora yelled.

Valor pinched the bridge of his nose and sighed heavily.

"Not this shit again. He doesn't like you, Flora. That deal was made when you were babies."

As I stared at Flora, something about her was not normal. My anger lessened as I watched her. Cassius glanced at me before explaining to Valor and his wife exactly what Flora did.

"Flora!" her mother gasped. "What were you planning on doing with that information?"

"Give it to her father," she sneered at me.

I stepped forward, and Flora's body shrank in its confidence. My head cocked to the side when I saw a small red mark on her skin, and red veins crept from it, seeping into her blood. It wasn't a sickness like I thought it would be. But some sort of magic.

"Flora," I whispered as her eyes found mine. When she looked at me, I could feel something evil lurking within her. Something foreign. "Where did you get that wound?" I pointed to it, and Cassius glanced with a frown.

"I don't see anything," he spoke.

"Flora, who were you around recently?" I demanded an answer. Her eyes shifted red, and she snarled at me like a rabid animal.

"Flora, sweetheart?" Her father came at her, but I refused to let him touch her.

When I glanced back at her, she looked possessed. Her eyes were red, but her smile was chilling. I glanced around and saw Cassius, and everyone was frozen to their spots.

"You little bitch," she ground out, but her voice was different, chilling. She had been poisoned, or something else was in control of her. "You're going to go to Ravenstone Coven; bring the bloodstone, or I will gut Cassius."

"I don't know where my bloodstone is."

"Find it," she hissed. "It's in your father's throne room."

"Who are you?" I asked.

She didn't respond. Then Flora fell to the floor. Her parents rushed her, not realizing they had been frozen. Cassius glanced at me.

"She was poisoned; she didn't do this." My healing magic surged forward and pumped through her body. "She'll be okay, but she will need lots of rest."

Then I used my magic to go to Cerithia. When I entered my room, Della was silently crying as Haden glared at her.

"You won't ever see me again," Della said to Haden without looking at him.

"Fine by me," he hissed.

I felt like shit to ignore their conversation, but this couldn't wait.

"Della I need you." I interrupted them. Cassius appeared a moment later.

"Thea, what's going on?" He frowned.

"You and Haden need to leave now," I spoke with fake irritation, hoping he would think I was angry with him and he'd leave.

"Are you upset about Flora?" he asked.

I turned with a glare.

"Get it through your head that I don't want you here. Leave!" I whispered harshly. "And take your friend with you." I glanced at Haden.

Cassius' eyes bounced between mine before frowning and taking Haden and himself away in his shadows. Damn it. My bond burned at how cruel I was to Cassius, but he needed to stay away.

"What's wrong?" Della looked at me.

I explained to her the wound and Flora's odd behavior. Della's face fell the moment I described the wound and what I felt from it. How they demanded my bloodstone.

"Thea, whoever did that was a blood witch. That is the mark of a blood possession."

What... no, they wouldn't do that to me.

"Are you sure?" I frowned, but somehow I already felt like I knew this. When Flora's eyes shone bright red, I knew it was a blood witch.

"I'm positive."

"Fuck." I used my magic to take Della and I to my father's throne room. We tore through the room, but the stone couldn't be found.

Fear gripped me because the woman had threatened Cassius. I was not risking him for anything, and when I found out who was responsible for this, I would gut her. My chest began to tighten. I couldn't breathe. My legs shook as I leaned against the desk.

"Thea?"

"I can't lose Cassius. Where the fuck is this bloodstone?"

Della moved toward me and forced my face so she could look into my eyes.

"I'm going to teach you how to do blood possession." She smiled.

CHAPTER 25

THEA

"Are you sure this is a good idea?" I looked at Della as she and I snuck into my father's room. I had frozen time in their room so they wouldn't wake up.

"It's fucking brilliant. You possess your father, and you will be able to control him and what he does. He will go get the stone for you and not know any wiser."

"That does sound fucking brilliant." I smiled.

I made my way around their giant bed to my father's side. He was lying on his back, sleeping peacefully. I lifted my hand so that I could focus on my fingers. A moment later, the tip of my pointer finger became a long pointed claw. I wiggled it and smiled at Della. She walked closer to me and watched as I took my pointer finger and held it above my father's collarbone and sank it into his flesh. It created a small puncture wound when I retracted my sharp fingernail.

I dug the claw into the tip of my finger, making it bleed, then let a drop of my blood fall onto my father's wound. My blood sank into the cut, and the wound healed in front of our eyes. Della and I glanced at each other; shit, that was easy. When I looked back at my father, he had the same red veins where I marked him that Flora did.

"Let's go to the throne room, and you can summon him from there." Della nodded as her star mist surrounded us. A moment later, I sat on my father's throne, and Della stood next to me. Closing my eyes, I called my father and told him to come to the throne room alone.

It only took a few minutes for my father to stroll into the room and shut the door. He stood staring blankly at me.

"This is actually kind of fucking creepy," I told Della. "Bring me the bloodstone," I demanded of him. My father blinked slowly, then walked to the throne I was sitting on. I stood up quickly, ready to fuck him up, but he lifted the cushion before lifting a small section of the wood under it, revealing a hidden compartment.

"It was protected by the same magic binding found in cuffs." Della's eyes widened. "No wonder you couldn't find it."

He handed it to me without hesitation.

"Go to bed." I waved him away and waited until he left the room before smiling at Della. My bloodstone shined red brightly in my hands, like it recognized it belonged to me. The stone was small but felt heavy in my palm. Suddenly its color changed to a dark purple. I glanced at Della for an explanation.

"It must change color when its energy is being used, or it's taking its true form because you are its owner?" Della looked at the stone that was shaped like a crescent moon. I could feel the energy from it fueling me and my magic. It was coursing through me so rapidly that I felt dizzy at first.

"Can any blood witch use this?" I asked.

"I'm not sure." She frowned. "We should go so we can figure out who the hell is up to all of this. I will be invisible to everyone but you."

Wisp appeared next to us and burned the same purple color as the bloodstone. I used Cassius' shadows to go to Ravenstone Coven. I was standing in the small, grassy village center. I glanced at the stone in my hand and shoved it into my pocket before using illusion magic to create a fake one in my hand.

"Oh, thank the moon you're here!" I turned and held out my dagger but lowered it when Genia was standing there. "Lyra has lost her fucking mind."

"What do you mean?" I frowned.

"She was acting strange and saying that she was taking what was promised to her. Then she killed a few of the witches, but we restrained her in Yerma's house."

Della shrugged her shoulders at me as we hurried to the house. When I walked in, a dozen witches surrounded a woman bound in a chair. I recognized Lyra as the blonde witch I met here last time. She was gagged and crying profusely. Wisp appeared next to her, her flames flashing red and black. Wisp was extremely distraught.

The other witches stared at me, but they wouldn't make eye contact with me. Lyra was the only one who was meeting my eyes. She shook her head no.

"Why did you possess Flora and go after Cassius?" I glared, but it was all for show. *Tell me what she is thinking,* I demanded from my magic.

Please. It wasn't me! It wasn't me; don't kill me.

I could hear her thoughts. Genia said it wouldn't work on them the last time I was here. But maybe she made it so it wouldn't. My eyes found Della, and I tried to communicate with her that something was wrong. I went to take the woman's gag out of her mouth, but Genia stopped me.

"What are you doing?" I asked. "I want to ask her why she did what she did."

"She will say anything to get out of this," Genia sighed. Her purple eyes were narrowing on me. When I tried to read her thoughts, it felt as though there was a wall up in her mind. Something in this room was keeping her thoughts from me. "We shall punish her for her rebellion against you, queen."

I flicked my wrist up and froze everyone but Della and Lyra. Lyra was hysterical as she realized everyone was frozen but her. I pulled the gag from her mouth.

"Please don't kill me. It's Genia, not me!"

"It's alright," I assured her. "I already know."

"You do?" She stopped crying.

I nodded and sighed heavily. What in the fuck was going on?

"Why is she doing this?"

"She lied to you when you came here. She had Yerma under a blood possession and was controlling her for years," Lyra stated. My mind flashed to when I saw Yerma's wound and thought it was infected. It was a blood witch mark. Fuck. "She's been in control of Yerma since we've been here. She is not letting any of us leave and bound our tongues with magic so we couldn't speak of it."

"But why?"

Lyra swallowed hard and looked away for a moment.

"Genia helped your father kill Bayla. He promised Genia that she could rule the blood witches. Genia and your father..." She glanced away from me.

"Are sleeping together," I said, disgusted.

She nodded.

"Genia had children with him."

I forgot about this. I had been too engrossed with Cassius and my curse. I had brothers.

"It was around the same time your mother was pregnant with you. The children were not powerful like you were, though. The twins were both boys, and male blood witches hardly ever inherit their mother's abilities. It's not impossible, just extremely unlikely. Both of them had elite magic, though. Your father never claimed them, but he did have them living in the castle with him."

My mind raced at this news. What twins were living at the castle with elite magic? Now would be a great time to remember my fucking life. I glanced at Della when she gasped.

"Are you talking about Kaz and Kai?" she asked Lyra.

"Yes."

My ability to breathe seized immediately. My Kaz and Kai, who I thought of as brothers, were my actual brothers. Their smiling faces popped into my mind, and with it, their elite magic marks. Ravens.

"Is Genia a blood witch or a Ravenstone witch?"

"Both; her father was from Ravenstone, and her mother was a blood witch. It's why she can change her eye color to match either coven."

"For fuck's sake." I turned from Lyra and began pacing around. "My father is a fucking slut." I glared at them as I completely lost my mind. "I will lose my shit if the twins are part of this."

"No, Kaz and Kai are nothing like Genia or Luren. They are so much like you. The three of you practically raised one another." Lyra frowned. I saw something in her eyes that reminded me of the way Cassius stared at me.

"Which one do you care for?" I asked. A frown took over her face. "I can see it in your eyes that you are missing one of them."

"Kaz." Tears filled her eyes. "They would never. This is all Genia and Luren. Genia cursed Exile through Yerma to make it seem like she had nothing to do with it just in case you ever came for us. Your father is using Genia for his gains, but she's doing the same."

I closed my eyes tightly and couldn't shake the images of the twins.

"Who else is involved?" I asked.

"Her other son." She shook her head and frowned. "Genia and the King of Kizar had Jesper together. The queen of Kizar couldn't have children, and Genia approached

Halvor and agreed to have an heir. She was hoping it would be a girl so that they would have strong powers, but Jesper was born without any. So, she had twins with your father, hoping that she would be blessed with a girl who was powerful like you. The twins have power but nothing close to what she wanted.

"We didn't know Jesper was her son until recently when he came to talk to her. I'm pretty sure it's why Jesper chased after you so much. Genia said that he needed to marry you because she knew of the prophecy and your powers. If you think your father is power-hungry, then double that, and that's how badly Genia wants everything. The only thing standing in her way is you. She is having Jesper marry Tally so that he can inherit all of Cerithia after the wedding. Genia is planning on killing your entire family."

Well, that pissed me off.

"No one will be killing my family except me," I declared. So Jesper was planning on screwing over my father. I didn't know what was better, my father being the leader of Elloryon or Jesper. "Forgive me, queen, but you made a big mistake when you came here last time. You told Genia she could have the blood witch coven if you died. So now she is betting on that. It's why she had you bring the bloodstone."

"But if I die, I will just go back to Exile."

"No, she is going to force you to give it to Cassius and then kill both of you."

"I need a fucking drink." Della breathed as she started rummaging through the kitchen until she found liquor and popped it open, taking a swig from it. "All of this lying and deceit is disgusting. I can't believe fae haven't become extinct yet."

"Alright... This has been a really fucking long day." I groaned and took the bottle from Della and took a swig to help calm my racing thoughts. "Here is what is going to happen. I'm going to pull you into the courtyard and pretend like I am punishing you, then I will fucking gut Genia. How does that sound to everyone?"

Gods, I kind of wanted Jesper to witness his mother's downfall. But I couldn't risk keeping her prisoner.

"Sounds good." Della and Lyra nodded. First, though, I grabbed Lyra's shirt and pulled it down so I could make sure she didn't have a blood mark. She didn't.

"Sorry, I had to make sure." I frowned at her. "You need to be hysterical when I unfreeze them."

Lyra immediately became hysterical before pausing.

"Let's do this; I want to see Genia get what she has coming to her. I want you to break the curse so Kaz can come home."

I saw Della frown at her words.

I nodded and put the gag in her mouth. When I glanced toward Della, she was frowning at Wisp, who was dark purple. I took a deep breath and got back in position as I unfroze everyone.

"You're right; let's punish her in the courtyard in front of everyone so they know I will not tolerate this." I nodded and wrapped Lyra up in my darkness gently and dragged her outside.

"Witches, everyone come out here now!" I bellowed. Witches poured from their cottages and stared frightened at Lyra. Genia's smile was wicked as I waited for everyone to be gathered. I glanced around at the horrified faces. These poor witches had been under this cruel woman's care.

"I want you all to witness what happens to anyone who rebels against me, but mostly who threatens my husband, Cassius."

"Husband!" Genia pretended like she didn't know. I smiled at her. "Sorry, we just didn't know that." She cleared her throat.

"That's right." I smiled as my eyes burned bright red in my fury. Tell me what she is thinking. I demanded my magic. *Stupid whore. Your father was right; you're as dumb as your whore mother. You don't deserve to be queen.*

"Let this be a lesson to each of you to not fuck with me. I will always be two steps ahead of you," I sneered.

Genia's eyes narrowed on me, but before she could do anything, I froze her again. The witches all whispered harshly as I let Lyra go.

"Please stay put if you'd like to witness Genia die; if you don't want to see this, now is your time to go."

I smiled when no one left. I stepped forward with my nails and punctured her above her collarbone before pricking my finger again and dripped blood into her wound. Smiling, I stepped back and unfroze her. Genia was confused at first when Lyra was no longer wrapped in my darkness. She glanced around when she noticed the shift in the air. Her eyes flashed to mine with anger.

"You Crimson whore," she spat at me.

I tossed my viper-handled dagger at her feet.

"Pick up the dagger, Genia, and stay alert for this. I want you to witness what your greed got you."

She bent down and wrapped her hand around the handle. Her eyes were wide with consciousness. Della was watching closely at the show. I smiled brightly at Genia when our eyes met.

"Before you die, I want you to know that I will make Jesper's death as painful as I can. He will be begging to die before I am done."

"Fuck you!" She tried to spit on me. "Your mother begged me and your father to not kill her. But just know that I made it unbearable for her."

My eyes flashed red, and my blood witch marks glowed brightly, illuminating the area around me. My magic escaped me and created a storm-like cloud above me. It crackled and popped like it had in Brim's home.

"Cut out your tongue, Genia," I demanded.

She was shaking her head as if she could stop my direction, but in the end, she couldn't. Genia cried loudly as she cut her tongue out. I walked around her, wanting to cause her immense pain.

"Cut off your left hand." I instructed her. She was sobbing but immediately started sawing her hand off at the wrist. I watched her closely until her hand hit the ground. I could hear the murmurs of the witches behind me, but I paid no attention to them.

Genia was losing a considerable amount of blood. She would die quickly, but she didn't deserve that. So, I used my fire magic to close up her wounds, making her cry harder.

"I want you to understand that this pain you are feeling right this second will only be a fraction of what Jesper will go through." I smiled at her when she shook her head no. "I'm tired of your existence. Gut yourself," I demanded.

Tears fell from her eyes as she lifted the blade and slid it into her stomach and cried out in pain. My darkness hummed at the sight. Genia slid the blade up toward her neck, her guts spilling in front of her as her eyes stared into mine.

I didn't blink until I saw the light in her eyes vanish for good. Stepping forward, I grabbed my dagger and wiped it on her dress before looking around.

"I apologize that I did not know that Genia was abusing all of you. As your queen, I vow to always protect the coven."

The witches bowed immediately before a cheer spread through them.

"I still have a prophecy to fulfill and a curse to break, so I would appreciate it if you all could stay here until everything is safe."

Their chatter died down, and they began whispering among themselves. Then Lyra stepped forward.

"We would like to witness the prophecy when it happens. Would it be possible to help or even watch?" She smiled.

I laughed.

"I think we can find something for you to do," I agreed before leaving.

CHAPTER 26

THEA

Wisp's bright flames were blinding when I opened my eyes. My gods, I don't think I had ever seen her shining like this. Then she faded, and it wasn't Wisp standing there. My mouth fell open when I realized a man was standing in the shadows. I grabbed a bronze statue and held it up.

"Back the fuck up!" I warned.

"Thea, it's alright," he whispered. "I'm not going to harm you."

The tall man with dark hair and friendly brown eyes emerged from the dark with his hands held up. Relief filled me, but then irritation. He was going to tell me exactly who he was. He said Bayla had sent him, and now I knew that was my dead mother.

"Says the man who magically appeared in my room," I hissed. "A man who refuses to tell me anything about who he is."

He was glowing slightly. He had a pretty gold aura around him that made me think of Petra's glow. He took a step toward me, and I threw the statue at him in a panic. He was much taller than me. Shit, he may be taller than Cassius. The statue went straight through him and hit the wall. My eyes widened as the man pinched the bridge of his nose and exhaled before laughing.

"You're laughing," I scoffed. "Why did that statue go through you and not hurt you?" I asked already knowing why.

"Because I'm already dead," he laughed harder.

"That's funny to you?" I glared.

"It's just that you are so much like your mother. Bayla had told me you were strong-willed, but for fuck's sake, she didn't say you were exactly like her."

A moment later Della appeared in my room, her hands on her hips and glaring at the man.

"You." She narrowed her eyes on him. "Where is she?"

I glanced at Della, confused.

"Ardella, please understand that we aren't trying to be difficult. You know, Bayla, when she wants something, she'll do anything to get it. She needs to see Thea break her curse."

The man looked back at me and smiled. I realized then who he was.

"You're Killian," I whispered.

"It's wonderful to meet you, Thea. You look just like your mother." He smiled at me like I would expect my father to—with pride and care.

"Where is she?" I asked.

His eyes drifted to Della before looking back at me.

"Hiding," his lips twitched when Della scoffed. "She does not want the goddess to force us to move on yet, so she refuses to show herself until absolutely necessary."

He moved toward me and stopped.

"She is close to you, always." He glanced at Della.

"Why can I see you?" I asked.

Della stepped forward.

"It's just like with Petra; you can see souls because I gave you part of mine. This is Killian's soul. When your mother comes out of hiding, she will appear as if she were still living, but with a glow to her as well."

That made sense, I suppose.

"Why are you here?" Della asked him.

"I wanted to make sure that Thea got my vision I sent to her and to make sure she knows it has not changed. Cassius is still going to die."

My gaze snapped up to his. He sent me the vision of Cassius dying. I stepped toward him, and he frowned at me.

"I'm assuming by the devastation on your face that you did get it. Bayla insisted that I send it to you and Brim so that it can be stopped."

"Are you a seer?" I asked.

"No, I was a fae with elite magic. I had the ability to see major events that would alter the lives of those important to me."

His words made my throat tight with emotion.

"I'm important to you," I asked.

Killian stepped forward and smiled.

"You are a part of Bayla, and that makes you invaluable. I have watched you for years, Thea; you are the daughter Bayla and I never had a chance to have. As far as I'm concerned, you are Bayla's daughter and mine. Your father is a total bastard. You are nothing like him and everything like Bayla. Besides your mother, you are the most important woman to me. It is why I had a vision of you; even in death, my magic wants to help you."

Tears filled my eyes as I stared at him. I could feel the sincerity in his words. Killian was everything I would have wished for in a father. I tried to hug him, but I stepped through him.

I turned around and saw him smiling brightly at me.

"A downside to being just a soul is we cannot touch the living. We are so proud of you."

I nodded as the tears streamed silently down my face.

"I have one other motive for coming." He looked at Della before returning his gaze to me. "Your mother has a message for you."

I perked up at this news.

"What is it?" I could hear the excitement in my voice.

"She knows that you are trying to break your curse without Cassius knowing, so perhaps the vision won't come true. She said the answer is simple. Give him the stone as he sleeps."

I opened my mouth to protest that it would not work, but I shut it and looked at Della. Was it really that simple?

"Would that work?"

Della looked at Killian with a perplexing expression.

"Yes, that would work. I don't see why that wouldn't."

Finally, an answer to this madness.

"I must get back to Bayla. We will see you soon, Thea."

"Thank you, Killian. Please tell my mother I said hello."

"I will." He smiled before leaving.

I looked up at Della, who was smiling.

"Your mother and Killian are hard to be upset with when they are so damn helpful," Della laughed.

"I want to go give Cassius the stone right now," I said. Della immediately stopped laughing and stared at me, nodding. "I cannot wait a second longer."

I slipped on my boots and took a deep breath.

"Let's do this." She smiled. It was far into the night, and I knew Cassius would be sleeping soundly like he always was when I visited late, but I was nervous that this wouldn't work.

Clenching the bloodstone tightly, I closed my eyes and pictured Cassius lying in his bed. When my shadows disappeared, I saw him sleeping soundly, and the sight made my chest squeeze with an emotion that was overwhelming.

Wisp was twirling in the corner, her new favorite color of purple. She didn't know what I was here for. Della watched from the corner. Slowly, I crept toward the bed. Cassius lay on his side, his arms stretched out towards the edge of his side of the bed.

His red crown tattoo lay visible, and it filled me with comfort. Maybe because it mirrored the black one I had. Gods, I hoped he was a hard sleeper. Slowly I lifted the bloodstone up so Wisp could see it, and she exploded.

Her purple flames burst into millions of tiny light particles floating through the air before she collected herself.

Her flames flashed dark green, and she twirled so fast through the room that I was thankful that Cassius didn't hear her commotion. It was clear that Wisp was excited. She wouldn't stop flashing a series of colors now. I gave her a small smile before I gently placed the stone in Cassius' hand.

"This is for you, Cassius Valeska," I whispered. "Gods and stars, please let this work," I whispered to myself. The bloodstone glowed bright purple in his hand to the point I worried it would wake him. Then the bloodstone stopped glowing altogether. Disappointment coursed through me. Tears sprang to my eyes as I grabbed the bloodstone from him.

I didn't feel any different. I glanced around, and Della smiled.

"It didn't work," I sighed.

Wisp was still dark green as she stopped twirling around at my words. Disappointment filled me. Cassius moved slightly, and I held my shaky breath.

"Little viper, am I dreaming?" he muttered. His sleepy golden eyes watched me but drifted back to sleep quickly. Emotions were too much.

Shadows wrapped around me, and a moment later I was kneeling in my bedroom. Wisp followed me, still seeming happy. The stone pulsed lightly in my hand as if to remind me that I hadn't broken the curse. I slid it into its hiding spot cut in the side of my mattress. Stupid fucking rock.

As soon as the thought disappeared, I began crying. Lightning cracked through the sky, and thunder boomed loud enough to drown out my sobs.

Wisp floated close to me.

"It was supposed to work," I told her. "It was supposed to break my curse so I could remember. I just want Cassius."

Wisp made an odd noise that had me looking up, but it wasn't Wisp. It was Della smiling brightly at me. Something about her was calming. Wisp twirled around her in a happy dance.

"Thea, you gave Cassius the stone." She smiled.

"It didn't work, Della. I don't feel different."

"Because I haven't given your memories back yet." She helped me off the floor and hugged me tightly. "I'm so fucking happy for you."

When I pulled back, I stared at her.

"So, it did work?"

"Yes, but I need to hear you say you love him and that you chose to forgive what he did."

My heart pounded as I smiled.

"I forgive Cassius for killing and cursing me. I love him more than anything," I cried softly.

She nodded as Wisp moved closer.

"You'll remember everything very soon. It took eight tries, eight long years, but I am so proud of you, Thea. You will still need to complete the prophecy; the realm of Elloryon is counting on you. Just be careful because this time if you die, you do not go back to Exile."

My brows creased as she looked at Wisp and nodded. Wisp's dark purple flames twirled around her, and when they stopped, it was me standing there. The wisp form of me was glowing brightly, but I was in awe of how peaceful I found it.

"It's me," I whispered.

"Wisp was your soul," Della confessed.

Suddenly it made sense why she was always lingering around Cassius. Because my soul loved him.

"Are you ready?"

"What for?"

"To remember."

Her star-colored eyes shined brightly at me. Then my wisp form walked towards me and smiled before she reached out and hugged me. Light exploded around me and shattered into small parts that illuminated like stars. I turned around to watch how beautiful it was. I felt peacefulness envelop me. It was the most beautiful thing I had ever seen. Then I saw Cassius standing in the middle of it, his hand stretched out toward me. Quickly, I went to him. As soon as my hand settled in his, all the lights stopped, and I was lying on the floor of my room in Cerithia, and then it all went dark.

★★☾★★

A bright purple light flashed in my eyes. Shit, that was blinding. As it faded away, I saw Cassius standing in front of me, smiling. He held out his hand for me again, and I took it without hesitation. He pulled me to him for a lingering kiss before pulling back.

"You did so fucking good, little viper."

Then he shoved me back, so I was tumbling through the sky. Darkness and stars surrounded me as I plummeted toward the ground. My hair whipped around me as the ground below me became bigger. Shit... I closed my eyes as I realized I was going to crash into it. My eyes cracked open when I didn't feel the wind all around me. I was hovering above the ground, and before I hit it, it stopped me and set me gently on the ground on my knees.

Gods, I felt terrible. My chest burned and ached with agony. My breathing was short, and I couldn't catch my breath. Where is Cassius? I wanted to be with him when

I died. I glanced at the elite fae fighting around me. My father attacked us while Cassius was gone. Sybil and the twins were surrounding me. My brothers.

"Thea!" I heard Cassius' voice boom around me.

Thank the moon.

I glanced around, too weak to move. I saw him moving toward me. He used his shadows to move across the field in a split second. He shot out his shadows to catch me before I fell to the ground. Gods, he was such a good husband. I would miss him until we could be together again, but I would wait an eternity for him.

Cassius was cradling my head. I felt so weak, so confused. His golden eyes took over my view. Why was he crying? Gods, I had fucking missed him. He had only been gone for a couple of days, but it felt like years. Cassius rubbed my hair from my face, sobs escaping him.

"My love," he said, panicked.

"I missed you," I whispered.

"I missed you too," he sobbed, but I wasn't sure why he was so sad.

"I love you so much."

Cassius leaned forward and kissed me. He lifted my viper handle dagger up as he spoke the words, "I love you more than anything. Please forgive me." Then he stabbed that *dagger straight into my heart, and all the pain and agony disappeared for the first time in years. I felt free.*

The memories plagued me so quickly at first. My childhood whipped past me in a blur, but then my memories slowed down when I met Cassius. Every word, every kiss, every touch played out in my mind. I watched it all in wonderment. How could I have forgotten a love like this? Our wedding played in front of my eyes, and the relentless ache of missing him filled my chest. How could I forget him or us?

Cassius was my husband. My mate. My fated mate, destined from the stars and made specifically for me to love. There was a pit in my chest as I watched it all. The trials, our life, my life now. I missed Cassius terribly.

But then a series of memories hit me that weren't my own. Cassius is lying in bed crying, begging the stars for me back. Cassius stared at portraits of him and me. Then it showed me staring at him like he was a stranger. I was seeing life through the eyes of Wisp, of my soul. My chest ached as I watched her look after Cassius and how distraught he was.

Stars, he didn't leave our bed for months when I died. He looked so lost and confused that I couldn't help the guilt that formed in my chest. He was so lonely—so hurt.

The next memories were Exile, followed by the trials. I watched myself die in the trials over and over. I watched Cassius staring at me like he loved me, and I looked at him like a stranger.

My mind raced with moments of my life I thought I would never remember again. Things I had prayed to remember over the years. Now they were back, and I realized how much I had been missing. All these precious moments with Cassius that had been forgotten. It would have been a horrible fate to forget these memories.

Cassius flashed through my mind like my curse knew how badly I wanted to remember him the most. Then everything went dark. I wanted Cassius to come back.

Slowly, voices started to penetrate the darkness. At first, I thought they were part of the memories, but then I realized that they were happening in real life. Part of me wanted to stay in this beautiful place and watch Cassius and me forever.

"Is she fucking dead yet?" Gwyn snapped. "We had all the healers we know come and look at her, and they can't find anything wrong with her."

"Gwyn, shut the fuck up," Jesper snapped. His voice made memories of him beating me break through the peaceful darkness I was suspended in.

I wanted to wake up. I didn't want to remember this. Sitting up quickly, I gasped loudly; everyone gathered around me as I lay in my bed, jumped and gasped.

"Fuck!" my father yelled as he straightened his ridiculous crown on top of his head. They all stared at me as I glanced around. It felt as if I was still dreaming, but I knew I wasn't. "Thea?"

I shook my head and stared at them before looking down at my arms. My marriage bond drew my attention, and I instantly felt like my chest would cave in on how much I wanted to see Cassius.

"Why are you all watching me sleep?" I glanced up at them.

Gwyn scoffed, and I ignored her.

"Sleep?" Jesper looked confused. "You've been passed out for ten days."

My memories felt like minutes to replay in front of my eyes, but in reality, it took days. Shaking my head, I tried to seem confused.

"I don't understand." I lied.

"We don't either." My father frowned. "We found you on the floor. Do you feel alright?"

I moved my stiff body but then nodded.

"Fine, although I feel tired. I don't remember feeling sick."

They all looked at each other, wondering what the fuck was going on, but they would never suspect what I had done. My family and Jesper had always underestimated me, and I never thought I would be happy about it, but I was in this moment.

"I'd like to shower and eat."

"Right, we will have the kitchen make food. It will be in the great room." My father nodded, and they all left wondering what the fuck happened.

As soon as the door shut, I smiled. My body was sore and stiff from being in bed for so long, but a hot bath would cure that.

Instinctively, I looked around for Wisp but remembered it was me. A new sense of happiness coursed through me. I knew I needed to plan how to fulfill the prophecy so that I could be with Cassius. My heart ached as I stepped into the scalding bath. Cassius watched me die over and over. He had to be so lost each time that happened.

How could he be so strong when I looked at him like I didn't know him? Like he was my enemy when he had never truly been.

I got out of the bath and stared at my clothing options. Disgust filled me as I put on my blue captain uniform. Taking a moment, I tried to get into the headspace to face the fae I hated the most in this realm. My behavior and words had to continue to be confused.

Taking a deep breath, I headed for the great room. They were all waiting for me like they fucking cared for me. The smell of the food filled the room, and I hurried to the seat at the end of the table away from them all. I ate like a starved man. Manners and politeness went straight out the window as I devoured everything in sight.

"Breathe before you choke," my father sighed.

I nodded and slowed down.

"So, what did I miss while I was sleeping?"

"Nothing." Jesper watched me. "But we have decided to attack Crimson."

I nodded because if I didn't, my magic would explode from me. My darkness begged to snap their fucking necks to protect what was mine.

"When should the men and I head out?" I didn't look at them because I worried they would see the anger in my eyes. So, I stared at my plate as I ate.

"Tonight," Gwyn spoke.

I glanced up at her. Tell me what she's thinking.

You need to be away from us as much as possible.

"That soon?" I questioned. Did they forget that I had been practically dead for ten days? My father looked me straight in the eyes.

"Yes, you need to break your curse and kill Cassius and all of Crimson's bloodline."

Verenna, Cassius, Rylan, Cassius's mother, Hatta, and the twin boys Sav and Tal popped into my mind. My family. Anger coursed through me, but I refused to let it show.

"Yes, it would be nice to remember," I answered. "I will prepare the men after I eat, and we will leave so we can arrive at nightfall tomorrow."

"Good." My father gave me a smile I knew was reserved for only me. A fake smile that was supposed to make me feel happy, but hatred filled me. I couldn't wait for the day I plunged my dagger into my father's heart. In the name of Crimson, in the name of my mother.

I hurried to eat because the tension was odd in the room as they all stared at me. I excused myself and headed to the training fields, excited to see Cassius soon, even if it was only in battle.

CHAPTER 27

CASSIUS

I had been in these damn woods for two days watching Thea and her men. Why were they out here? Luren had requested a meeting with me and my father for tomorrow, but Thea had been here for two or three days. The hair on the back of my neck stood up when I sensed her close to me. We hadn't seen each other in too long. She had been avoiding me since the incident with Flora. Della hadn't come around either. Wisp was missing.

Did she know that I had been out here every day and night watching her? I knew something happened when she saw Flora; something had scared her, and she acted mad at me. But why was she not visiting me anymore? I was worried. Something was going on, and she wasn't telling me. Did her father say or do something?

I saw her walk out of her tent and glance around the woods. It sent my chest into a frenzy. I wanted her to stop hiding from me. She walked the perimeter of her camp, stopping to glance into the woods where I was standing. She had to know I was here. I was never good at hiding from Thea. She was always able to see me.

She disappeared behind a tent, and I didn't see her emerge. I sent urgency through our bond, hoping that she wouldn't ignore it and come find me. My eyes lingered where she disappeared, but I didn't see her again. Damn it. I ran my fingers through my hair and sighed heavily.

"It's rude to stare," Thea's voice came from behind me.

I turned and saw she had her dagger out. But gods above, the moment Thea's eyes met mine, I felt like I was home. Like my heart and mind found what we had been missing for years.

"Little viper, how did you know I was here?" My eyes dragged over her. Gods, something about her seemed different.

"That's not important. What is important is that I found you." She gave me a glare that was not full of anger. I felt relieved; she wasn't upset with me.

Fuck, I had missed her so damn much. I took a step forward, not worried that she was holding a dagger at me. Her cheeks heated immediately when our eyes connected. Something lurked in their depths. Something familiar and comforting. Something that I hadn't seen for years. My heart raced as I stared at her.

"Blushing for me, my love?"

"Fight me," she demanded. "If you win, I'll let you go."

"And if I lose?" I smiled.

"I'll decide what I'll do with you."

Something about her words made my eyes flash black, and lust pumped through me. I charged at her, not giving her any time to think. My daggers were quick and unforgiving. She matched my every move unintentionally. I watched her readjust her stance and smile.

"You've been practicing."

"No, I was taking it easy on you before." She shook her head.

I laughed softly. She was flirting with me.

"Little viper, I knew you were letting me win so I'd kiss you." Her eyes shined playfully. "If I win, I want another kiss too."

"You won't win."

It didn't matter who won. We both knew what the other wanted for a prize. Thea kicked up her strikes. She was determined to win, and I would let her. Our daggers locked in an 'X' in front of us, pulling our bodies close. My eyes dropped to her mouth, but before I could kiss her, she leaned forward and pressed her lips to mine. Shit. It caught me off guard enough that she pulled back and kicked my chest, making me tumble away from her.

Gods, she was looking at me with no confusion or concern. Her guard was completely down. I paused for a moment. Thea looked at me like she did before she was cursed. Her big green eyes glanced over me as I stood staring at her.

"Couldn't wait to kiss me? You missed me that much, Thea?" I smiled.

"I was just distracting you." Her lie made my smile widen. I could feel her lust in our marriage bond. She was barely keeping herself in check.

I nodded as I rushed her again. This advance caught her off guard. One misstep and she was lying flat on her back with me on top of her, holding my dagger to her throat.

"Dead," I smiled triumphantly.

"Fuck," she breathed because this was too much. Our emotions barreled down the bonds, making both of us freeze. There was no mistaking how we were both feeling.

Her eyes traced over my face like she missed me. It was too much to watch. Thea's fire magic exploded out of her without permission and swarmed around us, making a shield from anyone who might come near us. I stared at her as she lifted her hands to pull me to her mouth. Then she kissed me like a starved woman. A deep moan escaped me as I deepened the kiss. Thea's body molded to mine as

I adjusted my body, so I was settled between her legs. My tongue dominated hers as she pushed her hips into mine. A moan left her, and I pressed harder against her, desperate to hear those noises she made for me.

"Cassius," she breathed as I pulled away from her mouth. My hand gripped her throat firmly so she couldn't move as my mouth crushed into hers again. Thea's hands ran through my hair as my hips rolled into hers.

Gods, I couldn't stop this. I needed her. My hands reached between us, and I undid my trousers as she pulled back and yanked her own trousers down. She only got one of her legs freed before she gave up on it. I sank into her with one hard thrust.

"Fuck," we muttered together.

She rolled her hips up to mine, and it was all the motivation I needed to take control. Her mouth seared mine with a consuming kiss before she pulled back. I rested on his hands so I could watch her face and sear this moment into my memory forever.

"Cassius, please."

"Tell me what you need, Thea; use your words," I demanded with a circle of my hips, and the motion made her eyes flutter shut and moan loudly into a mix of shadows and fire mist around us.

"Gods, I fucking love those noises you make for me," I groaned.

This was too much, but I didn't want it to end. I wanted to savor it and stay here with her forever.

"More, my love. I want to hear how much you like fucking me."

"Cassius," she moaned, but I cut off her sentence with another kiss.

"You're mine," I declared. "I can't wait for the day you remember. You feel how fucking perfect we are for each other, don't you? How much we belong together." My words made longing and lust pump through our bonds. "You can keep pretending like it doesn't consume you too," I whispered as my hips pounded into her without slowing. My hand came up and gripped her jaw tightly, so she was looking at me. My thumb rubbed over her red lips roughly, and she opened her mouth and bit my thumb. My moan was possessive, as I lost all ability to draw this out.

"One day you'll remember how hopelessly in love with you I am. How each breath I take is for you. How you possess me every waking moment."

I sent images of me on my knees in front of her down the bond, and she gripped my hips tighter with her legs. I swallowed down her moans, but then she pulled away.

"Wait... stop," she said frantically.

I immediately stilled and stared at her. Her eyes were wide with uncertainty.

"Shit." She shoved me off of her. "My father is here."

Thea was fixing her clothing but refusing to look at me. I swallowed hard as her grief hit me again.

"Little viper."

When she finally turned slightly towards me, I had already fixed my clothing. She looked terrified, but not of me. It's like she couldn't look at me because she was being reminded of something she didn't want to. I felt it through the bond, grief. But not just missing me grief. This was an all-consuming, devastating sense of losing me. It took my breath away.

"Cassius," she finally answered back.

"What's wrong?" I took a step toward her, but she held up her hand to stop me.

She shook her head as tears fell silently. "I can't tell you."

"You can tell me anything." I tried again.

"I love you." She frowned as if it were the last time we'd see each other.

Before I could respond, she summoned my shadows and wrapped them around her. When they disappeared, she was gone. I wasn't letting this go. I walked close to her camp, determined to go into her tent to confront her, but a commotion startled me as I rounded the corner. Fucking great.

"What are you doing here?" Thea glared at her father and Jesper.

She didn't know that they had called a meeting with Crimson. Why would they lie to her about it? They looked so out of place in her base camp. Their clothes were clean and pristine. Thea was covered in dirt and leaves from me.

"Why are you so filthy?" Jesper asked.

Thea ignored him, and I saw him clench his jaw at her blatant disrespect.

"We came to see how it was going." Her father glanced around as if he expected to see me sitting in camp with her.

"Why? You could get hurt out here." She didn't sound worried. Thea was pissed off.

Jesper scoffed and narrowed his eyes at her.

"You'd probably like that," he snapped.

"You didn't come out here for that, so what the hell do you want?" she demanded.

Jesper sneered toward her before Luren glared him down.

"Has Cassius made an appearance?" Luren asked.

"Of course not."

"Why were you in the woods when we got here?" Jesper stepped forward, and my shadows readied to fuck him up if she tried to hurt her.

"Scouting." She crossed her arms. Glancing over Jesper's shoulder, she stared straight at me. She gave me a small frown.

"It's what you do in a war, Jesper. You go into the woods and look for danger," she spoke to him like he was an idiot.

"Did you see anyone that shouldn't be here?" Luren's question made me smile. She glanced at me and gave me a small smile.

"Yes," she sighed. My heart raced thinking she was about to tell them about me. They both perked up. "Both of you. There is no reason for you two to be here. So, what is going on?"

I sighed, relieved.

"We got word that Cassius was planning on attacking you and killing you. We thought we would check."

These bastards.

"You two thought you would protect me from Cassius?" She laughed. "You are just a distraction to me and my men. I will not spare men to protect you while you lurk around."

"Well, too fucking bad. We were staying to make sure you're doing what you should be." Her father glared.

"Be my guest. Don't cry to me if we get attacked and you get wounded."

They ignored her and walked to the carriages they came in. My eyes were focused on Thea. I couldn't feel her through the bond again. I didn't want to leave her by herself with these two. Especially since they didn't tell her we were meeting tomorrow.

I sat down and watched her father and Jesper demand their tents be set up on either side of hers. Did they think that was going to keep me from sneaking in there? Luren glanced around disgusted when his robes got mud on them. For fuck's sake. It took the men hours to move the tents that were originally next to Thea's and set up Jesper and Luren's. What a waste of energy and time.

Thea kept her mouth shut and watched, uninterested. Thea yawned after eating dinner and stood.

"Going to bed already?" Jesper raised his brow at her.

"Yes, I've been up since first light, and we never know what tomorrow will bring."

"I'm a very light sleeper," Jesper warned. "I will hear if you sneak out, and my guards are stationed outside all night."

"Congratulations," she scoffed and went into her tent.

I used my shadows to head to Crimson to warn my father that Luren and Jesper didn't tell Thea about the meeting. Something was odd about all of this. But just as soon as I went to leave, I felt it—Thea's desire.

My eyes turned back toward her tent. I should leave. But then images of me kissing her and touching her barreled through the bond. I lost any ability to withstand her. My shadows brought me to the foot of her bed.

"Fuck," she whispered as she touched herself.

I knew the moment she sensed me in the tent with her. Her eyes opened, and she went to move her fingers away, but I used my shadows to stop her.

"Don't stop, my love," I whispered. "I want to watch."

Her eyes widened before she circled her fingers around her clit. My breathing was rough as my eyes bounced between her eyes and her hand. Fuck. I undid my trousers and slid them off before tossing my tunic to the side. I kneeled between her legs without touching her.

My hand stroked down my hard length as I watched. Her eyes stared into mine as I moved quicker. Gods, I needed more.

"Tell me what you think about when you touch yourself," I demanded.

"You," she breathed without hesitation.

I smiled.

"I picture all the ways I want you to touch me," she moaned softly when my hand rested on her thigh. "Your mouth devouring me, demanding I cum against it."

"Fuck," I muttered. She always knew what to say to make me lose any semblance of control.

"How good your cock feels filling me and how you know exactly what I need. But mostly I think of all the filthy things you say to me. That's my favorite."

Thea smiled brightly as I let out a long sigh, trying to control my need for her.

"You want to know what I'm thinking about?" I asked. She nodded.

"How good you play with yourself. I like watching you get off thinking about me. I like that I'm going to fuck you until you cum on my tongue and cock tonight with your father and Jesper acting like their presence will keep me from you."

She gasped as my hand ran down her thigh close to where she was playing with herself.

"You're going to be a good girl and not be loud," I demanded. "Jesper will never get to hear your pleasure. Can you do that?"

"Yes."

"Good." I leaned down without warning and licked up her pussy with an appreciative moan. She fisted my hair in her hands and held me there as she rolled her hips into my mouth. Thea's fingers gripped me so tightly, like she worried I would stop, but I wouldn't until she fell apart. I sucked her into my mouth, and she let out the prettiest noise of pleasure.

One of her hands disappeared, and when I looked up, I saw she held it over her mouth. I smiled against her as I shoved her hand away and clamped my shadows around her mouth. She whimpered as I wrapped my arms around her thighs and tugged her roughly against my mouth. She was close, but she was trying to hold out on me.

"Cum on my tongue and I'll fill your needy pussy with what you really want," I promised before sucking her back into my mouth. Thea's body shuddered as she called out behind my shadows as quietly as she could. Her breathing was choppy at best.

I moved quickly and slid into her without warning. Her pretty green eyes stared at me as her mouth hung open with pleasure.

"You know what I think about when I touch myself?" I asked.

Oh fuck, I was going to last two seconds.

"Your eyes," I breathed out. "You look at me as you take everything I give you, and I can see that you still want more. Your greedy eyes demand that I give you all of me."

Thea pulled me down to kiss me. My tongue dominated hers as my hand came up and squeezed her throat.

When I pulled back, I could hardly see through the black haze of my eyes shifting.

"You were made for me. Everything about you is perfect."

"Cassius..."

"Fuck, I love hearing you say my name," I moaned as my hand squeezed tighter and I pounded into her relentlessly.

"Please." She wasn't going to last much longer. When she looked up at me, I nearly came.

"Those eyes right there. Don't you dare look away from me."

"You feel so fucking good, Cassius."

Her eyes were fluttering closed as an orgasm built.

"Eyes on me, Thea, now."

"Fuck."

"You aren't going to be a good girl and keep quiet, are you?" I slowed my thrusts. My shadows burst around us. "There you go, my love; call out to the heavens all you want. No one but me will hear you."

"Cassius," she called out as her orgasm slammed into her. I didn't let up. My hips surged forward as she pulled me to her, rolling her hips to take all the pleasure from me that she could.

"Such a greedy fucking girl," I ground out.

My hips rolled into hers. She was going to cum again with me. Her eyes flashed black, and I smiled down at her. Thea's mouth fell open as small moans escaped her. Fuck, she needed to cum quickly because I was losing it.

"Cum with me." I pulled back and reached down, rubbing her clit. "You can cum again, can't you? That's what you want, isn't it?"

"Yes," she whimpered.

"So fucking beautiful," I groaned as our orgasms erupted at the same time. I buried myself deep inside of her as she clenched around me and came.

Our heavy breathing filled the tent, but my shadows still blocked us from anyone hearing. I kissed her neck as I wrapped my hands around her.

"I really fucking love you," I whispered.

"I love you too," she admitted. I rested on my hands as I glanced down at her. Her eyes looked at me like they used to. Did she break her curse? I wasn't sure how she would have.

"Say it again." I watched her mouth.

"I love you, Cassius Valeska."

My mouth pressed to hers before rolling off her and tugging her against me so I could live in this moment a little longer.

★★☽★★

I wasn't nervous the next morning because my father and I were meeting Jesper and Luren. I was worried that Thea seemed to have no idea that her father proposed a peace treaty with us. What was the point of it now after he had been so adamant against it? It was a trick, no doubt. But would he attack us now or wait until he thought we had our guards down?

My father glanced at me as we approached Luren and Jesper's camp. Our men were waiting in the woods out of sight. Thea would never allow us to get hurt either. My nerves were on high alert when I didn't see Thea standing with them. I glanced around the camp, hoping to see her, but I didn't.

We stopped about 20 feet in front of Luren and Jesper, who had a ridiculous amount of guards behind them. Like I couldn't kill all of them with my shadows within seconds. My eyes met Luren's, and all I thought of was Thea's green eyes. Then I glanced at Jesper and smirked when the image of Thea and I on his throne hit me.

"What are you smiling about?" Jesper hissed.

"It's a secret." I smiled.

Jesper's face reddened in his anger.

"We weren't sure you'd come," Luren spoke.

"If you're offering peace, then of course we would come. We do not want war." My father's voice was clipped. He hated Luren long before Thea and I were ever born. The man had killed his father to take his throne. Besides that, he was a terrible leader. Letting his fae starve and die because he was greedy.

"We—" A loud noise stopped all of us. Luren sighed when he realized what it was. "Thea." He acknowledged her as she walked up to us quickly. Her eyes were full of confusion when she saw me. Her body was tense as she glanced around us like she had no idea what she had just walked into. Her dagger was gripped in her hand, but I was confident it was to kill Jesper and her father if needed. Gods, she looked confused. What did she think was happening?

"What's going on?"

"Prince Cassius and King Rylan came to discuss peace negotiations."

Her eyes met mine.

Why would you offer peace now? What was he doing?

My eyes narrowed on her. Thea wasn't talking, but I could hear her plain as day in my mind. I stared at her as she tensed even more.

Fuck. This is a trick, Cassius. Why are you here? You're in danger by being here.

My body went still, and I couldn't stop staring at my wife as her thoughts flitted through my mind. Her eyes flashed red.

"It's alright, Thea; no need to be upset about it," Luren spoke.

Fucking moron, I wasn't upset about that. I hated that he acted as if he knew me.

"We will postpone our war for a year and try to reach a mutual agreement during that time," Jesper proposed.

"Six months." My father countered.

I couldn't even pretend to care about their conversation. We knew this was a ploy. Thea looked up at me, and I saw her flinch. Suddenly an image of me being killed played in my mind. *Cassius will die.*

My heart beat wildly in my chest as more images of me dying played through her mind. I closed my eyes and groaned as the images came in flashes.

"Are you alright?" Jesper asked me.

"Yes." I lied.

"Fine. We will agree to six months," Luren sighed. "It will be nice to focus on the wedding this week instead of wondering if you'll attack."

Thea stilled at this. A flash of her in a dress fighting flittered through my mind. Then it showed me getting hurt and Thea trying to save me, but she was too late.

The fucking wedding. I need to tell Della I know when Cassius is supposed to die.

When she looked at me this time, she didn't look away. I could feel an itch in my mind like she was trying to read my thoughts. But I don't think she could by the frown on her face. I was supposed to die. How did she know this?

"Deal." My father agreed. "We will pull back our troops immediately, and so will you."

"Deal." Luren stuck out his hand, and my father hesitated before shaking his hand back. Thea was staring at me, but I tried not to look at her. Jesper was watching me closely. I tried to read his mind but couldn't. When we were about to leave, I looked at her again. Her hand gripped the dagger in her hand tightly.

I will slice off his fucking head right now if he hurts Cassius. I will burn the whole realm down if my husband is taken from me.

Husband.

I took a small step toward her out of instinct but stopped. I could feel her anger and devastation in our marriage bond. Her eyes were wet with unshed tears as she looked at me.

I need to go to Exile and tell them I broke my curse before the wedding.

Her words rang in my mind.

She broke her curse.

When? How? Why didn't she tell me?

"Cassius?" My father pulled me out of my staring. I glanced at him. "Are you ready?"

"Yes." I glanced at them. "We'll see you at the wedding."

No, don't come to the wedding. You're going to die if you do.

My chest tightened with the sadness in her thoughts. But I wasted no time using my shadows and taking us all back to Crimson. As soon as my shadows disappeared, my father faced me.

"What's wrong?" he asked.

"I need to talk with you, Haden, Leer, and Zade in the throne room."

I didn't wait to see if they were following me. I began walking as fast as I could. My mind was reeling. My hands ran through my hair as I paced around the room. The door shutting jarred me from my racing thoughts.

"For fuck's sake, Cassius, what is wrong?" My father's voice was laced with worry.

"Thea broke her curse."

None of them reacted at first, too shocked to say or do anything. Then they smiled and let out sighs of relief. Haden was the one to notice I wasn't happy.

"Why aren't you smiling about this?" Haden asked, making all of them frown at me.

"She didn't tell me." I frowned. "When we were meeting Luren and Jesper, I heard her thoughts."

"Her thoughts?" Leer asked.

I nodded.

"Thea can read minds. It's a power she picked up somewhere. But when she gives me the stone, I get some of her powers. I guess I have the ability to read her mind, but I can't seem to read others."

"Okay, that's a lot, but why wouldn't she tell you?" Zade asked.

I swallowed hard, looking at my father.

"I think she's protecting me. She's having visions that I am going to die at the wedding."

The room fell completely silent. I couldn't hear anyone take a breath.

"What the fuck do you mean?" Haden asked angrily.

"She showed me images of me dying over and over again. She always tried to save me, but she couldn't. Thea doesn't want me to go to the wedding. So, I'm not going."

Haden began pacing back and forth. He was pissed.

"She's obviously keeping this secret because she thinks it will protect me."

"How long ago did she break her curse? And how did she do it without giving you the damn stone?" Haden questioned me like I knew the answers.

"I don't know when. But she had to give me the stone at some point. It is the only way to break the curse. Maybe she used illusion magic to disguise it as something else. I have no fucking clue; it's Thea. She is clever and smart. With her, anything is possible."

A new sense of longing hit me. Thea could remember me, her, and us and couldn't even celebrate it with me. Is this why she had been hiding? A war stormed inside of me. I was so damn proud of her, but now I knew if she died, I would lose her for good.

"Are you going to tell her that you know?" Leer asked.

"No." I frowned. "Thea has gone to lengths to make sure I didn't know, and I trust that she is doing it for our safety. Della knows too, which explains why she was being weird. They obviously think it's the best course of action, and I'm not going to question my wife."

"I can ask Ardella what is going on," Haden offered.

"No. Let's not tip them off that I know. Thea is stressed out about this."

If Thea was worried I was going to die, then I would stay away from the wedding.

Chapter 28

Thea

When my shadows moved away, Exile stood in front of me. It had been two days since my father called for a peace treaty with Crimson, and I was running out of time.

The shambled buildings and hot, sticky nighttime air felt like home when I glanced around. Emotions bubbled up as I glanced at the prison I lived in for years. My plan was almost in motion, so it was a good time to tell Sybil and everyone that I did it and soon they'd be able to go home. I gripped my bloodstone tightly in my hand, calling out to Lyra to come to me.

Slowly, I walked toward the town square, where Fallon held so many meetings. My heart was wild in my chest as I rang the bell. Excited anticipation coursed through me as I waited impatiently for everyone to arrive. Fae started spilling from their homes and towards where I stood.

Gods, I didn't realize that many of us survived. The number seemed off, like it was at least double what it was when I left.

They all stared at me with a sense of sadness, and I realized they thought I had died again. Sybil and the twins rushed to me, but I held up my hand.

"Hello everyone," I yelled out to them. "I've come to share some exciting news with all of you." I smiled at the crowd. "I broke—" My words died on my tongue when I saw her. The woman with her small child. The hair on my neck stood up as confusion hit me like an arrow. The mother with her small son, who begged me for food, stood in the crowd. Her son was holding onto the blanket I had stolen—the one I buried with them. They had died. Why were they here?

My eyes frantically flickered through the faces in the crowd. The man I had killed to protect Sybil in our home, whose eyes were white and possessed-looking, stared at me. The couple next to him made my chest tight with uncertainty. The woman who clung to her dead husband and took her own life was watching me. Was I in a dream? My focus moved back to the woman and her young son. The boy couldn't have been older than five, but we had been here for eight years. Was that part of Exile—no one aged?

"Thea..." Kaz's sad voice broke through my panic. "It's alright, maybe next time."

"I broke my curse," I spoke to all of them. "How are all of you alive? I watched several of you die. Why do the kids never get older?" Something was wrong.

Their faces looked sad and devastated even when I called them out. Part of me had expected anger because this was some sort of trick. I stepped backward as if that would protect me from what they would say to me.

"Thea, we can explain." Fallon was the one to talk first.

"I'll talk to her." Sybil stepped forward and grabbed my hand in a comforting way. "She deserves to hear it from me and the boys."

Fear gripped me.

"Why is no one happy? You all get to go home and live a normal life."

I was blabbering on, but my mind was not making sense. They all stared at me, and I felt a crushing sadness because something was wrong. Maybe I had broken the curse in the wrong way. Maybe I didn't do it, and this was all a sick and twisted dream.

I pulled my hand from Sybil's, worried that something bad was going to happen. No one left; they all watched as I sank down to sit on the makeshift stage. Sybil kneeled in front of me, tears already gathered in her pretty blue eyes. The twins each stood to one side of me like I might bolt.

"You did so good, Thea. We are so proud of you." She started.

They didn't look proud of me. No, they looked devastated.

"You're right, you did watch some of these fae die." Her eyes closed tightly, like it pained her to tell me what she needed to.

"I'm so sorry, Thea. I wish things could have been different, but they aren't, and now we can all move on."

Confusion settled deeper into my mind. My eyes shifted to the light breeze I felt. Della stood by as well, looking somber and heartbroken. Her star-colored eyes filled with guilt when she saw me.

"Why are you here?" I demanded an answer.

"It's alright, Thea; she is here for us," Sybil whispered.

Here for us.

"What the fuck does that mean?" I stood up. My emotions couldn't be held in as my fire mist exploded and twisted around me in an angry vortex.

"We all died." Kai was the one to finally say it.

My fire died immediately, and my darkness clawed its way up. The swirls on my skin glowed so damn bright it hurt my black eyes to see it.

"No," I said. "You aren't dead. You can't be dead." I started crying uncontrollably. Did I let them run out of food and supplies?

"Yes, we are. We died the day you were cursed." Kaz frowned at me. "You don't remember because you were dead too. Cassius was bargaining for you back. He doesn't know that we had been killed."

"You've been dead this whole time." My father was right. Sybil and the twins and everyone were dead. "Why didn't you tell me!"

"We couldn't." Sybil shook away her tears. "You needed a reason to fight, a reason to break your curse because you couldn't remember Cassius. But it was like we didn't have all of our memories either, or some of them twisted to make a different version of what happened. We didn't remember we were dead until Cassius saved us last year, and we couldn't tell you."

Ardella moved forward, and I wanted to spit at her for taking them from me. These fae had been my family for eight years. Sybil and the twins were my family long before that. When I had no one in Cerithia, it was them who saved me.

"Thea, that day in the clearing, Cassius and I made that deal to save your soul. My brother put all of these stupid rules in place, including you being kept in Exile. All of these fae you see asked to stay until you broke your curse. To make this better for you, so you weren't so lonely. I granted that to them because they felt like they owed you for saving them." Ardella's voice was still peaceful. My anger was slowly turning into a consuming grief.

"I didn't save them if they are all dead!" The ground shook with my devastation.

"You saved us from our father." Kaz squeezed my hand. "You risked everything to save us. Our father had all of us locked away in Cerithia, and he was planning to execute us, but you and Cassius stormed Cerithia and freed us. You did save us."

I looked over all the fae standing in front of me, watching me with a deep sense of sadness.

"When we first got to Exile, we couldn't remember anything that happened right before we got here. Our memories were gone too. It wasn't until Cassius came and made us leave Exile last year that we remembered. We didn't know that we were dead until a few days after leaving here, but we couldn't tell you. The curse prevented us from saying that, and we didn't rremember details of how everything happened," Sybil sobbed loudly to me. "Cassius could see us because Della allowed him to, to make sure you didn't find out until necessary."

My eyes squeezed tightly as tears streamed down my face. I shook my head as if that would make all of their words untrue.

"You once asked me who the other wisps were, and I lied," Della confessed. "It was them." Her hand swept around to all the elite magic fae watching us.

My head turned slowly as I stared at all of them. A sense of pride filled me. Slowly, they all shifted to wisp forms in front of my eyes. All around me, a rainbow of glowing orbs softly lit the night with a myriad of colors. Their lights pulsed gently, filling me with a sense of love before shifting back to their normal fae bodies.

"They protected you as much as they could," Ardella said, frowning down at me. "I wish I did not need to take them, but I simply cannot let them stay."

My eyes stung with deep emotion as I stood up and hugged Sybil and the twins tightly to me. How was I supposed to let them go? Sybil was like a mother, and the twins were my best friends...brothers. They turned towards Ardella.

"May we stay and talk to Thea for a little longer?" Kai asked. Ardella smiled and nodded.

Most of the fae shuffled into a guard formation. In the blink of an eye, all of the adults flashed in their crimson uniforms and saluted me.

"It was an honor to serve you in life and death, Captain Thea Valeska," Fallon called out, and they all smiled at me as I saluted them, and then they were all gone. Tears spilled from me as shock was coursing through me.

"Here, sit." Kaz helped me find my seat on the makeshift stage. Ardella stood there with them. At first, no one said anything.

"I don't want you guys to go," I sobbed. "You guys are my family."

"We wish we could stay too, but this is the way it has to be." Sybil gave me a sad smile. "We need to tell you what happened. It's part of the reason for your prophecy."

I nodded.

"Cassius tried desperately to help break the binding on your magic that your mother did when you were a child. He was so scared of losing you, so he said he was going to find the seer that foretold your prophecy. Cerithia had not made an attack for months, so we didn't expect them to while he was gone." Her eyes glazed over like she was reliving that day. "We were all living in Crimson by then, most of us as guards. You came and saved us when you realized what your father had been doing."

"You gathered all of us and brought us to Crimson," Kai began to speak. I nodded because I remembered that.

"Cassius had been gone for days when you insisted on going outside. You said something was wrong," Sybil said. Flashes of that morning started coming back to me. "When we got out there, Cerithia had already advanced on the castle. We still don't know how they got there without detection. But you immediately started fighting, and we tried to protect you." Sybil's voice was wavering.

"Cassius showed up right as your magic was about to kill you off for good. He said he knew what to do. So, we protected you two as you lay in the castle grounds. Then he stabbed you, and your magic exploded from you. We all went flying at the force of it. When we woke up, your father had already had us locked up."

"How?" They had elite magic.

"He used a witch that had been a rival of your mother."

"Our mother helped him," Kaz frowned.

"Don't worry, I made sure your mother suffered in death." My eyes flashed red as my brothers looked proud of me.

"They killed us all with a simple swipe of their hands. They couldn't get to you because Cassius and the gods were there. When Ardella realized we were all dead, she offered us a place with you or the option to move on. It was clear we chose you, always would." Kaz smiled.

Rage consumed me. My father had killed them all and tried to kill me. Shaking my head, I tried to control the darkness clawing its way out of me.

"Don't." Kaz grabbed my hand. "It's time to stop holding it in and let your powers all the way out, Thea. Then I want you to go and make them pay for what they took from us."

I nodded. Taking a deep breath, I closed my eyes and stopped trying to push the dark back inside. *Finally, it* whispered as I let it slither its way out of me. It turned and twisted up and around me, clawing its way into every part of me, and as it did, power surged through me. It rippled in waves around me, and there was no way to force it back inside of me now that it was free.

Sybil and the twins smiled at me when I glanced at them. My clothing had all turned black, and I had constant ribbons of darkness floating around me. My vision pulsed black. My veins were black under my pale skin.

"You have some work to do." Sybil smiled fondly at me. "It's our time to go."

"B-but Atticus, I promised him I would get you out and home to him."

Ardella stepped forward as Sybil's eyes filled with tears. I would have to tell him that she died years ago.

"Atticus is waiting for you, Sybil." Ardella smiled. "He did not want to live without you."

Sybil burst into tears at this news.

"But how did he know?" I asked. "I spoke to him not that long ago."

Della frowned at me.

"That was not Atticus you were talking to in the forest." Then who the fuck was it? "That little boy had illusion magic, and Cassius paid him to make him look like Atticus so he could talk to you. He thought you hated him for killing you and wanted to speak with you but didn't want to upset you."

"Clever boy," Sybil laughed. "I cannot wait to see Atticus," she muttered as she glanced at Ardella.

"We should go." Kaz frowned, and all I could think of was Lyra. Just then she appeared a short distance away.

"Wait," I whispered. Lyra was going to be devastated. Now with my memories back, I could remember how much she and Kaz loved each other. Kaz glanced at me oddly, but then turned when he heard Lyra.

"Kaz?" she whispered.

His chest seized when he saw her.

"Lyra." He ran at her, picked her up, and hugged her. I frowned as he kissed her, and she sobbed with happiness because she didn't know that it was goodbye. Kaz held her face as she talked and cried.

I couldn't hear what he said to her, but I didn't need to because a cry tore from her as she fell to her knees, screaming as if her heart had been ripped from her. Tears fell down my face as I watched him sink to his knees in front of her as she begged him not to leave her again.

I turned from them to give them privacy. Sybil hugged me first, then Kai. What did you say to someone for the last time? No words came to me, and I felt stupid for not knowing what to say.

Kai stepped forward and hugged me tightly again, giving me a kiss on the top of my head.

"Love you, sis," he whispered, but I could hear him crying. "I wish I could watch you make Cerithia pay for what they've done. Maybe we will get to know each other in another life." He pulled back and gave me his handsome smile once more.

"I love you too." I cried as he started to disappear. "I wish you didn't have to go."

He smiled. "Tell Cassius I said bye, and thanks for taking care of you." Kai took two steps backward from me and disappeared, and it was a knife through my chest.

Sybil smiled brightly and hugged me so tightly I thought she'd crack my ribs.

"You were never sick." I looked her over. She frowned and shook her head no.

"You needed a reason to leave and find a way to break the curse. I really did think I was, until Cassius saved us. I realized it was one of the memories that was twisted to make sense of everything."

"I'm sorry I was such a stubborn shit," I laughed softly as I cried.

Sybil laughed too and hugged me again.

"It was an honor to have known you, to call you a friend, family." She smiled. "You will do great things, Thea. Make sure you give Cassius a hug for me and keep that boy in line. He loves you so much, so I don't worry about you. He will take care of you with everything he has."

"I know. I love you, Sybil. I'll make my father and Jesper pay." I promised.

She squeezed my hand once more before stepping backward towards Ardella and disappearing.

When I turned to Kaz and Lyra, she was sobbing into his chest as he cried. A moment later he kissed her and grabbed her hand, walking over to where I stood.

"Thank you for letting me say goodbye to Lyra." His eyes found mine, and I nodded. He stepped forward and hugged me tightly. "Give them hell, Thea." Kaz smiled and gave me a kiss on the head like a big brother. He squeezed me in another hug, like he couldn't help himself. "And live for all of us."

"I promise."

He turned to Lyra, who shook her head and begged him not to go.

"I love you." He smiled at her as he wiped the tear from her cheek.

"I love you too." She cried.

He kissed her again and stepped away from her.

"Please, take me with you," she begged Ardella. "I do not want to be without him."

"Lyra, no." Kaz frowned. "You have a long life ahead of you."

"It means nothing without you!" Her voice was unwavering. "I have lived eight years alone, and I do not want to spend another without you. I want to go to the next life with you. Please, Kaz, you are my mate. Life doesn't feel good without you."

Mate. I didn't know they were mated.

Kaz cried silently as she broke apart in front of him.

"If you wish to go with him, I will take you," Ardella said.

"Lyra..." Kaz whispered, but she stood and hugged him tightly, kissing him.

"I'm going." She smiled. Lyra turned to me and bowed before hugging me. "I am sorry, Thea, but I cannot live without him."

I nodded because I understood.

"I hope our souls cross paths again." I smiled at them.

Lyra grabbed Kaz's hand, and they walked forward together, disappearing.

Della frowned at me.

"I am sorry that I didn't tell you." She looked so guilty, but I understood. I wouldn't have fought so hard to leave.

"I'm not angry with you; I'm angry at my father."

She smiled at me before she disappeared. I stood alone in Exile, and it felt so wrong. All my memories of my time here played in my mind, and they only fueled my rage and hatred for my father and Jesper. I hated them with everything I possessed.

I walked to mine and Sybil's home and sat at the table I made us. It was heart-wrenching to know what my own father did to my family. How could he be so cruel? Loud, heartbreaking sobs escaped me as all the memories from Exile crashed around me. I would have spent more time with them. I would have told them how much they meant to me every day if I had known that my time with them was limited. Glancing around the small home I shared with Sybil, I could picture her making bread.

I could picture Kaz and Kai telling me how I could beat their asses in a fight. My throat stung with emotions as the tears seemed never-ending. I didn't know how I could ever move past their loss. I sat in the silence of Exile reminiscing about my years here. Then my darkness dug its claws into me, not relenting. She wanted me to picture all the ways I could kill Cerithia's royal family and Jesper.

My mind raced with all the things I could do to make them pay, and after a long while, I smiled.

Their days were limited, but first I needed to meet with Falgon and Akecia's kings.

CHAPTER 29

THEA

The following day, I started my plan. My father had been watching me closer because my darkness was still not relenting. He demanded to know what was wrong, but I ignored him. I waited until it was far into the night before I paid a visit to Falgon and Akecia.

King Sybrien and King Valor were not impressed when I entered their kingdoms and kidnapped them. They both glared at me like I had lost my fucking mind, and they were right. Each hour that passed after going to Exile, my darkness seemed to get more and more unhinged. They were both sitting in Exile with me now. My magic held them to the chairs in mine and Sybil's home.

"You can scream all you want; no one will hear you." I sighed as I took gags from their mouths. "I'm not going to hurt you."

"Have you lost your fucking mind!" King Valor yelled. "My kingdom will destroy you."

I raised my brow at him because we both knew they wouldn't beat me. He slowly calmed down when I said nothing back. That, and he was loyal to Cassius and Crimson; he would never lay a hand on me.

"Thea, whatever you think you have to do, you don't. I know your father has convinced you that we are your enemy, but we aren't," King Sybrien said calmly. "You saved my wife and I. Why kill us now?"

I smiled at him. It was hard not to because he and his wife were such good friends with Cassius and I.

"I'm not going to hurt you," I said again. "I will release you if you promise to sit and talk with me."

They looked at one another before nodding. I released them, and they both stayed seated. King Sybrien's white hair practically shined in the darkness of Exile. King Valor's red hair reminded me of my fire.

"I'm sorry I... kidnapped you, but this is important, and I needed to speak to both of you together. Before the wedding."

They stared at me confused before Sybrien spoke.

"Your father doesn't know you are speaking to us."

"No."

I turned and sat in another chair I had dragged in here. Gods, I probably looked psychotic. I had startled myself when I returned after Della took elite fae from Exile. My eyes were solid black, with my darkness running in my blood, making my veins black under my pale skin. I was terrifying to behold.

"You have our attention." Valor's curiosity practically shined in his eyes. My darkness could feel the fear radiating off of him, but Sybrien's fear was nonexistent.

"You are aware of my prophecy."

"Yes." They nodded together.

"Good. I'm about to fulfill it."

At this, Sybrien's fear kicked in. Oops, poor choice of words.

"I'm not killing you, Sybrien, or you, Valor. Calm down; I can feel your fear." Sybrien's head tilted at me. Confusion was clear on his face. His dark eyes widened when he stared at me.

"By the stars, Thea, you remember." He stood and walked to me. "When did you break your curse?"

Valor's dark eyes practically popped from his skull.

"I didn't." I lied. "But I know I am going to kill my father and Jesper. I just needed you two to be aware because it will likely happen at the wedding. Does Jesper have any blood relatives?"

"No," Sy sat back down with a frown. I knew him well enough to know that he was suspicious of me. "He was an only child, and both sides of his family had illnesses, so he is the only one left. Why?"

"I wanted to know if I needed to kill anyone before the wedding. Once he marries Tally and I kill them, I will be the sole surviving member of his family, so I will inherit his lands."

Their eyes shined brightly at my words. Our realm would be so much better when they were gone.

"What do you need us for?"

"I needed to warn you about what will happen after Jesper and Tally marry and make sure Cassius stays out of it. And if something happens to me, Sybrien, I need you to give Cassius this." I passed him a letter. At first, he refused to take it, but I shoved it into his hand. "Please."

"Fine." He frowned. "But he will kill me if something happens and I knew of your plan." He was right; Cassius would be completely unhinged.

"I will wait until Tally and Jesper marry. Then I will kill all of them. My father, Gwyn, Jesper, and my half-sisters. By the law, I would then be the only bloodline left for both Cerithia and Kizar. Jesper was the last born of his bloodline, so it would automatically go to me as the last heir. I want to show that Crimson is an ally to Falgon and Akecia, so I want your kingdoms to split Kizar as Crimson's token of wanting peace for good."

They were both silent, and I thought maybe they would refuse. Then Sy and Valor smiled at me.

"Gods be damned, Thea, I can't wait to see this," Valor chuckled. "You have a fucking deal."

"I'm always on your side." Sybrien smiled. "Crimson is going to the wedding, but it was mostly to see you. I will make sure Cassius does not intervene."

I hesitated. *Cassius will die.*

"Thank you. I'm sorry I had to take you in the night. I just didn't want anyone to see us meet. But I want you all to know that my father is scheming something, so be on alert."

Valor's dark eyes glanced around the shambled house.

"Where are we?"

"In Exile." I frowned. "Let's get you both back home before someone notices."

They both stood, and I let shadows swarm around us and take us all back to their kingdoms. Valor was the first stop, then Sybrien. I went to leave, but Sybrien stopped me.

"Cassius will be so proud of you, Thea. He has been a mess without you, and he never stopped trying to get you back."

"I know." I smiled. "I'm very lucky. How have you been feeling?" Shit. I wasn't supposed to remember that he had been sick.

"You do remember." He frowned at me. "Why'd you lie?"

"Sy, please, you cannot tell anyone. Especially Cassius."

"He deserves to know." Sy looked at me oddly.

"He'll die if you tell him," I whispered. "A seer told me that Cassius will die if he knows I broke my curse. He will try to save me. You cannot tell him. If you do, he dies."

"Fuck." He ran his hand through his hair. "I promise I won't say anything; if anything, I will try to get him not to intervene."

"Thank you."

He gave me a hug.

"Now how are you and Petra feeling?"

"I'm the healthiest I've ever been. Thank you for saving me. I would've been dead already if you hadn't. And Petra is doing well; she is so excited she already has the baby room decorated," he chuckled.

"I'm glad you're still here. I have to go, but I'll see you in a few days."

Then I disappeared, but I didn't go to Cerithia. Cassius lay in our bed and slept soundly. Gods, how did I get so lucky to have him? I slipped off my boots and cloak. I admired him as he slept. He had always been so breathtaking to look at. I would never understand how I was so lucky to have him.

The stars blessed me with a great life the moment they made him for me. Quietly, I slipped into bed and lay so I was facing him. Slowly, my fingers traced over his warm chest before moving up to his face. Cassius slowly opened his eyes.

"This is a great way to wake up." He smiled as his gaze lingered on me. I gave him a soft smile as his fingers brushed my hair out of my face. Cassius watched me closely before he spoke again. "Is something wrong? "Why is your darkness clinging to you?"

"Everything is fine."

I could tell he wanted to argue, but he gave me a sad smile and nodded. I tried to read his mind, but I couldn't. Cassius' eyes traced over my face slowly, like he was seeing me for the first time in a long time. Fuck, I missed him so much. I couldn't wait to fulfill my prophecy at the wedding and be done with this. I just wanted to be with Cassius.

"I just wanted to see you," I whispered. "I've missed you." I wanted one more time to pretend like everything was fine. When I was near Cassius, it made me feel like nothing could go wrong. His fingers traced over my face as if he were trying to remember everything about me. Could he feel how terrified I was that we may never get a moment like this again?

"I've missed seeing your face every time I wake up," he whispered. Cassius seemed to hesitate before continuing. "No matter what happens in the future, I need you to know that you have been my reason for living. Every breath I take is for you. You have wrecked me in the best of ways, Thea. You have always been my purpose: to make you happy, to make sure you know you are loved. I hope I have done both of those things for you. I hope you never think of me and wonder if I loved you because I would have never been able to exist without loving you. I am *eternally* yours, and *nothing* will ever change that."

Tears streamed down my face because this oddly felt like him saying goodbye to me, but he had no idea what was supposed to happen to him at the wedding. I couldn't help the sob that escaped me as Cassius pulled me against his body and hugged me tightly. The weight of saving him and the realm felt all-consuming.

I did not want to lose him. I did not want to exist without him; I couldn't exist without him. Sobs escaped me as I held him to me tightly, like that would keep him from slipping through my fingers. His hands ran up and down my back as he kissed my head. Cassius held me silently and let me cry.

"I love you," I said softly.

"I know you do, my love, and you know I love you too."

I pulled back and stared into his pretty golden eyes. I tried to read his mind, but I couldn't.

"Why does it feel like you are saying goodbye?" I asked.

"I just want you to know that no matter what, I love you," he said before leaning forward and kissing me. "I know you're keeping something from me." He frowned. I knew he would never guess that I broke my curse. Cassius watched me closely like he was trying to see inside my head. I knew it wasn't fair to keep secrets from him.

I shook my head, but he gave me a sad smile.

"You don't have to tell me. I trust you more than anyone else. But if you think you are doing a good job hiding your sadness from me, you aren't. I can see it when you look at me that you are terrified. So keep your secrets, little viper, because I know you wouldn't keep them unless you absolutely had to."

My marriage bond demanded I tell him what was happening, but I couldn't. Why was he so damn understanding? I was so proud that he was mine. Slowly, I settled back against him. One of my favorite things I used to do with him was lay in bed and tell him how my day was or stories from my childhood. Cassius never seemed annoyed by my constant talking. In fact, he seemed content to just listen to my blabbering. I traced my fingers over his chest, smiling at the memories.

"This is nice," I said. "I feel like I am home when I am close to you."

Cassius' arm squeezed me tighter.

"You feel like home too, my love." After a moment Cassius chuckled softly.

I sat up and smiled at him. "What?"

"I know you don't remember, but you used to talk my ear off every night before bed." His eyes shined brightly. "It was one of my favorite things."

I creased my brows. It was crazy that we were both thinking about that at the same time.

"Well, I have a story for you if you want to hear one." My smile widened when he nodded eagerly. So I told him of when I escaped Exile and found myself back in Cerithia. Then I told him of my scouting trips to Crimson and seeing him for the first time and how something shifted inside of me when I first saw his face. Cassius smiled as he listened to all of it. The more I talked, the more everything else was forgotten. It felt like it did before the curse.

But then I made the mistake of looking Cassius directly in the eyes. My words faded when an image of him dying hit me. I flinched and looked away from him as panic swarmed my chest and made it impossible to breathe. My eyes closed tightly to try and get rid of the image, but it only seemed to get worse. Cassius grabbed me and pulled me to him when he realized I was upset.

"Are you alright?"

"I should go," I said in a panic. I went to slide out of bed, but Cassius stopped me and pulled me back so I was flush against him.

"Stay. Let's have this moment for a little longer. Everything feels normal when you are near me."

"Alright, I'll stay for a little bit." I agreed as I wrapped my arms around him. The scent of rain and forest surrounded me. Cassius' hand ran up and down my back as I tried desperately to memorize how he felt against me: the warmth of his body, his scent, the way his heart beat in a soft rhythm. Cassius turned so he was on his back, and I could rest my head on his chest.

My eyes were heavy as the presence of Cassius being close made me feel safe. I wished I could stay, but when Cassius' hand gradually stopped rubbing my back as he fell asleep, I stayed for only a few more minutes. The longer I stayed, the harder it would be to leave, and I still had things to do.

I sat up slowly, watching Cassius' chest rise and fall in steady breaths, hoping I would never see the day it stilled. Leaning forward, I gave him a chaste kiss and stood, slipping on my boots and cloak. Glancing over my shoulder one last time at Cassius, I stilled when he was staring at me.

"I love you." He smiled.

"I love you too, always."

Quickly, I summoned his shadows and left because if I didn't, I wouldn't be able to. Now that I knew Cassius was fine, I needed to go to one more place. My destination was the blood witches. When I got to the coven, they were all waiting for me. I'm assuming they had felt my urgency to meet with them.

Their eager eyes watched me as I walked into the courtyard, and they all bowed to me. I smiled.

"I broke my curse," I announced.

A gasp spread through them, and I could feel their pride and happiness consume me. They watched me wondering what I called them here for.

"I will be fulfilling the prophecy soon, and I would like you to help me. But first, I'm sure you all have noticed that Lyra is missing." They all nodded and looked worried. "All the fae of Exile were killed, including my brother Kaz, her mate. Lyra chose to go to the next life with him. My father and Genia killed those elite magic fae. They killed my mother."

The witches gasped and all looked up to the moon and muttered something. I was assuming it was a prayer for Lyra and Exile.

"How can we help? We want revenge for Lyra and all elite magic fae, for Bayla." A witch with silky black hair stepped forward.

"I need you all to visit the guards of Kizar and Cerithia and blood mark them."

I swear their red eyes glowed brightly at my demand. They were excited to help me get revenge.

"I know it is unlikely that you can get to all of them, but just get to as many as you can in the next two days. I will summon you to me when I am ready."

"We will do our best." The same witch bowed.

"I know you will. Do not kill any of them, and do not control them until I give you the command."

Their brows furrowed.

"If *we* blood mark them, then you can control them—even though you weren't the witch to mark them because you're the queen."

That was even better.

"Perfect." I smiled. "Start marking them, and I will still summon you when I'm ready to fulfill the prophecy. I have to go; call to me if you need me, and I'll come as soon as I can."

They bowed as my darkness swarmed around me, and I was taken back to the castle.

CHAPTER 30

CASSIUS

The wedding was tomorrow. I had been a wreck since Thea came here last. My marriage bond demanded that we go to her and bring her home. It wanted to take her and lock her in our home so that she could never escape, so we wouldn't lose her. Fear and anxiety gripped me. I had been pacing around our bedroom trying to figure out how I could help her without being in the way. I would die if she did. I could not survive without her.

She was fulfilling the prophecy tomorrow. I wanted to see her do it. Gods, I had waited years for her to kill those who hurt her. Fuck, it was harder to stay away from her than I thought it would be. I needed to protect her. I walked over to our wedding portrait and stared at it. Maybe I should check on her. I slipped on my clothes and summoned my shadows. When they disappeared, I stood in her room in Cerithia. But my anxiety only increased when Thea wasn't in bed. It was late as fuck; where was she? I silently slipped out of her room and crept around the castle, trying to locate her.

When I found her, I was more confused than I had been. Thea was walking down the hallway, where all the guards seemed to be frozen. They didn't move or blink. I stayed still when I saw her walk up to them, yanking down the collar of their uniform before she lifted her fingernail, which was sharp enough to pierce their skin. Then she dripped her own blood into the wound.

She was doing blood possession magic.

I had seen her do it once before.

I wish my father and Jesper knew their ending was coming tomorrow so they could live in fear.

I smiled at her thoughts. Then she started thinking of all the ways she could kill them. She had a lot of ideas. Her darkness burst out of her in a frenzy, probably excited to kill everyone. A moment later, she unfroze the guards but didn't move. She tilted her head like she could hear something. Shit. Hopefully, it wasn't me.

Then she kept walking without looking back at me. I sighed, relieved. She was fine. My marriage bond had calmed down since I had seen her. But a moment later I saw her pause at an open door and look in. Something like shock zipped down our marriage bond.

"Does Tally know you two are fucking each other?" she asked casually. A moment later, Jesper and Mae came from the room, disheveled and looking disgraceful. For fuck's sake, he was sleeping with Mae and Tally?

"What the fuck are you doing here?" Jesper sneered.

"What are you doing here?" Thea smiled back when his face froze with fear. Whatever he saw in Thea's eyes right now scared the shit out of him. Thea just smiled at him.

"Do your parents know that you're sleeping with Jesper?" she asked Mae.

"Fuck you, Thea," she hissed. "No one will believe you, Crimson whore."

I rolled my eyes.

"You really should come up with a better insult than that. I know it's hard for you to think with that pea-sized brain in your head, but do try a little harder." She insulted her. Mae charged at her, and it made Thea's smile widen. Thea changed her stance, getting ready to punch her, but Jesper stopped her.

"She would kick your ass, Mae." He gave her a pointed look.

"Of course, you're sticking up for her!" Mae yelled.

"Fine, go slap her and see what she does, but don't come crying to me when she hurts you," he sighed and dropped her. Mae looked at Thea and took a step forward before she stopped, thinking better of it.

"What's going on?" Gwyn's voice filled the space, and I was actually happy to hear it for once. My smile widened as I watched her reaction.

"I caught your daughter fucking Jesper on the table." Stars, Thea was not beating around the bush with this.

Gwyn's eyes frosted over at this news. Her eyes glanced at Mae with a burning rage.

"Mae, go to bed now," Gwyn snapped. "Disgraceful."

Mae stared at the floor as she rushed from the hallway. Gwyn looked at Jesper and glared.

"You are marrying Tally tomorrow and couldn't keep your dick in your pants the night before your own wedding?" she sneered.

For once, I was on her side. I watched as she walked toward him and slapped him across the face. Jesper's head turned at the impact of it. Shit, Gwyn's slap surprised both me and Thea.

"Gwyn," he started, and she slapped him again.

"If you hurt Tally, I will slit your throat while you sleep." Her voice held a special kind of hatred in it for Jesper. "Get the fuck out of my face," she hissed. Jesper glared at Thea, who just kept smiling at him. I could see her darkness was still clinging to her, which meant she was still worried about something. Gwyn turned to her and was tense.

"Why are you smiling so damn much?"

"Because..." Thea cocked her head to the side and looked directly into Gwyn's eyes. "Your precious Tally will be treated as well as my father treated you in your marriage."

This obviously pissed off Gwyn, who raised her hand and went to slap Thea, but Thea caught Gwyn's wrist and yanked her closer.

"I'll see you tomorrow for the wedding," she spoke as if it were a promise. "You better get some sleep. It's going to be a very long day."

Gwyn watched as Thea disappeared down the hallway and out of sight. Gwyn's face was red with anger when Luren came walking toward her with Jesper in tow. They stood in the hallway for a moment before Jesper spoke.

"She is being odd, Luren. I'm telling you something is not right with her," Jesper pleaded.

"Because she caught you and Mae?" Luren scoffed. "It's Thea; she has always been reactive."

"Jesper's right, dear. The way she talked to us and looked at us was like she used to." Gwyn backed up Jesper.

It was silent for a long moment.

"Maybe we should just kill her and try again after the wedding," Gwyn spoke.

Luren still said nothing. They were suspicious of Thea, and that terrified me.

"What would have happened? We have the stone; it is not possible that she broke her curse, so what are you suggesting?"

"Maybe she is having flashes of memories?" Gwyn whispered.

"Perhaps she knows that we are lying because she saw something. Maybe Cassius got to her," Jesper sighed. "Maybe Gwyn is right; we should kill her and try again. Something is not right."

"We have never been in this position before. I am not going to give up Thea because you two think something is wrong. Besides, after the wedding tomorrow, she will prove her loyalty to us, and if not, then we will start over again."

My brows creased. What would Thea be doing tomorrow at the wedding?

"She always picks Cassius. We shouldn't waste our time. Every year we should be hunting her down and just killing her instead of trying to convince her that we like her." It was Jesper who spoke such cruel words.

"Well, everyone has a weakness, and Thea's is Cassius. We will use it to our advantage. We will not lose."

"Are you sure you still have the stone?" Gwyn was the one who questioned it.

"Yes. Maybe she senses that you all hate her. Try a little harder to get over yourselves, and she'd be kinder to you," he suggested. "After Thea kills the royal families tomorrow, we will kill her, and Genia will take the blood witches, and we will control Elloryon. We have one night; let's not mess this up."

Fuck. They were going to slaughter the royal families tomorrow. Is this what Thea saw in her vision? If it were, I wouldn't be there, and neither would my family, so it would stop the vision from happening.

"I hate that you involved your whore in our business," Gwyn snapped at Luren.

"That's my fucking mother you're insulting." Jesper stepped toward her like he would kill her.

"I owed her after everything that happened. Either she gets something in return, or she makes things worse for us. Besides, having her lead the coven will only work to help serve us and our needs," Luren said, ignoring Jesper.

"What the fuck are you doing?" a guard spoke from beside me. I turned and stared at his angry face. "How did you get in here?"

"I wish you wouldn't have found me," I muttered before I wrapped my shadows around us as my dagger plunged into his heart. When the shadows disappeared, his dead body hit the forest floor. Shit.

I glanced around the woods and sighed heavily at how I had almost been caught. I took a heavy breath as I cleaned off my dagger. I summoned my shadows and went home, but as soon as they disappeared, I was met with a horrific scene.

"There you are." A Kizar guard smiled at me. "We've searched everywhere for you."

I watched my father, mother, and siblings struggling against their binds. My shadows burst out of me and tried to kill the man standing in front of me, but he smiled when I hit some sort of barrier.

"You can't get to me." His smile widened. "I'll trade all of them for you."

"Deal."

As soon as I said it, he lifted his hand, and his magic poured from him, wrapping around me so I couldn't move. My shadows seized around me. I struggled to try and break free when he didn't let my family go.

"Let them go!"

"No." The smug bastard looked around as if he expected to see someone else. "I think we killed all of the guards you had stationed, so there is no one to stop us."

Haden.

Leer.

Zade.

"Are you ready?" The man with long, greasy-looking blonde hair sneered at me. "We have a wedding to attend."

No.

I tried to break free. I couldn't go. But it was no use. I couldn't break free from whatever his magic was. When I wouldn't stop struggling, the man walked up to me and blew white powder in my face. My eyes and nose burned as I felt it coursing through me. It would knock me out in mere seconds, and I would be taken to a wedding where my wife knew I would die. My eyes were heavy, but I refused to give in. I used all of my strength to try and fight the tiredness I was feeling.

All I could think of was Thea living a life without me. She had always been stronger than me—she could live without me if I died—she could still exist if I didn't. If I didn't break free, then Thea would never forgive herself. The guilt would kill her, and I did not want her feeling like she didn't do enough to protect me. So I used everything in me to fight back. My shadows swarmed desperately inside of me trying to save me. One trendil of shadow escaped me and snapped the neck of the closest Kizar guard.

"Control him!" Someone yelled. But I was too focused on trying to kill the other guards to notice any threats. A guard blew more powder into my face, making me call out in pain when it burned violently in my eyes.

"You're quite the fighter." The man in charge smiled before he punched me in the face, making me lose all my fight.

"Thea, I'm sorry," I whispered as if she would hear me. Then everything went black.

CHAPTER 31

THEA

I scanned the guests of the wedding. It was customary for royal families to show up, especially for a wedding between two royal families. My father had come to check on me first thing this morning, which was odd. Then he surprised me with a dress—the one from my damn vision. Cassius was supposed to die today.

My father almost seemed surprised to see me in my room but played it off as making sure I was helping with the wedding. I didn't help, and there had been no plans for me to help, so I knew he was lying. Then Gwyn hovered around me all morning, and if she had to leave, Mae came to watch me.

Something odd was happening.

"Where is Cassius?" Sy asked without moving his lips.

"I assume they aren't coming to the wedding," I responded. Thank the gods and stars. If he stayed away today, then the vision wouldn't come true.

The sun was too hot for an outside wedding, but here we were, cooking in this heat. "My family has been odd all morning."

Sy sighed as his eyes glanced around at the ridiculous amount of fae here. Kizar and Cerithian fae mingled as the ceremony started. I couldn't focus on how ugly Tally's dress was or how Jesper stared at me when he should be focusing on his future wife.

"Well, that's probably for the best. Is the plan still a go?" he asked.

"Yes. I want to be done with this. Don't worry, I have it under control."

As the priestess spoke their vows, I felt an odd chill on my neck. I ignored it until it happened again. My eyes darted around the castle gardens, and I spotted him. Haden. He was hiding in the woods that lined the grounds. My heart stopped when I saw the blood running down from his nose. I turned forward so I wouldn't attract attention. I would slip away as soon as I got a moment.

"What's wrong?" Sy asked.

"Haden is in the woods wounded. He wants me to go to him."

Sy didn't respond at first.

"Well, that can't be a good sign."

"It's not."

A sinking pit formed in my stomach. I couldn't stand not knowing how Cassius was. I wanted to check on him this morning, but my family had hovered around me too much to sneak away.

"Fuck," he sighed as everyone cheered loudly at Tally and Jesper kissing. They were married, which meant my plan was already in play. "I will support you any way I can."

"Tell Valor that it's going to get messy."

Then I followed my family down the aisle like I was supposed to. However, it was easy to sneak away once the fae lined up to give their congratulations to the couple. I slipped from the crowd and headed straight to the woods.

"Haden?"

I didn't see him at first, but then he appeared bloodied more than I had even realized. Haden had a dagger out like he wasn't sure if I was here to kill him.

"Your father had Crimson attacked."

"Fuck," I sighed as my darkness exploded from me. It wanted us to burn everyone alive. "How bad is it?"

I turned to Haden, who stared at me oddly. His dagger fell to his side.

"Aren't you going to ask why I came to you?" he questioned.

I reached forward and healed his wounds.

"No," I sighed. "I was planning on fulfilling my prophecy today. This just pisses me off more."

Haden watched me oddly when I gave him a small smile.

"Cassius was right. You really broke your curse."

My whole body went rigid.

"Cassius knows?" I asked. I could hardly hear anything past my heart pounding in my ears. My vision pulsed red as visions of Cassius hit me over and over again. My throat was closing as fear ran through my veins and squeezed my lungs. I was going to pass the fuck out.

"Yes, he found out the morning he was doing the peace treaty with your father. He could hear your thoughts."

My darkness swarmed around me, making the trees sway in a frenzy. No, this couldn't be fucking happening. I tried everything to keep him safe. He *was* telling me goodbye when I visited him. Tears sprang into my eyes as his words sank into me. Cassius was saying goodbye because he knew that there was a real chance that he didn't make it out of this.

"He knows that you saw him dying today, so he was going to stay away, but Kizar and Cerithia attacked us last night. They are here somewhere."

"My vision is coming true, and I don't know how to stop it, Haden. I could never save him in time in my visions."

I glanced over his shoulder when I saw movement. I grabbed my dagger and held it out before she stepped out. Della held up her hands like she was showing me she wasn't armed. Her eyes immediately flickered to Haden, and I saw sadness and longing in them. Well, this was awkward knowing that he was her fated mate and that he fucking hated her.

"Della?" I dropped my dagger. "What are you doing here?"

"I've been waiting a long time to see you fulfill the prophecy. I didn't want to miss it. Besides, I will be needed once fae start dying." Her gaze wandered back to Haden.

Haden turned to see where she was, but his eyes flickered around like he couldn't see her. I looked at her for an answer.

"Ardella is here?" Haden asked me confused.

"Yes, she's standing right in front of me." I looked at her as she stared openly at him with devastation filling her eyes. "You can't see her?"

"No." He tried to hide the emotions but didn't do it quickly enough.

"He can't hear me either," Della whispered to me.

"Why?" I asked her, and Haden frowned.

"Because he told me that he never wanted to see my face again, and I realized the last time I saw him that he meant it. So, he will never have to see or hear from me again."

I frowned at her and felt my tears well in my eyes for her.

"Della..." I started, but she shook her head.

"What is she saying?" Haden frowned. "You can show yourself to me." He glanced around, but Della didn't appear to him. Haden closed his eyes tightly before turning them to the ground. When he looked back at me, I saw the heartbreak on his face.

"Cassius knows I broke my curse, and my father has him somewhere in the castle," I told her in a hurry.

"The vision..." she started.

"I know. I'm going to go see if I can free him. Will you make sure Haden is safe?"

"I will always make sure he is safe," she frowned.

Haden scoffed even though he couldn't hear her.

"Don't worry, Thea, I can't die." Haden glanced at me, then glared around us to show Della he was pissed off. His eyes held such hate for her. "Right, Ardella?"

She flinched at the use of her full name.

"You aren't the only one that the Goddess of Life cursed."

He snapped towards her, and I could feel her heart breaking from here. He was being cruel to her. "Remind me to ask you about that later," I muttered as I back to the crowd of the wedding guests.

"They have Cassius and the entire Crimson royal family." Haden frowned. "So many guards died. Cassius tried to negotiate his family's release in exchange for himself, but they ended up taking all of them."

Gods above, why was I cursed with such an evil father?

"Did Zade and Leer survive?" I glanced at him. Haden frowned.

"Leer is alright. Zade is wounded badly, but he should be alright."

My chest tightened at this news. My fire burst from me as grief hit me. Why? This would all end today. I would stop all this violence.

"I have to get back, but I will save Cassius and his family. I will kill everyone for Crimson, for Exile, and for my mother," I promised.

Haden and Della looked at me with pride as I turned and went back to the wedding reception. My family hadn't known I disappeared, but all I could think of was how happy they could be as they killed innocent fae.

When a guard found me in the hallway, on my way to find Cassius, he told me that the prisoners had been taken outside. I swallowed hard as I made my way outside but paused when I saw the amount of fae gathered. All I could picture was Cassius being taken from me. He knew.

My heart pounded violently. My hands clenched tightly as I walked toward the crowd slowly as if it were a dream—a nightmare. I didn't know what to expect.

This was not how I was going to do this. I wanted to do it without Cassius near me. He needed to stay out of it. What if they hurt him already? Would I know if Cassius died? I shook the thoughts from my mind.

Fulfill the prophecy. Prophecy. Prophecy. Prophecy.

My darkness was excited. It wanted the blood of every fae that had kept my husband from me. The sun blistered to an uncomfortable heat as I made my way toward my father.

"Thea, my dear, come join me." My father called from beside me. I hurried to him and looked at the arena-like structure I had seen in my vision. Gods, there had to be thousands of fae gathered here. My father must have used magic of some sort to transform it into an arena.

He had been planning this and didn't tell me.

Was he suspicious of me and my loyalties? When I reached my father, he stood with Jesper and the girls. He smiled at me proudly and it pissed me off.

"Father, what is going on?"

He grabbed my hand and squeezed it tightly in his before turning to the crowd.

"Fae of Cerithia and Kizar!" he bellowed. "Today is the day that my dear Thea fulfills her prophecy!"

The crowd went wild. I flinched at the noise. After a moment, my father raised his hands to silence them.

"Father?" I asked softly.

"Thea has tried to break her curse and come back home to us for eight years, but now... we bring her every royal family so that she can end this once and for all!"

All the families.

Just then the crowd of Cerithian guards split, and every royal family member kneeled, bloodied and tied up. My eyes met Sybrien's first before moving to Cassius' family—my family. My darkness burst from me without warning. My father smiled as if I were doing this because I wanted to kill them all. The guards holding Cassius shoved him so forcefully that he fell to the ground in front of the rest of the prisoners.

I took a step forward, ready to beat the shit out of the guard, but stopped. Cassius was kneeling with his family at the center of the royal families. My darkness immediately swarmed around me in angry black wisps of my magic. I'm sure my father thought it was a reaction to seeing Cassius and wanting revenge. But this was pure rage at the sight of my mate bleeding, bound, and looking at me like I would end him.

My eyes pulsed red with my rage. They flickered at each member of my family that was bound. Each one of them was terrified and hurt. Cassius stared at me oddly as if he were trying to tell me something. Tell me what Cassius is thinking, I begged my magic.

I'm sorry.

I could feel the tears sting my eyes.

You will let me die if you have to. You need to save everyone else, even if that means I do not live.

I shook my head no.

You can survive without me, my love. His eyes filled with tears as he stared at me. How could he think I could survive without him? *If something happens to me, it is not your fault. Don't blame yourself. It has been an honor to call you my wife, Thea. You have always been my purpose for living, but this is your destiny. This is your purpose. I love you. I will always be with you.*

Tears gathered in my eyes, and my throat burned as I tried to hold them in. Cassius was wrong. He was my destiny. He was my purpose. Cassius living—having a life with him was all I ever wanted. If he died, I would fulfill the prophecy before I followed him in death. I could never exist where Cassius did not.

"Cassius will be the first to die!" The crowd cheered, pulling me from his thoughts. I would fucking slaughter every single one of them. "And after everything he did to my Thea, she deserves to be the one to kill him and break her curse." He lied through his teeth.

Cassius struggled against his restraints as he glanced at me. My blood witch markings glowed brightly at the sight of him. Darkness clouded my mind as I stood and watched his golden eyes watch me with terror and longing. Fuck, I didn't like feeling his fear. He had never been scared of me before. My chest tightened when the guards I trained yanked up the Crimson family with more force than necessary. I took note of the guards so I could kill them too.

When I turned to Jesper, my family smiled at me. Cassius and his family were brought out to the front of the royal families, who all cried silently, thinking their fates were sealed. They were thrown to the ground, unable to catch themselves because of their bound hands. I took a step towards the guards to kill them but stopped. My father was making an announcement to the common fae who had gathered for the celebration. I heard nothing he said as I focused on Cassius' cut lip and the blood that dripped from it.

"Kill Cassius," my father suddenly demanded of me. Urging me to kill my husband—the last fae I would ever hurt. Cassius would not die today.

I smiled because I was almost done with this. Tonight, I would fall asleep in his bed and sleep soundly, knowing I killed every bastard that tricked me. My left leg took a step, revealing the slit in the dress, pulling my dagger from its hiding place. My viper-handled dagger sat heavy in my hand. My eyes stared at it, realizing that both Cassius and I had been stabbed by this blade, but now I would use it to kill everyone who tried to stop me.

There was no reasoning with me anymore. Everyone here had already sealed their fate. These disgusting fae of Cerithia and Kizar showing up to watch me slaughter innocent royal families. My rage could not be contained. Now their kingdoms would crumble, and I would stand in the rubble with Cassius. Together we would rebuild this realm.

"With pleasure." I smiled at Cassius as I stepped toward him menacingly. His golden eyes watched me, but he did not flinch at my appearance. His fear hit me and made me flinch in disgust with myself. Slowly, I walked around him as if I were inspecting my prey. I stopped when I was behind him, where he kneeled in the dirt.

I leaned down and held the dagger at his throat, my mouth brushing against the shell of his ear. I pulled the gag from his mouth. My eyes found my father, who looked as if he was about to win all of this.

"Any last words?" I asked loudly just for the show. The crowd went wild, but all I could focus on was the way Cassius trembled against me. I grabbed his hair and yanked it back, so his ear was against my mouth and my dagger was sitting at his throat.

Before he could answer, I let my darkness take over. It burst around me without being detected, and I smiled as it circled every fae so they wouldn't be able to leave.

"I love you," he whispered. I pulled his gag up over his mouth again.

"I love you too, husband," I answered back in a whisper, making him let out a sigh of relief. "This will be over soon, but you need to stay out of my way. I will not live without you. If you go, I will follow."

The tears silently slid down his cheeks as he shook his head no.

Once I was confident that I had everyone in my trap, I released the magic that allowed me to freeze everyone. At once, the entire gathering became absolutely still and quiet. I took a deep breath as I looked around, readying myself to fulfill my destiny.

I stood and walked toward Tally and Mae.

I wrapped them up in my darkness and carried them to where Cassius and all the other prisoners were kneeling, frozen in time.

My eyes immediately found Cassius' golden ones, and I smiled at him. My eyes were burning red, and my blood witch markings glowed brightly on my skin.

My darkness was in complete control as I smiled wickedly.

I moved toward Cassius and kneeled down, so I was face to face with him and unfroze him.

"I don't like feeling your fear." I lifted my hand and caressed his face as he pressed himself harder into my touch. "I need all of you safe and hidden by my illusion magic. I will not risk losing you."

I leaned forward and pressed my lips to his, then used my darkness to move all of the royal families to the side and out of the way. I stood, walking toward Tally and Mae as I unfroze them. It took them a confused moment to realize I had them. They glanced around and noticed that everyone around us was frozen.

"What are you doing?" Mae hissed.

"Father will kill all of them slowly in front of you before killing you, you Crimson whore!" Tally spit toward me as I smiled at her.

"You'll be dead first, Tally, but gods above, I wish I could torture you until you're begging for death."

Tally and Mae both stumbled backward, and I let them think they were going to get away. As soon as they almost made it back to their father, I wrapped them up in my darkness and forced them to kneel where Cassius and his father had been.

Come to Cerithia. I summoned the blood witches through the bloodstone that I now had hanging on a chain around my neck. It was tucked in the top of my dress, hidden.

I unfroze the prisoners so they could see what I was doing. My eyes glanced at Cassius as he watched me closely. I felt bad seeing them all tied and bound, but this was for the best. My eyes shifted to his younger brothers and the few other small children that were bound alongside him.

"Children, close your eyes," I demanded, and they all did. A moment later, my bloodstone pulsed violently around my neck as I forced illusion magic out. It spread in front of Cassius and all the real prisoners, making them disappear as if they weren't there at all. I smiled when I walked in front of Tally and Mae.

My illusion magic had made Tally look like Cassius and Mae look like the king of Crimson. My father wanted a show, and he would get one. I glanced to where I could feel Cassius watching me, hidden by my illusion magic.

"Illusion magic," I spoke to him. "No one can see any of you."

I glanced at Tally, who looked like Cassius, and smiled. "I just want you to know that I caught Jesper fucking Mae in the dining hall last night, and your parents both knew." She sobbed loudly, and it made me smile.

Then I took my spot behind Tally and held my dagger to her throat like I had been to Cassius only minutes ago. I unfroze everyone and smiled when my father and Gwyn glanced at me like I was about to destroy everything precious to me. They were none the wiser that Tally and Mae had assumed the identities of Cassius and his father.

"This is everything Thea has been working for, so Thea, please break your curse once and for all." My father urged me. "Make them suffer."

"Gladly!" I called out, but before I killed Tally, I leaned down to her ear. "I want you to know before I kill you that my husband, Cassius, and I will dance on the ruins of this shitty kingdom."

Tally started crying and begging behind her gag, but I just chuckled as my darkness begged me to do the honors.

So, I stood and tucked my dagger back in its sheath. Then, my darkness formed into a huge black cloud in front of me. The crowd made noises that let me know they approved of the show I was putting on.

Even though I knew this was really Tally in front of me, my darkness hesitated at the sight of a fake Cassius crying and begging in front of me. It's not him. He's safe.

Then my darkness reared back before ramming into Tally's back, piercing completely through her, making a hole big enough you could see through her. Tally didn't die right away. I could see her gasping for air, but she would never take a breath again. She slumped over dead, still looking like Cassius. I looked at my father, my breathing labored. My wicked smile widened because he looked fucking proud of me.

Gwyn smiled at me for the first time in my life where it wasn't her being a sarcastic bitch. I couldn't wait to see their faces when they realized it was their disgusting heirs I was killing. I focused on Mae, who looked at me horrified. I paused for a moment to take in the uncanniness of her looking like Rylan. Glancing around me, I realized that in a few moments, all of these fae would realize they cheered me on to kill Tally and Mae. I smiled.

Mae was shaking her head violently, trying to call out to her mother. My darkness took a step back as my fire came forth. I summoned a ball of fire in front of me, and the crowd died down. They were enjoying this. Sick fucks.

"Burn in hell, Mae," I whispered so only she could hear. I focused on her rapid breathing and summoned my fire to start inside of her chest. Mae stopped crying almost immediately. My fire was starting to burn brightly under her skin, cooking her from the inside out. A moment later, the flames exploded out of her, leaving a charred hole, and she fell over dead.

The crowd roared with applause. I turned to my father and sneered at him.

"Are you proud of me?" I asked. I could feel myself slipping farther and farther into my darkness. I was hardly in control of myself now.

"Our entire kingdom is proud of you!" My father raised his hands in the air and looked around proudly. Jesper looked at me as if he couldn't believe I just did that. My red eyes met his, and I glared, full of hatred.

He and my father would die last. The crowd was cheering my name. This was something I could have only dreamed of as a child—to belong here. Now I hated it. I hated every fae in front of me. But I let them cheer me on so that they would feel disgusted with themselves once they realized who I killed.

It was Jesper who realized something felt wrong about this. He always seemed to be the more observant one of the group. He seemed panicked as he turned around, looking for his wife. His eyes found mine, and I gave him a knowing smile.

"What did you do?" he snapped.

My father and Gwyn looked at Jesper like he had lost his mind. The crowd quieted down at the tension. I just stared at him.

"Jesper?" Gwyn asked.

"Where are Tally and Mae?" Jesper yelled.

My father and Gwyn immediately started looking around them but looked to me when they realized the girls were missing. The crowd didn't make a noise.

"Thea," my father said.

"You guys were watching me the whole time; I didn't do anything," I said innocently. "Except kill Cassius and Rylan, just like you asked me to."

I cocked my head to the side as I released the illusion magic and focused on Gwyn and my father, wanting to see every detail of their reactions. Their minds took a moment to register what they were looking at before their faces fell in horror at what they saw behind me.

CHAPTER 32

THEA

Gwyn's scream immediately filled the air. I turned to look at their dead bodies now that they weren't hidden by my illusion magic. My darkness hummed at the sight. Vengeance. When I returned my gaze to my father, his eyes were wild with hatred. I already pulled out my dagger. I took a step backward to stand between them and Cassius. My barrier magic released from me without permission to protect all of the prisoners. Jesper stared at Tally, barely giving her a second glance. His hard-pressed face looked like he was fucked, and he was right. But first I needed to get rid of everyone else. He and my father would get my wrath.

I shifted my gaze along the line of guards to see who would come and try to fight me first. I wanted a fight. They all stood frozen with fear, their weapons drawn at me.

Gwyn was the one who charged at me with a dagger of her own. Stupid woman. I swiped my hand around, evaporating all the weapons pointed at me with my fire mist.

"You stupid fucking bitch!" She screamed as she came at me. "We should have killed you when you were a child!"

Gwyn had probably never held a weapon in her life, so when she charged me, it was easy to stop her with one punch to her pretty face. She crumpled to the ground, but my fire mist was quick to wrap her up.

"I promised you that you would watch me kill your daughters one day," I sneered.

"They didn't do anything to you!" she yelled.

"They were cruel to me. They helped all of you kill me, lie to me, and cheat me out of my happiness." My fire lashed out and burned Gwyn, but only to cause her pain. My father seemed to just register what was happening.

"Kill the Crimson family and Thea!" he demanded from his guards.

"Whoever tries to stop me will die. If you leave, I will let you live!" I called out to the men I trained. Most of them stopped and debated whether or not they should fight me. Six kept moving towards me, and I shot Haden's frost magic at them, freezing them immediately. Kizar guards headed towards me, but with no weapons.

The crowd was yelling and wailing as they tried to run from me, but they realized they were all stuck here too. They wanted a show, so now they would get one.

One guard that had hesitated decided to be stupid and try to attack me. I dodged his attack easily, but he kept running past me, heading for Cassius. He hit my barrier, and I smiled wickedly at him as he fell to the ground on his back. I moved quicker than he did. A moment later I stood over him, my dagger pointed at him.

"That was very fucking stupid of you."

I summoned my darkness, lifting him off the ground, then speared the man through the chest, leaving a gaping hole big enough that I could see through him. Just like Tally. Glancing through the man's body, I could see Cassius and gave him a small smile, not quite registering the fact that he was seeing me through a torso. Cassius seemed to be in shock, but I don't think he had ever seen me completely taken away by my darkness.

I threw the man's dead body toward my father and Jesper. I was not in control of myself as I moved toward them. Gwyn still watched the chaos tangled in my fire mist, her feet dangling a few feet off the ground. My fire was still burning her, causing her painful sobs to fill the space around me. It only fueled my need for vengeance. My dagger sliced and stabbed through men like it was nothing.

My darkness humming at every heart I stopped, at every man I took down in the name of Crimson. For Cassius. For Exile. For my mother. For me.

My father and Jesper were circled by dozens of men. Cowards. I stopped and glanced at Gwyn.

"If you come over to me, Luren, I won't kill her. I'll trade you for her."

I knew my father would never sacrifice himself for anyone. Gwyn looked to my father, expecting him to step forward. He didn't move. I saw the sadness in her eyes, and it only made me happy to see her suffering. The fae in the colosseum still watched in shock, like they were safe from my wrath.

"That is the man you all follow blindly!" I yelled, causing it to turn almost silent. "A man who does not care about his wife, about his daughter, who does not care about any of you!" I was fucking seething. "You all disgust me. Who comes here to see the slaughter of innocent royal families?"

No one dared move.

Suddenly a dagger stabbed into my leg. Cassius' voice filled the space as he ran at my barrier magic. Immediately my chest seized as the images of my vision pulsed through my mind. It was happening. Was this what Brim saw too? Cassius' shadows swarmed around him, trying desperately to break out. His black eyes were full of hatred, but there was a deep fear too. Cassius' shadows ripped my barrier magic apart, and he headed straight for me.

No.

My heartbeat pounded in my ears. Time slowed down as I froze in fear. My vision plagued me over and over in my mind. I reached for him, but my darkness wouldn't release its hold on me.

Cassius, stop. I tried to release any of my magic, but it wouldn't. He wouldn't be able to stop himself. Our bond would demand he protect me at any cost.

"Thea!" Cassius' voice boomed.

It was happening. He was going to die. I could feel how frantic he was through our bond.

"Cassius, no!" I called out.

I tried to stop him with my magic again, but nothing came from me. Cassius was moving through the crowd of guards, his shadows ripping and tearing men apart who tried to stop him. His black eyes were focused on me. I had been so distracted by Cassius that I wasn't paying attention. It wasn't until I was falling to my knees that pain crippled me. My mouth fell open as the sword pierced through me. My father walked in front of me, smiling.

"You thought you could overpower me?"

"Thea!" Cassius became more frantic as he came for me. Sights and sounds became distorted as my blood flowed from my wound. I could feel the haziness creeping through me. All of my plans fell to the ground as I looked around in a daze. Time felt as if it had been slowed down. My gaze drifted from my father to focus on who stood directly behind him.

My mother.

She was beautiful. Like an angel, glowing brightly with Killian next to her. Her eyes were blood red as she tilted her head to the side to look at me. My breathing was labored. Each lungful of air sent waves of pain where the sword stabbed through me. My mother took two steps, so she was in front of me. She kneeled so we were at eye level.

"This is not how you die." Her voice was calm, but I could sense the fear coming from her. Everything was moving in slow motion around us still. "The dagger in your leg is stopping your magic." She reached down and yanked it from me, causing me to whimper in pain.

"This will hurt, sweetheart." She frowned with tears in her eyes as she looked behind me to where Killian disappeared. Before I could think of what she meant, the sword was yanked from me. A scream so vicious tore from me, causing ripples of power to explode from my body and knock everyone down. My magic exploded from me. "That's my girl. Heal yourself, and get Cassius contained." My mother smiled at me. Sybil's magic was already pumping through me violently, sealing the wound that would have killed me. I stood, my darkness in complete control of me. My body was engulfed in black flames as I looked around for my husband.

Cassius was kneeling...just like in my vision. A Kizar guard stood behind him with a sword. My darkness was already on its way.

"I love you," Cassius called out to me. There was a ringing in my ears as I heard Cassius saying goodbye to me. I did not allow myself to acknowledge my fear because it would paralyze me. My darkness was already wrapping up the Kizar guard that was about to kill Cassius. I sneered when he went to swing his sword, only to have my darkness force its way down his throat, making him drop the blade and fall to his knees.

Cassius glanced behind him at the man gripping his neck as my darkness blocked his airways, and then it seeped into his blood, turning his veins black. His eyes turned black as well before I turned the darkness inside of him into fire, making his body melt. Flames burst from his eye sockets as he fell over dead.

Cassius smiled at me, but then his smile dropped. I could hear someone coming up behind me, but a man was approaching Cassius too. All too quickly, clouds rolled over the sky, blocking the sun from reaching us. Lightning scattered across the sky. Della was doing something, but I didn't have time to think about it. I was too concerned with Cassius and the man approaching him.

"Watch out!" Haden's voice echoed as he ran toward Cassius. Cassius turned around right as a man charged him with a sword. He froze. Cassius didn't move a muscle. Why wasn't he moving? Then, starlight exploded around Haden and Cassius. I couldn't see them but figured Della was protecting them.

I could hear the heavy footsteps of the guard who was trying to sneak up on me was getting closer, so I turned and swung my daggers at him. The Kizar guard was small and not very quick on his feet. He swung too hard, causing his body to twist awkwardly but allowing me to step forward and pierce my dagger through his ribs. He fell over dead.

Frantically, I turned back to where Cassius and Haden had been, only to find my vision playing out right in front of my eyes again. Cassius' golden eyes stared at me as blood dripped from his cut brow. My father stood behind him, sword already coming toward Cassius. I tried to get to Cassius with my darkness, but nothing happened as it hit a barrier. The Kizar guard standing next to my father smiled.

"Cassius!" I yelled, but I was too late. The sword sliced into Cassius' neck; blood spilled from the wound as I tried desperately to get to him. I saw the moment his eyes went vacant. I refused to believe he was dead as my heart raced and tears flowed from my eyes. Cassius slumped to the ground. A scream tore from me, making the ground shake and crack below us, knocking my father and the guard down. Luren watched me, enjoying the anguish that was consuming me. I slid to my knees; my darkness expanded around Cassius and I.

"Please, open your eyes!" I begged. "Do not leave me!" My magic stormed above me. I could not control the emotions that ripped through my chest and nearly killed me on the spot. My hands covered the wound on his neck, trying to stop the blood gushing from it, but it was too much. My healing magic didn't come forward to heal him because it knew there was nothing to save. He was gone. Cassius was dead. "I'm sorry." I sobbed into his chest that no longer rose and fell with life. I gripped him tightly, refusing to let him go. My tears soaked his clothing, which was covered in his blood.

He was dead.

My husband was gone, and I couldn't even begin to comprehend what that meant. Images of Cassius smiling and laughing hit me like an arrow. I would never see that smile again. I would never hear him laugh. I would never know what it was like to have a life with Cassius. My father had ripped that away from me, just like he did with everything.

"Please," I begged his lifeless face. "I can't live without you!" A war of anger and sadness raged inside of me. Cassius deserved to live; he was everything good in this realm. He was every good piece of me. Without him I was nothing. My body was on fire, black flames burning angrily across my skin. I did not want to leave him alone on the ground like this. I curled against him, begging the stars to take me with him this very second because I couldn't breathe without him. I gripped his cold hand in mine.

I closed my hand tightly hoping when I opened then again that Cassius would be smiling at me, and this would be a bad dream. When I opened them, Cassius was still lying in a pool of his own blood not moving. His skin was too pale, his hand was too cold.

A soft golden glow caught my attention. His soul. I sat up and turned toward the glow, but it wasn't Cassius' soul that stared back at me. It was Haden.

"Haden? Where is Cassius' soul?"

Haden kneeled so that he was looking at me at eye level.

"Thea..."

"Tell me now!"

"Della overheard your father talking about killing Cassius to weaken you. The guard next to him can block magic and take down barriers. You wouldn't have been able to save him. So, I told Della that when they tried to kill Cassius, to make me look like him, and I would take his place so it could buy you enough time to kill that bastard."

I shook my head to try and understand what he was saying through the grief.

"Cassius isn't dead." He frowned. "Look at your marriage bond; it isn't broken." My gaze snapped to my crown bond. It was still intact.

"I don't..."

"Look at who you're holding in your lap," Haden demanded. When I did, it was no longer Cassius. It was Haden. "I tackled Cassius to the ground before the guard got him. Cassius is pissed, but he is safe behind an illusion barrier that Della put up. You must kill the guard next to your father, or he will get to Cassius again. His magic is what will allow your vision to happen."

"You said you couldn't die." Relief filled me for Cassius, but I didn't want to lose Haden either.

"I won't die permanently. Any moment my soul will go back to my body. I will be healed; you do not need to worry about me." Sadness flickered in his eyes. "Della always makes sure I come back to her."

He used her nickname. The thunder above us shook the ground as lightning lit the sky. I didn't need to know who was pissed. Della's starlight turned red as she appeared next to Haden. But she turned to me.

"Cassius is safe; just focus on the prophecy. Use that rage coursing through you to kill that bastard next to your father. They will know it's not Cassius that died in a moment. I can only change fae, not scenery like you can." Her eyes turned pure white before she gave Haden's soul a soft smile and gently put him back into his body.

I stood, letting my darkness fall away so I could find Cassius. My eyes met his black ones through Della's barrier. He was pissed. His hands were frozen together in front of him. Haden had restrained him.

"I love you," I said in a shaky voice even though he couldn't hear me.

Then I turned my focus to the man who had been standing next to my father. My father had retreated behind his wall of guards like that would save him. My eyes shifted to a blinding blue as I summoned Nev's light magic. I created a ball in my hand. As the guard was distracted by Della, my darkness crept along the ground and wrapped him up, forcing his mouth open. I stomped over to him barefoot as I burned my uncomfortable heels off my feet. I shoved the ball of light down his throat.

The man had no choice but to swallow it. I backed away from him and made the ball of light expand inside of him until his body exploded. Chunks of the man went flying into the crowd, but they still didn't dare move. Which was good, because I would cut the flesh from their bodies if they did. My red eyes flickered over to Cassius, who watched me as I put barrier magic, shadows, and my darkness around him. Would three layers of my magic overpower his need to get to me?

He didn't die. Relief filled me, but I knew that he was still in danger. I turned my focus back to where Gwyn had escaped and cowered behind my father. My darkness wrapped her up again and yanked her to me without lifting a damn finger. She cried and begged my father to save her.

Now that the fear of Cassius almost dying subsided, I was enraged—furious at the fae that thought our lives were just something to play with, furious that they tried to keep him from me. And enraged because I could have lost him.

"You all lied to me." My voice rang out through the stadium. No one spoke or made a fucking noise when they heard how pissed off I was. "You were cruel to me. But I can forgive that; after all, my father did not tell you all the truth about what happened. But what I cannot forgive is how you all condoned my family tricking me into killing him!" I pointed my finger at Cassius. His eyes were full of worry for me. "Cassius Valeska, my mate, my husband! Your future king!"

Chaos broke out at my declaration. No one could leave as my darkness swarmed around us without their knowledge. My bloodstone pulsed violently, giving me all the energy I would ever need.

"Husband..." Gwyn sobbed.

Cassius' eyes found mine, and he looked fucking proud to be mine.

"You broke your curse," Gwyn's eyes widened at the realization.

"That's right, Gwyn," I sneered. "I broke my curse weeks ago!" I yelled in her face. "But even before that, I could see you for what you were. A cruel, heartless bitch."

I turned to my father and Jesper. My mother was standing close to the blood witches, smiling proudly at me.

"This is for Crimson!" I yelled, making the chaos pause to watch me as I held up my dagger before plunging it into her stomach, yanking it up to her throat, cutting her open so her guts spilled at my feet. Her blood was splattering over me. My darkness pulsed violently as we stared Gwyn in the eyes until every fucking shred of light drained from her. And when it did, I tossed her dead body at my father. She landed at his feet with a thud.

My father yelled in his grief, but it couldn't be real, not when he wouldn't even trade himself for her. I would give myself, this realm, anything to save Cassius, and I wouldn't hesitate to do it. My father moved toward me but was still guarded. My eyes tracked his movements.

"Thea, I don't understand what you are doing."

"I am fulfilling the prophecy." I smiled at him. "Killing kings, crumbling kingdoms."

"But... b-but..."

"B-but nothing," I mocked him. "Your kingdom and now Kizar will belong to me, to Crimson, when I finish killing you and Jesper. Your fae will bow at the feet of their new king... Cassius. I smiled as my father's face reddened with rage.

My father glanced behind me to where Cassius and the Crimson royal family were now standing, still bound.

"It looks like Cassius will be dying after all." He smiled.

When I turned, I saw the man I killed earlier break through the barrier I had and pull Cassius from it. His magic didn't pulse as powerfully as it did earlier. The guard looked slightly different—a twin. He kicked Cassius' legs so that he fell to his knees. Fear seized me.

Cassius will die.

"If you move, I will slit his throat." The man threatened me as he held a sword to Cassius' neck. His ugly face held a hate-filled sneer.

"Drop your fucking dagger," he demanded. I did what he said because I didn't need it to kill him.

"You will stop this madness now," my father demanded.

My eyes focused on the man, on the threat to my husband, and I could feel magic bubbling up. I let it take control, and a moment later the noises of fear stopped. When I glanced up, everyone was frozen again but Cassius. My heart was beating wildly in my chest at how close that was.

Quickly, I walked to the man but leaned down first and gave Cassius a chaste kiss. Then I yanked the man's blade away from Cassius before I unfroze everyone so they could see me dragging the man by his hair. I quickly wrapped Cassius back up in my barrier magic and my darkness. The man thrashed around trying to get free, but my grip didn't loosen, and fear seeped into his dark eyes.

"What the fuck?" He tried to break free, but I only smiled at him.

"Thea..." My father started to speak.

I forced the man to his knees, so he was looking at Cassius.

"You should have never touched what belongs to me," I hissed. "I want you to look at my husband as I spill your blood for trying to hurt him," I said loud enough for everyone to hear.

Cassius' eyes found mine.

I smiled at Cassius as I grabbed the man's sword and swung hard, so the man's head flew away as it came off, leaving a bloody trail all the way to my father's feet. Cassius smiled brightly at me, and gods, he looked fucking proud of me.

When I turned, Jesper was trying to sneak away. I didn't know which one I wanted to kill first, him or my father. Guards surrounded them, but I only had to take a few steps toward them before most of them broke and ran. I stopped and glared at the guards that I trained. I didn't want to kill them.

"If you all walk away, I won't kill you. I just want Luren and Jesper." A few more of the guards ran, but some stayed, looking unsure. "You will not stop me from getting them, and you will lose your lives for nothing. You know my father does not care about any of you, but I do. I don't want to hurt you, but I *will* be killing Luren and Jesper, so step aside or die with them."

Most of them left.

About a dozen stood standing between me and my targets.

"You made your choice," I frowned as I summoned their blood marks. "You will all step aside and watch me slaughter Jesper and Luren." They all obeyed in formation. My father's eyes glanced around before looking at me. "Being a blood witch has its perks. Blood manipulation is so fun to use. In fact, I blood-marked you too."

My father stilled.

"You brought me a lovely gift." I pulled my bloodstone out and showed him. "Thanks."

My father didn't move, but Jesper turned and tried to run.

I used Cassius' shadows to move across the field directly in front of Jesper. He skidded to a stop and looked at me, horrified.

"Where are you going?" I asked. He turned and started toward the arena, but I moved through Cassius' shadows again, once more ending up right in front of him. This time, my darkness wrapped around his throat and slammed him into the ground, making it quake. Then it wrapped him up and dragged him along the ground behind me as I went toward my father. Luren continued to just stare at me without trying to run away.

He had accepted his fate.

I left Jesper tangled in my darkness on the ground as I stepped toward my father. The guards who refused to stop protecting Luren and Jesper would have to die. They chose their side, and it wasn't me. My darkness crept from me and snapped the necks of each guard. The sound of bones breaking made my father finally try to move.

"Luren, you will stay!" I demanded, and his feet planted to their spot because of the blood mark. His eyes that matched my own widened as he realized he was not in control of himself. I sent my darkness after him. It grabbed his wrists and ankles, lifting him a foot off the ground. He didn't try to fight, but fuck, his fear was pumping from him. I stopped a few feet away and glared at him.

"You are a disgusting excuse of a man, and I will spend the rest of my life scrubbing your very existence from this realm."

My father breathed heavily.

"You should have never underestimated me. You should have never kept me from Cassius."

"You're a traitorous whore just like your mother!"

The insult only made my blood witch markings glow with anger as my red eyes locked on him. I stepped closer to him.

"Do you want to know a secret?" I asked. He said nothing. "My mother is standing next to you."

His eyes widened as his chest rose and fell quickly.

"She didn't go to the next life just so she could watch you die. You took all the elite magic fae from me and killed them. You took Sybil and my brothers from me. So, for that, I will make this painful. And because you killed my mother, I will draw this out. When this is all over, I want you to know that your fae will realize how terrible you were when they see how great of a king Cassius will be."

"Fuck you!" he yelled. I stepped forward and pried his mouth open. Raising my dagger slowly, I waved it in front of his eyes, watching them widen in fear. Keeping my eyes locked onto his, I shoved my blade in his mouth and cut his tongue out.

"Much better now that I don't have to listen to you," I sighed. I threw his severed tongue at Jesper, hitting him in the face. He thrashed around in disgust as Luren's cries filled the silent air. The crowd of fae barely moved, probably worried I would slaughter them if they did. I gripped my viper-handled dagger and stabbed it into his thigh, making him cry out. I used my darkness to pry his eyes open so he couldn't look away.

"First, I will crumble your home." I summoned my fire, but my other magic mixed with it, creating a comet-like ball of angry power. The bloodstone pulsed violently as I drew upon its energy to expand the ball before I threw it toward the castle. The size of the ball of magic cast shadows over the fae watching as they all looked at the sky as if they were watching a shooting star. Every pair of eyes watched as the ball of magic soared over them and hit the side of my father's castle. The towers crumbled to the ground as screams of terror rang from the rubble. My magic ripped the castle apart in mere seconds, its stone and bricks exploding around us. My barrier magic swarmed around all of us as debris fell from the skies and my father's legacy crumbled. He was trying to close his eyes, but he would see everything. An angry cloud of smoke billowed up into the sky, overtaking the sun completely and making it seem as though it were about to storm.

"I will stab you for each fae in Exile that you slaughtered," I spoke as I slowly pressed my blade into his thigh.

My father cried, and I was just getting started. Just as I was about to start my stabbing, I looked over his shoulder at everyone watching. This would take too long. Sighing in disappointment, I knew I needed to not draw this out.

"Actually, I think we will do it this way," I said as I lifted my hand to summon my darkness. It transformed into dozens of sharp points before I urged it forward, cutting into my father's body without resistance. He screamed at the pain, but it wasn't enough. I pulled my darkness back when he started bleeding too much.

"Well, this won't work." I tisked and brought forth my fire magic and burned his wounds shut before doing it again and again. More screams of agony filled the space around us. I could feel death coming for him. But that was too kind of a punishment.

"This is for my mother. For Cassius. For Sybil. For Kaz. For Kai," I spoke angrily. "This is for Crimson!"

I held up my hands and squeezed my darkness around his wrists and ankles tighter before slowly pulling them in different directions. Luren's screams were deafening as his body was slowly torn apart. Limb by limb, my darkness ripped them from his body. I made sure it was slow, and only when I knew he was about to die did I pull so violently that my father's body fell into pieces at my feet.

More.

They deserved more punishment for what they had done. My breathing was wild as I stared at the pieces of Luren. I spit on him.

I was out of control when I turned and found Jesper still lying in my darkness. He was struggling, trying to break free, but he would never know what freedom felt like again. My darkness was angry, but more so than that, I was.

"I've been daydreaming of all the ways I could kill you, Jesper." I smiled when he started crying. "Nothing feels like it will be enough of a punishment for what you did to me."

All of the things that Jesper did to me came crashing down around me. My sanity snapped. I swiped my hand out so that my illusion magic recreated the cell in the bottom of the castle that he had tortured me in. I sat Jesper up and pinned his hands above him on the wall. Jesper was shaking his head no.

I used my magic to show everyone what he had done to me so they would understand why I was doing this. My memories of being tortured by Jesper played out in front of everyone. They watched in horror as my memories projected out. Walking forward, I used my dagger to cut his shirt off him. Then I started writing insults into his flesh.

He called out and thrashed.

"If you move, this will hurt worse for you," I hissed his own words to him. Jesper stilled, but I wanted this to hurt him. So, I dug my blade deeper so that he had no choice but to move. He called out as loud as he could. A moment later, I stood with puffy breaths. I smiled at the words 'Crimson's bitch' carved into the middle of his chest, among others.

"I just want you to know that I fucked Cassius on your throne after I slaughtered your guards." My eyes shined brightly as his eyes filled with hatred.

"*I* killed all of your guards. *I* killed the assassins you sent for Petra and Sy." I leaned down so I could stare at him. "And *I* made your piece-of-shit mother gut herself in front of *my* coven. She died painfully as I promised her that I would make your death even worse than hers."

Jesper was saying something behind my darkness that had him silenced. He was getting sluggish and hardly awake. That wouldn't do. My hand swiped around us again, and now the illusion magic made us appear in a washroom. A nice, warm bath was drawn for Jesper. With my darkness, I lifted him up and put him in the water. Once again, I used my magic to show all the fae present what Jesper had done to me. I didn't look to see what they all thought. I didn't care what they thought, but I wanted them to understand that they condoned this behavior.

"You're filthy," I muttered at him, my own voice sounding like a stranger.

I released my darkness from his mouth so I could hear his pain and suffering. I stepped toward him, and he cried out for me to stop, but I wouldn't, not until his heart stopped beating.

Glancing up at the illusion magic I played for all the fae, I saw them watching in horror as Jesper grabbed my head and held me under the water.

"Time to return the favor." I smiled and stepped forward, grabbing Jesper's head and shoving him down into the water. Jesper thrashed under me, but I held him down until he started to stop moving, then yanked him back up. He inhaled another deep breath out of instinct, and I shoved him below the surface of the water immediately.

When he stopped fighting, I pulled him up and took a step back. Jesper glanced at me, and his terror swarmed me when he looked at my face. I was sure I was terrifying everyone around me, but I didn't care.

"Thea..." Jesper breathed. "It was all your father's idea," he cried.

I cocked my head to the side and stared at him like he was an idiot. Jesper stared back at me, probably thinking he was putting on a brave face. But I knew better.

"My father did not make you beat me or torture me. You did all of that on your own, Jesper. You didn't need to be involved in the kingdom's scams and deceit. You chose to do that, and now that greed will be the reason you die today."

"I knew we should have fucking killed you!" he yelled. "I told your father that you were a lost cause, but he wanted to keep doing this stupid shit every year. I just wanted to kill you every year so that Cassius could never have you. I should have slaughtered his whole family while you were in Exile!"

I laughed.

"You?" I scoffed. "Weak. Pathetic. Coward. Useless. Dumb. Fragile man. You would never be able to get close to Cassius. He would have your body ripped into tiny pieces before you even knew it was coming."

"Well, I still outpowered you at one point," he sneered.

I clapped a big round of applause for the asshole.

"Congratulations, Jesper; you tricked me when I had no memories. You caged me like an animal only because you barbed my magic inside of me. Only because I let you barb it inside of me to save those I love. You used poison to weaken me. You were always a sorry excuse for a man. I'm sure your father died disappointed that you were his only heir."

Jesper's nostrils flared at my comment. It looked like I struck a nerve.

"And now, your kingdom will belong to me as the last heir of the Cerithian throne. As your sister by marriage, I will inherit all of it. But don't worry; I don't want your land. It will be split between Falgon and Akecia. Crimson will keep Cerithia. I will wipe your existence off of this realm after today. It will be as though you never existed."

Jesper's jaw clenched so tightly as if he wanted to say something to me, but he didn't know what he wanted to say.

"Fuck you!" He spit toward me.

I stepped forward and slapped him across the face. Jesper stared at me.

"Just kill me already," he demanded.

"But I'm having so much fun."

Jesper finally looked away from me. My darkness lashed out and pried his mouth open. It formed a dagger-like edge and reached in, ripping his tongue from him. Jesper's bathwater turned red as he thrashed around in agony. His death would be painful and drawn out. I'm sure the fae here would recoil in disgust, but they needed to know what happened when they fucked with me or my family. A moment later I summoned my fire magic and released it toward the bath full of water, making it rise in temperature.

"Let's get your bath at a nice, hot temperature."

Jesper tried to crawl out when he realized how warm his bath was getting. Slowly, I raised the temperature of the water, boiling him alive. His screams begging for death only fueled me to slow down his death. Jesper's death was going to be agonizing, and somehow it still felt like he deserved worse; my whole family had deserved worse.

If anyone spoke around us, I did not hear them. I was too focused on Jesper's pain and pleading. When his skin started bubbling from the heat, I would use Haden's frost magic to cool the water down, only to do it all over again. His skin blistered and melted off of his bones and muscles slowly. His bathwater turned more red as he bled out.

The sight of his body was disgusting. His skin and body had practically melted into fae soup in the tub. I moved toward him when I could feel death coming for him. I stared at him in the eyes.

"Tell my family I said hi when you get to hell."

Jesper was gasping for a breath he would never catch. But even now I wanted to take away his air, so I shoved him under the water, making sure his last lungful was water. When he didn't fight back, I pulled him out. He was dead. His whole body slowly submerged into the water when my magic released him. My darkness swarmed around me; I was out of control, and I didn't know how to stop. More. I wanted more vengeance.

Maybe I should kill all the fae in the arena. My dress blew in the warm gusts of wind. It was covered in blood. My toes curled on the dirt beneath them. Dust filled my lungs as I readied my magic for more blood.

Chapter 33

Thea

"Thea," Cassius' voice pierced straight through the darkness. "My love."

I turned slowly and saw him and all the other prisoners now unbound behind the barrier I put up. Cassius stared at me like he was worried. Closing my eyes, I shook my head, trying to pull out of this rage I was feeling. Gods, what would they all think of me?

I wanted more vengeance. This wasn't enough of a punishment. If I could bring them back to life and kill them again, I would.

"I love you," he called out to me.

My eyes opened, and I stared at him.

"You did so fucking good, Thea." He smiled at me.

He was proud of me, not scared. I stepped toward him, shattering the illusion magic I had around me. The illusion splintered and shattered like glass around us, showing the true massacre in the field. I saw that the crowd was still trapped in their seats as I glanced around. My shield magic dropped, and Cassius ran to me. His arms wrapped around me and lifted me from the ground as he buried his face into my neck.

"I love you," he whispered. "I've missed you so much."

Cassius pulled back for a moment and then embraced me in a soul-consuming kiss. Gods, I had missed him. All those emotions that I had bottled up from Exile came crashing down around me. Tears spilled from my eyes as I held him to me. Cassius pulled back and grasped my face in his hands.

"I love you so much." I grabbed his face in my hands and stared into those captivating golden eyes.

"You fucking did it." He stared at me in disbelief. "I don't know if I'm really processing that you did it," he chuckled softly. The crowd started getting restless. Cassius glanced around at them. "What are you going to do about them?"

I stared at all their faces; they looked terrified.

Stepping forward, I spoke. "Cerithia will now be part of the Crimson Kingdom! We will not be at war with the other kingdoms. We will live in peace. We will treat all fae with respect and make sure everyone can afford to live. We will not tolerate hate or rebellion. Today, we move forward and forget that my family ever existed. The Valeska family will treat you with respect and kindness, but we expect the same in return!"

The crowd glanced around at one another. I knew someone would object or say something snarky. It shouldn't have surprised me that it was a few noblemen.

"You're a monster!" one yelled.

"We will never accept you as our queen!" another retorted.

I flicked my wrist and evaporated them with my fire magic. Their bodies turning into ash and floating away in the wind.

"I suggest you all bow to your queen!" I yelled. "If any of you do not bow, I will send you straight to hell with my family." I pointed to the dead bodies, and slowly the guards bent their knees and bowed in front of me. Cassius stepped up with me and hugged me. "And bow before your new king, my husband, Cassius Valeska of Crimson!"

I released the magic around them and watched every fae kneel as Cassius stood next to me, holding my hand tightly in his. My eyes took in the blood witches as they smiled and bowed deeply.

"This will be the last warning I ever give. We will not tolerate rebellion or hate in our kingdom. Our realm deserves to live in peace, and that is what we will work on moving forward. If you are caught trying to rebel, you will be killed immediately."

All the fae nodded as I spoke.

"You're all free to go."

They left, some quickly, and others took their time. It would take a lot of time to build up trust with them to get the kingdom functioning like Crimson. I walked to the blood witches.

"Thank you for getting the blood marks done. If you guys hadn't done that, I would have been swarmed by every guard in the castle. I owe you."

"Are you kidding?" One of them said, "That was fucking amazing."

I smiled as my eyes shifted to Killian and my mother. They smiled at me like proud parents. I wished I could hug them. Memories of my mother and I filled my mind. She always gave the best hugs, and she always knew what to say. What was I supposed to do without her?

"Don't cry," she whispered.

"I don't want you to go. I already lost you once. I already lost my brothers and Sybil," I cried.

"But you have Cassius, and together you will make a family of your own. You already started, Thea. Look at everyone here who cares for you. Everyone who fought beside you and rooted for you to win. You have a family, one that loves you." She stepped toward me. "Killian and I are so proud of you, but please do not dwell on the fact we aren't here. We will move into the next life together; we will not be alone.

"I wish to the stars and the moon that you could be my daughter in every life, Thea. You are my greatest accomplishment; I will feel your loss in every life. Cassius will love you enough so that you do not feel like you are missing anything. He is so wonderful." My mother smiled.

Della appeared next to me.

"It's time," Della whispered.

Tears fell from me as I stared at my mother and Killian hugging each other.

"Thank you for staying with me. I love you." I cried.

"I love you too. Promise me you will be okay." My mother's voice cracked as tears streamed down her face.

"I promise."

Killian held her tightly as Della reached for them. I watched them until they disappeared. The blood witches watched me, waiting for direction. But I didn't know how to be a queen.

"You may set up the coven wherever is best fit for you. I will need time to readjust to everything, and I will be doing that at Crimson's castle."

"Then we shall go close to Crimson with you, and don't worry; we can care for ourselves until you are ready." A witch named Farah smiled.

"I appreciate you all being understanding."

They bowed to me and stood but bowed again when Cassius approached.

Sy and Petra ran over to us and pulled me in for a hug.

"Thank the fucking stars for you, Thea." Sy pulled back and smiled brightly at me. I had missed my friends. The rest of the royal families came over to say thank you and congratulate me on breaking my curse. It was all too overwhelming.

"We will take care of everything here, Thea. You do not need to worry about anything but resting and being with Cassius," Rylan said as he hugged me. "We are beyond the moon that you are back home."

"Thank you." Relief filled me. I was exhausted and just wanted to be alone with Cassius. When I looked behind me, Cassius was watching me with an expression I couldn't decipher.

"Let's go home." He grabbed my hand and squeezed it softly. I nodded as he used his shadows to move us and our family back to Crimson. I immediately went to Haden and hugged him.

"Thank you," I whispered. "You saved Cassius today, and I will always be indebted to you for that."

Haden hugged me tightly against him. I released my healing magic for him, but he didn't have any wounds to heal.

"It's what family does—protects each other," he said with a smile as he pulled back. His blue eyes glanced at Cassius before looking at me. "You should probably go talk to your husband before he combusts," he chuckled.

When I turned, Cassius' eyes were glued to me. They were full of questions and hesitation. I stepped toward him, and he held his hand out so I could take it before he led us to our room.

As soon as we walked into our space, I felt so much better. I pulled the bloodstone from around my neck and set it on the counter. Cassius' eyes lingered on the stone before looking at me. I thought he would ask questions, but he just dragged me to the washroom and started the shower.

Cassius smiled at me as he helped me undress.

I did the same for him before we climbed into the shower. Cassius turned me so I was facing him. He leaned forward and gave me a chaste kiss before washing my hair for me. Tension released from my muscles the more he touched me. When he was done rinsing my hair, he stared at me, uncertain.

"What's wrong?" I frowned.

"I keep waiting for this dream to end and wake up to you still not remembering who I am." He sounded so scared.

"That's never going to happen, Cassius." I ran my fingers over his cheek and pulled him to me for a kiss. "I'm sorry I didn't tell you I broke the curse."

"About that..." he narrowed his eyes at me. "How did you break it? You never gave me the stone."

I smiled.

"One night I realized I could use your shadow magic to move to different places quickly. I had used your magic to visit Crimson sometimes. So, I gave it to you as you slept."

Cassius smiled.

"Did you spy on me as I slept, my love?"

"Yes," I whispered. "I could not stand to be away from you all the time. I knew I would give you the bloodstone the day you told me that it was how I would break my curse; I just didn't know where it was. And then I couldn't tell you because Brim and I had a vision of you dying. When I got stabbed by the dagger today, you were going to help me, and my father was going to behead you. So, I didn't tell you. I hope you understand why I couldn't tell you."

Cassius stared at me for a long moment. Emotions filled his eyes as he watched me.

"When did you break it?"

"Do you remember when I found you in the woods spying on my camp, and I told you if you beat me in a fight, I would let you go?"

"Yes." His eyes flashed black at the memory.

"I broke the curse not long before then. I couldn't stay away from you. I needed you. I couldn't stop myself from kissing you or touching you."

His brows furrowed.

"I had thought you broke it that day," he confessed. "You looked at me differently. You didn't look confused about your desire for me, but I thought I lost my mind. I thought there was no way you broke it," he chuckled. "I should have known that with you, anything is possible."

His eyes glanced over my face.

"When I was standing with Luren and Jesper in camp talking about a peace treaty, I heard your voice."

I glanced at him, confused.

"In my mind, I heard it. You weren't saying anything, but I could hear your thoughts. I truly thought I had lost my fucking mind."

Was that why I couldn't hear his thoughts that day?

"You must have gotten that as part of my powers when I gave you the bloodstone." I smiled. "Are you upset I didn't come back to you immediately?" I swallowed the lump in my throat.

"No." He pulled me to him and hugged me as he kissed my forehead. "I always knew you'd break it and make it home to me. But you were right to keep it from me. I would have tried to protect you and probably gotten in the way. I tried today. If Haden hadn't saved me, I would've died because I couldn't focus on anything but protecting you.

"The way you destroyed your family and Jesper today was... fucking amazing. I have never been more proud to have you as a mate than when I was watching you punish every single one of them. Fuck, I was in awe of you, little viper. I will always be in awe of you."

I stood on my tippy toes and kissed him, pulling him to me with need. Cassius tilted his head so he could deepen the kiss. His tongue dominated mine as he pushed me into the shower wall. His hands skimming down my body with a hum of approval.

I moaned when his fingers pushed into me.

"Always ready for me," he muttered as he kissed down my neck, biting softly. He tangled his free hand into my hair and forced me to look at him. Cassius teased me by leaning forward as if he would kiss me, but he paused. His breath fanned over my face as his eyes took in everything about me. His fingers pushed inside of me at an unbearable pace as his thumb rubbed against my clit.

"Fuck," I moaned.

Cassius smiled as his shadows crept away from him without permission. His eyes flashed black before he leaned forward and gave me a consuming kiss. He pulled back.

"Do you want to cum on my fingers or mouth first?" he asked.

Gods, I was already close. I opened my mouth to answer him, but nothing came out. Cassius stopped moving.

"Use your words, wife. Fingers or mouth?"

"Mouth," I breathed as he smiled and sank to his knees in front of me. He hooked my leg over his shoulder and immediately licked me before sucking me into his mouth. My hands gripped his hair as I rolled my hips against his tongue.

Cassius hummed his approval against me, making me whimper at how fucking good this felt. Cassius pushed his fingers inside of me as his tongue swirled my clit.

"Cassius," I breathed.

He pulled away and glanced up at me, his black eyes taking my breath away. Gods, this image of him would be ingrained into my mind forever.

"Once you cum on my mouth, you can have my cock, my love." But he didn't move. He watched my face as his fingers kept sliding into me. "You look so fucking beautiful like this," he breathed.

"Please," I muttered as my eyes bounced between his fingers sinking into me and his face watching me. His thumb circled my sensitive nerves, and I squeezed my eyes shut.

"Eyes on me," he demanded. I opened them and moaned loudly.

"It feels too good," I whined.

"You can take it." He smiled.

"Cassius, I need more," I begged. "I need your mouth on me."

He smiled as he watched me.

"You'll get my mouth, greedy girl."

He pushed his fingers into me deeper, and I called out at the pleasure it brought. Cassius finally leaned forward and withdrew his fingers to replace them with his tongue. Cassius licked and devoured me as if he were a starving man. His hands spread me farther apart. Fuck. Fuck. Fuck.

"Don't stop," I begged. Cassius groaned against me as my orgasm crashed around me. My fingers tangled in his dark hair as I held him against me so I could ride out the waves of pleasure against his mouth.

A moment later I released him, and he stood, lifting me up so he could sink into me.

"Fuck...Cassius."

"Gods, I fucking missed you. I love it when you lose yourself to me," he muttered. He stared into my eyes as his hips surged into me without pause. I was going to cum again. His hand gripped my breast before teasing my nipple. Then he leaned forward and bit where my neck and shoulder meet, and I came loudly. I was begging and pleading, but Cassius didn't stop.

"Again. You can give me one more, Thea."

I shook my head that I couldn't, but I knew I could. He gripped my jaw in his hand and forced his tongue against mine.

"You can cum again, can't you, my love?" He squeezed my jaw tighter.

I shook my head, yes.

"Good girl. You will take me until I'm done with you." He pushed harder into me. "I want to hear you screaming for me. Don't worry; no one will hear you. Our magic has blocked anyone from hearing those noises that belong to me."

"Cassius."

"Thea," he answered me.

"You feel so good," I moaned.

"And you feel like heaven," he ground out. "I could fuck you for the rest of our existence, and I would never get enough of you. You're mine, and no one will ever take you from me again. Now cum for me, wife."

"Fuck..." I called out without care. I clenched around Cassius as his hips slammed into me faster as he chased his own release. "Cassius!"

"That's it; let the realm know who your undoing is," he muttered out of breath before slamming into me one last time. My heart pounded violently as I struggled to breathe. Cassius turned us so his back was on the wall, still holding me as he slid down it and sat with me straddling his hips. The water was getting cold, but I didn't care.

Cassius' chest rose and fell in quick succession.

"For fuck's sake, we might not leave our room for a year. I don't think I can tire of having you," he muttered.

I lifted my eyes to meet his before kissing him. Emotions clogged my throat as tears filled my eyes. When I pulled away, Cassius wiped the tears streaming silently down my cheeks.

"What's wrong?"

"I just love you so much that it feels... all-consuming," I confessed. "I love you so fucking much."

Cassius pushed the wet hair from my face.

"I'll love you until my last breath, and then I will love you all over again in the lives to follow. We will love each other until the stars fall from the sky and the realm ceases to exist, and even then that will not keep me from you. Even if the universe ceases to exist, our love never will; it will outlast time itself."

6 MONTHS LATER- THEA

"Cassius, what is with you today?" I laughed softly. He had blindfolded me this morning, and to my great disappointment, it wasn't for bedroom fun.

He helped me get dressed and led me out of the castle without saying a word, but I could feel his excitement through the bond, and honestly, he was practically shaking with giddiness. I hadn't seen him this excited since the day he proposed to me.

"Are you proposing to me again or something?" I asked as we rode Onyx.

Cassius' lips pressed against my neck, nipping my skin and sending a jolt of desire through me.

"No," he chuckled. "But this might be the best surprise I ever give you, and I've been working on it for three years."

"Three years?" I tried to look over my shoulder toward him as if I could see him through the blindfold. Cassius claimed my mouth with his.

"Yes."

My heart rate picked up as I leaned back into Cassius and tried to think of what he had been up to. Wouldn't I have noticed he was doing something these past six months since I broke my curse?

"You're thinking very hard, my love. Just relax; we're almost there."

I smiled to myself as Onyx picked up speed. We hadn't been riding for long. So, we were still in Crimson. A moment later, I heard the waterfall of our favorite place. Maybe he had planned a special date? Suddenly, Onyx stopped. Cassius' shadows wrapped around me gently and set me on my feet. He dragged me along with him for a moment before stopping. He moved me so I was in front of him, gripping my shoulders to steady me.

I smiled as he pulled the blindfold off. My eyes adjusted to the sunlight before they focused on his pretty golden eyes that seemed to be shining brightly. His big smile made my heart clench tightly with anticipation.

"Cassius?" I chuckled as I looked at the waterfall to the left. His hands held me in place, so I couldn't turn around.

"Do you remember when I asked you to marry me here?" He watched me closely.

"Yes, of course. It was perfect." I leaned up and gave him a hard, lingering kiss. When I pulled back, his eyes swirled slightly with black.

"Do you remember what you told me afterward?"

My brows furrowed as I tried to remember what I said, but I couldn't. I shook my head.

"You told me that you could wake up every morning to this view and fall asleep to the sound of the waterfall."

I did say that. Realization filled me.

"You didn't..."

"Oh, I did," he said with a proud smile. "Hold on, I want to see your face when you see our home for the first time."

He moved behind me, and my body hummed with eagerness. Gods, what the hell was taking him so long?

"Alright, my love, turn around."

I turned quickly, and Cassius stood with his arms spread out and a smile filled with excitement. Behind him stood a beautiful black stone home. It was two stories, but just as intimidating as the Crimson castle. The side of the home facing the waterfall was nearly all glass, so the view was unobstructed.

My eyes didn't know where to look first as I stepped forward quickly. To the left of our home was a garden so vast that I had to stop because I was in awe of it. He had replicated some of my favorite fountains from the castle. There was a pretty stone pathway and archways made of shrubs, and the sheer amount of flowers was breathtaking.

"Cassius…"

"Do you like it?"

"Like it? I love it. You did all of this for me?"

He stepped forward and wrapped me up in his arms.

"Of course. Now let me give you a tour of the inside. I decorated it as best as I could. But Sybil helped before, so we can change anything you don't like."

He grabbed my hand and dragged me inside. The home was open and large. There was a large wooden table to our left that could seat our entire family. My eyes shifted to the large living space to the right. It had dark green couches and a large fireplace. My heart stopped when I saw what hung on the wall above it.

It was a large portrait. Cassius and I stood in the center; it was clear it was supposed to be our wedding day. On his side, his parents and siblings stood. On my side, he had them paint my mother, Killian, Sybil, and the twins. Tears streamed down my face as I moved toward it. It was so good to see their faces. Gods, I fucking missed them.

Cassius' arms wrapped around me from behind and held me as I stared at it.

"I love you," I whispered as I turned in his embrace. "I love you so fucking much."

"I love—" I cut him off with an all-consuming kiss. Cassius moaned against me as he deepened the kiss, but then pulled away. "You. We will finish this kiss after I show you everything else."

He promised. I looked over his shoulder, and my mouth fell open at the sight of the waterfall.

"Come on, little viper."

He dragged me up the wide staircase.

"Upstairs are the bedrooms."

I looked down the hallway; there were two doors on the right and four on the other side. He led us through the first door on the side with the waterfall. Our room was decorated in forest green, with the same wall of windows so we could see the waterfall. It had a private washroom, a large closet, and a seating area with a fireplace and small library.

"This is so perfect, Cassius."

He smiled.

"What are the other five doors?"

"One is a washroom, and the rest are for our kids. I didn't know how many you wanted, so I figured four bedrooms, but if we need more, we can add on."

Suddenly an image I hadn't pictured flooded my mind. Little boys running around with dark hair and mischievous golden eyes like their father. My chest tightened at the thought of having our own little family.

"Four will work." I smiled and walked to one of the rooms and saw it was empty, but my heart raced at the idea of it being filled with a mini version of Cassius one day.

"We never talked about it, but you said you wanted kids once." His voice was tight with emotion as he spoke. I turned to look at him.

"After I've had you to myself for a while, then we can have a few little Cassiuses running around." I agreed. His eyes widened like he was picturing it.

"I pictured hell-raising, mini-Theas," he chuckled.

"Maybe we will have both." I glanced at the room, smiling, before shutting the door. "Gods, help us when we do," I laughed.

Cassius grabbed me and dragged me back to our room. We stood in front of the windows, admiring the scenery.

"Do you know what I am looking forward to?" Cassius finally broke the silence. I looked at him as he stared at me. "Just regular days with you. Days where we lay in bed and do nothing. Just being together. I'm looking forward to you and me having time alone, having fun together."

"Me too." I stared at him and felt that overwhelming sense of love filling me. I loved him so much that words failed to describe it.

"I'm so lucky to have you, Cassius. I know I say I love you all the time, but if I could find a better way to explain how much you mean to me, I would. My life would have been nothing without you. I would have been nothing without you. I will spend the rest of our existence loving you. I would go through everything again if you were my prize at the end of it."

He blinked rapidly as wetness pooled in his eyes.

"You don't have to say it out loud, my love; I hear you thinking about it all the time," he whispered. His hands came up and cupped my face, his thumbs rubbing across my cheeks to wipe the tears.

"I don't know how I feel about *that* being the power you got from me through the bloodstone." I pursed my lips, and his smile widened.

"You think about me all the time; how do you get anything done?" he teased.

I laughed loudly because I did things as fast as I could so I could see him. I couldn't stand to be away from him for more than a few hours.

"I have a secret I've been keeping."

"Bigger than a house?" I frowned.

"No." He released me. "I've been practicing for a week. Haden is usually with me so he can extinguish the fire if it gets out of hand."

My heart rate picked up.

Cassius lifted his hand, and a small ball of fire floated in it. My mouth fell open as he focused hard on it, and it moved across the room to the fireplace, igniting the wood on fire. My eyes snapped to his.

"Cassius... You got more powers? What else can you do?"

"That's it. Fire and mind reading, but only your mind still."

My eyes drifted down his body to the crown tattoo, and I smiled.

"I told my father that we will not be leaving our home for a month, and I meant it." Cassius breathed heavily as he stepped forward, wrapping his hand in my hair and pulling me to his mouth. I kissed him back, deepening it. Cassius moaned as I pulled away.

"You should've told him two months." I smiled.

"I'll tell him three." Cassius lunged at me.

DELLA 10 YEARS AGO

I walked aimlessly through the small village in Kizar undetected by anyone, always unseen. I took in the sight of all the fae as they laughed, kissed, hugged, and smiled at one another. I wondered what that was like—to be seen by another, let alone be smiled at.

There was nothing special about this place. It was one of the worst villages in Kizar, the poverty level extremely low, and most of the homes were falling apart. But I couldn't shake this feeling of urgency that filled me. I was meant to be here, but I found nothing that would make sense for me to be called back. This was a feeling I had never felt and therefore did not understand.

So, I walked around without purpose, jealous of the fae who lived, even in squalor, because they felt something. I only felt longing, longing for something else to fill my boring days. I was so lonely that I wasn't sure if life would ever bring me any sense of joy.

I summoned my star mist to take me to my home in the stars but stopped when I felt that tugging again; only this time it was more urgent. I turned around and saw nothing out of the ordinary. I frowned with disappointment as I turned forward. Something was wrong in this place, but I could not tell what it was. I made it a few steps forward when suddenly, I stopped dead in my tracks—just to stare at him.

Walking up the dirt path was a tall man who was fit and handsome. His dark blonde hair was chaotic as if he had been running his fingers through it. He was talking to a girl his age who had bright red hair. She looked at him in a way I didn't like—like he was hers. Gods, he was beautiful.

He was getting closer to me, but his face was turned toward the girl as they talked heatedly about something. I couldn't stop staring at him. I couldn't believe my eyes. It was him. I had waited for this moment, and it felt like it would never come. His smooth skin, his straight nose, which led to kissable lips and a perfect smile.

I realized he was smiling, and I finally snapped out of my gawking. He was going to walk straight into me, but it didn't matter. He would not see or feel me. So, I stayed where I was because I wanted to admire him longer. The red-haired woman was talking his ear off when I glanced up into pretty, dark blue-grey eyes that reminded me of a violent storm in the sea.

Shit, he was perfect.

I admired everything about him, staring far more than what would be deemed appropriate if he could actually see me. His brows furrowed as he looked toward me. But I just kept staring. Amusement filled his eyes as he smiled slightly. I wondered what the woman was saying to him to make him look happy. He stopped a few feet in front of me.

"Excuse me," he smiled down at me.

My eyes widened when I realized he was looking me in the eyes. I turned to see who he was talking to, but I was the only one standing there. I pointed to my chest, and his smile widened.

For the love of the stars, he could fucking see me, and I was staring. My cheeks heated.

"Who are you talking to?" The redhead raised her brow curiously.

The man turned to her and back to me.

"To her." His curious eyes drifted over my face slowly. Shit, did he like what he saw?

"Haden, there is no woman in front of you."

He looked at the redhead.

"Kira, she's right here." He pointed at me. I could see her eyes searching for me, but she wouldn't find me, not unless I wanted her to, but he could. My heart felt like it was going to explode into a million pieces. I could not believe it was him.

Haden.

Mine.

I smiled at him when his stormy eyes met mine.

"You don't see her?" He frowned.

"No, maybe your father hit you a little too hard in the head because there is no one in front of you, and others are starting to stare."

He didn't look away from me, like he couldn't.

"Her eyes look like the stars," he whispered to himself.

I smiled.

"Seriously, Haden, everyone is staring."

He looked away from me and looked at the fae watching him talk to someone who wasn't there. They all looked at him like he was a freak, and that pissed me off—a lot. He swallowed hard as he side-stepped around me and kept walking. I turned to watch him leave, feeling a deep sense of longing for him.

After a minute he turned to see if I was still there. He smiled brightly at me when he saw I was still watching him.

I smiled back, thanking the stars that they gave me a perfect mate.

Secrets & Curses Of Fate will be released in 2025.

SHAY TAYLOR

Subscribe to my newsletter for updates
on new projects, giveaways, and more.
www.authorshaytaylor.com

Follow me on TikTok and Instagram
@shaytaylorauthor